Mountaineer Page

Second Book of the Aethereal Knights' Tales

Mountaineer Page

Copyright © 2020 by William Cornelison

Cover Illustration by Hannah Werner

Printed in the United States of America

ISBN: 978-1-7343415-3-9 (Paperback)
ISBN: 978-1-7343415-4-6 (ebook)

Second Edition

10 9 8 7 6 5 4 3 2

Mountaineer Page

Second Book of the Aethereal Knights' Tales

William Cornelison

Warring Magic Books

The Aethereal Knights' Tales

~ Chapters ~

A belief is a spell beyond comprehension.

With its power, people challenge monstrous things,

foster strength in the hesitant,

and bolster their inner will when needed most.

It hardens resolve into steel and the body into stone,

leading to the performance of great feats and changes.

That is why faith of any kind can grow so strong.

But the human mind, like that of their faith, and even the land itself,

shall tear and crumble into the depths of the abyss

should the limits be tested enough.

And as it is natural for the land to change with the seasons,

so, too, is it for the mind to be shaped by growth.

To challenge a devoted faith and risk everything for one's own

means to walk away from it all the stronger.

~ First Chapter ~

Another New Day

The spring months in the kingdom of Ederea were always the most prosperous. A plentiful autumn and a restful winter having passed, farmers once again began watching over and tending to their crops to ensure another bountiful harvest. Fishermen took advantage of the fish migrations ripping through their waters to make their biggest catches of the year. With fish being the country's main food source, they made almost as much money as the nobility who looked after the people.

Many of the country's holidays happened during those glorious months. With the weather at its finest, nice and hot but not quite blistering, the people kept around any large body of water to stay refreshed in the tropical heat.

Smiles spread throughout the country at this grand time of year.

Even the knights became laidback and found time to relax. But there was always something for the warriors to do. Many who were not always on the watch for brigands and pirates travelled to the training facilities to see the growth their pages have made.

Most Ederean pages learned the art of warfare and the knight's code in isolated facilities built on deserted islands. Each one was protected by magical barriers held in place by finely crafted charms to keep trespassers out and guarded by elite knights chosen for their skill and prestige.

Every facility had its own unique methods of training pages, as well as differences in terrain. Most of them had perfectly constructed fortresses in the remote areas of the islands with the best possible training conditions and the most competent knights responsible for their training. One island, however, was made a facility without disrupting the wildlife, left overrun by the largest, most savage beasts, making it the most dangerous facility in the archipelago: Des Meurtal.

Unlike the other training facilities, Des Meurtal did not have any protective structures built to house the pages. They lived in conditions so perilous that they went throughout their days worn ragged, barely able to rest at night. Those who returned from the perilous island were said to become the strongest knights in the country's history, but the edict of the land was unforgivably harsh. For the pages, it was either survive and overcome or wane and die.

Many of the children chosen to train in Des Meurtal were exceptional, especially one committed youth named Luchs.

Luchs spent every waking moment bettering his body and mind so he may someday protect the kingdom. The various dangers of Des Meurtal offered the perfect chances for building muscle and practicing teamwork, especially when they needed to fend off aggressive animals or weather frightful storms. There was nothing to read on the island, and the commandant responsible for their upbringing never taught them personally—his philosophy being that the young must grow their own way to be strong.

A sharp lad five-and-ten years of age, Luchs learned about every danger there was to know about through reconnaissance, observation, listening in on the knights guarding the island. And after the long, challenging days, he spent the evenings reciting the knight's code he learned from the knight who recommended him word for word.

It was a vibrant, peaceful morning when he next awoke. He slept in a narrow opening beneath the rocky cliff close to the eastern beach. The slumber was an uncomfortable one both due to the confined space and the nightmare that shook him awake, but he was grateful to awaken to the glimmering golden rays peering in the cave from the outside. The horizon was a blazing blue so radiant it nicely complimented the calm ocean water below.

Luchs sat up from his bed of leaves and grass, stretching out his back and arms as much as possible before gathering his gear and stepping outside. He was a large lad for his age, even among the bulky children born in Ederea, which made slinking through the opening a little trying. His round head was full of shaggy, unkempt brown hair and in his thick skull were two marsh-green eyes. The frayed clothes he wore barely fit, but it was all he had to wear.

Without any shelter, the pages either had to build their own out of branches and rocks or learn to endure the harsh elements and sleep where predators could not reach or would not typically go. Very few were lucky enough to find the naturally formed shelter Luchs and his friends had.

Aside from their clothes, each page was given a single weapon and a small buckler shield that needed to last until a knight came to take them for their squire. If their equipment was lost or destroyed, there was little choice but to go look for what the knights hid around the island.

Before concerning himself with the dangers he would find that day, Luchs joined the two lads sitting leisurely on the beach. They were his comrades and the only friends he made on the savage island. He was greeted by a wave from the sharp-eyed Aloysius Aucolin, a taller youth with bright red hair. Rufus Labont, the short, dark-haired kid who arrived on the island two years ago, turned and did the same as soon as he saw him. The three young men all wore the same messy olive uniforms padded with thin leather and lined with white spiral patterns on the arms.

"Ho there, Luchs! 'Tis a nice morning, eh?" Rufus stated.

Luchs nodded and turned to Aloysius, who tossed a stick of old jerky his way. He sank his teeth into the dry meat as soon as he caught it. The taste was rough and gamey, but it stimulated the tired taste buds and left a strong aftertaste that woke the rest of his mind up. When he first tasted the rough flavor, he thought he would never get used to it, but after four years he was eating a different kind of dried meat each morning courtesy of Aloysius, who dried the leftover game from their hunts for a later time.

"Good wolf jerky. Just wish the meat was not dry as the sand."

Foul tasting as it was, they could not be picky. Food was sometimes scarce, and the growing lads needed energy to combat the aggressive wildlife and ornery pages looking for a fight.

Life on Des Meurtal existed around one conflict after another. From the moment they arrived, the children were put into one of five factions that challenged each other for territory and resources. It was a means of simulating actual warfare so the children could learn tactics in the heat of battle and how to show restraint. Gaining strength was a necessity, but knights without control over their actions made for poor soldiers. Giving them actual weapons instead of ones shaved down for practice purposes offered greater incentive to learn said control, as well as allow their muscles to adjust to the heft of their tools all the quicker.

"We are running low, so we'll need to go on another hunt," Aloysius stated. "What'll it be, gentlemen—more wolf, or maybe boar or venison?"

"How about we go for something small this time?" Rufus interrupted. "The rodents here have some tasty meat." It was not out of cowardice that he complained; he genuinely liked the meat of smaller game. Although smaller in stature than many his age, Rufus was a scrappy fighter capable of confronting enemies twice his size. Many underestimated him, though, and learned the hard way how their first impressions were sorely mistaken.

"Come now, Rufus. Bigger prey means a tougher fight. No wonder the other pages like to target you," Luchs commented.

"I like a scuffle as much as anyone else," Rufus stated, "but I also like the food I eat to have a good taste."

"Too bad we don't have any fancy spices to satisfy your picky pallet," Aloysius teased.

"You just don't know where to look."

"Oh sure. You've been here for a few years, Rufus. You must know where all of the best herbs and spices grow, aye?" Luchs teased.

He opened his mouth to say something, but instead he sat with his mouth hung agape. His mien slowly grew into that of a fool's bafflement and quickly became vengeful when his friends chuckled.

As someone who never concealed his erratic emotions well, Rufus was often the one to bring laughter to his faction. When days were tough and they grew weary, Luchs and Aloysius were grateful to have him around. Their experience on Des Meurtal would have been miserable if they did not know how to laugh.

"Whose turn is it to go hunting anyway?" Rufus blurted out, attempting to shift focus onto something else.

To help each other survive on the dangerous island, factions assigned certain tasks to each of their members, such as hunting and searching for suitable places to move camp in case it was overrun by enemies. The pages attacked one another daily to perfect their warfare tactics, so there was also the need for others to remain behind to protect their territory.

Since Luchs' faction only had three knights-in-training left, they were the most vulnerable to attack, but delegating duties was much easier for them. When their larder ran low, they took turns bringing back fresh game while the two remaining guarded their territory.

Aware it was his turn, Luchs took one last look at the ocean and inhaled the refreshing salty air, still groggy from being forced out of slumber. Then, taking an axe in hand, he got back on his feet and trudged straight inland for the dense forest.

"Bring back something plump and juicy!" That could only mean either a rat or vole coming from Rufus—such strange taste in meat.

Luchs turned back flashing a broad smile. "Only if I can find it, you scrawny slacker!"

Des Meurtal's immense forest spread throughout most of the island, and it was claimed by the deathly strong animals that lived there. One would have to cross through armed or leave without their innards. It left little option for where the pages and knights could set up camp and go hunt.

The challenge of traversing the forest made it all the more enjoyable for Luchs; animals proved more of a challenge than the other pages.

He even dragged his axe over the ground, hoping to attract attention from anything nearby.

Not many were as brash about facing danger as Luchs. His combat skills were on par with the other pages, but what he really took pride in was his body's unnaturally dense muscles and tough skin. They were thicker than a boar's hardened backside, acting like a natural armor capable of taking more hits than feasibly possible. Even with only a few plates of leather padding covering him, he felt capable of taking on an entire faction single-handed.

It was his durable body that impressed the nobles responsible for training pages. Heavy blows bounced off of him, weapons that cut or tore met resistance that kept them from leaving lasting damage, and blood stopped seeping through the wounds in a matter of seconds even in the heat of battle. Many accused him of using a charm or magic enchantment to appear more bodily able, possibly out of jealousy or disdain. It was almost offensive, though Luchs thought the same when he first discovered it himself. He honestly thought he was influenced by some hex when a knife accidentally cut his thumb without shedding a drop of blood.

Luchs got so distracted strolling down the not-so-sound memory lane that he lost track of where he was. Whenever hoping for more fragments of his forgotten past to return, he often lost focus of the present.

Never once had he mentioned to his comrades that he was an amnesiac. He barely remembered the time he spent held captive. Everything was a blur to him. The beatings, the humiliation, the abuse and torture—everything inflicted upon him by the people who stole him from his old life warped his mind, utterly erasing everything that happened before he was rescued by the Ederean military. Everything he knew was either told to him by the generous family who took the broken child in or deeply ingrained in his psyche and invoked by nightmares.

The memories of his earlier life were gone, but he was saved by the Vertueux family before any more of his mind had slipped away. How they tenderly cared for him, each member of the family treating the deep injuries and blackened sores, helping the body readjust to natural movement, was always fresh in Luchs' mind. He still remembered the gentle hands that tenderly held his body and wiped away the tears that constantly flowed, that supported him while he was taught to walk and speak and even use utensils again.

Five years passed since they rescued Luchs, and he was grateful for every moment spent for his sake.

The only clue he had of his past was the name written on his arm with his own blood.

"Hm. What have we here?"

That voice, that dry, ragged voice, sent shivers straight down his axe-wielding arm. It made him wish he was still lost in his own thoughts, especially since the voice sounded so blasé. If there was anyone else in the area looking for a fight before, they had long since left.

Knowing full well he would regret ignoring the horrendous voice, Luchs turned to the trees at his left to find a man donned in bleak armor relaxing against a finely grown trunk before approaching him nonchalantly. He carried a broadsword with a long blade and a curved edge near the guard, a crest of a sneering ogre at the center of the weapon's neck. That man was Commandant Gilbrand Brunlier, the knight responsible for everyone training on Des Meurtal, his facility.

Many of the knights on the island were rather stout. Men with large, strong bodies were respected in Ederea. Among such men, Commandant Brunlier was a feared behemoth standing at ten feet in an unsightly slouch.

Luchs forced down the tension welling up in his throat as Commandant Brunlier stepped past the bushes. The closer he got, the more intimidating he appeared. Seeing him made it easy to believe that giants truly existed at some point in history, and that he was blood-linked to them.

"Out for the hunt, I s'pose?"

"A-Aye, Commandant Brunlier. The boars like to graze around this time of day. I thought to help myself to one."

"Oh? That so?" The commandant paused to yawn, which made Luchs gulp. He was more dangerous when bored. "Well, those beasts will probably feed for some time now. What say we have a bit of sport first?"

His subordinates feared him for more than his substantial height. The horrible battles he fought in left the entire right side of his face a scarred mess, the black eyepatch covering up the worst of it. Not only was it terrifying, it also showed just how strong he truly was to survive it all. Everyone dreaded encountering Commandant Brunlier. Whenever any of the pages met him, he forced them to spar with him for a few minutes. For him, it was an exercise to keep from falling asleep; the pages themselves struggled to keep their limbs sparring against him for so long.

Even if it meant their lives, no one dared refuse him. Anyone who refused a challenge of physical strength threw themselves into complete disgrace. It was the worst possible shame for a knight, even for their juniors who were expected to grow as strong and versatile as they.

After coming so far, shaming himself and the family who cared for him was unacceptable. Silently offering a prayer to the gods, Luchs braced for the worst holding his axe high off the ground.

"That's a good lad," said Commandant Brunlier. "Come at me!" He always preferred for his opponents to make the first strike in single combat. He would be thought overconfident for allowing the enemy to make the first strike were he not so terribly strong.

Obeying the command from his superior, Luchs charged directly for him, carrying the axe with both hands and hurling it into a hard swing straight for the large man's ribcage. Commandant Brunlier responded with speed unbecoming of his size, guarding with the broadsword at its blade's sharpest. After sparks flew from the connected metal, Luchs quickly lurched backwards to avoid the behemoth's imminent swing.

Wielding a battleaxe made Luchs' movements more sluggish than they normally were. Unless he timed his attacks perfectly and reacted accordingly, he would not walk away unscathed.

Commandant Brunlier's reflexes reacted to the lad's retreat, not allowing him to get far without leaving behind a cut. It was hardly deep, and blood seeped from the opening for only a moment before it stopped. That was the commandant's way to fight—hack at the enemy until scarcely anything remained. When up against Luchs, those wounds inflicted closed as soon as they opened, and that tended to leave the commandant with a sour disposition. Those two sparred several times over the years, and every time they had, Luchs always saw this bitter look on the man's face whenever blood stopped flowing from the gashes he made. He struck Luchs as a cruel sort to enjoy bloodshedding as he had.

It left Luchs unsettled to see it, but this time the look he saw on the commandant's face was that of amusement.

Already looking for the finishing blow, Commandant Brunlier thrust his sword directly for Luchs' heart. The lad was not foolish enough to leave any of his vitals exposed; although if his body was hard, that did not make it invincible. He quickly turned the axe at its side and brought it to his chest, improvising a rather broad shield.

Pressing the free hand against the axe's smooth surface, Luchs managed to withstand the mighty blow. Despite the quick thinking put into the protection, the commandant's raw power pushed him back, forcing him to dig his heels into the soil. He was almost thrown on his back the impact was so strong. And Commandant Brunlier kept applying more force in his swings, his muscles never shaking from overexertion. The crooked smile he wore shook Luchs to the core.

It insulted him how the enemy still held back while he was giving it his all remaining on the defensive, implying he was nothing against the commandant.

No man allowed their pride to be trampled on by anyone regardless of their rank and status. Young as he was, four years' time on the savage island cut off from civilization, training his body and senses for the battlefield, made him someone not to be trifled with.

Luchs pressed his weight against his axe in meeting the commandant's force and fighting it off with his own strength. Every muscle in his body trembled in opposition to the crushing pressure threatening to trample him if one misstep was taken. He remained resolute against the avalanche of power, showing no signs of crumbling under its mighty downpour. With one thrust that tore his muscles, Luchs shoved his arm forward, breaking Commandant Brunlier's attack and throwing him back. The commandant faltered backward, catching himself on his right foot.

Taking his chance, Luchs rushed at his foe while he still left an opening and hurled his axe skyward in a brutal uppercut.

Neither of them moved until slowly the eye patch strapped onto Commandant Brunlier's face fluttered off with a whisk of wind, revealing skin stained red by old blood dried across an empty crater. Droplets of crimson leaked from the cut under the empty eye socket.

But no more than that.

Standing with his back arched, Commandant Brunlier managed to escape further disfiguration by drawing his sword against Luchs' axe before the cut became deep. Even after the attack nearly cleaved his head, he kept his frightful sneer and even spread it, showing every tooth in his mouth.

The unsettling expression discouraged Luchs. By the time he realized his mistake, it was already too late. His strength wavered, and the behemoth brushed him aside with a simple flick of his sword.

He closed in too fast, the great behemoth moving in and pressing the lad to the ground, holding his sword to his neck. Luchs remained perfectly still to keep from being skewered by the cold metal.

It barely began and it was already over.

Right as he began to think he was actually going to be killed, the sword hanging over him for so long, Commandant Brunlier pulled it away. Air finally returned to Luchs' lungs upon him stepping back, that grisly pressure no longer threatening to crush him.

"Good defense. Yer reactions are getting faster."

When sitting up, Luchs noticed the commandant was not walking away to offer him a little space, but to fetch the eyepatch he lost.

Thankfully, he decided to take it back. His expressions were almost demonic without the hollow crater covered up.

"And ye've gotten more muscle on ye. Not many lads yer age can scathe me."

The veteran's terrifying appearance aside, praise from him meant plenty. With his strength at such unreal heights, he did not bother wasting it on the weak. It was next to impossible to impress someone of his stature. And the words he uttered were never lies nor flattery, making them all the more valuable.

"Well then, I'll be off now. Watch out for them boars, lad."

Luchs watched the commandant disappear through the trees with these mixed feelings of humiliation and relief. Grueling as it was to fight against him, he never regretted it once.

He never said much aside from his desire for a good bout and commenting on how well or poor the pages progressed. Many only thought him a brute who liked to pick on the weak, but Luchs learned a great deal from him just from exchanging blows.

It was through their clashes that Luchs found what he needed to improve his fighting style. The fact that no one could oppose him with brute strength alone taught Luchs that power in a fight was not everything. He left few openings after an attack and struck fast and true, teaching him to time the attacks and counter promptly. Everything involving defense Luchs learned from him.

Out of everything, there was one lesson he learned: defense made for a perfect offense if used wisely.

Reminding himself of that, Luchs got back on his feet and looked toward the open sky through the gaps in the trees, having lost his bearings after the clash.

The skies were almost clear apart from the few clouds that drifted hither and thither. It promised another grand sunny day.

Days of sunshine on end were not unusual in Ederea. They sometimes made one yearn for a little rain.

After finding the sun's position, he glanced back to the clear paths around him and headed in the western direction. He kept his pace quick, more eager for a successful hunt after losing again.

The hunt proved fruitful.

Not many boars were grazing together in the fields, but the ones in the open were plump—and capable of defending themselves. Luchs purposely chose the biggest one he could find to exert some energy, still miffed about his defeat. That boar offered a fine fight, but it was nowhere near as challenging as the monstrosity he faced off against earlier. One of the beast's tusks snapped off with a strike of the axe close to its snout and was thrown on its side, vulnerable to one final swoop to the throat.

When had it come to the point where the only thing on the island capable of giving him a challenge was the commandant? It was a relief to know he had become that strong, but he sometimes dreaded what he would have to do to get stronger.

Getting disheartened about it would do no good, so he looked back to his catch and quickly changed his attitude. *Thinking that way will ruin the meal this beast will make*, he thought jovially, and we can't have that.

The prize weighed heavily against him the further he lugged it. It was difficult to carry since the dead weight pressed over him like the boulder that nearly crushed him the year before. Judging by its immense size and weight, the meat would last both him and his friends the night and leave plenty of leftover jerky for the next week or so. Just thinking of the taste provoked his already agitated stomach to snarl.

Despite the fantasies of what tastes his catch would have after being cooked running through his mind, Luchs kept a sharp lookout for any insatiable, savage beasts—and the animals—that would try to steal his rightfully earned meat. Many factions have tried to rob each other of their catches over the years because there was not enough prey to go around. Everyone was aware of how many animals inhabited the island and knew not to hunt them if their numbers were too low.

The factions organized themselves like armies. Whenever they fought over something, they considered it "going to war," and those who emerged victorious took the spoils: weapons, material, and even food.

Although each faction had very few in numbers, the fights were always strenuous. There were rarely ever casualties, so the fighting never lessened.

Meaning an attack could happen at any time.

Fighting off five or six enemies while dragging a three hundred pound boar on his back, oddly enough, sounded like an interesting challenge.

As he kept trudging through the forest path, lugging the boar every third step, something unusual caught his eye. Carved in the broad tree to his right was this bizarre symbol that looked like a person's head with an arrow jabbed straight across the cranium.

It was not unusual to see symbols and the like carved into things from trees to stone. There were five styles of well-known markers that indicated whose territory was where—lion heads for the Féroce, soaring hawks for the Chevalerie, wolf claws for the Devoir, twin axes for the Loi, and a crown for the Vaincre. But a marker of a skull? That was something entirely different from the markers meant to alert the pages not to step into another's territory. Was it some sort of sign fabricated to mark one of the places Commandant Brunlier liked to go? The symbolism seemed appropriate, but the mark was too small for anyone to get a good look at while casually strolling by.

Curious as he was about what it meant, it would be best to think on that while in his faction's territory.

He took a shortcut through a few bushes and slid down a steep hill behind them, where he was welcomed by a band of ten pages covered in bloody cuts and black bruises. They were obviously in the middle of retreating from an excursion they set out on. Considering they all gave him such ugly looks before passing him by and leaving for their own territory, they had to have just gotten into a fight with his faction.

Glancing briefly at each face and recounting them once more, Luchs faintly recognized the group as the Chevalerie faction, a group of pages that invade his territory often with hardly any successful raids. They normally attacked other territories with six or seven pages.

Each one of them gave an irked reaction upon noticing him, then turned back toward the path they were on and went on their way. Luchs sighed, still hoping for a little more exercise, when they were but blurs in the distance.

Were he still new to the island, he would have had suspicions about a few turning back to steal his prize after they had admitted defeat. There was no need for that. No one ever did anything so disgraceful after failing in their conquests.

Pride ran deep in Ederean veins as naturally as blood.

He headed straight for the shore where Aloysius and Rufus sat in wait, hunched over and tending to their shallow cuts with filthy old rags they constantly washed in the nearby river and reused. It took some time for the three to figure out how to fight off an excess of enemies and come out on top, but they eventually learned to conceal themselves often during the light hours and put an effective ambush into play once an enemy stepped foot into their territory. Guerilla tactics were never a favorite of Luchs', but they came in handy when engaging a larger group.

Luchs smiled. Even though those two grunted and heaved from fatigue, having fought off more than thrice as many opponents, they were beaming with pride.

"Luchs!" Rufus, who had fewer injuries to treat, waved at his approaching friend. "Where have you been? All the fun happened without—" He fell silent, eyes popping open and mouth dropping in awe at the hefty carcass that grew larger the closer it drew his way. When they were only ten feet apart, Luchs could see the drool dripping from his open jaw.

"That beast will taste all the sweeter after that brawl," Aloysius boded, still rubbing his injured foot.

Luchs grinned. "I'm tempted not to share any after you two varlets kept all the fun for yourselves."

"Ah, don't be that way, Luchs," Rufus joined in the joke. "We never keep our catches from you, and you're the one always biting off more than you can chew." That last part was definitely not about food.

Seeing those two so fatigued must have been infectious because Luchs began to feel it as well. Hauling that boar over the sand put more pressure on his back and weighed down his arms until they ached. Moments ago, he felt capable of continuing a few more feet after repeatedly telling himself he could. It irked him how his stamina gave out so suddenly.

When he looked ready to collapse, both of his friends ignored their injuries and rushed over to his side before the boar's weight crushed him. Each wrapping an arm around its plump neck, they held it up long enough for the hunter to move away. None of them had the strength to move it far and left it where they dropped it for the time being.

Luchs turned around and fell limply onto his back as soon as he could. Normally, showing such fatigue in front of anyone would have made him ashamed of himself. A knight must be able to carry on in war even if it meant his last breath, after all. But not many have ever clashed with Commandant Brunlier and still had the energy to do anything else, especially hunting.

There was something to be proud of even in that defeat.

Aloysius turned to the sky, then took a deep breath and sighed in relief. "I think we've earned ourselves a little meal. What say you, lads?"

No arguments from Luchs or Rufus.

While Aloysius went back to his hiding spot to find the carving knife he fashioned out of stone, Rufus joined his burly friend on the sand for a little rest. It was always the same routine with those three; those two would keep watch while Aloysius prepared their food since he knew more about cooking than they.

Even when they needed rest, they could not let their guard down at the risk of leaving themselves vulnerable to attack. It was their rule to keep weapons and wits about them at all times. With their faction being so small, there was not much they could do on the defensive.

Luchs turned his attention to the ever-expansive sky while he rested. Just looking blankly at the brilliant blue scattering its pure white clouds, feeling the majestic winds wash over him like waves, made him feel at ease after the day's strife.

Being so close to the ocean always felt strange to him, but it was a welcome strangeness.

"So," Rufus spoke, breaking the pleasant spell, "find anything interesting out there?" He was always interested in the things people found all over Des Meurtal. It was hard to blame him. There were sometimes weapons buried behind bushes or underneath stumps, for instance. The only thing no one wanted to hear about was finding another page having left their world for the Elysium.

Luchs shook his head, forgetting it was still in the sand. "Nay, nothing of interest."

"Come on, Luchs. Don't go lying to me. With all the time you've spent amongst the trees, you had to have found something."

Luchs glanced to his right, directly at Rufus. "Aside from this weird carving, there was only a behemoth that got in the way of my hunt."

Rufus made an interesting sound that conveyed pity. No one enjoyed their time entertaining Commandant Brunlier, least of all the smaller pages. "What of this carving? What's that about?"

"Not sure. It was just this unusual skull with an arrow through its head. Do you think the other factions are trying to make a new marker?"

"That hardly sounds right. Those symbols last as long as the faction exists, and they're hard to get rid of since we get new pages here every six months or so. If they changed whenever someone wanted it, it wouldn't be easy knowing whose territory is where."

"So what do you think it could be? A prank?"

"It could be that, or maybe..." Suddenly serious, Rufus sat up to look from one possible infantry point to the next, as if expecting spies. Then he leaned in close and faintly whispered, "Pirates!"

To which Luchs laughed heartily at. He wondered what foolish notion the lunatic was about to spout but never expected something so ludicrous. "Pirates? You lost your senses, mate? Everyone knows pirates can't cross these waters. There's a protective spell surrounding the entire island. Ships without the proper charms can't possibly pass through, at least that's what the knights always say."

"Mayhap, but we never know when it might fall. You've heard the rumors, aye?"

"About magic disappearing from the land? Malarkey! I've seen mages perform spectacular feats people could only hope to do. That sort of power could never just disappear."

"Believe it or don't, but I still say pirates could invade these shores if they notice the opportunity."

If only it were ever uncovered.

Luchs would not mind if what Rufus said was actually true. It would be a rare treat to put his training to use and apprehend genuine criminals. Granted, the other inexperienced pages gave him a bit of sport and the random encounters with the commandant reinforced his resolve with humility, but he needed to implement what he knew against experienced fighters, see how well he could subdue them.

That would have to wait until he left Des Meurtal and became a squire to a knight. And how he looked forward to that day!

~ Second Chapter ~

Wavering Judgment

There have been significantly fewer attacks on Féroce territory lately, leaving plenty of time for Luchs and his faction to spar with one another. The other factions on the island were not as active as they usually were and kept to themselves these past three days, never attempting to raid their campsite.

Luchs did not care what the other factions did if they posed no threat to his own, and so far, there was none, apparent or otherwise.

Preparing for any kind of battle was of the utmost importance to the Féroce faction. There were not enough of them to invade another's territory, and even if they scanned the area beforehand, their guerilla attacks were not as effective in enemy territory. Being ready for anything was an absolute must.

There was never a reason to fear enemy factions allying with one another. Everyone was much too competitive to consider such a thing. An exception was made once before, but unless the Devoir began acting out of hand again, there would likely never be another one.

Those three days were too good to waste. While the calm lasted, they sparred against each other with every weapon in their possession. Whenever they had the chance, Luchs, Rufus, and Aloysius traded weapons they appropriated from other pages they bested and practiced together.

Luchs was not too fond of the exercise when he first came to Des Meurtal, but after seven months of listening to Aloysius constantly rant about how dire it was to be proficient with every weapon, the idea grew on him. Mastering multiple weapons without any instructional guidance was not easy, but it was as Aloysius said: "There are times when a warrior doesn't have a choice about what he can use or what needs to be done." Were he to lose one in combat and need another, he could not be picky about which tools to use, if there were any.

Getting used to every weapon was trying, but there were advantages to it. Along the line, Luchs learned better uses for one weapon from handling others. It never occurred to him learning to fight with secondary weapons would allow him to open his mind to new techniques.

It was amusing how Aloysius' own advice backfired on him when his turn to spar with Luchs came.

Rufus laughed so hard watching Aloysius get thrown on his back that he rolled over in the sand and started choking on some.

After helping Aloysius up and making sure neither of them gave the other any serious injuries, Luchs dropped his axe and went to collect some of the ocean water in a rusty old helm. He walked back to his gagging friend at a slower pace just to toy with him. And when Rufus began leaping around like his head would explode, Aloysius held him down while Luchs poured the water down his throat.

It was hilarious watching Rufus jump free and run around like a chicken that lost its head, spitting out the last of the salt water and coughing hard enough to hack up a lung. He leaned against an old palm tree, struggling to get his breathing under control.

"What in the gods' names," he rasped before pausing to wheeze, "made you think *that* was a good idea?"

"Well, you're not floundering anymore, are you?" Luchs stated. "Best be thankful I got you any water."

"Why didn't you just toss me my waterskin?"

Aloysius chortled. "Where's the fun in that?"

When he was done spitting out the sea's taste, Rufus walked back over to where his two friends carelessly dropped their weapons and picked up the axe. "Right then, my turn! Who's going to be my first victim?" That surly response carried more than the heavy stench lingering from last night's boar jerky.

Neither were ready to jump forward and be his sparring partner. Many pages who lost their temper training often lost restraint when handling their weapons. The most they could do was confront the ornery lad before he did something regrettable.

When it looked like Rufus was reaching the end of his patience, Aloysius stepped up and fetched his sword. "Don't go falling off your rocker, mate. I will help calm you down," he declared nonchalantly. "Luchs, why don't you go off to the forest and see what you can find? Bring back whatever's good."

"Aye. But both of you better be alive when I get back."

"Worry not. I will fare better against him than I had with you."

Luchs said nothing. Instead of provoking either of them to do more damage to the other, he rushed for the upturned lifeboat where they kept their weapon stash. He quickly swiped a bow and its quiver, and a spare sword, then went to the forest before Rufus decided he wanted to fight him. It made him uneasy leaving Aloysius alone to quell their friend's temper.

This was not the first time something like this happened. The three got into more fights pestering one another than they had from other factions. Most of their injuries came from each other. Fortunately, they never once came close to anything fatal. Their disputes were always settled and their friendship renewed after pounding some sense into one another.

It always gave Luchs infuriating headaches to see his brothers-in-arms at each other's throats. Despite that, he was grateful Aloysius decided to take him on. Rufus was leaner than them, but knew how to handle himself well in a fight even with weapons he was not used to.

Those were some finer details one had to notice before taking someone on. Quick decisions must be made and actions taken almost the moment before. Aloysius knew that better than either of his younger friends, making him more likely to put out Rufus' temper and walk away with fewer injuries. His knowledge and capability made both of them follow him as their leader.

So long as neither killed the other, all would be well.

The forest was calm with an atmosphere serene. It was tempting to relax and take it all in, but he dared not let his guard down. Luchs kept his eyes peeled for any dangers that would befall him—enemy pages, hungry beasts, traps anyone was smart enough to make, or worse yet, the commandant. He hoped to find more stray weapons the knights left hidden in plain sight for the pages. Their "armory," as the faction tended to call it, was becoming a home for broken weapons.

While on the lookout, Luchs thought to keep an eye out for any more of those strange carvings. Whenever there was one marker, there were always more not far from the first. Once he got a grip of himself, Rufus would be more than happy to see them and further tell his ludicrous theory.

Pirates, indeed.

Luchs examined nearly every tree he came across until entering unfamiliar territory.

He went far from his territory deep into the forest without finding anything. It was probably a practical joke like he earlier suspected, a way to unnerve those who passed by it. Scare tactics were very effective means of warding off the weak-willed or overly cautious.

But the more Luchs thought of it, the less it made sense. The marker he found was almost a speck. If it were really meant to ward someone off, it would have to be bigger, more obvious to the eye.

All of that thinking only gave him the headache he wanted to avoid. Whatever it was, he could find out after finding more of the skull markers.

After that, he could grab Rufus and Aloysius and have them see for themselves.

Unfortunately, there was not a single skull marker to be found. For a while, Luchs wondered if he had taken a wrong turn. Even for someone who spent the better part of four years exploring Des Meurtal, it was sometimes difficult to distinguish the different parts of the great forest. The problem with a mental map was its contents could easily change and offer false information if not properly managed.

Luchs retraced his steps, realized where the misstep was made, and turned back to return to the path.

He did not get far. He stopped as soon as he heard the rustle of leaves, the bushes shaking for a moment before everything went quiet. Someone was there, and they knew they were already exposed, but tried not to make sudden moves after Luchs took his bow in hand and reached for an arrow. If he was doing anything, it would have to be something requiring slow, soft movements that would not instigate letting the arrow fly.

"Come out with your hands up!" Luchs demanded.

There was no doubt that it was a person concealed in the foliage. It had to be something too large to remain in the small space without stirring a few branches, and it had to be intelligent or cautious enough to know to remain still.

Luchs managed to keep a steady hand until an arm shot out of the shade and grabbed hold of an adjacent tree, dragging the body connected to it out of the darkness. His hand tensed up against the quill when he saw who it belonged to. He knew him.

That messy, long blonde hair, those tired brown eyes, that small, distinguishing scar at his chin—he was one of the Devoir faction.

The Devoir was the most aggressive faction on Des Meurtal, each member a barbarian thirsty for blood. Their tactics were cowardly, their morals diminished from ill use, their judgment border-lining insanity. Four years prior, the Devoir earned their terrible reputation by breaking the one edict Commandant Brunlier enforced: one must never kill their rivals. They were the exception that brought the other factions together for the first time. They were crafty, making their victims appear to be have been mauled by wild animals or took the wrong turn and met with a fatal fall. Such tricks did them little good.

They were found out. The other factions rallied against them. And following the grueling defeat against the united factions, Commandant Brunlier confronted the one responsible for the madness and ensured that the lapse in judgment would not happen again.

That was one of them, one of the animals that began the carnage by killing members of the Féroce simply to prove their strength. It took all of Luchs' willpower to keep from letting an arrow loose at the sight of him.

"Oh..." the Devoir sighed. "It's just you."

How could he behave so calmly after everything he had done to Luchs' faction? It was sickening!

Tempting as it was to let anger guide his actions and release the arrow, he resisted. Acting on malice was against the knight's code, as was attacking someone who was unarmed. The Devoir held his empty hands up as he stood before Luchs.

He had a sword on his person but did not take it in hand. To Luchs, it meant he was unarmed.

"Off with you! Get back to your horde if you know what's good for you."

Luchs was expecting some sort of taunting or comeback about how weak he was for not taking the kill. There was none of that.

The page stood silent for a second, then veered an uncomfortable grimace. "Can't." He remained silent for a moment more, letting that response sink into Luchs' broad skull while ridiculously shaking his hands to gesture that he kept himself unarmed.

He did not want a fight—hard as it was to believe. Even after the senseless killing stopped, the Devoir still resorted to ruthless, almost desperate acts to keep others factions under their thumb. Luchs was not willing to drop his arrow so soon.

"I need to look for Cain."

"The Mad Prince?"

Everyone knew of the page who ushered control of the Devoir years ago, ordering the killing spree, as the Mad Prince of Des Meurtal for his brutality and inspiring his own to follow in his twisted example. Even after being removed from power, he still remained influential over his faction's actions.

This worried Luchs terribly. If the Mad Prince was on his own, there was no telling what sort of chaos he would reap.

"He's missing. So are five others in our faction."

That worried him even more. It was odd enough for one of his own to think him missing, but for several others to be gone with him? It was too suspicious.

"Missing? Nonsense. He had to have let his underlings know what he is planning." There was no hiding Luchs' disdain as he spoke.

"There's no plan. They've been gone for three days. The rest of the faction has been searching for them since. ...I doubt this matters to you, Féroce. It probably brings you joy hearing unrest has spread among your competition."

Normally, it would be pleasing news, but this was too unusual. There could be a great many reasons why someone had not returned to their hideaway after so long. The enemy page seemed too bothered by it all, as though he knew something unsavory. The way he put it made it sound like it was not just his faction being affected by the change in events, and it did not sound like an act.

"And the other factions do care?"

"You are so focused on your own faction that you don't know what's been going on? I suppose that's our fault too." For a moment, there were strands of guilt brushed over the Devoir page's face. But that could not be. They never showed guilt or mercy. "The Chevalerie, Loi, and Vaincre are missing pages as well. No one knows what became of them. The leaders of each faction decided on a truce so we can find them. Someone tried to warn you Féroce about it, but I heard you chased them off."

The page then paused, trading his mildly neutral stare for one of suspicion. His right hand slowly reached for the sword at his back. Luchs' right hand trembled trying to resist the urge to fire the arrow. He would not make a move until the enemy properly armed himself.

Then, much to Luchs' amazement, the Devoir pulled it away before so much as grasping the hilt. "Nay. You wouldn't do it, not after the hell we put you through."

There it was again. That pained look of guilt plastered over the Devoir page's face once more. Was he truly reflecting on what happened? With all that he had seen them do for the sake of victory, Luchs was not certain they could feel remorse.

"Look, I just need to continue my search. Will you let me be off?"

This page was beginning to irk him. The fact that he bothered asking instead of doing as he pleased as he had done in the past made him all the more difficult to appraise.

Let him be on his way, Luchs first thought.

It was not like they were in his faction's territory. But the pitiful act the page put on made it so he could not take an eye off him. To put on an entirely new front after the years of gruesome façades was much too suspicious. He could not just let him go free.

"You can go, all right. And I'm coming with."

It was not that he believed in what the Devoir page was saying, rather that he was being cautious of it. If what he said was true, it was in Luchs' best interest as a page to find out what happened to everyone. Horrid as they were, the Devoir was still a faction of pages promised to the Ederean crown, and no knight worthy of his shield would leave his fellow knights to unsavory fates were a choice given. If this was a hoax and the page was plotting something, as he suspected, however, then it was all the more important to keep that Devoir close and put him in his place should he step out of line.

While the enemy page seemed as confused and cautious of Luchs as he was of him, he simply shrugged and walked past him undaunted. Either everything was going according to his plan or it gave him some relief knowing there was someone with him during the search.

If pages were disappearing, then why traverse the forest alone and risk vanishing himself? He would have asked, but Luchs sought to keep any conversation between him and the enemy to a minimum.

The forest's atmosphere became progressively less inviting as the two trudged through the pass. The trees came to cast away the sunlight behind their branches, blanketing the ground in shadow. The birdsong disappeared, leaving an unsettling silence. Only the faintest gasps of wind were heard every now and then. It was astonishing how a few simple changes turned the illusion of a botanical paradise into one of an enchanted grove where mortals were not meant to tread.

The two pages searched the area while keeping as much distance between each other as possible. Nothing appeared out of the ordinary. No human tracks dented the earth with ugly impressions. No weapons scarred the trees or marked the small hill they walked down. The grove was unsullied, unaffected by the presence of man.

Even though the island had been used as a makeshift battlefield for a little over a decade, this isolated area of the forest was still beautiful. The wonders of nature never ceased to amaze.

The Devoir did not look at the natural majesty around them the same way. For nearly every tree they passed, his eyes lost some of that neutral expression and darkened into a morbid brown. His mouth wrinkled into a little frown and it gave a brief view of his clenched teeth whenever they failed to uncover anything. His worry gradually became a vile discontent.

It was hard to look at the Devoir and see anything apart from anxiety. Though he would not let go of the past, Luchs could not deny that he saw so much vexing emotion.

Devoir pages were known for deceit, but they also put the Mad Prince before anything. While it all could very well be a trap, Luchs felt much less skeptical about the possibility of the disappearances being a trick.

The air, warm and comforting, suddenly turned cold when a wicked chill blew through the trees and down his neck.

Curious, Luchs looked to the sky through partings between the trees, their leaves shaking. It was as clear as it had been for days with scarcely any clouds in sight apart from the few wisps flying by. Everything looked normal, and the air was still humid. Whatever it was should have been dismissed as a little prank from Zyleec, child god of the wind, but there was something Luchs could not quite overlook, something frightened him.

The thought of a potential storm brought him to a halt.

Des Meurtal had a bizarre ecosystem that made exploring virtually impossible after a storm. Brief showers did not matter as much as when a downpour created a flood. The mighty giants making up Des Meurtal's forest could do nothing in against heavy rainfall to protect the soil. The ground would absorb every drop of water and turn the solid earth into a gelatinous surface that popped if someone took so much as a single misstep, drenching them in muddy water too thick to trudge through. The only places to move unhindered through were the sandy beaches and rocky bluffs, but even then, it was not safe. Large waves rolled into the shores and mighty gales brewed across the bluffs sweeping everything away in mere instances. Hunting became impossible when that happened, and no one was safe unless they found a well-grounded place to hide until the storm passed.

No one knew why the unusual phenomena happened, only that everyone needed to act when they did.

The signs above showed none of that would happen so soon. But the memory of that chill kept making him second guess it all.

"Nothing!"

The enemy page lost his composure after so much time without any sign of the lost. His face contorted from clenching his teeth and bitterly glaring at everything he saw. Frustration growing, he began stomping frantically about and kicking a tree at its base.

"Still nothing! Where the blazes did they go? The varlets didn't just upright vanish. They've got to be here somewhere."

The tone of his voice, it sounded frightened. His eyes bounced so frantically every which way that they looked ready to pop from his skull. Sweat fell from his jawline and off his earlobes. His hands trembled feverishly. It was hard to look away from.

It made Luchs think on something Sir Trenent, the knight who saved him, said once before:

"To know a person's anger is to know something about them."

In his breathing, his tense, hunched posture, his jittery eyes, there was an unquestionable fear. He was terrified of not finding his faction, one page in particular. It was then that Luchs stopped looking at him with disdain and contempt, seeing the page as just another lad with fears.

They were not in the best of places for him to lash out. Luchs stepped up to him and put a hand to his shoulder. A twitch jolted through his thick hands when the Devoir, panicked, reached for his sword only to stop when he realized it was only his reluctant companion.

"Keep your wits about you!"

The Devoir stared at him for a moment, still engrossed in their fruitless efforts, then took a deep breath. He was still uneasy and trembled while trying to contain his apprehensions, but the serene forest air calmed him enough to unclench his muscles and let the strain on both mind and body diminish.

"What's got you acting so crazy?"

The Devoir's uneasy eyes fixed themselves with disdain as he rebuffed the burly page's offer for help and repulsed his grip on his shoulder. "My comrades may be in danger, Féroce. I have to find them."

"'Tis your Mad Prince?"

He made that abruptly clear earlier. Instead of simply saying something happened to his faction, he pointed out their leader above all others.

While it should not have been very surprising, Luchs' rebuttal left the Devoir speechless for a moment. Still gruff and agitated, he turned away pacing toward the end of the path, shaking his head in refusal. He kept moving down the path another ten feet before stopping to look back at him and struggled to pick up the pieces of the broken mask depicting resolution.

Then he caved. "We're responsible for Cain. The commandant made that very clear after the mess we made." That seemed to be all he was willing to say until he saw the raised eyebrow on Luchs' face; it was apparent that he needed further explanation. Again, he caved. "He wasn't the only one punished when the knights came to judge us. He took his lumps, aye, and then some, but much of the blame for what happened fell on us for listening to him in the first place. 'Instead of letting the maggot lead ye by a stick, ye should have taken it and beat him with it for such idiocy,' he said. Then he left the burden of watching over that lunatic— making sure he did not do or made anyone do something foolhardy—on us!" The pent-up grievances finally being laid bare, the Devoir stood shaking, almost fatigued, after keeping in so much tension. "If he kills, even when we try to stop him, we get blamed. If he goes missing, that's our fault too. If he dies..." He took another breath as he clenched a fist again. "Fie! This is my problem, not yours. Just go back to your faction and let them know what's been happening."

Once again, he walked down the path, this time without stopping to wait for Luchs to follow.

It never occurred to Luchs to pursue the Devoir or let him go. He simply remained where he was, motionless and staring at the spot the lad walked away from.

It was little wonder he was such a wreck. All of that pressure, all of that responsibility Commandant Brunlier foisted upon him and the rest of his faction drove him mad with fear over the punishment that awaited them should they fail again. If how he spoke was of any indication, the task was unforgiving.

Listening to him gripe about his problems when they committed the unforgivable made a vein in Luchs' head throb grotesquely. It was as annoying as a festering tick gnawing at the skin for nourishment. And yet, when he chose to cast him away with the suggestion to put his own before a rival, it made Luchs wonder what was going on in his head. There was something about him that he resonated with, something that made him regret letting him wander off alone.

In that irate, raspy voice was the shambles of pride.

Although feeling he would kick himself for it later, Luchs dashed deeper into the dark forest to catch up with him.

The surroundings became eerier as more fragments of sunlight had been cut off by the profuse green canopy overhead. Creeping vines hung from the branches; some resembled threatening serpents in the cover of darkness while others bundled together into natural curtains.

And then, it happened—the ghostly whispers.

Luchs stopped in place and turned around to where he heard the first, then looked to a tree with a hollow cavity in its trunk, then faced the outstretched forked paths ahead.

Those whispers were always heard in that corner of the forest at every time of day no matter the weather. Rarely anyone on the island ventured there, whether at sunlight or sunset, so to avoid the spirits they thought haunted the area.

Luchs did not believe in specters or spooks of any kind. The whispers were an effect of the winds blowing through the unusual plants and trees around him. He knew that, but stopping and looking wherever he heard them was a reflex he could not shake.

Choosing to ignore them, he retraced his steps and turned to the numerous possible directions the Devoir could have gone. To have gone so far so quickly meant he had to have started sprinting at one point. Luchs took slow steps while crossing the broad path in search of fresh footprints. The fading sunlight made it so he had to crouch down every now and then to make certain he did not miss anything.

Then he found it—a set of prints at the path in the leftmost fork. They blended in well with the shadows, the first few sets barely left behind by any force like its owner attempted to mask his presence. Past a fair distance, they had more depth, more weight pressed into the ground, until it looked like he had started running.

Running toward something? Or away from it?

Not wasting any time, Luchs ran in that direction.

Rushing through the lukewarm air made the eerie whispers sound all the louder, much to his chagrin. Some of them almost sounded clear enough to make out a few syllables or words. It gave him goosebumps hearing what he did. He cursed again and again for letting the bizarre phenomenon get to him. At the very least, the scream up ahead broke the stream of whispers.

Signs of a struggle were laid out down the twisted path. Tracks trampled the ground in violent desperation, not just one pair but a second joining in around the dead tree resembling a grasping hand. The new set was definitely human, but much larger and took longer strides than the other, and more weight was put into the steps making them easier to see. Their size dictated they belonged to an adult, but the prints were of bare feet, not from the boots the knights wore.

Another bloody scream resounded in the distance. It was not just anyone. That pained outburst belonged to the Devoir page he had been following.

Luchs dashed through the thicket in hopes of finding the Devoir before he met his end. It no longer mattered whether he was an ally or an enemy. He could not have him dying.

After crossing a faint patch of dim bronze blossoms grown underneath the shade of a tree, he was close enough to whatever conflict that ensued to hear the *clang, clang* of metal coarsely meeting metal. The pursuer had a weapon on hand, and the Devoir was faltering against him.

In his sprint, Luchs slung his bow off his shoulder, quickly taking it in hand along with one of the few arrows in his quiver. Whatever foe it was must be incredibly dangerous if he posed a threat to a Devoir. He needed to move fast and leave his mark where it hurt.

The foliage around him grew close together densely as he kept moving. The leaves turned so dark as to appear pitch-black.

And as he broke through the botanical barricade blocking his path, he found the Devoir squaring off against his pursuer. Going toe-to-toe with him was this big, surly, snaggle-toothed brute batting at him with a thick scimitar. The hunched stature this stranger held made him appear more ogre than man. One look at him and Luchs knew a single arrow would not be enough to fell him.

Who was that ogre, and where did he come from? He looked nearly as formidable as the commandant himself. There was no way someone so deformed could have remained hidden away without someone noticing.

The ogre's size gave Luchs a substantial target, but seeing as he had such thick skin, he doubted how deep an arrow would go. Aiming for the torso would be best and even that might not be enough. So long as the ogre kept moving his arms, puncturing a weak point would be trying.

The situation was not yet helpless. The Devoir stood his ground against the horrendous man, though not as many of his faction would have. He kept on the defensive for the most part by holding his sword out with his hand against the flat of the blade, swinging it with both hands only when there was a real opening. Odd as it was to see an Ederean page using a reserved stance, it would keep him alive long enough for Luchs to find a weak point. There was still hope so long as he kept resisting. A chance would come, and Luchs was ready for it with an arrow drawn and nocked against the bow.

The Devoir tried taking the offensive back again by rushing straight for the enemy. He ducked down when the blade slew horizontally for his neck, then attempted to throw his foe off balance by shoving him. A perfect opportunity presented itself and he drew his sword skyward to cleave through the ogre with great ferocity. The ogre drew his blade in before metal met skin and held the lad at bay. It was a duel of brute force from then on, one where the outcome grew one-sided as the much larger adversary easily pushed the other down.

The crimson marks steadily spreading on the Devoir's left shoulder and staining his right hip glistened in the dim sunlight. He would not last long.

And still he fought.

The page rolled to his weakened side, slipping away from the scimitar's slam, slowing both of them down a moment. Wincing from the sudden action, he barely had the focus to look toward the ogre as he raised his curved blade and moved in to take the final blow, exposing his blubbery neck at the side.

Luchs, his eyes drawing wide open at the chance, let the arrow fly at that exact moment, piercing the vulnerable swell of fat near the stranger's bloated windpipe. Wasting nary a moment, he charged from his cover while his target uncontrollably writhed in pain and tackled the brute with all his strength. Even the most skillful warriors could easily be bested by those much weaker than they if thrown off balance. With the momentum he picked up, Luchs kept pushing the ogre until slamming him into a tree trunk as strong as a stone wall.

Blood spat from the ogre's mouth and squirted from the hole in his neck upon the impact. The sweltered mass slowly crumbled, letting out a loud grinding sound as it slicked against the healthy trunk.

While not the most gallant way to stop an enemy, it was satisfying to know he was able to pull it off. Luchs took slow steps away from the stranger to ensure he would not follow, then hustled over to the Devoir, who struggled to get off the ground. Gripping the bleeding page by the shoulder startled him, urging a quick lift from his sword before he realized who it was.

"On your feet."

He looked ready to argue for a moment, but the Devoir followed Luchs' lead mustering every bit of his fleeting strength. His legs were shaky and looked ready to buckle over even with the support offered to him.

"I ... didn't need your help."

If only to save face, the Devoir maintained balance and pushed Luchs hands off of him, grunting heavily from the simple action.

"Aye, sure you didn't," sarcastically rebuked Luchs when he glanced at the blood splotched onto his fingers. "What's this then? Crushed berries?"

"'Tisn't the time to jest! We need to tell the knights."

If anything, it tickled Luchs to see how much fire the Devoir was showing, unlike before. But he was right. Whoever that was, he was no knight, not without a shield from a superior, not with his lack of armor and decent clothing. Some mad interloper somehow got onto the island without anyone noticing and tried to kill someone. For all they knew, he could have been responsible for the vanishing pages.

They turned back toward the path they came from, Luchs tacitly offering to catch the Devoir if he fell over by remaining within a distance of his shadow. The walk back to their factions would be a long one—and it was about to get longer.

Leaves steadily swayed and rustled overhead, causing their hair to stand on end. A low, heavy creak from behind urged them to reach for their weapons, and the low moan that followed made their blood run cold. Whatever injury and pain earlier inflicted seemed to somehow fade as the ogre rose to his feet and ripped the arrow from his neck.

When reaching for another arrow, Luchs realized his bow was no longer in his hand, but near the ogre's fat feet. How it slipped from his grasp was beyond him.

"You still raring to go?"

But he did not focus on that. The threat was back on his feet and steadily stomped toward them malevolently. Until it was removed, their focus could not break.

With the Devoir in his current condition, it might have been more tactical to escape, but if they did, they would never forgive themselves.

Knights did not run from a fight nor did they turn their back on an enemy. Knights fought the evil that dared disturb the peace—or whatever it should be called on Des Meurtal—and punished them to the extent they deserved.

The Devoir, taking his sword in both hands, readied a reserved stance once more. "Don't mock me!"

Grinning, Luchs drew his sword.

Groaning so tensely it sounded like a growl, the ogre charged at the two with his scimitar eager to taste blood. The ground practically shook from every step he took, further displaying just how much power that was under his belt. The pages ran in different directions when he came in so close to divide his attention, confusing him for a moment. Luchs, eager to end it quickly, dove at the ogre. He swung his sword while drawing his free arm aside in perfect synch, the joined movement allowing both to move quicker. The ogre, meeting the blade with his scimitar, tried swiping Luchs away with a single flick, focused on ending the child he first set his eyes on. But Luchs held his ground, not willing to give the ogre the opportunity to pick them off one by one. Sparks flew when the sharpened metal gnashed together. The clash would have already been settled if it were left to brute strength. While the ogre would normally overpower him, the wounds already inflicted left him dazed and his movements clumsy.

Leaving nothing to chance, the Devoir clenched his sword in his hands and lunged at the enemy's exposed back. The ogre, seeing immediate action was needed, used his gargantuan size as further leverage against Luchs, sweeping him aside and kept moving with the swing of his curved sword in time to intercept the darting Devoir before his weapon met flesh. The impact was so fierce it knocked the sword from his hand and the already fatigued page on his back.

The heinous man loomed closer to him, his shadow banishing the meager light around him. Raising the scimitar high left himself exposed to Luchs, who, in desperation to save his ally, rushed at the ogre. He heard the approach as he had with the less beefy child and turned to swing.

Dragging out the fight after losing blood so profusely made his moves more sluggish, easier to perceive, allowing Luchs to pivot aside the angled slash. Then, as the ogre prepared for the final blow, Luchs seized his opportunity and thrust his sword into the ogre's ribcage. There was enough force behind the blade to tear through his muscles and, a torrent of blood erupting from his chest, skewer his heart.

With hands gripped painfully onto the hilt, the blade connected to the bleeding body, he could feel everything happening in that moment. The ogre's massive, deformed muscles trembled agonizingly. His throaty breathing grew weaker. And as the ogre struggled to raise his scimitar again and take the page with him, all control of his body broke until movement could only be imagined.

With that, the ogre breathed his last.

After he was certain the enemy had been slain, Luchs took a few heavy steps back, drawing his sword from the fresh corpse, and fell back onto the grass. His legs trembled violently, as did his arms, which made the sword rattle and the freshly spilled blood dribble and spatter. Haggard breath forced its way past his lips. His heart palpitated painfully against his chest. The scent of blood, wafting against his nose, twisted and blurred his vision into a mess of crimson.

"Hey, Féroce!"

It took a moment for him to remember he was not alone. He shook his head slightly before looking to the Devoir, who had been watching the struggle from where he had been left. There was that bizarre look in his eyes again, but there was something else: relief.

"You all right?"

There was much less bleakness in his voice than when they met earlier. Luchs was much too rattled to give the shifts in that page's attitudes and countenance any real thought. For now, at least, he took his kindness as just that.

"Aye... I will be. Just need a moment."

The Devoir gave a brief, tart chortle, but he tried to hold it back. It seemed the distress in Luchs was obvious in his eyes.

Not wishing to look the startled child any longer, Luchs forced himself to be still, clenching his hands and teeth tight, then stood again. There was no point in getting so worked up over the death of a man who tried to murder them.

Both pages mustered the strength to stand once more, fighting off fatigue, injury, and weakness. Luchs needed a few moments to keep his legs from shaking so much.

The Devoir approached the ogre, looking at him with contempt, and took one of his arms over his shoulder. "We ought to bring this back with us. The commandant will want to see."

It was a good idea. Neither recognized the dead man and doubted anyone else would either. It needed to be investigated immediately.

Luchs walked up to the man he felled, took the other arm over his shoulder, and the two began marching down the path they came from.

~ Third Chapter ~

Taking Back Des Meurtal

The knights were in an uproar when presented with the corpse of the unknown man. They immediately sent word for everyone to gather and left to locate Commandant Brunlier. Several remained with Luchs and the Devoir to bombard them with questions as they tended to their wounds.

Luchs did most of the talking, though there was not much to offer.

They did not know who the man was, where he came from, why he suddenly appeared, or what connection he had to the disappearing pages. The questioning only left more to ponder on.

The knights returned with Commandant Brunlier and the remaining pages, all notified of their unwanted guest. Every faction gathered to witness what they thought impossible. They were all dumbfounded by what they saw, and they were even more surprised that two pages were able to bring down such a sizeable monstrosity.

While the knights attempted to figure out who the intruder was, Luchs and the Devoir were ordered to rest.

Rufus and Aloysius were completely beside themselves when they met up with their comrade. They asked him many questions, such as why he was with a Devoir of all people. After everything that happened, though, he did not have the energy to deal with them.

He slipped away from the others when he found the chance, but he could not keep still sitting under the tree he retreated to. His arms and legs would not stop trembling no matter how hard he tried to fight it. He could not relax since plunging his sword into the ogre's abdomen, feeling the life drain from him as blood trickled down its blade. The fear and despair he felt as everything slipped away and faded into nothingness pooled down the blade and into Luchs.

Thinking back on it, he felt pathetic. It was just like when he first arrived on Des Meurtal.

There was another time Luchs had to take the life of another person to stay alive, and it was just as horrific. It was during his first year on the island, the lad a new page with nothing more than the basic knowledge for combat and survival. Barely a few days passed after his arrival, and he had been pulled into the chaos wrought by the Devoir faction's rampant murders. At the time, he knew nothing of how poorly the faction was doing against their adversaries, only that one of them had gone mad after assuming control.

The act of simulating warfare became war itself. Anxiety pumped through his veins instead of blood. Tension made his muscles into stone, yet his reflexes and reaction time became snake-like. It did not get any easier when the other factions decided it was time to retaliate.

When the time came to stop the Devoir faction, the four other factions marched together to the heart of the forest where the Devoir had taken refuge among the tall trees and capricious creepers. The other four groups had the equivalent of twelve strapping lads all combatting another at their best. The sun shined high above their heads, glaring through the cover of the trees, and the air was bone dry. The pages drew on until pain and fatigue gripped them, pulling their bodies down to the blistery ground. When the Devoir pages could no longer resist, the others bound them with the creepers to keep them from getting back up and killing.

Luchs got separated from his faction during the chaos and faced off against two experienced pages alone. They pursued him into a dark thicket, surrounding him, then cornered him, cutting off his only escape, against the bars of a woodsy cage.

Panic overlapped his thoughts, clouding his mind with fear and desperation. With the enemies closing in, he frantically fought back, wanting the thoughts of cages and chains they pressed into his mind to be purged.

Luchs was unsure what had happened after that. During the conflict, he had been enveloped by fright and the terrible, inhumane images he had been haunted by for a year. And when he came to, the first thing he noticed was the sword he held piercing through the chest of the lad with freckles and a big forehead. The lad's blood coated his sword and spattered on his hands and face, staining his skin with the thick crimson. Its stench crawled into his nostrils, warping his thoughts and sight with despairing colors. As the blood drained from the lad's body, Luchs felt the terror in his trembling muscles, the vibrations creeping through the sword and into his hands, until all that remained fell into a dark, avaricious void.

It was absolutely horrifying.

Four long years had passed since then, and he still reacted so harrowingly to the death he inflicted upon another. With all the time spent on this dangerous island, he thought he would have become numb to death, but it still tormented him to take the life of a person.

He never told another soul of that experience. A knight that could not bring himself to kill, that froze when he did, would be a laughing stock. It would keep the knight's shield he coveted out of reach forever.

"Hey."

While he attempted to work through the dread and force his body to remain still, someone went against his wishes to be left alone. It no longer fazed him that the Devoir he saved approached him so casually. Apparently, the page was more interested in him than looking at the corpse that nearly slain him. He stared down at him with those dark, tired eyes as though eying a wounded pup.

Disrespectful as it was, Luchs did himself no favors looking so pathetic. How it irked him to be pitied by him.

"You mind me joining you?"

After what happened, it did not matter that he tried getting so close. Luchs just shrugged, not willing to offer more than that.

The Devoir took that as acceptance and sat down by a root fencing the two apart. Moments passed without a word said, just the clamor from those eying the corpse and the wisps of trembling winds.

Turning focus toward the change in the wind current was the only thing that kept Luchs calm. He could not shake the feeling something was unusual in how it abruptly soared past the island in small gusts, gusts that kept growing stronger. Making preparations for a potential storm occurred to him, but the way events played out made thinking about it trivial.

"Still thinking about it?"

Luchs looked the Devoir's way after hearing his question. His voice wavered against his ears with a ring of sympathy. Although he had heard it a few times before, this was the only time Luchs had not let it fall upon deaf ears.

"What are you babbling about?"

The Devoir did not take the mild snapping reaction personally. He shrugged it off without much care and went on. "The kill. It's still gnawing at you." If it was so obvious, there was little point in offering a response. The bitter silence was all he needed to be sure. "Biting your tongue won't make you look any stronger. Trust me."

"And a varlet like you would know?"

"Aye, I know. I've spilled more blood following orders than you have, no doubt, and I hated doing it."

The page eased his body against the tall spruce. The dreary way he looked at the sky and the lax position he took made him look like a soldier who spent the days intensely training but was not satisfied with the results. "You can't imagine how much it pained me to do it."

"Then why did you—"

"No matter what you think of my faction," the Devoir interrupted with a firm, strong tone, then went on in a much less brutal voice, "we are not without hearts." Such a statement was seen as nothing short of hypocrisy, but the way he carried himself made it hard to think him a liar. His voice was tired yet resolute, his expression tensing up when he first spoke. "Who do you think got us into this? 'Twas all because of Cain.

"We were content training with the others before he took over—just sparring, hunting, and taking territory. But it was not enough for him. He wanted a name for himself before leaving this place, and he aimed to take one through true warfare. The maniac asserted himself as leader of the Devoir and made us kill our competition, saying we cannot grow as real knights unless we took lives instead of sparing them ... and threatening to take ours unless we complied.

"Cain made us ignore our consciences. 'Twas because of him that I killed pages I once sparred confidently with. 'Twas because of him that we've earned ourselves reputations as blackhearts, as monsters! It tore us all apart."

Every word he spoke was tortured, riddled with guilt and shame. There could be no denying just how much he despised everything he did.

To be led by such a monster, someone who forced them to kill or be killed, even for a short time, must have been like being pushed in the direction of an angry bear with a knife held to his back if there were any attempts to flee. The entire faction was in unrest the entire time, the Mad Prince making it so there would be no real sanctuary for them. Such an evil page.

But there was only one.

"Why didn't you drive him out of the faction together with your comrades?" Luchs asked. "You could have revolted."

The Devoir shook his head. "'Twasn't so simple. Not when our leader is son to the island's own monster."

Luchs, wide-eyed as a mackerel floundering on land, turned his attention to the perturbed group gathered around the corpse and looked to the commandant, who stared at the empty husk.

A child of Commandant Brunlier.

He never thought the commandant had family of his own.

It all made sense. They could not refuse Cain's orders out of fear he would torment them, and they could not oust Cain out of fear of what the commandant—the man who beat his pages for sport—would do to them. And going to the other factions for help could not happen after what they had done. The many who opposed Cain were trapped in their own trial for survival where no one would escape unscathed in body or mind.

"We thought Commandant Brunlier approved of his son's insanity. We didn't know what to do. We were scared out of our minds. All we could think of then was getting out of that mess with our heads." The Devoir turned to face Luchs, seriousness written plainly over his tired face. "I'm not making excuses. I know what we did was unforgivable. All I'm saying is, I know how hard killing can be. How you're reacting right now, it means you value life, even that of someone who tried to take yours."

His words left Luchs speechless. All this time, he thought of his reaction to taking human life as a weakness, something he needed to shake if he wanted to earn his shield. To see those moments as mourning the life he took made him feel less deplorable.

Knights valued life, after all, but they also needed to take life in order to protect the weak and innocent. Unless he found a way to manage his dread over ending his enemies, he would not make a worthy knight.

He looked back at the Devoir baffled, but still tried to keep a proud demeanor. Although he was responsible for ending many a good page, he also had his own battle to suffer through. It was about survival. He did all he could to protect his life so that he could return home alive.

He could not, Luchs realized, be faulted for doing that.

Even if our training is meant to put us against each other, we're supposed to be united in the end.

"Luchs," he stated. "My name is Luchs."

The Devoir stared at him, surprised he was willing to offer an introduction. Meeting him halfway, he smiled and returned the favor. "And mine is Maxime."

The two remained seated underneath the tree for some time and discussed each other's notions and insights on what they experienced when they took a life. Both of them seemed to experience a similar sensation, for the most part, where they felt their enemy's life melting through them and taking a part of themselves away when it left. The sensation was terribly cold yet burned like an unholy fire. It was terrifying, leaving them hollow for mere moments, and left scarred soon after.

Strange as it seemed, discussing it made them feel less abhorrent over what happened.

Everyone gathered around the commandant when Maxime began mentioning methods to overcome those gripping sensations. They put their discussion on hold to see what got them so excited.

When everyone gathered, Commandant Brunlier crouched down by the corpse, which had been flipped onto its stomach. Below the shoulder blades, buried beneath a layer of rolled-up fat, and a smidgen to the left of the proximal point of the spine was a brand shaped like a skull shackled by the neck with a scar at the right eye.

"An escaped convict!?" shouted one of the younger knights.

Whenever a criminal was caught, they were branded after their sentencing to be easier to find should they manage to escape from their punishment. That one must have put up quite the fight for the brander to miss the back of his neck so far off.

The stranger's presence alone was enough to rattle anyone, but to learn he was a criminal nearly made the pages panic.

The commandant angrily knocked the corpse aside with his boot. "And I doubt he was alone." His tone reverberated a hostility rarely heard from the bored behemoth.

Most of the pages there were well-educated about criminal activity before being sent to the island; they knew the odds of a single Ederean criminal travelling alone so far to the edge of the country was slim. The land forming the Ederean Archipelago was too secure for criminals to remain on land for too long. It was why many resorted to piracy.

"To show their hides as the generals send a ship our way. If'n they arrive with pirates running loose, my authority here will be put into question, the training done here thought misbegotten. The lads won't be closer to a shield than when they arrived."

Shock settled among the pages, followed by disbelief, until finally rage set in. If that did not motivate them to step up and ready themselves to get rid of the invaders, nothing would.

The commandant turned to face his subordinates and pages with strong dedication and unruly ferocity. His already gravelly voice rattled unsavorily when he groaned, and as he spoke, it resembled something of a beastly roar. "Men, lads, arm yerselves with everything ye can find! We set out to hunt down the rest of these swine before the next sunrise. By the time the ship arrives, we'll have the heads of these convicts to present—a grand accomplishment for ye all to bring home. There will be no restraint, no holding back. These are no longer training grounds, but a war zone! Now go! Be ready before I hunt ye down too!"

Not a single person remained once Commandant Brunlier finished barking orders to his impromptu army. They all scattered in every direction, searching for any useful weaponry kept hidden out of sight. Several of the knights moved towards the camp that was their center of operations. Luchs and Maxime were about to set out themselves when—

"Lads," Commandant Brunlier barked. They looked his way to find the behemoth marching up to them. "I hear ye be the ones who brought me this gift." His left hand gestured to the corpse that was left to decompose.

The pages stood, Luchs helping Maxime until he could keep on his feet by himself, then they explained what happened. Their story amused him.

"Show me where ye found it."

By his order, the two backtracked to the dark grove where they faced off against the ogre. It did not take as long without the dead weight slowing them down. They kept note of the landmarks—the hollow tree with a ravenous face, the patch of bronze blossoms—anticipating the need to return. The march was an uncomfortable one with the behemoth accompanying them. Unnerving as his presence was, the commandant would no doubt frighten off any dangers that came their way.

They came to the dark grove where the fight took place. The pages were ordered to remain there while the commandant inspected the area.

Staying there made the memory of that heinous sensation Luchs earlier felt fester in his mind. His eyes were fixated on the spot where he slayed the ogre. Looking down at it made time stand still, the terrible dread still lingering, as though the man who died was still suffering.

"Still shaky about it?"

It seemed the foreboding weakness he felt showed.

Maxime looked at him pitifully. "Dwelling on it won't do you any good. You'll end up filling that head of yours with dread."

"Are you telling me to just forget it?" Luchs growled.

Maxime shook his head. "I didn't say forget, just *don't dwell.*" He emphasized the last words carefully, and without spite. "The more you think about what you felt, the more of a hold it has on you. Men who can't move forward make for poor soldiers."

"Says a lad who is yet a man or soldier." Luchs could not help saying as much, but he remembered Maxime took more lives, spilled more blood, than he did. "Your first kill, what was it like?"

Maxime picked up a small rock the size of his palm. He tossed it at a melon-like fruit hanging from the branch above him, knocking it off its stem. When it smashed onto the ground, he picked up a piece and sampled the soft, moist golden insides. It had to have been tasty for him to smack his lips.

"A lot like yours. Even after Cain had his power taken away, it still got to me. I can't change what I did, and letting it pick at my mind only drove me mad."

"So what did you do? How do you move forward?"

"I think about why I became a page." Maxime sat there, reflecting on what he said, staring at nothing. When he came to, he took another bite of the melon. "You weren't forced into this, were you?"

"Course not! I asked for this. I asked to be a page."

Maxime stared at Luchs while he ate the melon, then looked to be in thought after he swallowed. "So why did you ask for it?"

Answering his question with more questions annoyed Luchs. But it made him think.

Sir Trenent, Liliiun, Agnes, Ulrin, Jilié—the Vertueux family looked after and protected him when his world had been shattered along with his mind. So many wonderful people treated his wounds and took care of him, a stranger, without a care for who he was or where he came from.

All of their efforts would have been for naught were he to be felled in preparing himself to set back out into the world.

The dread he felt remembering the kill committed in the dark grove diminished in light of those fond memories. Was that the answer? Fighting to live for them? To fulfill his promise to repay their kindness by honoring their name?

He did not know, but it was something worth holding onto.

Commandant Brunlier found what he needed and returned to the meeting place where everyone gathered with Luchs and Maxime. He informed them that he narrowed down the few possible hiding places the enemy could hold themselves in without detection, all of which existed past the grove.

They marched northwest for the bog beyond the forest. Many hesitated to proceed once they reached it. The bog was forbidden territory for good reason. The terrain was loose, unstable, and dangerous to walk across. One wrong step and someone would wind up swallowed by the thick, miry waters. Three pages and a knight were already lost to the treacherous pit since Des Meurtal became a facility, and everyone was warned time and again never to go there.

No one thought the invaders would hide there, but it was the best way to approach the other possible hiding places without getting detected.

Everyone moved through the bog in small groups of at least three so they could aid each other should one of them get stuck in the muck, but not groups so large that the scant stable ground around them would cave in and swallow them. The Féroce faction moved well ahead of everyone else with Luchs' intuition to guide them where it was safest. With every step he took, he felt the ground a small diameter around him and how strong it was. He had some trouble himself due to his weight constantly dragging him down, the loose, sloppy earth trying to integrate him.

Once everyone got through, it was a straight path to their mark.

The only other places a large group could remain hidden on the island without being noticed were the small mountain and a sharp cliff overlooking the ocean. Since the mountain would take more time to comb through, they marched to the cliffs.

The ground rose steeply as they walked on, making it a challenge for many to follow without stopping for breath. Fewer trees grew along the path, exposing the sky which, much unlike before, looked dark and bleak. Clouds have rolled in to block out much of the sun's light. Several layers were darkened enough to suspect a storm. Rain had yet to fall despite how much moisture there was in the air.

From where they crossed, the steep cliff looked no different than smooth ground. There was nowhere to go except off the cliff, a ninety-foot drop into the ocean. Anyone fool enough to do that would have to be hopelessly desperate. A curious Rufus rushed over to the jagged edge— excitable as ever—so he could get a look at what was down there.

Nothing but sharp rocks made sharper by crashing waves.

Careful about masking their presence, Aloysius kept right on his tail ready to cup a hand over his mouth if he decided to yell something absurd for a laugh.

"The sailors who discovered this land called this the Leviathan's Maw," Commandant Brunlier stated nonchalantly. The pages looked his way when he approached and took a look down himself. "The cliff below opens into a gaping wide maw like the jaws of the beast itself." It was not a simple conversation he was striking up. His knights caught on that he suspected their enemies have hidden themselves inside the Maw.

There had to be a way to scale down without clinging to the edge since someone managed to find their way to the surface, but even the knights familiar with the island knew no direct path down.

Every group split up to search for a path while Commandant Brunlier stood unwavering near the cliff's edge. The Féroce took to the northern side with remnants of the Chevalerie and Vaincre factions; the southern side was left to the Loi and Devoir. The ground seemed relatively smooth all around, a large stone protruding from the compact earth hither and thither, but no path in plain sight led down the cliffside.

Believing the sharp stone spires might be masking something else, Luchs suggested searching around them. Rufus and Aloysius, in agreement and not having much luck on their ends, followed his lead and began searching them, but they quickly took the lead themselves when he stopped behind them.

The wind became too much to ignore. An eerie gust bellowed, carrying the sound of ghastly moaning, as if a spirit haunted the place. Wind flow was often strong around such high places overlooking the sea, but the ominous gust felt too strong streaming over his cheeks, brushing back his hair, drying out his eyes. Turning his attention to the open sky, he tried to make sense of it. He kept eying the clouds, those thick black smears just narrowly above the sun. The scattered ones were nothing; it was the cluster of dark clouds clawing its way from the horizon toward the island that made him shudder.

It was a bad sign.

"Men! Over here!"

Everyone rushed over to the soldier who excitably called them. He managed to uncover a compact passage that drew down the cliffside hidden between two stone mounds. It was just barely wide enough for the interloper to slip through.

The commandant inspected the natural staircase with intrigue, a wide, toothy sneer sprouting over his face. The cramped space did not seem to concern him. He hunched his back and bent down, taking the first step. "Never saw the inside of the Maw meself. Who would've thought it would take *this* to finally make it?" Everyone remained silent while Commandant Brunlier savored the moment. He was almost calm enough to appear content. Of course, with the hunt drawing near, that nearly pleased expression soon changed to a grin revealing a primal ferocity. "Our victory shall be all the sweeter. Onward!"

And so, the soldiers and pages orderly marched down the small passage, following their commandant's lead. The path had not been in use for long. Much of the rubble underfoot was slick and smooth and would likely be difficult to cross if rain fell.

That very possibility troubling him, Luchs glanced up at the sky whenever the path seemed clear enough for him to turn away from for at least a moment. The clouds began to roll in, darkness casting out the light fading in the distance. Just a glance at them and Luchs knew the chances of a storm were absolute. The darkness had clawed its way closer to Des Meurtal as they reached to lower end of the cliff walls.

At the rate it was approaching, it would swallow them mid-battle.

"I don't like the looks of this."

Aloysius overheard those worrisome words despite strong winds shooting up the cliffside, though not well. "Did you say something, Luchs?"

"You see those clouds there? They bring a storm—a big one!"

"What damage do you think it'll bring?"

"Not sure. But the winds are already strong, and the air's getting heavier. Either it'll be swift and devastating, or linger for days to come."

His leader did not like the sound of this, and neither did the few listening in on them. They could not likely turn back, though.

Any battle, even one where the gods punished good men-at-arms with chaotic winds and piercing rain, must be seen through until the end. Every soldier must fight through blistering sunny days, harrowing rainfall, ghastly winds, even monstrous sea waves in the name of the exalted du Joiec bloodline to be called true knights. It fell onto them to punish those who dared oppose the laws of the kingdom, no matter the situation.

All Luchs hoped for was to surmount the invaders before the elements turned against them.

The impromptu army soon reached the bottom of the path and discovered the menacing cave down the throat of a leviathan's head. Lodged inside of it was a ship. It was a grand ship built from wood as dark as the night sky, bearing flags with no colors on its masts, and armed with several cannons around the gun deck.

Without a doubt, it was a pirate ship.

"And here I was only jesting," Rufus muttered to himself.

It was a surprise to Aloysius and Luchs too. No one else took it any better either. They lived as they had on the island believing the magic shielding it would allow their training to go on uninterrupted. It was a critical blow to their faith, even after already witnessing one man slink through. Even a few knights were left speechless by the sight.

Since they knew what they were dealing with, there was no need to make any change in plans. They were convicts who disturbed the law of the land for their personal gain and needed to be punished. The knighted held onto their faith knowing that. The pages, wanting to appear as capable, held their weapons firm. As for their commandant, no one could pry the sword from his hand even if he fell in battle.

The knight carrying a spyglass on hand took a look at the ship's structure, then put it away. "A few are keeping watch, but it looks like most of the crew is resting. If we make a quiet approach, we may retake the island without many casualties."

Those words reassured a few yet rattled the rest. They invaded their island and turned one of their own loose to massacre the pages. Retribution was in order, not just capture but total, crushing defeat.

While there were others in disagreement over this, there were also the cannons to consider. Not seeing a way he could toy with the pirates beforehand, Commandant Brunlier made the call for a stealthy approach. Hungry for blood as he was, the man was not so foolhardy that he would risk himself and his comrades being blasted to smithereens.

From the maw of the cavern lay a rough tongue of a path leading down into the ghastly gullet covered in stone spires above and below. The natural sounds of the wind and stirring waters echoing against the walls imitated the sound of a growling beast, leaving the army hesitant to move. The march into the Leviathan's Maw took considerable patience. Water drenched every surface, the faint *splish, splash* and *drip, drip* echoing through the cavern, making it difficult to move in silence. Too many moving at once too quickly would give them away immediately, but they needed to remain hidden for as long as possible, so they could not linger in the open. The stalled march, the alarming waves crashing against the island, the slow, audible drips from fallen droplets—it was enough to make a jittery lad lose patience and recklessly charge in.

The army made it to a makeshift dock with two planks bridging a way to the ship. The path was clear, but before they could sneak aboard, a deafening horn sounded from the crow's nest. They were spotted.

"Forward, now!"

Commandant Brunlier led the charge across the plank and onto the ship. About half of their army, including many pages and a few knights, managed to join him before the man who sounded the alarm hurled an axe at the planks, shattering them and cutting off the way aboard. Several pirates already joined their attackers on deck and moved to intercept them. They were quick to operate, perhaps anticipating the attack.

Enemies from above were dangerous if left alone. A few pages arming themselves with bows nocked their arrows and let them loose at the pirates perched at the crow's nests. It took a few tries, but Maxime and another page with a keen eye managed to shoot them down before they could cause any more trouble.

A change of plans was needed. Everyone searched for another way to board the enemy vessel, keeping in groups so they would not be alone if ambushed. Fortunately, they found the perfect opportunity. Near the end of the cavern was a massive slab of land where the ground made a gentle slope over the deck of the ship.

"What are you waiting for?" Aloysius shouted. He assumed everyone noticed the same fortuitous opportunity, and those that had not would soon enough. "Move it!"

What was left of their force rushed for the slope, eager to help out their comrades before the enemy's numbers overwhelmed them. Luchs kept an eye on the path and had the other scanning his surroundings for abnormal activity, the buckler in his left hand held before him the entire way, wary of sudden attacks. If they were so organized, there could be other countermeasures in place.

And it seemed he was right to fear so.

The pirates, not wanting to withstand the entire army's force united, took drastic action. Several men took the ropes strapped to the mast and swung on them, using the momentum to hurl them atop the slope. Many more slunk out of the shadows and surrounded the lads. There were three pirates for every page.

The odds were against them, but they did not back down. A few bold pages even continued charging for the wall of burly, scarred men, shifting past the swing of their swords and ramming into them. They tackled the pirates off the ledge and flattening them onto the ship's deck. As for the rest, they gathered together to rely on one another when their enemies closed in.

The pirates were quick to encircle their victims. The pages followed the knights' lead when the pirates got within swinging distance and struck hard while they raised their weapons. Ten sea rats fell from letting overconfidence get the best of them. The remaining were much more careful and resilient.

Luchs charged at the nearest pirate. That one was a portly yet robust fighter who carried a large axe. His movements were slow but accurate, something he proved after Luchs rushed at him, using his axe handle to shield him from the page's sword and shove him away. The portly pirate then threw his axe in a horizontal slice, eager to decapitate him. Luchs swung his sword at the axe's handle, shoving it back with great force. The enemy was strong, but not so much that he had to strain himself fighting him back.

"Little—" The pirate grew agitated at the smaller warrior managing to hold him back, and moved in to swing low when one of the knights jumped into the fight and swung his broad halberd across his fat ribs. It ripped apart his heart, blood furiously gushing out of his abdomen.

The scent of blood wafting against his nostrils made Luchs go rigid again. It was getting worse. Just the mere aspects of death were beginning to make him freeze, becoming consumed by the dread.

More were bound to die in the conflict, enemies and allies alike, and nothing could be done about that. He gritted his teeth in fright and frustration both, desperate for a way to overcome the sinister sensation ensnaring him.

"Luchs!"

Another pirate drew near Luchs while he was in his daze and readied to take his life. Had Rufus not jumped in from the side and carved through the man with his small, angular axe, he would have been done for. Rufus then threw his fist into the man's gut and knocked him off the ledge. He turned back to face his comrade, a nasty gash over his left eye, his breathing frantic. Even after losing his depth perception, he still had enough focus to butcher a person, whereas Luchs could barely ignore one death to prevent his own.

"What's going on with you?" Rufus asked breathlessly. "Get it together, mate! We can't be losing you here."

He remained by his side as more pirates came their way.

Breathing more frantically, Luchs fought to take control of his body again and charged at his enemies with his buckler out and sword held aside. When he saw a weapon aimed his way, he held the buckler up to intercept and throw it back, then moved in to thrust his sword.

But he hesitated.

That hesitation was enough for the enemy to react and ready himself to take Luchs' life. Again, Rufus came to his rescue. Although his attacks were not enough to kill, he kept many enemies off their backs and managed to cripple a few enough so they could not keep up the fight.

It happened so many times that Luchs became sickened with himself. Relying on a comrade was one thing, but it seemed more like he was fighting the battle for him. If he did not want to be a lesser knight, he needed to shake the dread and fight back.

The two of them were doing well. The enemy numbers were slowly being reduced. But as their enemies had, they became overconfident and unfocused. Out of the blue came an arrow fired by an enemy archer, an arrow that struck Rufus in his shoulder. The shock made him drop his weapon, leaving him defenseless in front of his enemy.

Luchs rushed to his comrade's side, praying to the gods for the strength to get to him in time. At that moment, he did not see that man as a person, but as a threat and imminent danger to one of his own. Fear for his friend's life gave him the push he needed to fight the dread holding him back and guard Rufus' body with his own.

He barely felt conscious for the brief second where he thrust his sword into the man's abdomen. The vague dread became so much more harrowing, coiling around him like chains, crushing him. Time slowed and the world turned dark. His body trembled, the terrifying sensations once again invading his mind and paralyzing him. His breathing stopped and he heard only the dying gasps that came from his victim ... and those startling breaths from behind. It was Rufus, the one he moved to protect.

If he stopped there, then that breath would be snuffed out, and his friend, too, would be dragged into the void.

Nay. I won't allow it!

Fighting through the heavy, oppressive dread, Luchs shoved his blade deeper into the pirate's abdomen, using all his body weight to drive it all the way through. He twisted his sword a bit to tear through whatever organs he penetrated, spattering blood over his arms.

Tense and rigid, Luchs pulled his weapon from the now empty body and stood with great determination and will before the remaining pirates who dared threaten his vulnerable ally. He held the bloodstained sword at his enemies with conviction. "Come at me!"

~ Fourth Chapter ~

Opposing the Storm

Luchs was more determined to fight than ever. With Rufus injured and the others busy fighting for their own lives, he was the only one he could count on to protect his friend. Any who dared get too close to him was quickly struck down. He skewered his foes, tore through their guts, bashed their skulls in. The blood that flew fed the dread, but he refused to relent and kept on fighting.

If he had to lose anything, he did not want it to be a friend.

It was only a matter of time until the rest of the knights and pages fought through the pirate horde and joined their comrades aboard the ship.

The pirates were still fighting back, but their forces were easily overwhelmed by the numbers storming their ship and were surrounded, ultimately defeated.

The only ones who kept fighting were Commandant Brunlier and a rugged man wearing a leather jacket and a tattered black bandana who wielded an elegant yet crudely thick rapier. The commandant was much more enthusiastic with the bout against the pirate than he had been sparring against his pages. That pirate—possibly their captain—fought closer on par with him than most knights the commandant trained with.

Their blades clashed with one another in a rapid frenzy of steel flashes. The pirate's arms shook from the impacts endured from Commandant Brunlier's timbering swing, but he endured and fought back for his life.

The pirate was more dexterous than his massive foe. While the commandant had superior strength, the pirate was much quicker, and struck back with precise strikes. They both had strengths that kept them matched against each other. And yet, despite the pirate captain offering the fight of his life, the commandant acted as though it were just another exercise. His hoarse voice howled this disturbing laughter that resonated with the cave walls and seeped fear into those who listened.

Holding his sword murderously, he watched carefully as the pirate captain prepared a fatal blow. His grin turned wicked as he read his enemy's movement. When the pirate thrust his sword, the commandant stepped aside and used his empty hand to shove him against the tall mast, then moved in and threw his sword down at his head. Panicked, the pirate captain held his sword to intercept, using enough opposing force to just stop that sword from grazing his nose.

"A deft hand ye got there," said Commandant Brunlier. Although his voice sounded somewhat composed, there was a wild excitement about him. It gave the others the impression of how much he looked forward to ending his adversary. Then he boded in a heavy tone, "How much longer do ye think it'll hold?" He was toying with the man, pressing his sword against the rapier firmly until his enemy crumbled to his knees.

The behemoth had his prey in his jaws. There was no escape.

But that did not stop the pirate captain from trying. He heaved his body to the side, but before he could roll away, the commandant's sword fell over the pirate's leg and carved it off. He crumbled onto the floor, crying out in sheer agony, and attempted to hold his mutilated muscles together as blood stained the deck.

No longer seeing the need for a weapon in hand, Commandant Brunlier sheathed his sword. He stepped lightly around the pirate writhing in agony on the floor. "Must admit, I'm impressed. A life of running across the seas has made ye an admirable swordsman. But a rat is still a rat." His loud, powerful stomping across the deck shook the entire ship.

No, that could not be him. Everyone was so caught up in the bout that no one noticed the waters underneath begin stirring in a frenzy.

As the pirate struggled to slink off of the floor, Commandant Brunlier grasped his neck in his hand and pulled him up, then slammed him against the mast. "How did ye reach these shores? The spell should've kept you lot out."

The pirate captain, either from pain and shock or pride, would not say a word. He just breathed dryly and hastily, then, out of spite, spat a drop of blood at the behemoth's cheek.

The commandant was not a man known for his patience. His hand tightened around the pirate's throat slowly for every few seconds he went without an answer. All of the pressure put into it eventually squeezed a pitiful squawk out of him.

"We don't know of any spell!" one of the captive pirates squealed when there looked to be little life left in his captain's eyes.

Everyone looked to this slouching, red-bearded man with a face half as long as a horse's and swelled badly from abuse. That was one of the more cowardly pirates who ran like a headless hen at the first sign of danger. The other pirates silently complained when that spoke up, but did nothing out of fear of being immediately sentenced.

The commandant glanced his only eye to the horsey pirate. He looked to be miffed, then smiled for a somehow more sinister effect. "Speaking up for yer captain? Good. Then keep at it! How did ye find this island?" Showing he would take action otherwise, he pressed his thumb firmly against the captain's throat enough for him to wince in pain.

The horsey pirate swallowed hard before responding. "We didn't know the island was here. We just happened upon it by chance."

"By chance, ye say? Ye just chose to sail our way?"

"'Twasn't by choice! We were desperate. Just tryin' to get away!"

"From who? Ederean soldiers?"

Enlightening as the interrogation was, Luchs could not ignore the noise from outside the cave. He slipped away while everyone was fixated on the banter and made way for the stern deck where he could get a better view of everything.

"Worse—a witch!"

He stopped halfway up the stairs and turned back their way.

"A witch?"

"'Tis truth! We've met her ... and we've enraged her." The looks on the other captive pirates said everything. Their ghastly expressions were riddled with fright, a fright Luchs had once seen looking in his reflection after waking from a nightmare. They faced something horrific. It had to be from what the horse-faced one was speaking of. "We tried to make off with somethin' of hers, we did. 'Twas some kind of book, a magic one. The cap'n figured he could've used it for plunder ... but we underestimated her. Most of us were killed, slaughtered by her power. The lot of us here got away, but not afore she cursed us." It was getting harder to listen in as the winds blew tempestuously through the Maw's opening. "We've been chased by a terrible storm ever since. Every day we docked was one the storm got closer to us. We thought we were leavin' Ederea's waters, but instead we ended up gettin' shipwrecked, trapped in this damned cave!"

So it was misfortune, not skill, that guided their ship into the Leviathan's Maw. It would explain why part of the hull had been pierced underneath.

Chased by ... a storm?

Something like that would be too much to believe unless he saw it for himself.

Luchs kept scaling the stairs. With the wind blowing so strongly, he could not hear anything said below. No one else seemed fazed by the wind brewing outside and flooding into the cave. There might have been a steady flow streaming into the cave even as they fought, but it grew louder, stronger, more oppressive. Were they so fixated on the pirates that they were blind to what was going on around them?

He made way for the railing to get the best view of the Maw's opening. The closer he got to the open water, the more he heard it vibrantly crash against itself, waves joining waves, smashing into hard rock. It was much more rancorous, much more destructive than when they scaled down the cliff wall.

He could not help but tremble at what he saw.

Darkness rolled across the sky, and would soon swallow Des Meurtal. The eye inside the swirling clouds peered down at the island, ravenous and vengeful, illuminated be streaks of violet light. The winds lashed out in a violent flurry. And the waves beneath them became jagged razors hatefully tearing into the land.

Storms at sea were brewed by the gods Zyleec and Lady Untae as they worked to shape the everchanging world, as was their role. What phenomena they orchestrated were meant to serve as trials for mortals to prove their strength and tenacity. Survivors were granted boons and opportunity while the doomed were brought to Lady Cural, who guided their souls to the Elysium.

Dangerous as they were, the storms brewed by the gods had a majesty to them that made them beautiful. Luchs had seen many, and he was fascinated with them all.

But the approaching storm, a mass of wickedness, was no work of the gods.

He ran back to the deck to find the knights mocking the prisoners.

"'Tis only a matter of time until the storm sweeps over the island. When that happens, we're done!"

The others laughed at the pirate who spoke, thinking him insane.

"He speaks the truth!" Everyone looked Luchs' way with the same surprise and scrutiny they faced the pirate with. His outburst was not well appreciated by the knights, but they withheld reprimanding him for the moment so he could explain himself. "Can't you feel it? The winds are screaming, the waves below us raging. Look and see for yourselves! They're right. This storm could bring down the entire—"

"Enough with your blathering!" demanded one of the knights.

"Listen to what he says," Aloysius interjected.

"Aye! Luchs knows storms better than any of us," added Rufus. "If'n he says something is wrong, then something is *definitely* wrong."

"Enough, the lot of you! I'll not have you encouraging these—"

"Laszlo."

The only thing to keep the knight from lashing out was a simple call of his name from the commandant. He looked back at his leader.

After getting what he wanted, Commandant Brunlier released the pirate captain, the man's groans letting his crew know he yet lived. A few of the knights remained beside the pirate captain with lances held scarcely above his head.

Standing confident, Luchs remained steady as the living terror approached. "Ye know storms, lad? And what does yer gut tell ye about this one?"

"Just as they claimed. The storm will wash Des Meurtal away and us along with it."

Commandant Brunlier fixed his cold eye on him for a time, then he walked up the steps to the stern deck and gazed at the outside. He stayed atop the steps, assessing what he saw.

"Laszlo, Dimitri, Raemon," he called his knights. Those he named approached him with a clenched fist over their hearts for respect. "A crisis be upon us. Take a page or two and fetch three of the Mirage Locks."

The knights were all uncertain about this.

"Commandant, the charms are scattered across Des Meurtal. Even if this storm is that fierce, there won't be enough time—"

"Yet ye're keen on wasting time questioning me? Go fetch the Mirage Locks. *Now!*"

They did as commanded before he tore their heads off.

Commandant Brunlier demanded the pirates tell them where their gangplanks were kept and sent a few pages to retrieve them. By the time their exit was made, the knights had chosen the pages to follow them— two Chevalerie with Sir Dimitri, a Loi with Sir Raemon, and Luchs and one of the Devoir with Sir Laszlo.

The groups set out immediately upon deciding their destinations. One would head to the mountain, one to the south of the island, and one to the east. All they needed to do was secure their targets and return before time ran out.

Scaling back up the cliffside was much more difficult than the climb down. They struggled to withstand the constant bursts of wind, and the spray from the ocean waves made the walls difficult to cling to. They were constantly in danger of falling into the fangs of the sea, and a few nearly had before they were halfway up the cliff. Luchs and the Loi, being the quickest to act, pulled up the pages who nearly fell into the briny deep.

Arduous as the climb was, they managed to make it up the passage. Everyone became discouraged at how much the wind picked up, and it would only keep getting stronger, but they kept their wits about them. They raced to their designated objectives; while Sir Raemon set off toward the mountain edge and Sir Dimitri to the beaches, Sir Laszlo took Luchs and the Devoir back toward the way they came past the bog.

The Mirage Locks—the magical stones used to form the barrier around Des Meurtal and create the illusion that the island did not exist, forcing trespassers away from the shallow waters.

Everyone saw one of the Locks at least once. It was hard to believe something so small contained enough power to conceal and protect the entire island. If Luchs did not see the veil peel away for the ship he rode in on years ago, he would not have believed it.

But someone managed to slip through the barrier, a sign that the magic in the Locks was waning. How could they use three of the four Mirage Locks to protect themselves from the coming storm?

Curious as he was of what Commandant Brunlier had in mind, Luchs kept focused on the storm approaching Des Meurtal. Every now and then, he could feel a strong push at his back putting more spring in his step; the violent winds grew stronger, as predicted.

What they really needed to worry about was the rain. Once that came, there would be little time left to get to safety before the worst hit.

The pages struggled to push through the wind and hesitated to move once they crossed a path of trees.

"Don't falter! Keep moving!"

Sir Laszlo sensed their fear. He, on the other hand, kept advancing strongly like the impending storm did not scare him at all. With that kind of man leading the way, they could only follow his example.

Either by the push of strong winds or their quick feet, they reached the end of the path of trees and eventually came across a ruined keep. Time and the unfavorable conditions of Des Meurtal left what would have been a magnificent keep in shambles: walls crumbled, towers toppled, the entire thing left little more than a pile of rubble. The knights stationed themselves there whenever they were not out patrolling the island or observing the warring pages, most likely to check on the Mirage Lock that was the easiest to access.

Exhausted as they were, there was no time to rest. The air was getting heavier and the clouds came closer. They were short on time.

Sir Laszlo kept close to the keep wall as the two pages stood hunched over to catch their breath. Instead of heading straight for the entrance, he inspected the walls, drawing his hands across them until he found the spot where a stone fell into the structure. A large patch of the rocky wall crumbled down, revealing a staircase.

"Wait here," Sir Laszlo ordered before entering the staircase.

The path was well hidden. Every stone that made up the wall had been put in place like an intricate puzzle, leaving no gap or opening to suspect there was anything behind it. The extra measure seemed subtle and unnecessary, but the chain of magic linking the Mirage Locks never broke, so it must have been effective.

Since they had a moment to rest, Luchs turned to the skies, to the terrifying vortex above. While still a fair distance from the island, its reach of black clouds had surrounded the island as it pulled closer. The violet light crackling within the vortex grew more erratic the closer it came.

Luchs turned back to the ground, not sure why he thought seeing how close destruction was would help.

Sir Laszlo quickly returned with a smooth stone dimly lit in an emerald glow in hand. "We have what we came for. Now let's move. Back to the Maw!"

They ran back the direction they came.

It took more effort to run against the wind. Every now and then, branches and grass flew at their faces, blinding them as much as the forceful winds dried their eyes out.

Trudging through the open grassland was a struggle, but their advance started to make progress after dragging themselves past a gathering of trees. The trees provided some cover from the wind, making it a little easier to move.

It was not without complications, though. Their wobbling trunks and rattling leaves kept Luchs on his toes. He heard their roots steadily being tugged by the storm's might when he stood next to one.

They nearly passed through before—

Creak! Snap! Groah!

A tree had been torn in two and fell over Luchs like a hammer. It moved too fast to react to before its gargantuan shadow expanded around him. Before it could crush him, something knocked him against the wind, shoving him from where he stood. His face stung and his back ached, but he still lived.

He stood quickly and looked back to see what happened, and fell short of breath when he saw Sir Laszlo underneath the tree, the trunk crushing his legs. Both he and the Devoir rushed to his aid and grabbed the bottom of the trunk, pulling it up with all their might. It was not too big but still dense and heavy. The pages, both strong and well-built, managed to lift the hefty trunk and move it away from Sir Laszlo. Valiant though their efforts were, they were in vain. His legs had been completely broken, one of them with a bone protruding outward.

Sir Laszlo groaned. "Lads... The Lock..." They came close once he started speaking. "Take this back to the Maw." He held the stone to them with an unsteady hand.

"What about you?"

"Forget me. They need the Mirage Locks," he barked, interrupting the page he saved. "Get it back to them!"

Without an argument, the Devoir snatched the charm from his trembling hand, but instead of taking off with it, he took Luchs' hand and dropped it into his palm. "Go. I'll take care of Sir Laszlo."

Taken aback, Luchs watched the Devoir kneel by the knight's side, taking one of his arms over his shoulder.

"You'll never get him back to the Maw like this. How—"

"I'll take him back to the keep and hide there. Stop wasting time and take the Lock before the bloody storm swallows the others! Go!"

As much as Luchs wanted to protest, they were out of time. Rain began to fall. If he did not move, no one would survive the storm. The Leviathan's Maw would flood and everyone would drown. So he left the two behind and raced through the trees, trying hard not to look back. All he could do was hope the ruined keep could withstand the storm's fury.

The winds became so strong that even moving was a grueling challenge. It took all of Luchs' strength and willpower to bear the torment of marching on.

Every wisp of wind lashed at him like a whip, causing his muscles to lock up. Images from his nightmares were invoked, and when he opened his eyes, he could have sworn he saw the real things striking at him.

Too much was at stake for him to surrender to his fears. He endured and marched on, and soon found himself in a familiar environment. The land rose underneath his feet, curving upward. It was the cliffside where they discovered the Leviathan's Maw.

The struggle was far from over. When he began to scale down the passage, he saw that the waves were already climbing to high levels and soaked the path in slippery brine.

He kept moving. He had to. The Maw was deep and the ship was lodged in place. There was still a chance to make it in time.

He clung desperately to the cliff wall to avoid losing his footing. His free hand gripped into the earth, his feet pressed into gaps between stones.

With the wind raging and the waves crashing along the cliffside, he could not afford to move carelessly. One misstep and he would be consumed by the sea.

Just a little farther. Just a little more...!

Luchs forced his way down the path, fighting the elements and his mind. He held strong, believing he would reach his comrades in time.

Once he stepped foot onto the lowest climb of the passage, a sharp wave drew over the rock wall at the edge and crashed against him with bone-crushing force.

Another terrifyingly familiar sensation made his body lock up, but being so close to the Maw, he shook off the pain and kept crawling along the wall.

No matter how durable his body was, it still had its limits. Fatigue would claim him if anything else hit him like that.

He kept dragging one foot after the other, barely slinking by, until finally seeing the gap in the cliffs. Everyone was waiting. With that in mind, he abandoned caution and put in one last sprint for the Leviathan's Maw. He could see people in his haste, two having climbed up the Maw and perched precariously behind the left and right fangs.

And there was another standing foolishly in the open path. It was Commandant Brunlier.

He shouted something, but the wind drowned out his voice. It had to be an order telling him to hurry. Luchs could tell that much from listening to the wave behind him swell to tremendous heights. It might have been his twisted imagination, but Luchs could feel it was made of malice.

Giving it all he had, he charged straight for the commandant until his legs burned, holding the Mirage Lock firmly in his left hand. He dared not look back to see how large the wave had grown, no matter how terrifying it was hearing it rise so high behind him. If he looked, he would lose the mettle he had left.

"The Lock! Hurry with the Lock!" the commandant bellowed.

As he closed in, the wave began its descent, tearing apart everything in its wake. Their doom drawing closer and closer, Luchs pushed himself to run with the wind to the commandant, who stood with his hand outstretched for the Mirage Lock. With one final kick at the ground, he was close enough to reach Commandant Brunlier.

He snatched the stone from his hand as the lad ran past him and slammed it into the ground.

A dazzling light sparked from the Mirage Lock and the ones held by those hiding behind the fangs. Rings of that light formed around the three and connected with each other. The energy intensified once the magic established a link, sending sparks of intense energy flying all around, until the intangible force over the Leviathan's Maw became a solid barrier, one that withstood the monstrous claw of water. The entire cavern trembled from the impact, but not a drop leaked through the barrier.

His mission finally at an end, Luchs fell to his knees. His breathing was loud and haggard, and his legs turned to jelly, but he beamed with pride having returned in the nick of time. His faction rushed to him, their expressions riddled with worry while they helped him aboard the ship for a well-deserved rest.

In his tired daze, he saw other pages surrounding Sir Dimitri and Sir Raemon and their chosen entourage before a small group rushed his way. They were curious about what was happening outside.

Maxime was the only one focused on something else. "Luchs, where's Stéphane?" He spoke of his fellow Devoir.

Exhausted though he was, he knew he had to say something. "Sir Laszlo got hurt. The lad stayed behind to save him." He explained everything, leaving not a scintilla of detail out. It was hard for the Devoir to take, but no one blamed Luchs. They all had a mission to follow regardless of the costs. It would have been an insult to them if he had ignored their wishes and neglected the task at hand.

"Gods, watch over them," Maxime prayed.

Luchs told the pages of the things he saw. Afterwards, they told him what happened when he left and what they found out.

That the pirates managed to infiltrate Des Meurtal meant that the Mirage Locks lost the power to keep them at bay. Commandant Brunlier understood as much, but he also knew the stones' magic affected an incredibly wide range. When brought within closer proximities, they had just enough power to protect them.

There was no way to know how long the barrier would hold. They could only hope that the storm passed before the Mirage Locks lost what was left of their power.

The pages were all instructed on how to channel power in the Mirages Locks with simple illumination charms the knights held. Some had more potential than others, but most of the pages learned how to properly use the Mirage Locks; those who had not still practiced, not wanting to be left out. Those three could not hold the spell for the entire storm.

In the meantime, the pages rested to reserve their energy and conversed with one another to quell their anxiousness. The pirates' food storage had plenty to offer and would supply everyone, even the prisoners held in the brig, with enough rations for about a week.

Luchs wished to practice channeling magic as well, but the knights insisted that he rest. His faction coaxed him to do the same.

To distract himself, he asked the other pages and knights what they experienced in retrieving their Mirage Locks.

Sir Dimitri and his two Chevalerie ventured to the southern beaches to find the Mirage Lock buried underneath thick stone slabs and held in a small chest. The waters there were not as vicious as those clawing at the cliffs, but they were still large and reached several yards into the shore.

"'Twas a nightmare," Sir Dimitri boded. "The waters attacked us like ravenous beasts, threatening to drag us into the pack. If'n brave Ruben wasn't there to snag the Lock, the lot of us would have drowned trying to fish it up."

Then there was Sir Raemon and the Loi he took to the mountain. Their Mirage Lock was hidden in a stone pillar enchanted to look like a tree. Along the mountain where the land was more elevated, the winds raged about more savagely than in the fields, taking everything from the earth, playing with it like an energetic child, before throwing it all away with abandon.

"'Twas as if lil' Lord Zyleec himself was playing with the mountain," the Loi sighed. "And I thought child gods were supposed to be delightful."

All of their voices were worn and their tones dark. To think they laughed at the pirates and scoffed at Luchs for agreeing with them hours earlier.

Several hours passed. Over a dozen knights and pages took over maintaining the Mirage Locks' spell. The only one who continued without rest was the commandant. Many passed the time just by staring at him, wondering how long he would put himself through the abuse. They saw from the others that the process left a strain on both the mind and body. A few openly complained over their numb limbs and blurred vision. It was miraculous he had the strength to hold on so long, but there had to be a limit. How much longer would that be?

And when would the storm end? The deathly loud crashes and the rhythmic rain that echoed through the cave from the outside let everyone know it had not settled down at all.

The air inside the Maw was frigid. A few pages tried building a fire, but the moisture in the air kept their wood from holding a flame for long. Their bodies were thick, but the heat drained from them quickly.

They were all so glum and devoid of hope.

"Fie!" Rufus grew tired of the dreary atmosphere. He had been quiet while recovering from his time maintaining the spell, but he always hated a dull crowd. "The lot of us curled up here, cowering, helpless! 'Tisn't the way the time should go by."

"And what do you propose we do? Ain't like there's much choice," complained one of the Loi.

"'Ain't much choice,'" Rufus mimicked in a whiny voice. "You know how pathetic you sound right now? Ha! My forebearers would be laughing their teeth off if they saw you pansies like this." He stood from his place between Aloysius and one of the Chevalerie and walked across the ship's deck, picking up a discarded hatchet. "When my grandda was in his prime, he'd keep the spirits of his fellow men alive by taking anything he could find and dance with it like a fool." And wave the hatchet he did, imitating the flamboyant, winding swings his grandfather must have done. "Did he feel a loss for his dignity? Nay! It kept everyone's spirits up and lively enough to react to it, not lying around dead like you sorry lot."

Everyone jolted backward when he started closing in.

"Quit waving that around, you ninny!" Luchs shouted when the blade was swung his way. The enthusiasm was fine, but he did not have to get so close.

He heard but did not think of stopping the performance. Rufus spun the handle in his palm, his arm waving it hither and thither in what almost looked like practiced motions instead of random flailing. Had he done it before? Neither Luchs nor Aloysius ever saw him perform in that way during their time together.

"Don't get your britches bunched up. Not like I'll behead anyone. I've been doing this before I could even—" Just then, the hatchet slipped from his dexterous fingers, flying at the knight resting against the main mast of the ship. It struck wood just a hair's length from the man's skull. Rufus' feet scuffled toward the gangplanks before he even realized escape came to his mind, weary of the knight's ferocious gaze. "Ah-ha... Mayhap I could use some practice."

Gaggles of rough laughter broke out as everyone watched Rufus sprint for land with the knight he nearly decapitated close behind.

A moment of rambunctiousness proved he was right. Letting the time pass in dead silence while the storm razed the island would only drive them mad. So instead of sitting around or wastefully burning their energy with strenuous activity, the pages all passed the time telling each other what they hoped for the future. With the future looking so bleak, nothing else gave them any comfort.

Aloysius looked up to the stalactites above. "I always hoped to follow my father's footsteps and become a tactician. The lives of every soldier on the battlefield rests in his wise hands. What more important role could there be?" It was more like he did not want to trust just anyone with his own life. He heard stories from his military family about those who readily sacrificed their soldiers like pawns—like his father. As necessary as a soldier's sacrifice was, senselessly sending men to their deaths did not sit right by him.

"Decent enough, but why pursue your father's role when you can surpass him?" Maxime stated. "As for me, I'm aiming for the top. I'm going to be a general!"

A determined spirit chasing a big dream, that one.

A Loi by the name of Hetan spoke up next. "I just wanna protect my home from pirates. They killed my ma and pa... I don't want them killing anyone else." It was a noble wish.

Everyone had fine reasons for striving for a knight's shield. As for Luchs, he wanted to honor the family who rescued him from a cursed fate. Compared to their wishes, his could have been seen as minuscule, he speculated. But it was not to him.

Eyes turned to him eventually after the others spoke up, and he humbly stated, "I just want my family to be proud of me."

He was not blood-linked to the Vertueux family, but they were the only family he knew, perhaps the only one he would ever know, and he wanted them to know their efforts for his sake were not for nothing.

~ Fifth Chapter ~

Acceptance

The storm lasted eleven days without rest. Every waking moment was plagued with the deathly sounds of destruction orchestrated by rancorous winds, vicious waves, thrown debris, and the roars of thunder. The waves tore at the land and assaulted the magic barrier held up by the Mirage Locks. Provisions were deteriorating and there was little to sustain everyone after the eighth day. It was astounding they had the strength to hold their defense for so long.

Finally, on the twelfth dawn, the storm died down.

At long last, they finally left the cave. The sun shining was a gift from the gods after being left to wither in the dark for so long. A few dreaded they would rot in the Leviathan's Maw after going so many days without its radiance. All of that struggle was worth it just to see the golden glimmer once again.

Everyone emerged from the Leviathan's Maw half-starved and barely able to hold themselves upright, but with a renewed love for life. Fortunately, no one starved to death.

The thought of lost life pushed Luchs to run back to the keep where he left his party. Not a moment passed throughout the storm without thinking of what terrible fate they suffered through.

They had the protection of the Maw and the Mirage Locks, but those two only had the crumbling keep to cover them.

Eleven days in that hell...

He dared not entertain the thought of their demise nor would he cling to near-false hope of their survival. He needed to see with his own eyes what became of them.

The entire island had been completely ravaged by the storm's rampage. Circling the bog was much more arduous after the rain expanded its mired body tenfold. Only the mightiest trees still stood, the rest torn asunder, while the other plants had been drenched in salt water. Even the ground had been ripped from its place, leaving behind ghastly gaps in the earth.

After racing across the tattered land for what felt like forever, Luchs reached the keep and, to his utter astonishment, saw it still stood tall. Gashes covered the keep like scars on a body.

He ran to the keep and called out for Sir Laszlo and Stéphane as he searched for a way in. The entrance had collapsed, but so had a few parts of the walls. He found his way inside climbing through one of those holes.

With the keep's upper level gone and most of the ground level buried, the only place left to search was the basement. The way down had been covered by a few stone slabs that Luchs easily pushed out of the way, revealing badly carved steps drenched in rainwater. The corridor led to a broken-down door where he found the two he left behind lying beside empty barrels used to store food.

The Devoir page had curled up in a ball into the corner. He had all but wasted away. Whatever food they had was not enough. His girth was shriveled up, his stomach hollowed in. His tunic was gone, and the trousers he wore could easily slip off him if he were to move too much, though that did not seem likely. His arms and legs were more bones than meat. And at the corners of his mouth were splotches of dried blood.

Alas, Sir Laszlo had long since passed. His body, cold and decayed blue, sat inches apart from the page. The legs that got crushed to save Luchs had been dressed in torn wraps of olive cloth; the page trapped with him must have attempted to keep him from bleeding out.

Luchs closed his eyes and shook his head when images of the knight slowly dying entered his mind. The Devoir still barely drew breath. He needed help.

"Stéphane!" He stepped up and gripped the Devoir's shoulder. "Can you hear me?" he barked as he shook him.

He said nothing, but slid open his eyes a bit, revealing a faint glimmer of life. That was as good an answer as any.

Luchs turned around and reached back, taking hold of the lad's arms and having them wrap around his shoulders. "Hang tight."

He made a run back for the Maw. His lungs burned like fire and his legs ached terribly, but he still kept running. The lad had waited for help long enough.

Nearly an hour had passed when the Devoir finally woke up enough to utter a few words. It was best to keep him from going back under and risk never waking up again. To that end, Luchs tried talking to the page as he ran. He asked him questions, enough for him to stay awake for a long while.

His name was Stéphane Solicer. He was part of a family of simple farmers. Their lives were peaceful until a group of mercenaries began pilfering their livestock, claiming it to be a tax for their protection. Stéphane and his family hated the mercenaries, but they were not strong enough to protect themselves. The Ederean military could not always protect every civilian, and they would not pay the rogues to be rid of them. That was why he chose to enlist as a page. He hoped to rise up in the ranks and organize something that could protect his family and others from lowlifes who preyed on good people.

He was an admirable person to take on such a burden for the sake of his family—all the more reason to keep him from fading.

The run was more grueling on the way back. Luchs felt his lungs flare and his legs nearly give out. But he managed, and soon Stéphane got the help he needed. The pages each gave a scrap of their remaining rations to him, hoping to put some meat back on his bones. One even gave the tunic off his back to cover his freezing body. It was amazing how deadly experiences could bring people closer.

The burden of guilt lessened, Luchs finally allowed himself a moment of peace and rest atop the Maw's cliffs. He needed some time in the fresh air after being confined in the cave. The air was unburdened of heavy rains and the sky was clear once again, returning tranquility to the island. So long as he did not look back at the devastation behind him, it was perfectly relaxing.

After climbing back up the cliffside a third time, it was impossible not to see what little remained. The vast stretch of green was all but deforested, only a few dozen trees remaining. Chunks of earth were scattered throughout the island and even littered the water. Even the mighty mountain had been rent asunder. Even the wisping winds sounded unsettlingly different, tattered, broken.

The only ones to roam Des Meurtal were the knights and pages. What became of the animals? Had they all been carried off by the tempestuous winds and torrents? Did they hide someplace the humans could not? Perhaps some had resorted to cannibalism in a desperate attempt to avoid starvation.

Magic was disappearing from the world—a given fact now—and yet it was the work of the arcane arts that destroyed Des Meurtal.

What's going on out there? Luchs thought as he stared at the still sea.

Four days passed since the storm ended, and everyone kept to the pirate's ship for shelter. There was nothing to hunt or forage for. The storm had swept away everything and left the soil drenched in salt water. All they had to eat was what little remained on the ship—and an occasional scallop.

The pages tried not to be too active. All the knights had them do was keep an eye on the prisoners and keep a lookout for ships on the horizon. A ship from the capital had been expected to arrive but had doubtlessly been thrown off course by the storm. Their hopes rode on surviving until that ship came.

Stéphane was recovering well, but he needed to lean on someone to walk. Luchs watched over him and helped him recuperate, feeling responsible for his state, and Rufus and Aloysius, loyal to their own, felt obligated to do the same.

The other pages helped in whatever way they could, too, if only to pester him about what happened when he attempted to rescue Sir Laszlo. He refused to say anything about it. And when the knights returned with Sir Laszlo's remains, he turned white as a ghost and closed himself off from everyone.

The knights seemed to know—or at least speculated—what happened given the mixed looks of revulsion and pity they gave him.

The sixth day was trying. Their food and fresh water supply had run out. What little morsels they fed on was not enough to sustain their hunger. Tempting as it was to go out and search for anything that survived, they could not risk needlessly wasting energy.

The sun shone bright that day, its radiant rays drying the island. The unexpected heatwave made it grueling for those on lookout duty staring aimlessly at the horizon. It was not any more comfortable for those who cloistered themselves within the Leviathan's Maw. Hunger and thirst plagued them, sitting in the briny air dried out their tongues begging for water, and riled up their already snarling stomachs.

It was either sit out in the sun and roast or dwell in the cave and further provoke their starving bodies.

Late in the day, a small shadow crept over the horizon. Although he thought it a hallucination, Luchs dismissed the notion after rubbing an arm over his eyes. It was a ship. Help had finally arrived.

"Commandant! They're here!" he shouted down the cliffside. He nearly ran into the page that climbed the path to relieve him of duty, who followed him down to see what the panic was about. He shouted "They're here!" until reaching the Maw and alerting the knights.

The pages quickly gathered and followed Commandant Brunlier to the northwest beach, leaving behind a few knights to guard the prisoners that yet lived. Marching under the sun was not as overwhelming after learning there was hope. The pages all marched across the ruined island with purpose, carrying themselves like actual soldiers now that they knew they had a future once more. When stepping foot on the drenched beach, they stood upright at perfect attention for the soldiers.

The massive ship pulled into the shore shortly after their arrival and dropped anchor at the nearby shoal cape. A large gangplank dropped from the main deck, slamming into the coalesced, miry sand. Down the plank came the knights, many donned in bronze and silver armor, scurrying over to the expecting knights and pages in panic.

"What in the gods' names happened here!?" the ship's captain, Commodore Odilon, bellowed. The veteran navy officer was a rotund man and shorter than a typical Ederean—around five and a half feet. "The island! She's ru'ned!"

Deafening as ever, he is, Luchs thought to himself.

Everyone else muttered the same thing between themselves, careful not to be overheard by the knights.

Commandant Brunlier wiped off the spit sprayed on his face and blankly stared at the portly man. "Yer eyesight's not failed ye yet, I see," he japed coldly. The behemoth and dwarf never liked each other and were not shy about showing it. "I'll be quick: we had to subdue invading pirates, got caught in a hexed storm, and spent well over a week trapped in the Leviathan's Maw."

"Pirates?" blurted out one of the not-so-merry men.

"You daft, Brunlier?" another barked. "No pirate ever crossed through these waters without a Mirage—"

The commandant scoffed. "'bout that, those stones be near useless now. Their power has gone flat." His words sent them all into disarray. They behaved like the pages when they first found out about it themselves, especially the high-strung commodore. "The lads here can tell ye all ye want. In the meantime, Odilon, come along and bring some of yer men. Some sea rats still need sentencing."

With the island they returned to in shambles, they did not know what else to do. Several of the knights followed the commandant into the ruined Des Meurtal carrying weapons and manacles.

Those who remained recognized the pages' malnourishment and guided them onto their vessel for some food. Their larder contained more food than the pirates had, enough for the hungry children. The pages only helped themselves to enough food to quiet their noisy bellies, fearful of going without meals again.

Luchs grabbed some strips of dried meat and refilled his waterskin before heading back up to the ship's deck. The air felt much more refreshing after the sun began to sink over the horizon.

He was about to join the pages when someone came up to him.

"Ho there, Luchs!"

An arm wrapped around his shoulder and pulled him toward the man connected to it, holding him in a rowdy bear hug. While being jostled about, Luchs looked up at the man to see a suave face sprouting bristly crimson-red hair, eyebrows, and sideburns. His brown eyes beamed with joy.

"Good to see you too, Ulrin!"

It was Ulrin Vertueux, the eldest son of Sir Trenent Vertueux, the knight who saved Luchs from the slavers who imprisoned him.

Luchs squirmed out of his tight hold and looked back up at him with a broad grin. The knight stood tall before him, though not as much as he had since last seeing him four years ago.

Ulrin put a hand to Luchs' shoulder, patting it firmly. "Quite the weed, you are! And excellently built. 'Tis good to see life on Des Meurtal has made quite a man out of you."

Hearing words spoken with such pride coaxed Luchs' broad smile to show more teeth. "'Tis kind of you to say, but I'm not a man yet."

"Mayhap not, but you're certainly close!" Ulrin cheerfully patted the lad's shoulder again. "You and these lads here faced things that would make anyone less than that soil their breeches. Pirates. A storm brewed by an angry witch. And, from what I've heard, you played an important role in the insanity."

Luchs almost looked like a cackling idiot his smile grew so large. He admitted to finding the pirate who separated from his crew with Maxime, as well as convincing everyone to treat the storm as a threat and retrieving a Mirage Lock.

The smile on Ulrin's face showed greater elation the more he heard of the accomplishments. "Aye, aye! Wonderful work, lad. Wonderful!"

Rather than rejoining the others, Luchs and Ulrin kept by the railing while they talked, hoping to catch up with one another. As always, there was much for Ulrin to tell about: the islands he ventured to, the pirates he fought, the lovely ladies he kept company—and he tended to go on and on about that.

By the time the moon began glistening over the dusk sky and the glimmers of the sunlight vanished, Commandant Brunlier returned with the knights he escorted to the Leviathan's Maw, and the pirates they captured bound in chains. A quick count showed there were at least fifteen still drawing breath, at least for the time being.

Luchs caught Commandant Brunlier and Commodore Odilon talking as they scaled the gangplank behind the convicts, with the commodore gruffly stating, "Well, ye can't run yer 'facility' on a shriveled-up island," when he came within earshot. "No beasts to hunt. Nothing to use for shelter. Land that *eats ye!* 'Tis nothing short of a miracle ye survived this long."

"Then there be no choice."

"Aye."

Their intrigue piqued, the pages fixed their attention on the veterans while they took their prisoners to the brig. Several talked about what they could have meant until they returned to the deck.

"Lads," Commodore Odilon took the lead, "with Des Meurtal in shambles, ye've no hope of keeping yer training up here. We'll be sailing for Shoafond where ye'll be left in the royal guard's care until it can be decided on where we'll put ye."

The pages cheered upon hearing the news. Everyone had been to the capital, Shoafond, at least once after their families enlisted them for page training. It was a beautiful city built atop a highland cliff overlooking the ocean. Streams of fresh water branched throughout the city from an underground spring that never ran dry. There was always fish along the coast and the skies were ever clear and sunny. The only problems had there were whatever the townspeople brought themselves.

"Now enough bellyaching, landlubbers! Get this vessel ready to set sail. Whether the skies be golden glittered or bathed in twilight, nothing keeps an Ederean from taking to the sea!"

That grizzly remark from Commodore Odilon was all it took for the men to hustle to their stations as fast as startled yaks. In mere moments, the anchor was raised, the sails unfurled, and their vessel had taken to the seas once more.

The commodore took the wheel after the ship left Des Meurtal's waters. Much of the crew retired to the berth with the exhausted knights and pages after finishing their duties.

The night skies were clear and the waves calm, but enduring the harrowing storm left Luchs wary that it would all come alive and attack again. He remained on deck for a while longer, letting the frisky sea air sate his worries.

Footsteps creaked across the deck from the staircase leading to the berth. Scaling it was Ulrin.

"Keeping sleep at bay won't do you good, Luchs." He walked over to him at a slow pace, steady like the waves. "You should be resting after that misadventure. There are plenty hammocks left, if'n that's what you're fretting over."

Luchs turned his way bearing a thin smile. "Nay, 'tisn't that. I just want to take in the sound of the waves for a while more."

He seemed to understand, but Ulin did not return below. Instead, he joined Luchs by the railing, leaning over it. "Can't blame you for being fearful of another devilish squall. What was it like?"

"Like the sea and sky wanted to devour us... To think there is someone out there with the power to brew a storm, let alone one so monstrous."

"Aye. Hard to believe, I know. There are only a handful of mages I know in the kingdom, and none of them wield that kind of power. 'Tis terrifying to imagine, truly is."

He took the words from Luchs' mouth. Had he not already been plagued by nightmares, he would have been tumbling in his sleep from twisted images of torrential giants and sirens born of the sickle winds.

"Five years have passed. Still no luck with finding your memories?"

Luchs shook his head drearily. "Nay. Just those bloody nightmares."

"'Tis a shame, seeing as the only things you dream of are from your imprisonment. Those dastards really left their mark on you."

A dreary silence filled the air between the two. That sad tale always left an awkwardness between him and the Vertueux family whenever he failed to uncover anything. It was to be expected, but they could never get used to it.

A massive shadow blocked out the moonlight. Turning skyward, Luchs saw it had been from Commandant Brunlier standing tall in one of the crow's nests.

"I knew Gilbrand's loss weighed on him more than he led on. Never seen the man so distraught."

Ulrin's words had startled Luchs. Commandant Brunlier, distraught? The mountain of a man never wore a dreary expression in the four years he knew him and always had an atmosphere of sheer fighting spirit. Even when the commandant fought against the pirates, he carried himself as he always had.

Ulrin, noticing Luchs' disbelief, smirked and glanced back at the crow's nest. "Gilbrand isn't the sort to take someone's work. You'd sooner see him dancing with the dolphins buck naked, you would."

Luchs looked the commandant's way once more, but turned back to the shimmering waves so as not to get caught looking at him. "I heard one of the pages killed was his son."

Ulrin nodded. "Cain was Gilbrand's only son. Oh, he has daughters aplenty, but not one who will inherit the family name when they marry. He always said it never bothered him, but I always doubted."

That would definitely be a cause for distress among fathers in a patriarchal kingdom. Some families got along well enough by marrying off their daughters and accepting dowries from the son's family. There were exceptions, but in most cases, unless a family had a son, they could not preserve their family name.

"I wager he'll return to his family and mourn for a short time, then take a more active position than teaching pages."

"And what'll happen to us?"

It took a moment of thought before Ulrin responded. "The pages will likely be sent to a different facility. Mayhap they will wind up with Lord Clarten, who rarely trains so many at once." That aloud thought brought him to think deeper on the matter. He spent some time mumbling to himself and scratching his sideburn. Luchs wondered what could be going through his mind while taking the time to appreciate the waters. "You know, I don't see his methods agreeing with you. He focuses on teaching regulation more than the necessities that make a knight."

Intrigued, he looked to Ulrin, a bewildered look on his face. "It sounds like you don't approve of him."

"Not many do. I thank Lady Sundralla you wound up with Gilbrand instead of him. At least in Des Meurtal, you were able to learn how to survive in dangerous environments and band together with your brothers-in-arms when need be. That's what pages should be learning!

"I don't like the thought of you ending up a mere foot soldier. 'Tisn't much opportunity for you with him." Ulrin nodded again. "Aye, that settles it then. I'll just have to make you my squire."

A sudden proclamation, and one Luchs did not see coming. His eyes widened like saucers. "You want me to be your squire?" It was something he hoped for, though never thought would actually come to pass.

Watching him grin at his response only broadened those hopes. "I've been meaning to find someone to take under my wing. Someone bold, determined, with the heart of a lion and courage unyielding. You fit the bill just fine. You're ready, says I," Ulrin said. "What say you?"

A lot has happened since arriving at Des Meurtal four years ago. And in that time, Luchs learned firsthand about the basics and necessities for survival, combat, mastering the terrain around him, and making strategic decisions. He was more than ready, and he knew it.

Beaming with confidence, he nodded and declared, "Aye, I'm ready!"

The voyage was an enjoyable one. Rarely having the chance to ride a ship, the pages all took the time to learn firsthand about how the crew worked and what they did to keep everything running smoothly.

Since they were no longer in Commandant Brunlier's care, they stopped referring to each other by their faction names. There were no more Féroce or Devoir, Chevalerie, Vaincre, or Loi—just fellow pages learning with each other instead of fighting. Any feud formed during the time on Des Meurtal dissolved like sea form.

They were still halfway from their destination after six days of sailing, and low on food since taking in the additional passengers. An islet named Untaseau was not far from their position. Commodore Odilon seized the opportunity to dock and restock their larder.

Untaseau was originally a small land the faithful used to pay homage to Untae, the goddess of the sea and bringer of ocean life. A small chapel had been built there for sailors to visit and pray to the goddess for a safe voyage. It was once a quiet islet many priests and clerics journeyed to for solitude when they were unsure of dire changes in their lives, but it turned into a prosperous place to establish trade somewhere along the line.

While the commodore and his hearty crew paid the docking fee and began to discuss business with local fishermen, Luchs and Ulrin took their leave.

It would not be difficult to find their way off land later. Untaseau was their home. All they had to do was request a ship from the head of House Vertueux and they would be on their way to the capital. It was House Vertueux that managed the major fishing routes and trade with the rest of the country. Minor nobility as they were, they were still important to the people of the islet.

The people of the islet did not need much. Their hardy appetites were sated by the plump fish that swam around Untaseau and even the sea slugs that fed on the limestone deposits close to the bluff. Trade with the other islands across the country, however, ensured that they were safe from the threat of piracy. And with that security, they could give their families safe and happy lives in the humble little hamlet.

Past the bustling pier stood a small village with simple houses and merchants' stores. The paths were full of people roaming about. Some were idly chatting with merchants, others were enjoying themselves with their neighbors. The children out and about were playing together without a care in the world.

Luchs took kindly to the people of Untaseau. They were all friendly sorts. When word got out that the Vertueux family took in an ill lad, they all flocked to the modest chateau behind the village, offering baskets of fruits and fish and meats aplenty, along with their prayers that he recovered soon. He did not know who anyone was or why they cared for his health, but he was thankful for all of them and gladly expressed that once he was well enough to visit them.

"Ah, look who's back!" called out a well-built woman carrying a basket of clothes. "Good to see you home safe, lads."

Ulrin nodded to the woman with a kindly smile. "A pleasure to see you as well, ma'am."

"What's this?" A man behind a seafood stall got a good look at the two after handing a customer a selection of sea slugs. "Could that be Luchs? How you've grown! Paula! Get a look at this lad."

A young lady at the other counter under the shade of a tree turned around and smiled brightly. "Oh, look at you! You definitely look better than when the nobles first found you."

"You look right fine yourself, miss," Luchs complimented.

There were friendly, boisterous greetings from every villager young and old, tall and small, busy and ambling as they strolled through the streets. It was a welcome change from always watching out for stray arrows, falling blades, and territorial animals at every turn.

After meeting practically every living soul there, Luchs and Ulrin marched past the village. Going the rest of the way on foot was no trouble. The chateau was close, tucked away behind a few clusters of trees. People often passed it on their way to the chapel on the other edge of the islet.

The walls surrounding the Vertueux Chateau were quite tall, slick and without cracks, making them impossible to climb, but not the least bit foreboding. They were built to safeguard the family and the islet's innocents within should invaders come, not to give the villagers the impression of ruling tyrants. A few guards stood at the front gate, offering a kind greeting and a salute when Luchs and Ulrin approached.

The chateau was a fairly modest one, only a single story but stretched out significantly. There were plenty of rooms with decent space for the nobility and servants both. The heart of the manor was the huge banquet hall where many a delightful festivity had been carried out. The good people of the islet, as well as many Edereans across the archipelago, relished in celebrating joyous occasions like the birthdays of nobles and royalty and the remarkable feats of the gods in the past. There was no better way to celebrate than everyone gathering together for food and merriment.

Luchs hurried inside, eager to see if everything was still the same.

"Ah, how nostalgic!"

Even having already lived there for a time before enlisting, Luchs was always so amazed by his other home. The ceiling reached an impressive height, much like the trees that used to stand on Des Meurtal. The halls stretched far, lined with ornaments given to the family as thanks for their islet's trade. Facing the entrance was this massive stuffed black bear standing in a threatening position at twelve feet with its claws held out, its muzzle baring its fangs—a trophy hunted by Lord Jean-Luc Vertueux in his prime. It was easy to see the power and respect the minor noble family held just by exploring their halls. Every day Luchs thanked Lady Sundralla for being gifted the luck of being brought into their lives.

"I take it Father is in his quarters." Luchs looked Ulrin's way when he spoke. "Let's go see."

The two walked toward the hall past the bear whereupon they

bumped into a young lass some two-and-ten years of age. Her curly red hair bounced when she jolted back, surprised to have run into someone, and her hazel eyes beamed when she saw who was in front of her. "Is that you, Luchs?" The lass ecstatically smiled upon realizing it was him, then leaped at and hugged him. "'Tis been so long!"

Luchs laughed and wrapped an arm around her. "Aye, much too long. You've grown, little sprout."

She was Jilié Vertueux, third child of the household and the youngest sister. Five years prior, she was a little flower that always lit up a room with her smile. Now the lass stood before Luchs a good four foot eleven and had a bit of meat on her bones, but she still looked adorable in her dress and her cheeks still glowed a sweet berry-red.

"How about some love for your brother?" Ulrin stepped up to the lass and mussed her hair when she finally let Luchs go.

Jilié laughed, then scurried back and stood before her elder brother with hands on her hips. "Always trying to cut in, aren't you, Big Brother? You don't get to be the center of attention all the time, you devil!" she jested before leaping in to hug him, and let go sooner than she did for Luchs.

Noticing this, Ulrin grinned and chortled. "Still fancy Luchs here more than you care for me, aye?"

It was no secret the cheery lass had been smitten with Luchs when they first found him. She used to always hang around him with twinkling eyes and rosy cheeks and keep him company wherever he went. She constantly insisted that he was a prince who came into her life to make her a princess.

Flattering as it was, Luchs could only see her in a sibling manner.

And, considering the angry blush and her fierce stare, it seemed she came to think the same way. "Oh, stow it, Ulrin!"

"Good to see you two still get along fine," Luchs said in a laugh. "Have you seen Sir Trenent, Jilié?"

She nodded. "He's reading letters in his quarters, mostly the ones from Liliiun. Come on, he'll be thrilled to see you!" She took Luchs by the hand, dragging him down the hall she came from. Then she looked back to her brother. "Oh, and you too, Ulrin."

They talked a little bit as they walked. As it turned out, Jilié's older sister, Liliiun, had gotten married in the time Luchs had been gone. Liliiun was a very maternal woman when she looked after Luchs, always making sure he was tucked comfortably into bed, offering drinks and snacks, coddling him whenever he woke from one of his nightmares. She had to be two-and-twenty years by now. According to Jilié, she wedded a marquis who operated one of the page training facilities and managed construction over warships.

"What was his name again...? Barda— Bari— Ack, whatever. Someone important, she said."

Seeing as the man took her loving sister away, it was no surprise Jilié did not care for whoever he was.

At the end of the hall stood two thick doors at least ten feet tall with fine carvings of vines and berries along the sides and door handles. Ulrin showed them inside, shoving both doors open. Inside was a man with dark brown hair and a shaggy beard sitting at a desk, staring sternly at the parchment in his hand. He looked up when they entered and traded the gruff countenance for a jollier one. "Aha! Ulrin, Luchs! Welcome home, lads!" Sir Trenent stood and walked over to the two with open arms, showing off a lean yet muscular frame; he resembled his eldest somewhat. He pulled each of them in with an arm and pat their backs.

They laughed with him in the embrace and looked at him with delight.

"I heard Grandfather finally made you head of the family," Ulrin stated. "Guess that makes you *Lord* Vertueux now, aye?" He thought to tease his father by putting more emphasis on his new title.

The man smiled. "Aye. Though I'll miss patrolling the country with my comrades, this means I get to spend more of my time here, see the rest of the family grow. And how about you, *Sir* Ulrin?" He teased his son back. "I heard you saved a town from being pillaged. Good on you, lad!"

"And there's more to be happy about." Ulrin stepped back and cupped a hand over Luchs' shoulder. "I've made Luchs here my squire."

That statement brought a brilliant spark of jubilation to Sir Trenent's big blue eyes. He broke out in laughter sounding triumphant. "Aha! My son, finally taking his first squire. And Luchs, stepping up in the ranks. Ah, 'tis a good thing Untae's Day is nearly upon us 'cause I feel like celebrating!"

It was thought at one time in history all the water in the world had rotted, and the one who restored it was the goddess who watched over the ocean. There have been arguments regarding which day she saved the world, but all of that arguing made people forget why they wanted to celebrate in the first place, so everyone settled for one day to finally honor Untae together.

The door behind them creaked open not long after Sir Trenent pulled them in for another bear hug. A woman with curled dark red hair wearing a rustic beige dress stepped into the room, holding onto the hand of a young lad about five years of age. It was the children's mother, Agnes Vertueux, and the youngest of the family, Cael. She seemed to have arrived with something on her mind, but lost focus when her eyes rested on Luchs and her eldest.

"My Ulrin! Little Luchs! Now, why didn't you lads tell me you've come home?"

They let go of the happy father and walked up to her with open arms, another embrace to be shared. Cael looked at the two older men with bewilderment and slight irritation from his mother letting him go for them. Seeing his displeasure, Luchs let Agnes go and bent down to the lad's level. The last time he saw him was when he was not even a year-old babe. "You've grown some yourself, Cael. A right handsome laddie, you are." He raised a hand to fuzz the child's hair, but Cael backed away and clung to his mother's dress, staring at Luchs meekly.

I suppose 'tis natural he doesn't remember me.

The mother laughed adoringly. "Oh, don't be like that, Cael. You remember Luchs, aye? He helped me take care of you like the rest of the family."

There were no words from the lad, but Luchs did not take it harshly. Sir Trenent's laughter filled the room in his child's place, as did his jolly proclamation filling his lovely wife in on what their eldest son just told him. His voice rang so loud the servants through the halls must have heard it all as well.

The baroness was as elated to hear it from her husband as he was to hear it from Ulrin, clapping her hands gleefully before moving in to hug them again. Tired of being left out, Jilié leaped on her mother, wanting to join her embrace. Even little Cael clung to his mother's leg and sister's waist wanting to be a part of the family merriment.

It might not have been the same without Liliiun, but being with the Vertueux family again stirred a feeling of security and satisfaction Luchs had nearly forgotten living out in the wilderness for four years. It was not the fortuity of being with capable comrades-in-arms but something more: family.

Sometimes, he could not believe how the Vertueux family accepted him even after five years. When he first woke without any idea of who he was, no knowledge of home or family when they all had theirs, he thought he was alone. Being given a place in their family was the only thing that comforted him for a long time. It was more than he could ask of them.

Still, there were things he wanted to know about himself that none of them could give, things that he needed to find out.

~ Sixth Chapter ~
Changing Tides

Untae's Day was wonderful. The festivities planned by the Vertueux family were wholesome fun for everyone. Plenty of food had been provided for all to partake in. Men threw hatchets at targets painted on barrels. Women put on graceful, dramatic performances of the goddess of the sea restoring the world's life-giving water. Everyone all came together to dance freely to the invigorating music played by the bards.

The main event of the evening was Luchs standing proudly before the crowd of people and telling them stories of Des Meurtal. They all knew how dangerous the island was and dreaded ever sending a child they knew there. Of course, the story that excited everyone the most was of the battle against the pirates and the cursed storm that devastated the island. He spared the more gory details out of courtesy for the children, but he regaled them all with a hearty approach and a loud voice, gripping them with a heavy tone and reflective anticipation.

Everyone praised him for surviving the madness as much as for being made a squire. To give one's life to their country was one of man's greatest virtues, and they all wanted him to recognize that. The blacksmith even offered one of his finest shields at a very generous price—he still had to make his living—for him to use until he earned the shield that came with a knighthood. Since it was a special occasion, the baron Trenent Vertueux did not mind spending the extra lev for a present and a wish for good luck.

Never had a night gone by any quicker it was so enjoyable.

The next morning, Luchs and Ulrin made ready to leave for Shoafond. Arrangements had been made by the baron when they arrived a few days ago, and their vessel was shipshape and ready to sail the morrow after the festival. Unfortunate as it was to leave after just arriving, Sir Ulrin was expected back at the capital soon. It would not reflect well on him if he kept his superiors waiting.

The crew gathered before sunrise, inspecting their ship one last time before setting out. The entirety of House Vertueux came to see their champions off, even the servants and the old baron Jean-Luc. Many of the other sailors even held off their own departures briefly to wish the two luck. Jilié clung to her brother and Luchs stubbornly and told them not to be gone for as long again. As much as they relished in the thought of returning home soon, they knew better than to hang on to false hope. There was no knowing when the kingdom would need of them, after all. But they made the promise to return as soon as humanly possible.

"My grandson did this family proud time and again in his work, lad," elderly Jean-Luc grumbled in addressing Luchs. "Being in his service, you'd best show your worth yourself." The elderly man had a lot of salt in him and was as tough as any commandant and gruff as a boar. He had his fairer moments, rare as they were.

Sir Trenent gripped his father's shoulder firmly. "Don't go getting in his head, old man. Luchs will be fine. He'll only be of help."

Before long, the ship's captain approached the family and gave them to okay for their departure. The two soldiers spared only a moment to embrace the family before finally ascending the gangplank. The sails were unfurled not long after making it on deck, and the gangplank was drawn back and stored. Luchs and Ulrin waved to their family and watched them do the same, along with many good men and women who joined them that morning, until they floated out of view. After an hour or so, Untaseau was but a speck on the horizon.

Upon taking his eyes off the isle, Luchs got a good look at the sky. The sun shone brightly with promising golden rays painted across a delicate blue canvas. No clouds dark or light disturbed the fine view. A few gulls soared past the sails looking for land to roost at. The wind blew strongly against the sails, carrying the vessel at an optimal speed. It was a fine day for sailing.

Most of the Ederean kingdom comprised of a chain of islands that stretched for hundreds of miles in a breach between the continent. The islands used to train pages were near the edges of the archipelago; at the far southeast was Des Meurtal—or what remained of it. The archipelago's inner islands were the most populated. And at the heart of it all was the capital: Shoafond.

From Untaseau, it took approximately three days to reach Shoafond. The skies remained clear and the waters steady the entire way, and the winds were always against their sails.

Despite the fine progress, Luchs remained uneasy. The storm crafted by the witch that the pirates warned of stole breath from Zyleec and ripped the clouds from his domain. He could feel it with every gust that blew against him that the winds had lost their power.

Was it merely the elements trying to regain strength like a winded man after a fight, or was it an omen of worse things to come?

Paranoid thinking, he thought at first, only to think on it more.

Ulrin noticed his anxiety and tried to keep his mind distracted by working the body.

There were moments when the squire aided the crew in maintaining the ship or observed the navigator. After ensuring everything was running smoothly, he would spar with his meister knight.

When they fought, Luchs took bold advances against his foe, forcing Ulrin to keep his wits about him. But the knight never broke a sweat, his experience and trained muscles always keeping him ahead. Every move he made was swift and coordinated, his learned technique proving more fluent and effective than the rough swordplay his squire picked up on Des Meurtal. Life on the wildland taught him a great deal about the necessities of cooperation and always being ready to react, but no one directly taught the pages how to fight properly.

"Gilbrand obviously hadn't done you any favors. We'll have to temper that technique of yours before much else."

"Good. That way I'll catch up with you all the faster," Luchs confidently boasted.

Thanks to Ulrin, the voyage was an enjoyable one but passed by very quickly. They arrived at their destination before he knew it.

A massive shadow swept over their vessel, a great stretch of land looming high above their heads. The ship made berth alongside a dock constructed of wood so bright it almost shimmered in the sun while not buried in the shade.

The side of a grand cliff protruding out of the cascading waters was a strange place to construct part of a city. A great many buildings and bridges had been built clustered together along the perfectly vertical wall. A few waterfalls flowed from the impressive heights, the white waters meeting the deep blue with a soft but clear *whoosh*.

The crew disembarked and met the dockworkers with blithe grins. Ulrin paid the dockmaster his due fee before being introduced to two geldings, one of chestnut fur and the other of fine silver.

It appeared that they were expected.

After bidding the crew who carried them there farewell, Ulrin climbed atop the larger chestnut mount. Luchs attempted to mimic his meister knight, but his clumsy body slipping off the thinner silver gelding only showed how little experience he had with horses as well. He flopped over the horse like a dying fish until finally squirming onto the saddle. Not wishing to linger there any longer, he guided his mount to move along the well-built boardwalk, leaving behind that embarrassment with the laughter of the dockworkers.

The wooden streets of the city's cliffside were bustling with activity, but the civilians still knew to make way for incoming horses. Horses were beasts of burden not owned by many in the Ederean Archipelago except merchants, the high class, and the military. It was not difficult to tell who the riders were between the three given a little thought to what they had and what they lacked.

More people roamed the streets in the developed area atop the cliff. Just as many buildings sat atop the cliffside and bridges spread across the rivers flowing over it, but there was space aplenty there compared to the cliffside district. The scrambling people there were not as busy, and a few of them spared the time to offer Ulrin a hearty hello.

Luchs could not help notice that many of those few were lovely young women. They fawned over the knight and swooned when he returned a wave.

He began to remember a conversation Sir Trenent had with his son regarding marriage. It started out easygoing, then turned rowdy, and ended with the baron marching off to enjoy the rest of their celebration.

After going so high up, the air had a refreshing taste and became thirst-quenching. Simply inhaling coated the tongue in the thinnest layer of water. Luchs had nearly forgotten how much moisture the waterfalls of Shoafond sent into the air, and they were heading directly to the source.

The horses went into a strong trot over the hill past the city, breaking into a run as the roads began to stretch and curve left. A cloud of mist came into view, so had a massive crater beneath it where water fell from every corner, crashing down to the grand basin. And over the waters stood a solitary plateau with a grand castle crafted from ancient marble atop it. Its radiance, the sunlight illuminating its walls, shone over the mighty waters like a divine treasure in an unreachable trove. Riding downhill, they came to see the six bridges joining the plateau with the island in two stacked Y-patterns.

The horses crossed over the bridge stretching from the castle's southeastern point after a long while of steady galloping, slowing into a trot. The falls underneath roared mightily, the water in the air washing over them. Approaching the royal palace felt empowering. Taking in the sight of the fantastic monument and embracing the atmosphere was enough to feel ready to charge fearlessly into battle.

At the center of the tremendously long bridge stood the gate that blocked their entry to the castle. Those who were turned away either returned the way they came or plummeted into the falls from the massive gap left by a closed drawbridge. The soldiers stationed atop the gate eyed them through the mist and began moving about quickly. It was a matter of seconds before the drawbridge was lowered, completing the path.

Their vision had to be superb to see so well through the heavy mist.

Past the gate, the path extended and eventually broke into several forks made by small garden plots filled with healthy shrubs, trees, and blossoming flowers. The installation of life within the castle walls brought a stunning change in the atmosphere compared to the outside, something more relaxing and rejuvenating.

The path directly in front of them led straight into the castle. About halfway there, Ulrin dismounted and kept moving on foot. Luchs followed suit, wanting to follow his meister knight's lead. Soon enough, the mist parted enough to reveal an arched entryway. Several more guards stood there armed with halberds, a few approaching after taking notice of the knight and his squire.

"Welcome back, Lieutenant Ulrin."

Their greeting left Luchs speechless. He only stared at Ulrin while a soldier took the reins for the chestnut gelding and blindly obeyed when the other took the silver horse from him. As the knight watched the soldiers guide the horses to a proper hold and then march on, he came to realize his squire was not following. He seemed perplexed, but his expression quickly eased into a confident yet playful smile.

"Did I forget to mention? I'm the lieutenant of the Sea Drake Company."

Luchs groaned and scowled at Ulrin. "You tell me of all the maidens you flirt with and neglect to tell me you work directly under the general of the First Company!?"

Ulrin just laughed off his squire's frustrations.

There was little point in staying mad at him over that. After all, they were in Castle Ederea!

The soldiers who remained saluted to Ulrin and his squire, their fists clenched over their hearts, when they marched their way.

The inside of the castle was as splendorous as the out. A curved staircase ascended to the left along the hall, adorned by a long verdant carpet lined down the hall and a matching banner with the royal family's sigil hanging over the trail. An occasional suit of armor stood at attention along the path and lanterns were fixed onto the wall, each holding a dim gray stone. Luchs remembered how those stones glowed at night when capturing even the briefest speck of moonlight. They glowed so brilliantly it was hard to believe they were not magic in nature.

Even within the castle walls, the air tasted refreshing. The mist did not follow them inside, but breathing it in was still such a delight.

The long stretch connected with the castle's vestibule, where a few distinguished gentlemen waited at the bottom of a widespread staircase. They all wore similar armor with the kingdom's symbol, the broad head of a mighty sea drake, on their shoulder plates, except for the tall man in fancy attire outfitted with several plates of bronze armor. He had a dominant countenance that demanded respect and eyes that could pierce through stone.

Ulrin chortled a little upon seeing them. "Quite the reception you've made for me, General, sir. Had I not known better, I'd say you wanted me discharged."

The knights turned their way with rapt attention, even the stern one at the center. He kept silent until his lieutenant and the child with him approached and stood before him. "Gone unexpectedly another few days though you were, it hardly calls for your removal." Keeping that smug look, the man pulled out a sheet of parchment from his pockets. Judging by the small claw marks, it had to have come via carrier bird. "Word from Lord Vertueux came long before you. I see no reason to keep a man from celebrating Untaseau's most sacred day right after stepping foot on the isle he calls home."

"And the entourage?"

"Lads missing their favorite lieutenant," the general scoffed. "And now that they have—off with you lot! Back to your stations before I have you running laps across the bridges until you drop."

The knights were off before their general could finish giving orders, scattering in different directions. One crossed Ulrin, offering a friendly jab on the shoulder and a smile before returning to his duties.

The general pried his attention from his second-in-command to look at the child beside him. "Your new squire, I take it?" He reached a hand out to Luchs with a smile less intimidating than his earlier expression. "A pleasure, lad. General Eurieg Esperance."

Luchs took his hand firmly, showing a little of his brawn in the grip, as was customary when greeting another man. "'Tis an honor, General Esperance."

The smile on the man's face sprouted into a grin. "Strong, and respectable too. A fine pick, Lieutenant. I only hope he knows how to keep his head in battle."

To that, Ulrin could only chortle. He reached out and gripped his squire's shoulder confidently. "Luchs here's survived Gilbrand's little 'facility' and far worse. No doubt he'll be a fine asset to the kingdom and make a grand knight."

Luchs could not help grinning from their praise.

General Esperance seemed pleased by the answer. "Ah, a page of Des Meurtal. That itself says enough of your resilience, but you will need more than that if you wish to be considered a knight in the future. The role of the company you are now a part of is to ensure Ederea's peace is preserved. Absolute perfection is expected of us all, no matter your standing in life."

"Always the stick in the mud, eh, Eurieg?" his second-in-command responded less formally. "Instead of pressuring my squire so soon, why don't you fill us in on what we missed when the others returned?"

Offering a nod, General Esperance turned around to scale the stairs with the lieutenant and his squire in tow. The staircase was much more grandiose than the one they scaled before, an elegant design put into the railing with finely crafted hawks engraved at the base, and the carpet on the steps traced with lines of gold catching more light than the one they walked on earlier. The climb to the top of the stairway split into two different staircases; they took the one on the right.

It was not long before they reached a hall with level ground. Just like the lower ones, it was lined with several luminous lanterns and a few suits of armor. To the right were windows that gave a view of the city. Even looking on from there, it was obvious how many people roamed the streets.

Down the hall, another soldier and a lad walked directly toward them. They were an odd pair.

The man had paler skin than most would see on an Ederean, longer hair and thinner eyes, too, which were a deep black. A good look made it clear he was not an ordinary soldier. He wore no armor but instead thick, dark clothing that fit comfortably yet firmly around his limbs. There was no mistaking him for a civilian, not when he was armed with two swords at the hips and one on his back.

The lad was just as unusual. Given his russet skin tone, he could have been from one of the southern isles, but Luchs never heard of southerners with white hair before. He wore some abdominal armor over his simple clothes, but it was leather, not metal. The strangest thing about him had to be the thick amber scarf wrapped around his neck and lower face, burying everything beneath his eyes. As he approached, Luchs noticed his eyes, those bitter blue droplets, looked more suitable for an animal than a person.

Whatever their business, they passed by without a word said or a remark of their existence.

W-What the—

When they passed, the air had been smothered in a horrifying chill. It gnawed at Luchs' body, bit into his skin like thousands of tiny fangs, reminding him of coldest nights in the dank Leviathan's Maw.

It was only for the briefest time when they crossed paths, and yet it was so cold he could not help but stop in place. The others did not seem to notice. Once again, Luchs wished he was not so aware of the changes in the air around him.

He turned back to the strange twosome, to the lad in particular.

It came from him. How?

Not wanting to get separated from Ulrin and his new general, he rushed back to them.

General Esperance glanced his way, then at the strange twosome, and then turned back to the path in front of them.

General Esperance guided them through the expansive halls of the castle until they came across a path with no windows. At the end was a simple wooden door adorned with long, thick metal hinges that looked to be flowers in bloom. He opened the door for his subordinates, showing them inside.

The room within was small and moderately lit by five lanterns hanging at each corner of the room and over the doorway. A sturdy desk sat before them by the wall where the kingdom's flag hung proudly. Three tall bookshelves full of what appeared to be important documents stood against the right wall, and in front of them was a lad who sifted through the shelves, organizing their contents.

The lad turned to face the door upon hearing it open. "Welcome back, Gene— Luchs?"

Luchs blinked. He did not recall meeting him, but the small scar beneath his chin reminded him of someone. "Maxime?"

Not much time passed since leaving Des Meurtal and yet Maxime looked so different. His blonde hair had been trimmed for a classier, less raggedy appearance, looking less filth-ridden and greasy than before. The terror and grief that once filled his eyes gone, there was the glimmer of life and energy in its place. Such subtle changes made him look like an entirely different person.

Placing the papers in his hands down, he marched over to the door with a smile and jocularly jabbed his former foe on the shoulder.

"I didn't think to see you so soon."

Luchs grinned and returned the playful jab.

General Esperance smiled. "So you met my squire already. Good. No need for introductions."

Shocked and awed, Luchs quickly turned to the general and then back to Maxime. "You? His squire?"

His smile was a weary one. "Aye. I didn't believe it myself when he offered. Nearly lost my head, I did."

Ulrin seemed as perplexed as the squires. "Why the sudden change of heart? When last I brought it up, you said you've 'no need for a squire.'"

The general took to his desk while his subordinates and squire entertained one another, sitting with a respectable posture. "I do not look kindly upon pages who've yet to learn what it really means to follow orders, as you are aware. The latest crop of 'Devoir' pages, as Commandant Brunlier called them, however, begrudgingly learned how difficult it can be to follow another's will. And I found Maxime to be the most resilient of his little faction. He deserves the chance to learn further."

Maxime became red in the cheeks from hearing his praise.

It was strange to see him behaving rather meekly after witnessing how ferocious he was in a fight. Luchs could not help but chuckle.

"And if he fails to continue meeting your near-impossible expectations?"

The few documents on the desk were in General Esperance's hands before he continued to the conversation. He sifted through them leisurely but read quickly. "Then he will be sent to a training facility until another knight deems him fit to serve," he curtly responded, then shifted a glance at his squire. "Maxime, you are now familiar with Castle Ederea?"

"Aye, General."

"Then show Ulrin's squire around while I brief him."

Following those orders, the two squires left the general's quarters and travelled down to the castle's lower areas. At Luchs' request, Maxime guided him toward the castle's archives while showing him the other facilities en route to it.

From the windows past the general's quarters, they had a grand view of the training grounds behind the castle. Soldiers trained within a ring of water formed by two small streams flowing inside the grooves of carved stone. They all practiced simple repetitions of swinging and thrusting their weapons underneath the scorching sun. From what Maxime said, those soldiers would continue the repetitions for at least an hour before engaging each other in combat exercises.

On the lower level was a storage room used for stockpiling weapons. Racks were cluttered with spears, buckets full of swords. There were even suits of armor that held onto weapons that could only be considered works of a master craftsman, perhaps meant to be wielded by high-ranking knights. That one area was so large it stretched from one hall on the east side to the one on the west.

After going so deep into the castle, they stumbled upon a dark stairwell leading into the depths of the plateau. Unlike the other stairwells, there were small trails of water that leaked from the ceiling and pooled down the edges of the hall. The luminous stones adorning the walls set the flowing water aglow in a faint cyan light. Ominous as it first appeared, the light had a strangely calming effect.

The flow of water from the waterfalls outside could be faintly heard there and grew louder the further they descended.

The walk lasted a while, whether it was from the stairwell being so long or the pure light entrancing Luchs enough to lose track of time. At the bottom was a door with a cryptic rune at its center, one that glowed like the stones. Maxime took the door's thin handle and pushed it open.

Sunlight sliced through the dark space as the way opened to what first appeared to be an exposed treasure trove. Instead of walls, six strong stone pillars held up the roof of the cavernous room, allowing the outside light to illuminate the space. Like in the stairwell, water flowed freely inside, filling small indentions in the floor and collecting together at its center, condensing into another mighty, roaring waterfall upon reaching the edge of the space and flowing outside.

Luchs was in awe as he tried to process how, after going into the darkest reaches of the castle, they ended up outside.

Castle Ederea truly was extraordinary.

Within the cavernous space were bookcases arranged into a maze that spread out to the mighty pillars that held the stone mouth open. The small circular steps before the door led to a pedestal with a tome as thick as a log on top of it.

Unfazed by the wonder before him, one he had likely already seen, Maxime stepped down to the pedestal. "A grand place, and not one without guidance." He opened the tome and began flipping through the pages. It must be used as some kind of directory.

Luchs followed his guide and caught a quick glimpse at a few words from a page before it was turned. Strangely enough, he noticed that many of the pages were mostly blank.

"Why is it incomplete?"

"General Esperance told me this castle had been built centuries, maybe millennia, before the kingdom's founding. Most of the records here stood the tests of time, written in a forgotten language. Still, the wisest kings and scholars thought the vast knowledge here too precious to discard, so many of the shelves here are occupied by indecipherable apocrypha, at least until someone manages to translate them." Maxime turned to face Luchs. "There is still plenty we can read. Do you have any requests?"

"Are there any maps here?"

It was not long until Maxime found what he was after. When he did, he closed the tome and walked into the maze of bookshelves, gesturing for his companion to follow.

The placement of the shelves seemed inconvenient. Accessing the needed text or document would no doubt be trying, even with the directory tome in place.

When they reached the opening to the outside, Luchs noticed something unusual. The sun's rays shot through the massive gaps in a burning glare. When he moved to cover his eyes, he saw something he did not expect: a faded reflection. What stood before him was not a tear in the wall but a window. The ridges of the clear surface suggested it to be a crystalline substance that unless approached closely would be difficult to notice. Luchs reached a hand out to press against the barrier and found the surface to be thin yet incredibly durable.

"This is incredible!"

Maxime's cheerful smile was reflected on the crystalline wall. "I had a similar reaction myself."

"What is this?"

"I haven't the slightest idea. There have been things found here that baffled and amazed the conqueror who claimed this land. This entire castle is thought to be a monument left by the gods." The grin he wore grew broader. "What better place to rule over a country?"

Looking past his reflection, he saw the mighty waterfalls surrounding the castle crash down into the basin below. It was a better view than from atop the bridges. From there, he could see the white waters meet with the pool of deep blue.

As captivating as the view was, they were in the middle of something, so Luchs half-hesitantly stepped away from the window.

The shelves they searched for were not far from the window. One had a small plaque at the head that read Maps.

It took some time, but Luchs found a tome completely comprised of maps including Ederean territories, countries conquered in the past, and various other nations, such as their Vermalian and Brungonian neighbors. Every page contained maps drawn with exquisite detail and lists of side notes on each region.

Ederea looked like the start of a swirling vortex—excluding its mainland territory to the east and west—with Shoafond at the eye of the storm. After the main page depicting the Ederean Archipelago, the rest of the section on the country contained details on each individual island. Not knowing exactly what he was looking for, Luchs just flipped through the pages hoping anything he might find something familiar.

He had skimmed through half of the tome before Maxime pulled him out of the pages. There was still much he needed to see.

Since Luchs had not practiced swordplay yet, Maxime suggested they spend some time training and showed him to the training grounds.

Many soldiers were still performing their exercises. The squires did not see it right to interrupt their training. Instead, they introduced themselves to the knight leading the exercises and humbly requested the use of a few weapons for their own training. The knight looked at Luchs skeptically since he did not yet bear any semblance to a squire nor had he recognized him, but he nodded when turning back to Maxime. He offered them any weapon they knew how to wield and directed them to a plot near the gardens.

They each took a sword—Maxime held his in both hands, and Luchs paired his with his new shield.

They headed toward the gardens, stepping through the tall topiary arch covered by thick vines and golden flowers in bloom. A wide clearing spread before them, promising plenty of space for a little fight. No one seemed to be nearby, so there would be no one to disturb. Both lads held their weapons at their foe, taking wide stances, ready to react at a moment's notice. They have learned extensively the advantages and drawbacks both of making the first move in a fight. It was true that moving quickly enough would secure an upper hand, but an adept fighter would be able to react accordingly, even counter.

Not one to be patient, Luchs took charge.

The two sparred against each other until exhaustion overcame them. Luchs was kneeling, tightly clenching his sword hilt and shield handle; Maxime leaned limply against the sword he pressed into the soil.

Between breaths of exasperation, there were brief moments of laughter from both of them.

Luchs enjoyed how his muscles burned from exercise, how sweat trickled against his skin and clothes. It was how he knew he was truly alive, something he endlessly craved. His opponent seemed to share his feelings. A smile never left his face, no matter how weary he was.

Brushes of humid air cooled their weary bodies. The late-day sun gleamed along the metal of their weapons. A few flower petals blew across the wind before landing someplace out of sight.

It was not a bad aftermath for a sparring session. Luchs would have pondered on how the aftermath of his first battle as a squire would be if he were not so tired.

Fighting his fatigue, Maxime gripped at the hilt and guard of his sword and lifted it and himself off up. "Crivens! How is it that you're fiercer still than when we tried killing each other?"

Such praise made Luchs laugh. "I'm no slouch. A fortnight's rest wouldn't be enough to stray my strength," he said while attempting to pull himself off the ground.

The lads stood tall as they gradually sheathed their weapons. Feeling the breeze brush against their legs purged the flaming fatigue from them in cool waves. They marched to meet the other, carrying themselves with however much dignity they could keep, and reached out to firmly grasp and shake hands, showing each other gratitude for an exciting fight.

Leaving their match with a winner undecided was unsatisfying, but there would be no sense in fighting beyond that point.

Instead of leaving, they decided to stroll around the gardens to keep their sore muscles moving. Luchs teased Maxime about wanting to be there to look at any passing maidens, not flowers. Maxime looked like he wanted to retort, but could not help stammering while redfaced. When he could speak properly again, he assured him that was not it.

"The gardens here are beautiful and I want to admire them. Who knows when we'll be called to battle or how long we'll remain trapped in a world of blood before seeing this again? As one who survived Des Meurtal, I'll not pass up a chance to engage in pleasantries like this if given the chance."

He made a fine point. Although Des Meurtal once had beauty to itself, many found it impossible to appreciate after spending the days struggling to survive.

They came across small patches of beautifully chromatic flowers. Tall trees stood among them, gentle giants beside the delicate nymphs, retaining a decent territory from one another. The flora grew healthy from the sun's powerful rays and the plentiful water in the mist, and the air smelled and tasted divine because of it.

A few birds soared through the air before perching onto a branch. They wasted no time in preening their fine golden wings. Not long ago, Luchs would only have thought about how tasty those birds would have been. Seeing them as captivating creatures instead was a nice change, as was the chance to appreciate the beauty of it all.

The blow of the wind. The rustling of tree branches. The exquisite aroma of flowers wafting in the breeze. The beauteous voice humming—

Humming?

Luchs had no idea that there were others in the gardens. They probably came after the sparring finished or entered through a different area outside their notice.

The lads turned to where the sweet voice came from, noticing a small path leading to a vast bed of radiant flowers. There they saw, at its center, a few lovely young women and a younger lass about their age tending to the flowers. The women had frilly garments typically worn by maids that served in the castle. And the lass, she was something else entirely. She had beautiful porcelain features and dazzling silver starlight hair with curls that bounced whenever she moved to touch the flowers. She did not pick any, only took them into her gentle palm and graciously caressed their little petals. Those big, pearly eyes of hers looked down at them as though they were precious children. The lass almost appeared to be a nymph queen tending to her beloved subjects in her rightful place. She wore a dress of silk colored cerulean with golden strands accentuating her slim figure. Fine treasures adorned her person—a jeweled necklace around her neck, a tiara atop her head.

The squires dared not disturb the tranquil scene. It was beauty belonging to the women there, a small world of tranquility that allowed them a moment of peace. Breaking the tranquility would be uncouth of them.

Maxime smiled. "I recognize that tune. My mum used to sing it to my little brothers, and mayhap myself at one point. You think she is trying to soothe them?"

"Soothe? You speak like she thinks the plants people."

"Mayhap she does." Maxime mulled something over quietly. He kept his eyes on the lass and the ladies beside her, his hand propped under his chin and his elbow resting on his free arm. "Could she be...?"

"Something on your mind?"

"Just a passing thought. I don't think it matters much."

They took in the sight of the lovely lass and the ladies for a moment more before turning away to head back. Behind them came Ulrin.

"Finished playing in the daisies, lads?"

"You think sparring with this varlet is easy?" Luchs asked, pointing a thumb at his friend. "So I was right to think you never trained on Des Meurtal then."

Ulrin looked at the lovely ladies behind them, then back at them. He seemed surprised for a moment in between. "Here I thought you were helping the ladies over yonder tend to the flowers."

What was that? No remark on their women's allure? No attempt to go and flirt with them? Such behavior was very unlike the philanderer. He only did so if he knew he should not.

"Ulrin, do you know them?"

There was a brief look back, but he tried not to let his eyes linger. "Those ladies there? A little. 'Tis best you leave them be."

Maxine caught on to what Luchs implied quickly and afterwards said, "What of the lass?"

"Oh, her. If you lads hoped to meet her, you're out of luck. The ladies there," he pointed to the women in servants' attire, particularly the tall one with stern eyes, "they don't let squires near the princess."

The squires looked back at the silver lass. Given the attire and demeanor, it was understandable she was of high class. But the princess? Out in the gardens with her handmaidens and no guards? Hearing that nearly made Luchs jump.

Maxime, on the other hand, seemed only slightly surprised. "Huh. So I was right after all. Princess Camellia du Joiec... I wondered what His Majesty's heir would be like since meeting him," he mumbled to himself.

Luchs took a good look at the lass he now saw as a princess. She was clearly gentle and caring to hold the petals of a flower without damaging them. If she was that way with flowers, perhaps she was the same with her subjects. He took the time to carve her visage into his memory while Princess Camellia took the hand of one of her handmaidens and followed them out the gardens.

She was to be Ederea's future, the next ruler. Her loyal knights, Luchs included, would be trusted to protect her life.

Hopefully, he would be ready before that time came.

~ Seventh Chapter ~

Trembling

There was much to learn about life in Castle Ederea.

After being fitted for a uniform, Luchs was shown the many duties the knights performed. Secure as the castle was being suspended within a pit of waterfalls, every area had been overseen by soldiers. The centuries of procedure performed in the times when a conqueror sat on the throne have not been forgotten.

Guards regularly patrolled the halls, ensuring everything was as it should be. Several keeps were set up across the Crown Plateau for the soldiers to recuperate and so there was always someone to respond to trouble should it occur. The six bridges linking the plateau to the rest of the island were always under heavy surveillance at the drawbridge gates.

If they were not at work somewhere in the castle, the knights patrolled the city to ensure order was maintained.

As a squire, Luchs followed his meister knight and did as he did unless ordered otherwise. His first few days were spent having Ulrin show him how things were done and learning the routes to and around the city.

Minor situations were handled by the knights available. Threats to the castle were handled by the captain of the king's guard. Whenever dire news came, the king's nine generals were informed, and those present decided on what actions to take. And should someone infiltrate the castle, they would be captured and brought before the king for their punishment. Criminals were not kept within the castle walls but rather in dungeons built behind the mighty waterfalls, often referred to as the Cage Falls.

After Luchs had familiarized himself with the castle, they set out for him to get to know the city. Shoafond was a peaceful haven. The port where they came into the city from was busy from dawn to dusk with ships being loaded and unloaded of precious cargo by the heartiest men. The buildings near the hillside mostly belonged to merchants selling fine catches and fresh produce, but there was also an inn and housing for the more successful businessmen. Miles of land peppered with houses and slivers of rivers stretched from there to the edge of the city. A chapel stood between the city and the castle, offering sanctuary and guidance to those in need of understanding the gods' work in the world and finding their place in it.

The citizens were kind and lively, often approaching the knights on duty for friendly banter when otherwise unoccupied.

Of course, there were times when someone thought to test the law.

Around his second week in the capital, Luchs had the chance to capture a criminal. It was nothing too problematic—just a meager thief. He swiped a few radishes from an unsuspecting grocer. Theft of any kind was a crime, and acknowledging this, Luchs gave chase. His prey was a slippery one, cutting through corners too narrow for him to cross. He did not escape, though. A few other knights who caught wind of the theft managed to intercept him.

He was just a lad, a young thing no older than ten years. He was frail, emaciated from hunger. The pitiful look on his face when he stood before Ulrin almost made Luchs regret going after him.

It was shocking to hear he wanted the king to get involved. But when he saw how the king responded, his opinion changed.

The king was infuriated seeing his knights manhandling a child and demanded he be shown courtesy while in his court. Princess Camellia was there, too, and watched the men with disappointment. Although a crime had been committed, he was still but a child.

Aware of the situation as he was, the king looked at the lad like an outraged father waiting for an explanation.

The lad felt he had no choice in what he had done. He was starving, as was his sister. They needed to eat and had no means of getting food honestly, not after losing their mother.

His punishment was made quickly after hearing that. For such a small offense, the lad was charged with working under the grocer he stole from until earning his forgiveness. And so that the lad would not run away, he and his sister were kept in the care of one of his soldiers while he worked off the debt. The arrangement was not just fair, it was generous. The children were given a roof over their heads and even provided eatable meals during their punishment.

A strange way to punish someone, Luchs first thought.

But what would happen to him after being turned over to the grocer? It might have been few vegetables, but he worried whether or not the grocer would be forgiving.

He tried to shake it off, to forget about it for a time.

Then the next day, he stopped by the grocer's stand. The lad was there, grabbing everyone's attention with a show of his pitiable eyes and meek calls asking people to buy their produce. While lacking in confidence, he seemed to be well, much better than he was the previous day. Even the grocer seemed content.

"Mad?" the grocer echoed when Luchs asked about the theft. He then cackled. "Aye, for a wee bit. But I'll not fault the lad for trying to feed himself and the lassie. Besides, I've more business now 'cause of the wee one. Tell His Majesty all is forgiven and the children are more than welcome to stay with us if they still need a roof."

It was a relief to know everything would be well with them, but Luchs could not help think it had been settled much too smoothly.

On route back to the castle, he asked Ulrin how the king was so certain that would work.

"King Godefroy is no saint, but he recognizes when someone needs an open hand or a firm trouncing. The lad looked in need of both."

It seemed simple enough—too simple. How was he so sure the grocer would not have trounced the lad himself for the theft?

The skepticism made sense to Ulrin, but he still smiled and laughed. "I've told you before how His Majesty's ancestors were conquerors, aye? The du Joiec didn't just win battles and take land, they won the hearts of the people and took their troubles onto themselves. All of the wars to win greater prosperity took great tolls on every nation they ruled, so the du Joiec did all they could to lessen the strain by having the people help one another—commoners, soldiers, even nobility. The conqueror's time has long passed, but the people still remember how important it is to hold each other high when times are hard. King Godefroy wants the people to retain that memory as he has. Of course, not everyone will act on that, but some will."

It was a wonderful belief. And it was fantastic how so many shared it. He saw the people of Untaseau act on it as well during his recovery.

Hearing how the Edereans' generosity came to be made him look at what he learned from the knight's code and showed him he still had much to learn.

A month passed without much incident. Mornings were filled with the exercises Luchs practiced alongside the other soldiers. The middays typically involved patrolling and reviewing various aspects such as battle tactics and knightly decorum. And evenings were mostly spent polishing his and Ulrin's armor and weapons before resting for the night.

A few thefts made things exciting until they were dealt with, the criminals caught and sentenced. Luchs managed to be of help in pursuing one of them, but once again lost the catch to someone else.

There was little time for him to act on his own. On the days he could scrounge up some time for himself, Luchs spent as long as possible looking through old maps in the archives.

With no real leads from them, he began looking into historical documents. It was more of a longshot than looking through maps for places with names that might sound familiar. It was likely just a huge waste of time. But he was desperate.

Every day that went by with the terrible gap in his memories made him feel more lost. He had to remember who he was, and finding out where he came from might have been the first step. With all of that information at his disposal, there had to be something, anything to point him in the right direction.

But he never found anything. Nothing ever reminded him of anything.

The lack of answers always agitated him. The best thing to do after that was train, get the frustration out through physical exertion.

One day, Luchs and Ulrin were with a group of knights and their squires in the training grounds. Everyone paired off and switched partners every now and again, fighting against each other with all they had. Luchs already squared off against ten squires and came out on top every time. The knights were so impressed they had one of them see how much abuse he could give to someone bigger than him.

It was a rough bout, but Luchs held his own against the knight like a real warrior. He took plenty of abuse, nicks of the blade grazing his skin, brutal bludgeonings that knocked him off his feet whenever he got careless. The way his body held together and the impossibly quick rate his blood stopped spilling astonished everyone, as did the strength and cunning he put into his attacks.

Everyone cheered and hollered seeing him fight.

"You've got yourself a live one, Ulrin!" a stout knight stated.

"A strong one at that," said the one Luchs just beat. "Des Meurtal must've had a hard time with him."

Both meister knight and squire were beaming with pride. The other squires surrounded Luchs, patting and playfully punching him on the shoulder and laughing at the fun they had sparring against him. A few jealous remarks were made, but mostly in good fun.

Strong and durable as he was, there was still much he needed to learn. The men gave him advice on the best ways to hold a sword and showed him stances for single- and two-handed swordsmanship. After trying everything once, Luchs found he needed plenty of practice to follow such strict methods. And he was eager to learn it all.

After their sparring session ended, General Esperance came along to break up the merriment. Everyone stood at attention and saluted as soon as they realized he was there.

"Lieutenant, with me." And of course, that meant him and his squire.

They left the training grounds quickly and took the direct route to the throne room. Maxime was waiting for them by the entrance.

Even having already been there once, Luchs was still in awe at the grand style of the throne room. Past the two grandiose doors was a hall so spacious that the ceiling could barely be seen. Two rows of silver columns complementing the polished marble floor stretched to the end of the hall, bordering a cerulean carpet with gold trimming. Each column depicted a story from ages past, but no one knew when those times were or who was carved into them. At the edge of the hall rested two ornate thrones, one smaller and less imposing than the other, where the king and queen would address important matters. And behind the mighty thrones was a massive window—although it looked more like the wall had been removed entirely—that offered a view of Shoafond's magnificent lowlands.

King Godefroy awaited them on the larger throne of silver and sapphires, and next to him was Princess Camellia on the smaller throne meant for the late queen.

Ulrin once mentioned the late queen's daughter had been taking initiative in certain affairs so she may learn how to be a proper ruler when the time came.

Four men and a couple of lads stood before their rulers: two generals, their lieutenants, and three squires.

General Esperance and his entourage marched to meet them, then turned to their king and princess and saluted them promptly. Everyone stood at ease once King Godefroy raised a hand off the throne's armrest.

He looked too tense for his summons to mean anything good.

King Godefroy du Joiec II was a burly man with muscles rippling against the rich cloth he wore. His dark brown hair was thick and shaggy, his beard matching it nicely. The regal robes he donned almost concealed the top and trousers barely containing his physique.

Every time he looked at him, Luchs had been reminded that he was a mighty warrior before ascending to the throne. His dreary scowl, a stark contrast to the joy that typically glimmered in his ebony eyes, almost made him shudder.

He said nothing until the guards at the throne room's entrance secured the doors. "Good of you all to make it," he began grimly. "We have a matter on our hands that requires all of your attention. There have been a terrible number of attacks in our archipelago as of late, attacks made by ships of unknown origin."

"Might they be pirates?" interrupted a general. "I heard there have been more infesting our waters recently."

King Godefroy shook his head. "Nay, they are no mere pirates. These enemies are too well-organized and too many in number. The other generals are on high alert because of what happened to General Aigle." He lowered his head when mentioning one of his nine generals, his countenance wrinkled from stress. "He is still recovering after the ambush on his fleet. Few escaped with their lives, nary a ship lasting against the assault."

An entire fleet ambushed? The men were awestruck, their mouths hanging agape. They could not believe anyone had the audacity to attack Ederean naval forces. And to think they emerged from the skirmish victorious—it was inconceivable. The Ederean military had the strongest naval force in the world. Even Vermalio's and Pterna's might paled in comparison. To have that power suddenly outmatched by another was a huge blow to their pride.

"Unknown forces that can match our own ships, even outright attacking us... 'Tis a grave situation," another general grumbled.

"Not to mention an outrageous insult!" General Esperance snarled.

"I'm glad we understand. Then there's no questioning that action must be taken. If these enemies have the gall to attack us unprovoked, we cannot guarantee they won't treat civilians with less hostility. They are a threat we need to sink before they come too far into our archipelago." Before going on, King Godefroy stood from his throne and took out a slip of parchment from his left sleeve, showing it to everyone abruptly. It was a letter. Several spots were damp from the salty sea breeze, drops of blood dried by the signature. "This missive states they come from the north. Securing our territory there is our first priority. General la Mabél, you'll join General Troteu in the northwest. General Leteo, to the northeast."

Neither party remained after hearing their duties. It was not seen as disrespect toward the king, more of a desire to get the job done and not leave a moment wasted.

Upon their dismissal, King Godefroy turned to General Esperance with a stare heavier than before. "General Esperance, I need you in Prévinn with Admiral Barbossa. Should the facility fall—"

General Esperance nodded. "Understood, Your Majesty."

The four left the throne room as quickly as the others.

Luchs recalled the name Prévinn from when he read the maps in the archives. It was a wide isle located to the far north of Shoafond. The land was flat and level, the only high risings it had was from the large facility constructed at its southern edge.

"General," Maxime spoke, "what was King Godefroy going to say?"

He said nothing right away, trying to assess everything that had happened. Then, he took a deep breath, exhaled, and said, "Prévinn serves many purposes, but its primary role is to support the construction of ships, specifically the warships we use to safeguard our waters. If the enemy takes it, they will be able to use those ships against us."

Preparations were made forthwith. Every member of the Sea Drake Company present in Shoafond took up arms and made way to the docks. They sailed for Prévinn before the day's end.

Not a single ship, hostile or otherwise, sailed their way during the voyage. The waters remained steady and the skies clear. There was nary a sign of trouble on the flagship, but everyone kept looking. They could not help it, not after seeing the last few to board back at port.

Luchs recognized them from his first day. It was the same strange twosome he crossed paths with before, the warrior in dark garb and the small lad. Everyone looked their way aghast, but their eyes were at their feet, at a small white fox that walked beside the lad.

Foxes were said to bring bad luck. They were a favorite of Lady Malute, the goddess of misfortune, who delighted in the trouble they caused.

Several men tried removing the fox until it hid behind the small lad. They dared not make any sudden moves when they saw him reach for the sword at his side. He bore a vicious glare promising trouble. The ship's captain protested against the beast's presence, as did General Esperance and every other man on board.

"I've tolerated much from you, Executioner," the general rebuked the man, "but bringing a fox, of all things, in our presence now of all times is unacceptable. Disembark at once!"

"And who are you to order me around?"

It was bewildering to see the man speak so disrespectfully to a general.

"King's orders: we're to join you against this enemy. And that fox follows the kid wherever he goes. If you don't like it, see if you can make him get rid of it."

The man spoke no more on the matter and walked past everyone. The lad followed, as did the fox.

General Esperance, for as flustered as he was, did not argue and gave the order to set sail before the fox jinxed them.

It was hard to believe someone as dignified as him would allow anyone to speak to him in such a way. He called the man Executioner. Luchs mulled that moment over, trying to make sense of it.

From what Ulrin later explained, the executioners were men who served directly under the Ederean king. They were warriors responsible for eliminating those who committed the worst of crimes. Since the times of the first conqueror, executions have been carried out in the dark, away from prying eyes. Making a spectacle of a man's death was abhorrent, a sin in and of itself. Only rarely did Edereans praise the death of an enemy rather than the effort of the one who felled them.

A man normally earned the role by proving himself a soldier of pristine character, judgment, and caliber.

However, that man, Wolfram Sörrign, attained his role simply by displaying his skills before the king after appearing out of nowhere. It was not uncommon to earn the role in that way, but those executioners were typically well-known, respectable Edereans; there was no record of Wolfram Sörrign's life. The only things people knew of him were that his combat skills were second-to-none and that he secluded himself somewhere on the Crown Plateau when not on a task from the king.

The lad that followed him was just as unusual. All anyone knew about him was that King Godefroy and Princess Camellia brought him to Ederea with them after returning from Vermalio almost a year ago. He rarely spoke and did not train with the others. No one understood how he became a squire to Executioner Sörrign, only that it was recognized by the king.

Seeing how wary everyone was of the lad, Luchs took it upon himself to ensure he was never out of sight. He rarely did anything. Most of the time, he stood at the bow of the ship with his fox, looking out at the waves.

Before he realized it, they arrived at Prévinn.

A tall fortress loomed over the horizon and a massive port stretched beneath it. Several warships sailed around the isle, acting as a barricade to repel hostile ships. They were all much larger than the Sea Drake Company's ships, their main decks at the height of the flagship's first sail.

The Sea Drake Company's ships were drawn in by a lad at the docks signaling for them to follow. The captains turned their ships to follow, steering their vessels carefully through the crowded waters. They managed to quickly dock with his help.

Waiting for them at the docks was a stout man wearing the proud attire of a well-decorated admiral underneath thick plates of armor. His facial features were round and his gut was full. The muscles on his body showed he knew his way in a battle. Auburn hair grew atop his head and over his jaw. The rigid gaze from his brown eyes could frighten the small and weak.

"Admiral Barbossa." General Esperance pounded his chest in salute to the imposing man, who saluted him back. "I trust you know why we're here."

"Aye, the unknown attackers. 'Tis the talk of the archipelago," the admiral gruffly put. He looked over the soldiers brought before him as though looking at a selection of stallions.

"I'd say we have nothing to fear. You've more than two thousand good men within these walls, as well as a fleet of the king's most trusted company. Our strengths combined will protect your facility from those barbarians."

Admiral Barbossa grumbled something curt before turning his way and nodded. "Aye, that it will. Come. I've much to show you."

General Esperance and his men followed their host inside the facility. Those already familiar with it dispersed, following servants that walked in the directions of the barracks.

The tall iron gates had already been opened in anticipation of the First Company's arrival, leading to a massive courtyard. At least a hundred knights, squires, and even pages were inside doing repetitions, some with swords, others with spears, still others with axes. They paired up and began sparring with one another when directed to by the one leading their exercises.

Everyone went their separate ways, engaging in different areas of the facility, until only General Esperance, Ulrin, and their squires remained in Admiral Barbossa's company. He explained the plan to them while on their way to his quarters, going over the details thoroughly. It was a defense protocol used for the past hundred years, so he was confident it would prove effective.

They had discussed how the ships would be placed when—

"As I live and breathe. Little Luchs!"

He stopped in place upon heading the familiar, kindly voice. Standing in the hall at his left, bright-eyed and giddy, was an ebon-haired maiden in an eye-catching dress.

"Liliiun?"

It definitely was. For as much as she matured, he knew it was the same woman who attentively nursed him back to health five years ago.

She hurriedly walked up to him and quickly brought him into her arms, caressing his head. "'Tis so good to see you again, little Luchs!" She stepped back so to get a better look at him. "My, how you've grown. You're much too big for me to mollycoddle anymore," she said while patting his matted hair.

"Good to see you too." It took him a moment before he realized the others were watching. While General Esperance remained stone-faced, Ulrin and even Maxime grinned at the familial display.

That attention would normally embarrass him, but Liliiun's presence made him think. "Wait, Admiral Barbossa is the marquis you married?"

Ulrin chuckled a little seeing the lad so surprised. It seemed he knew.

Ack, you lout! Luchs thought bitterly.

"So this is the wonder child you've told me of, dearie?" said Admiral Barbossa.

Liliiun often shared her praise for Luchs surviving his ordeal when he was still healing. It seemed she told her new husband as well.

"Certainly looks like a survivor." He somehow seemed imposing even when speaking kindly of another. "Why don't you escort my darling wife around, keep her company? I'll have your meister knight inform you of the plan later."

Liliiun, in her excitement, took Luchs by the hand before he could reply and showed him down the hall. The lad promised to catch up with them later before being dragged away.

The halls of the fortress were oddly comfortable for a military facility, likely because a marquis called it home. The walls had been adorned with

~ 124 ~

paintings and other luxurious décor, and plants grew in pots beside doors and along windowsills. Some suits of armor stood idle by the walls and small silk banners hung above the doors they crossed that Liliiun explained served as guides for the soldiers.

Charming as the halls were, Luchs did not pay much attention to them. He could not look past what a beauty Liliiun had become. Everything about her was so radiant: her hair long and flowing, her skin gleaming and smooth, her smile angelic. When he caught himself admiring her curves, he shook his head and tried to distract himself.

"Liliiun, if you don't mind me asking, how did you end up marrying Admiral Barbossa?"

Her smile showed she did not mind. "'Twas surprising, surely, to hear Father arranged to have me marry—said something about needing the lev and support, he did. I didn't really mind, not so long as the man knew his manners and was kind. And I learned he certainly was after sailing here to meet him in person. I was hesitant for a while, but..." She smiled, likely thinking of a time the married couple shared, inadvertently making Luchs feel a hint of envy. "He knew how to treat a lady. Loud and brusque as he behaves as an admiral, he proved himself to be a man I'm glad to spend my life with."

Liliiun cupped a hand to her cheek thinking of the special day she had. "Ah, I wish you were there with the rest of the family, Luchs. The ceremony was wonderful. The bards played the most divine music. I think you would have liked the dancing. Oh, and the dress! Mother had the most wonderful dress made for the occasion! It made me look like a queen, and it felt as though I was wearing angel wings."

The longer she talked about her dress, the more he could picture her in it. He shook his head frantically before she finished speaking, trying to clear his head.

She's practically your sister, Luchs, he kept thinking. *You mustn't think like that. She's ... practically your sister. And she's married!*

How he struggled to keep a steady expression when she looked down at him.

"Oh, listen to me gabbing on. Surely, you must have had more exciting times during your training."

"Aye, you could say that," he put vaguely. His page training made him think of the disaster that ravaged Des Meurtal, and he did not want to share that with her.

Their conversations continued on as they walked outside. They stepped through a tall staircase leading to the top of a wall that overlooked the gates to the pier. Everyone below scampered about, working hard to ensure everything was prepared for incoming attacks. Sunlight glared at them from the right, bringing them to look to the courtyard where soldiers gathered. Some inspected weapons, some tended to the mounts in the stables.

Looking down at them made Luchs feel confident, but when turning to Liliiun, he saw she was troubled. The frown across her face showed concern for what might happen, for those that might be lost. She was always considerate to a fault, even toward people she did not know.

It was difficult seeing her that way. Her sadness seeped through their locked hands, pricking at his heart. He gave her hand a little squeeze to calm her. Gentle as it was, the comforting press managed to stir her from her morose thoughts. She glanced down at him bewildered, looking like she had forgotten where she was, what she had been doing. They stared at one another for a moment, trying to assess the other, then Liliiun's lips curled into that sweet, sweet smile, and she squeezed Luchs' hand back, returning the comfort given to her.

"'Twas a wonderful thing, you coming into our lives. You make a wonderful little brother."

Luchs grinned broadly, the color in his cheeks giving away how happy she made him.

A touching moment it was. Sadly, it came to an end.

Loud horns sounded from the distance, a deep bellowing that knocked at their craniums. The foreboding sound alerted the men below to quickly take up arms.

Luchs made haste towing Liliiun back inside. "Come on."

Everyone worried over the possibility of the threat making its way to Prévinn, but this soon? When they themselves just arrived?

Stern as he was, Liliiun tore herself from his grip, then moved past him while gazing his way with a smile. Although hesitant, she uttered, "Go to Ulrin. He'll be in the barbican," a little uncertainly, then firmly said, "Keep each other alive!" She only allowed that to be left said before hurrying back inside, trying not to look back.

It made more sense to follow her words rather than chase after her. Liliiun knew the facility, so she must have known what to do in case danger befell them.

He trusted she would be safe and tried to figure out where to go.

Luchs rushed through Prévinn's facility in search of his meister knight and general. Many of the halls looked the same; he wished he paid more attention to what had Liliiun said about the fortress instead of gawking at her. Some of the knights on their way to the frontline shepherded him in their direction, not caring who he was with. He had his sword and carried a shield, so they thought him prepared.

Suppose everyone's going that way, Luchs reasoned.

Fortunately, they knew where to go. He joined them in the barbican that led further inland. The Sea Drake general stood on a stone platform ensuring all eyes would be on him.

General Esperance looked over the troops with a skeptical eye, veering one way and the next, estimating each warrior's mettle with but a glance. Everyone kept their posture straight and their weapons held firmly, not wanting to appear out of place.

"Men," General Esperance barked stalwartly, "Admiral Barbossa tasked himself with overseeing the fleet of ships. As such, control over the ground troops falls to me!" He remained silent a moment, waiting to see if anyone opposed. No one dared speak up.

"I'm sure you all know well the significance this facility carries and the consequences that will follow should it fall, so I won't waste precious time mincing words on what is at stake. I'll only leave you with this."

Taking his sword in hand, he raised it high and bellowed, "Let's throw those bloody swine back into the hell they crawled out of!"

The knights all roared boisterously at his coarse words, raising their firsts and shaking their weapons in cheer. Even Luchs got caught up in the excitement listening to those few yet empowering words.

"Gather in your factions and await my command. We advance once Admiral Barbossa has sent the enemy our way!"

Everyone scattered either to claim their equipment or prep their mounts. Some squires slammed their helms against one another to show off before the battle began.

Executioner Sörrign and his squire were there too. The executioner approached General Esperance, much to his chagrin, while the squire and his pet went to the stables. The other men tried to avoid the white beast as they mounted their steeds.

Luchs suspected it was not the jinxed animal they needed to be wary of. A deathly chill filled the air whenever that lad was around, lingering wherever he rested. Some believed the air would freeze when the witch god of death drew near. Perhaps death followed him.

"There you are, Luchs!" Ulrin came up to him from behind wielding a lance with a wave-like blade. It was a beautiful weapon, one he carried into every battle.

He filled his squire in on what was discussed in his absence.

The soldiers stationed in Prévinn followed a strict procedure to rout invaders. First, the finest of warships set sail in waves, creating a wall that forced enemy ships back and sunk the ones too stubborn to turn away. The enemy vessels would either drown or make for the exposed northern shore to avoid the cannon fire and storm the fortress, falling into their trap. Once they hurried inland in pointless hope of taking the fortress before the ships returned to land, preferably after passing the great lake in the isle's center, the cavalry would be sent in to slay the rest.

They only needed to wait until the watchmen gave word of the enemy's position, and the final phase of the defensive strike could begin. The knights were eager for the coming battle, so much that they shook

~ 128 ~

their weapons. Even the normally easy-going Ulrin had trouble keeping a steady hold of his spear.

Having only gotten off of a battlefield recently, Luchs worried about showing hesitation in a crucial moment again. But this was not just about his own survival. The kingdom needed Prévinn to remain standing. And so it would!

"They've reached the lake!" a watchman shouted.

General Esperance sent the first wave of men forward to intercept the enemy. The mounted soldiers were the first to advance. Horse hooves resounded against the ground like thunder, shaking it from underneath the soldiers yet to run.

Maxime and Luchs were anxious to get out there. As the general's and lieutenant's squires, they were to ride out with the main force alongside their meister knights. Restraining themselves was difficult when some of their own already set out to meet danger.

In this stage of the strategy, the first wave of soldiers rode out to meet the enemy and prevent them from advancing further. The second wave would set out to provide aid and further pressure the enemy. And once the enemy began to lose ground, the third and final waves would be sent out to finish them off. The rest of the soldiers would remain behind in the barbican to act as the last line of defense only to ride out upon seeing factions stray from the enemy's main force, picking them off one by one.

Soon, the watchmen informed General Esperance of the first wave engaging the enemy.

"Excellent. Ready the second—" He fell silent when he heard a strange whistling sound in the air that grew louder by the second.

A watchman looked back out at the battlefield as a massive blob of fire crashed into his post, consuming the entire platform. The other watchmen attempted to run to the lower levels before fire rained down upon them, knocking them off the ledges.

Those below ran away from the explosions, avoiding the flying embers and debris, but someone forced himself through the fleeing masses.

It was the executioner's squire.

When there was no one else to run past, he stopped several feet from the explosions, looking ready to strike at something. Suddenly, the warmth in the air had been smothered by a terrible chill. Upon striking his palm to the ground, a shivering wind burst throughout the area and a wave of white powder flowed from the spot he struck, hitting the sturdy stone wall.

Everyone was in awe at the display of power. Their eyes were on the unusual white powder, a soft-looking element that caught the falling men in a plush hold yet crumbled around them upon contact. The cold sweep of air snuffed out the thick embers scattered about.

The men who fell struggled to get out of the powder, trembling and hugging themselves. Several men rushed over to help but halted a few feet from the strange substance; it was colder than the wind it rode in on.

Luchs turned the dark lad's way as Executioner Sörrign approached him. They only exchanged a few words, then made for the horses, eager to join the fight.

Luchs looked back at the men caught in the cold sweep. Surprising as the squire's method was, he managed to save everyone, but most of them leaned on others for support, unable to avoid complete injury.

"Fie! They've a mage on their side," General Esperance barked. "The situation has changed. All troops, we ride together. Now!"

With a mage threatening them, it was too risky to move by the original plan. Remaining in the barbican itself was dangerous since their magic reached that far. The entire facility was in danger from one man.

He needed to be eliminated.

Every member of the intercepting force charged out to meet their comrades and push back the enemy. Luchs rode on a small stallion alongside his meister knight, determined and ready to fight.

Witnessing the clash unfold before him put a damper on his determination. Despite the Ederean's superior numbers, the enemy forces managed to slay numerous soldiers. Many corpses were littered across the field, much of them wearing Ederea's symbol.

The bizarre thing was that many of the enemies were not men, but animals—wolves, boars, bears, even mountain lions. They were attacking the soldiers and their mounts alongside the invaders.

It did not matter who or what they were. Be they man, beast, or demon, those radical forces attacked Ederea and needed to be punished.

A wolf sighted the two in their charge and leaped after Ulrin, who quickly pierced the beast's abdomen with his spear. Favoring unmounted combat, he then leaped off his horse with skill and dexterity enough to keep from hindering his steed's charge across the battlefield, trampling the enemies underfoot.

Luchs tried to follow his lead and roll off his mount, but ended up on his back. He barely found his footing before an enemy drew near. The man wielded an axe, bringing it down at Luchs the moment he saw it. He leaped back to avoid getting beheaded, then drew his sword from the scabbard on his back as the enemy raised his broad weapon. Luchs moved forward quickly, a feint to make the man hurl his axe down, where he then moved to the side and pierced his heart deftly.

Dread plagued him once more, as it had in the past, but only for the briefest moments. He withdrew his weapon before he felt the heart stop and the body getting heavier, letting the body fall.

There was no time to waste focusing on the dead.

Several more enemies charged his way aiming to cut down everything in their path. Their weapons were sharp and well-crafted, but none of them could end the squire. They did not expect Luchs' muscles to hold as well as his armor, the confusion allowing him to take the finishing blow before they could react.

Although his wounds closed quickly, the cold steel shot waves of pain through his body, slowing him for a moment. The remaining enemies moved in to avenge their comrades but fell to a few bold Edereans leaping in to aid him.

Several animals charged his way, but they seemed only interested in attacking those closest to them. Fortunately for him, the knights had the majority of their attention.

One came close to him, but it ignored him in favor of the enemy soldiers, tearing them asunder in flashes of white. Archers at the rear of their respective groups tried to shoot at it but failed to hit something so quick. It took a moment for Luchs to notice the flash of white resembled a fox.

A white fox...?

It was the fox belonging to the executioner's squire.

He thought he had started hallucinating from sunstroke. It was hard to believe he saw the beastie dash through the field faster than the warhorses and tear whole limbs off of the enemies. It got close enough at one point for him to see the severed arm it held in its monstrously sharp fangs.

Striking as it was, Luchs focused on the enemies in front of him. He searched for Ulrin after losing track of him. So many got in his way, the bodies ever obscuring the sight of his meister knight on the rare occasion he saw him. Fight through them though he did, he could never meet with him.

The best thing to do was to locate the enemy mage and take him out. The fiery blasts lobed at the fortress have lessened considerably as the battle dragged on, likely because he was forced to engage Ederean soldiers. There were so many enemies to beat back and so many of them wore such flamboyant garb that it was impossible to sift the weapon wielders apart from one sorcerer.

But he noticed something interesting while fending enemies off. Every now and then, Luchs could feel this uncanny shift in the air, a subtle yet forceful change that sent shivers down his spine.

He kept his wits about him as he dashed through the battlefield, heading toward where the shifting came from.

A robust swordsman charged straight for him, brandishing an immense blade that looked like it could tear a stallion in two. He held the weapon at his side and swiftly, deftly swung it at Luchs, meeting the significantly smaller sword in the squire's hands. The weight from the weapon alone would have been dangerous enough, but guided by the warrior's thick muscles made the power thrown harrowing. It took all Luchs had to hold it back. Blocking took much of his energy and his sword nearly snapped from the pressure applied from both sides.

Surviving on the battlefield without a proper weapon would be next to impossible. He had a few daggers strapped between armor plates for emergency use, but such feeble weapons would do next to nothing against the foe right in front of him.

But Lord Ralias and Lady Sundralla did not favor the man. An archer noticed the squire facing such an unfavorable foe and fired an arrow at an artery. It nearly slew him in that moment, but the warrior still struggled to keep fighting. Before he could make another move, Luchs moved in and slit the man's torso. He turned the archer's way and quickly pounded his chest to show thanks before moving through the battlefield once more.

Flashes of light and waves of deathly smog erupted in the distance. It was not long before he found who he was looking for.

Marooned by the lake, distanced from his allies and most of his foes, was a massive sasquatch of a man in a heavy cowl who flung flames from his hands. His body was that of a warrior yet the devastating power he wielded was that of a sorcerer. Many brave knights attempted to oppose the mage, but none walked away. Only one still fought against him.

Executioner Sörrign himself faced the enemy mage with ferocity, agility, and great power of his own. In his grasp, he held a sword unlike any other: a longsword reflecting a heavenly light.

Luchs witnessed the executioner battle the enemy mage with waves of the sword so quick and strong, so expertly controlled, that it was artful. The large weapon clashed with the forceful energy forming around the mage's hands repetitively in quick, concise strikes. The mage attempted to push him back, but the force behind his magic equated to that of the light around the weapon. He instead retreated, hurling condensed spheres of his power from a distance. The divinely-lit sword in the executioner's hands, when swung, shot the golden light from its steel, neutralizing the energy it came in contact with.

He has magic too!?

It was as much of a shock as it was a relief. With two magic users in their midst, the enemy had no hope of taking Prévinn.

Judging by the mage's reaction, that repetition would eventually lead him to defeat. It was only a matter of time—time someone needed to buy the executioner.

Two more enemies approached Luchs while the executioner and mage combated one another. One moved in too quickly for him to react to.

Before steel carved into his flesh, General Esperance came out of nowhere and slew the attacker with his sword. He then charged at the other soldier, intent on slaying him before he recovered from seeing his ally killed.

The short sword in that warrior's grasp was not as sturdy as the longsword the general held, but the hand that guided it was adept. He was a swift once, able to match General Esperance's attacks accordingly. They intercepted each other, pushing their blades back stubbornly against the other like angry yaks. Their struggle continued long and hard, the weapons pressing against each other enough to shave a few sparks from the blades.

They could have stepped back and continued waving their swords at one another, but they simply did not want to. Pride in men was stubborn and, as proven when the general managed one last push to overpower the warrior's defense and tear through his shoulder, destructive.

With his enemy dead, General Esperance turned back to Luchs in frustration. "Never allow yourself to be distracted in battle. It will prove to be your end."

Luchs was ashamed that he allowed himself to be taken by surprise. He wanted to look away but knew not to disrespect his general like that.

"Of all the irresponsible... Losing his squire like this."

Something told him they were in for some terrible drills later.

Maxime ran back to his meister knight's side after helping another knight dispose of an enemy. He asked Luchs if he was okay, but went without an answer. They were beset by more enemy soldiers and a few beasts with their eyes on the mighty war veteran.

More capable protectors rushed back to their mage, but they were all beset by the Ederean army. Casualties were suffered on both sides, most of them belonging to the invaders who struggled to take back the advantage they had.

Roars from the mighty knights echoed throughout the battlefield, all anxious for their anticipated victory. Those triumphant cries were soon drowned out by a terrible booming that tore apart the clouds above.

The world became swallowed by crackling and eruptions as masts of profane light shot out of the sky, tearing apart the gargantuan warships surrounding the isle. Everyone, even the invaders, watched as the ships in view had been decimated in mere moments.

Terrified, Luchs turned to where the mage had been and found him impaled by the executioner's sword. The executioner drew his weapon skyward, cleaving his foe in twain and shattering his skull, when he noticed the devastation.

If not him, Luchs scarcely managed to let the thought pass in his mind muddied by dread, *then who is doing this!?*

It did not stop with the ships. More masts of light shot down at the battlefield, entrapping and burning those caught in them. Each one came an instant after the last, claiming as many just lives as the invaders took.

Hearing crackling overhead, before Luchs could think, he ran to Maxime and shoved him out of the way, letting the mast that fell from above strike him instead.

The other masts vanished nearly as quickly as they came, but seconds, minutes have passed as his body and armor were being seared away. His screams were drowned out in the roar of energy as the terrible images from his nightmares emerged in his mind, the lurid magic prying them from his psyche for him to experience again. An eternity of suffering had been hammered down upon him in one instant.

He could not recall when the spell hit, nor could he hope to know when it was finished with him, the pain having rent his mind. There was no sound. His vision blurred until everything became a smear. All sensation had faded.

The last thing he felt was the ground trembling beneath him before that, too, disappeared.

* * *

Agh... The agony... I've never felt pain grip me like this before. So why does it feel ... familiar? Those nightmares...

I hate this. Why must the only pieces of my past be of torture? Makes the effort of looking for it such a waste, if'n that's all there was.

Ack! I'd prefer a blade to the gut to this burning. Wait, burning...? Ah, that's right. I was struck down by a magic spell. So I'm dead. Then this must be the Elysium that Ulrin and Liliiun always told me of. A pity. I couldn't even bid them farewell—and after all they've done for me.

Wait. What is this? 'Tisn't a garden. There are no flowers or trees or any other blessed souls enjoying a blissful afterlife. Just me ... in a quarry of dried rubble and cold dirt.

This can't be the Elysium. So where am I?

What's happening? The ground! The ground is moving! I-It's opening up before me. It's going to swallow me! ...No. No, it's refilling on its own. It's building up, sculpting something of itself.

Aah! The cliffs above are being torn apart! So many boulders are falling, but they're all falling ... up? They form islands in the mute golden sky above.

This place is madness. I need to get away from here!

Why can't I move? My body, it's not budging. Why do the cliffs fly when I am pressed down by nothing!?

To have victory taken away so suddenly, and now this? Nay. I must leave this place. This won't be where my soul remains for eternity!

Aye. Aye, I can move my arms. Now just ... the legs. Just a little more. Just need to pick myself up a little more.

What was that? Where did those voices come from? I hear whispers from somewhere. No, they're everywhere! They're all over, and they're closing in!

What is happening to the piled-up rubble? The stones keep clumping together, building itself higher and higher. What is it making itself into?

U-Unbelievable! 'Tis so high up that it's touching the sky. It looks like a body, the body of a burly giant. It almost looks to be strapped in armor. Just what is this thing?

I feel it.

Every one of them. All those voices ... belonging to children and the grown, men and women, all inside that rock armor. But how can the voices of so many come from one body? Mayhap they can fit inside, but not all of them could possibly speak together so clearly.

It's looking down at me—I can feel it! Those eyes hiding in the darkness of the stone armor are looking down at me.

A soul who has dwelled in a mortal shell of great power. You lived as a strong one, both in body and spirit. This I see in you, mortal child.

It can tell what I was? And so strong and imposing. Could it be—

"Are you ... a god?"

No god am I, merely a voice of nature bound to your realm. The world of the mortal realm is held together by the earth, and the earth is held together by my will. I am called Terrae.

Not a god yet it wields such power?

There was a battle before your demise, one which you needn't have taken part in. Why did you offer your life to fight in it?

Why? I was a soldier. I had to fight. For the country ... a country that may not even have been my homeland. But it is home to the people who cared for me, people I cared for. And not all of them could fight.

"They've endangered many good people, innocent people who didn't suspect or desire any conflict. I didn't want more to suffer because of them. I had to do something for them, for the people I loved."

Why is it silent? Why doesn't the colossus speak up or even move? Why ask that of me? What could this being possibly want of my own personal need to fight?

Aah! Oh, thank the gods. 'Twasn't thunder, just that thing exhaling.

Luchs Lau.

...What did it say?

Come. Approach me. Should I move, the earth of the mortal realm shall tear and reform.

I have a bad feeling about this, but refusing this thing may rouse its ire. Best do as it says.

Rrgh...! The air is heavier than the stones floating above. But I'm not backing down. It'll just take a little nudge. Left foot. Right foot. Left. Right. L-Left! Right... Gah! All right, I've done it. I'm right underneath it. Crivens, but this thing up close makes Castle Ederea look puny. Why does it want me so close anyway?

Luchs Lau, noble soul made unyielding shield to the weak, I bestow my gift of mastery over the earthen element to you. May it serve your exemplary deeds well.

Whoa, stop! Get back. Take your hand away. You'll crush me!

Help!

~ Eighth Chapter ~
Back to the Wild

The ordeal with Terrae exhausted Luchs' mind, yet it continued to wander down paths he did not realize were there. Everything was a blur at first, and it made less sense as it cleared.

He found himself in an orchard with trees bearing delicious fruits. There were elderberries, huckleberries, and even some unusual gourd-like shells that hung from the branches as easily as the tiny berries called goilda, sometimes known as ivory fruit for its pale complexion. Mountains aplenty surrounded the orchard and the village built near it. For a time, he was picking berries and putting them in a wicker basket, and when it was full, he carried it, balancing it atop his head, to the humble house neighboring the orchard.

Inside were three people: his grandfather, mother, and elder sister.

The grandfather was wrinkled like a grape left in the sun and thinned, but he was no frail codger. He lived many long years fighting as a mercenary, the fiercest in the mountains, before settling down and starting a family.

Frail and petite, the mother was a sickly one who could scarcely perform regular tasks on her own. She had been ill since her husband passed away and barely had the energy to do much straining work or walk far from the village. Even eating became so taxing that she barely ate more than a slice of bread and a handful of berries per meal.

Then there was the sister, an energetic lass just a few years older than Luchs who enjoyed running about and chasing things. She was a big help in the orchard; making a game of collecting the fruit and gathering river water always pushed her to try so hard. She sometimes acted like the happy hunting hound their neighbor let her play with.

Everyone looked happy to see Luchs. His elder sister playfully snatched the basket from him, helping herself to a few berries. The adults laughed, then urged the children to sit down and eat.

Their life together was peaceful, one of hardship for certain, but one they were all satisfied with. Alas, it did not last.

Strangers came to their village one day, something that rarely ever happened. Their presence unnerved everyone. They rode in on horses, carried many weapons, wore such strange clothing. It was clear even to a child that they were not simply exploring the mountains.

One of their pack walked into the village alone.

Luchs' mother and grandfather went to meet them after ordering him and his sister to remain inside. A key member of the village council, his mother needed to address matters with outsiders alongside her fellow councilmen, and his grandfather needed to ensure she had someone to hold her up just in case.

He did not know what was going on or what to expect, but those strangers scared Luchs. The outsiders gathered together, covered underneath the shadows cast from the peaks above, were intimidating enough just standing in place.

And his sister agreed. She took him by the hand and led him outside, taking him away from whatever went on.

The protests he made reminding her of what their mother said fell on deaf ears. She looked at her little brother with a cheery smile and spoke candidly of going exploring and having fun while the grownups took care of their business.

It was a lovely day, so it would have been a shame to waste the time inside. He went along with her into the dense forest where they loved to play. It was very enjoyable. But then she took him farther away from the village, crossing the area where the cliffs were terribly steep.

She started to scare him, taking him so far from home, without their grandfather to watch over them. He wanted to know where they were going, unappreciative of the vague remarks of having fun when she barely paid heed to anything.

Angry and frightened, Luchs thrashed about, trying to wrench his wrist from her grasp. He broke free, and slipped down a cliff in doing so. Dirt and rock grated at his back, arms, and face as he tumbled down the mountain wall, until landing on his back against flat ground.

The fall would have battered and broken most, but he stood back up as if he merely tripped over a stone. It was not the worst fall he ever had.

His sister called out to him, asking if he was all right, then shouted for him to stay put, saying that she would find a way down to him.

The lucid dream turned into a nightmare when he noticed the first to find him was not his sister, but rather who they were running from—the outsiders. The images became more grueling from then on. He only recognized being in a cage with many more unfortunate souls. Then came the torture—the whips and clubs, the chains and shackles, the knives and needles, the threats of what was to come upon them arriving someplace whose name passed his ringing ears. Everything he knew slowly slipped away with every cruelty inflicted upon him.

Those terrifying visions stirred Luchs from slumber.

His whole body ached, even his eyes. It took a moment before he made out the stone roof above. He was back inside the fortress, lying in a comfortable bed. The room he was in appeared more extravagant than the other facilities in the military base, plenty of fancy décor and rich fabrics lying all around. It had to be where visiting nobles would rest.

Agh, how'd I end up here? While he thought on that, a heavy scent of strong herbs wafted over his sinuses. The smell was all over his chest and forearms, and seeped through the tight bandages wrapped around them. *Must have been hurt worse than I thought.*

He tried getting up, but a sharp pain shooting through his muscles and bones pinned him down. He almost managed to sit upright before falling back onto the cushiony pillow. The fear that he would fall apart coaxed him to stop struggling and stay still. Injuries that serious needed rest.

He stared blankly at the ceiling and gave some thought to that new dream. It was not just torturous images and sensations this time. He remembered who he was, his family, the mountain village he grew up in and had been taken from. "Lau..." It was strange saying his long-forgotten family name after so long. It did not roll as easily off the tongue as it used to, even though it was so short.

"Awake, I see."

Alarmed by the break in silence, Luchs tried turning his head to find whoever spoke. He never heard that voice before, one so quiet yet carrying a certain firmness. A meek manservant perhaps?

Upon finding some strength, he turned his head to find Executioner Sörrign's squire sitting in a chair across from him.

The dark lad sat there, staring passively at Luchs. "I expected you to be out longer. You are quite the resilient one." He spoke with an accent Luchs heard from foreigners who had a difficulty speaking Abioan, but his pronunciation was decent enough to understand.

Feeling the lad was looking down on him, Luchs found it in him to sit up despite the tearing discomfort. It felt strange for pain and soreness to linger for so long; it never happened before. "What're you here for, laddie?" he asked, his voice a bit hoarse. "Shouldn't you be with the executioner?"

"I was ordered to watch over you, wait until you awoke. You must be confused after facing such an ordeal."

"Ordeal? A bit dramatic, aren't you? 'Twas but a battle. Loads of men die fighting to protect their country. I'm better off than the ones that didn't make it ... so I wouldn't call it an ordeal."

The dark lad stared at Luchs while he spoke. He looked to be barely listening yet seemed intrigued nonetheless. His somewhat vacant stare was off-putting. With his expression dim and his mouth covered beneath the scarf, it was hard to tell what he was thinking.

"You don't remember yet."

"What're you on about?"

"The sudden death. Finding yourself in a world unimaginable. Awakening to find yourself not as you once were," the lad gravely mused. "Give it a moment. You'll recall the spirit clearly."

Spirit?

Breath welled up in Luchs' throat and his eyes spread wide. Suddenly, his lost past was not the most important thing that came to mind. He recalled the terrible amethyst light and his body burning, then the quarry where the ground flew and his body remained heavy. And then, there was the stone giant.

Overwhelmed and confused, Luchs raised a hand to the bundle of bandages over his chest and tore them off. He stopped breathing for a moment, which gave him a good look at his abs, seared with burn scars so deep that the lightly tanned skin faded, becoming white as bone. It was painful to look at. Given how they formed, there had to be more around the rest of his bound torso and forearms, perhaps much deeper too.

Terrae.

It was his doing. If it were not for the entity, his body would not have held together. He remembered seeing others being entirely erased by the deathly light.

Luchs tried to calm himself and looked back at the lad. "How do you know about that?"

"It is a familiar experience for a Nascitte like myself."

"Nascitte?"

The lad nodded. "Beings with strong ties to nature that are revived from the dead by the hands of the spirits who command it. You died and were revived by the very same spirit you met. You are now a Nascitte."

Even after having been through it, hearing it from someone else made it sound like madness. More than that, listening to someone talk as though he was there made Luchs all the more irritable—not to mention how he spoke of it so calmly, like it was nothing.

"So ... what does that mean for me?" the scarred squire asked in a shaken tone.

"Look out the window."

Behind Luchs stood a wide window that overlooked a majority of central Prévinn. The dazzling morning sun shone through the glass and kept him warm. He barely noticed it in his daze when he woke and looked surprised to see it, but not as much as by what was outside. A dark, gaping fissure had torn across the field of luscious green, cutting a hole deep into the isle. It opened up like the maw of an infernal monster. There did not look like there was a bottom, as if it stretched to the gate of the seven hells.

"That fissure opened in response to your revival and the spirit taking a stronger hold of this world through you."

"Wait— You're saying ... I did that!? How many—"

"Fell in?" the dark lad interrupted. "None, save those already dead."

Thank Lady Sundralla for that impeccable stroke of luck.

"The damage could have been worse, and that's what troubles me. A Nascitte just revived has a difficult time controlling their newfound power, the Second Verse. Imagine the devastation your Second Verse might have caused had fissure it opened been bigger."

He would rather not. Looking at that fissure and hearing that even more devastation could have followed made him dread the entire isle being swallowed. And the thought of it all happening, all of the people on Prévinn falling into the depths, by his hand—

The frightful thoughts came to a halt when pain sparked across his right shoulder. He turned back to see the dark lad's fist parting his side. "Don't panic," he stifled with a stern tone. "An unsteady mind cannot keep control of the Second Verse. Keep control of your emotions." The cold stare he gave Luchs did more than help control his emotions, it froze them.

Those glacial eyes pierced him, and after staring at them for so long, he saw how there almost looked to be cracks in them, cracks over a glimmering surface. What inhuman eyes.

"Your body still needs time to recover. It would be best for you to stay in bed until we leave."

Luchs blinked. "Leave? *We*? What're you talking about?"

"As you are now, it's too dangerous to leave you on a populated island. The two of us are to depart for another so I may train you to control your Second Verse."

Sent to another deserted island?

The thought sent shivers down Luchs' spine, which made him wince from the pain. It took him four years to get off Des Meurtal, and that was dumb luck. Returning to civilization after so long overjoyed him, and now he was being sent away again—to be instructed by a puny lad no less.

As if sensing the disbelief and frustration within him, the dark lad cut Luchs off before he could respond. "No one can understand the strain and tension the Second Verse has on a person more than someone who already has it. It's a more complex power than almost any magic. Like it or not, I am your best chance at taking control."

It was hard to accept, but he could not entirely deny what he had been told either. He knew about the spirit that revived him, of the power that tore the isle in two, and even how unpredictable said power, the Second Verse, could be.

Either he trusted him or risked tearing the land apart.

When he began contemplating how his life could have taken so many disturbing turns, a commotion began roaring outside.

Luchs leaned over to the windowsill and looked down. Everyone was running frantically back into the facility as if attempting to flee from something. Then, a tumultuous wave of unease shot through his body.

"Another tremendous surge of magic..."

Monotonously as he put it, the lad was right. The clouds above broke apart as they had when that disastrous spell came and decimated their forces. As the sky blacked from the gathering magic, another mast of profane light shot down from it directly into the barbican. But nothing was destroyed. Instead, the light gathered and created a new shape, a cloaked figured draped head to toe in long, thick robes that stood as tall as the stone walls. Those who could not get away from the blast gathered around it, arming themselves in anticipation of another attack. The hooded person was transparent, though, a mere illusion unable to get hurt or inflict pain.

"Hear me, vermin who have infested our once sacred land." A majestic voice echoed loudly enough to be heard throughout the entire facility. The hooded figured reached up for the cowl draped over its head and, upon a swift, haughty removal, revealed the face of a woman. Her face was smooth, her cheeks beautifully formed, her head devoid of hair, and a long, almost pointed nose sat between her furious eyes. "I am Gatreah, High Priestess of the almighty Convent of One and acolyte to The Divine One, Kyros. I commend you for surviving the incursions made by our holy armies. It was a fine prelude. But what follows shall be your undoing." No one did anything while the illusion spoke. A great many recoiled when she gazed down at them like a furious mother would at a misbehaving child. Her voice and demeanor were equally domineering and venomous. "You have only yourselves to blame for this. You Ederean vermin have long rejected the ways of the true god and filled your minds with the lies of your paltry deities. We left that well alone and decided to keep our salvation to ourselves. But you insisted on meddling in our affairs against the scavengers who desecrated our sacred texts and dared to condemn us for casting righteous judgment. The line has been drawn! Since you wish to further oppress our endeavors, we of the Convent shall ravage your land in holy war. We shall bathe the archipelago in the light of Kyros and cleanse it of your poisonous ways. And when the dust settles, when the stain of your sin has been expelled, it will be we of the Convent who shall rule this land once more. Your fate is sealed!"

With her threat given, the illusion flickered a blinding flare before fading away. Everyone was in awe at the display of power and knew her words to be dangerous.

The men below were all in disarray. Luchs saw his general and Ulrin had rushed down there to see the spectacle for themselves. They struggled to keep the troops in check.

Whoever that woman was, she declared war on Ederea. If she did not have the magic to back up her imperious tirade, they would have thought her insane. But she had the power and was obviously not shy about using it on them.

All the more reason for Luchs to take control of the Second Verse before it, too, threatened the country.

Later that same day, the two squires were put on one of the few ships that survived the assault. Luchs was still sore and had a hard time moving. Ulrin and Liliiun were worried for him, but instead of fretting over the trial he would face, they made certain the ship had every necessity to help him heal during the voyage.

General Esperance and Admiral Barbossa briefly gave Luchs their best wishes before he left. As appreciative as he was for it, Luchs could barely look the general in eye, ashamed of how he saw him in battle. It was hard to tell what he was thinking with that stoic stare of his.

For many a day, Luchs lay in a simple bed in a private cabin and let the rocking waves relax him. Everything he needed had been brought to him by a squire with an enthusiastic and humorous smile. It would have been awkward being brought food and medicinal herbs were it not for the trite, audacious remarks the squire made about his condition. He knew how to make someone laugh.

The executioner's squire checked in on him periodically, his fox in tow. His name was Vandelas and, apparently, he called his pet Snowflake. He shared little more than that and barely spoke when not asked a question.

The voyage was long but very relaxing. He only felt uncomfortable when it came time to eat. No matter what he was given—dried fruits, bread, meat, even fish—it was all bland. None of it had any flavor whatsoever. He would not reject what was offered to him and trouble the others, but it still bothered him.

Instead, he confided in Vandelas. It did not seem like a coincidence that he could not taste anything after being revived. And his confidant agreed. Although uncertain as to why it happened, they deduced that Terrae's influence somehow robbed him of his sense of taste.

By the time they arrived at their destination, Luchs regained enough strength to move on his own. The first thing he did was rush outside to see where he would be living for the time being.

The islet before him was little more than a speck on the blue sea, peppered with tropical trees across the surface. It amazed Luchs how feeble it was. It stretched out for, at most, five miles. The islet's foundation looked ghastly, as if it might collapse at any moment.

When the crew dropped the gangplank, a small part of the risen land crumbled into the water. The ones who set the plank watched nervously as the earth was swallowed by the briny blue. Even Vandelas assumed caution while stepping across with his pet jinx.

Seeing how squeamish everyone behaved made Luchs nervous about taking the first step.

"Hurry along," ordered Vandelas. "One more body won't break the island."

That attitude made Luchs groan. "Easy for you to say. You barely weigh anything more than that fox of yours."

He walked across the gangplank carefully, taking slow steps so the little support that held it up would not cave. The wood creaked and wobbled beneath his feet with every step. Every sound and movement made him all the more nervous until he finally reached the ledge.

The ship set out the moment they disembarked.

It was no surprise that they did not want to remain. Talk went around the ship about the dangers of Emiet. Islands tended to gain and lose landmass with time, but this islet crumbled like an old piece of bread in a bucket. More and more of it was lost by the day, everything vanishing little by little. There were no animals save for the passing gulls, leaving few options for what to eat.

From what General Esperance explained before their departure, they were to remain on Emiet for a month while Vandelas instructed Luchs on how to keep his dangerous power from running rampant.

Luchs faced the islet to see what awaited them. Many of the shaggy trees arched over each other, letting their long leaves and branches sway with the breeze. A few moss-covered stones lay hither and thither. Emiet was somewhat habitable in part to the coconuts that hung and fell from palm trees, the fruits growing from a few bushes, even the heads of edible-looking leafy plants growing in patches of damp soil.

He hoped there was more to offer inland. Coconut milk never agreed with him.

They marched into the scarce woodland in search of a suitable place to make camp. The foliage looked much healthier the deeper they went, the leaves a brighter hue and their bases fuller, much stronger. Nothing grew too close together, leaving plenty of sunlight for the plants to soak up. Some of the shrubs and trees bore fruit, nothing like he ever saw before, in little bushels. It all looked edible. Chances were, though, that it would not last them long if they took everything carelessly.

Anyplace looked suitable for a campsite, but Vandelas kept moving. It irked Luchs that he would not pick a spot and get on with his training. If it were not for the general's orders to follow his instructions, he would have made camp himself.

"No matter how I look at it, I still don't get it."

Loud and confrontational as Luchs was, Vandelas did not respond.

"Ulrin and the general told me you saved me—plucked me from the fissure as it opened around me. But I think 'tis malarkey. You've barely grown out of a laddie's body, and calling those lumps on your arms muscles is generous."

He was not the first to say such things. Many have pointed out the lad's shortcomings whenever crossing his path during their voyage to Prévinn. He looked too feeble to be of any threat to anyone, he took no precaution to secure it with suitable armor, and he dressed strangely. Why the scarf? The Ederean archipelago was hot year-round.

And yet he saved him.

"How could you have hauled me out of there?"

Without looking back, Vandelas listlessly answered, "I ran to it. I jumped in. I threw your body on my back. And I climbed out. That's all."

And he spoke of it as if it were no feat at all! Seeing someone so small acting so mighty yet impassive made the vein in Luchs' head throb. He did not know why it irked him so, just that he could not resist acting on it.

A brisk walk took them to the middle of the islet where Vandelas finally decided to stop. He looked disoriented swaying subtly where he stepped. The fox stepped briskly around him and looked up at his drained mien. Luchs would have scoffed at the supposedly strong lad looking ready to collapse were he not startled by the thin vapor wafting from his body. "I'm fine. I'm fine," he huffed. "Just a little winded." He walked over to the tree providing the most shade. A chill ran through the air as he sat down and a layer of ice formed beneath him. He was much more comfortable atop the chilling surface, legs bent, his hands resting on his knees.

Once he took a deep breath and exhaled, spewing a puff of white air, he looked as impassive as before. He took a brief look at his surroundings, peacefully taking everything in, then glanced back Luchs' way. "See that rock there?" Past the trees and lying next to a small shrub sat a rock roughly the size of a cannonball. "Bring it here."

An abrupt demand and an annoying one. "I thought we came here so you could teach me control of this Second Verse."

"Bring it here."

The melancholy child was not going to go any further unless his words were followed.

Luchs sighed gruffly and lazily walked over to the rock, hefting it off the ground. It was thick and dense as a mace, and easily filled the hands that carried it. When dropped to the ground, it shook the surface a bit and scattered some loose soil.

It made Luchs feel oddly superior carrying the heavy stone before the lanky lad without a breath of exertion. "There's your stone. Now start taking this seriously."

Again, no reaction to his assertive words. Instead, Vandelas turned to his little pet, stirring some excitement from the fluffy creature, its ears perked up. "Snowflake, please break it."

That wee thing? Break that rock?

The thought was so hysterical that it made Luchs burst into crazed laughter. He drew a hand over his chest, clenching his cuirass.

When he opened his eyes, he nearly stopped breathing altogether. The creature stood, growling heavily, as a cerulean light flickered from atop its forehead. Behind tufts of fluffy white fur, a small stone glowed with that light as it spread across the fox's body, its white fur catching the light magnificently. Its body changed, shifted, even expanded. The puffy tail lengthened. Its legs broadened, taking a graceful, trim shape. Those nubs for claws grew as long and sharp as daggers, just like the fangs in its growing muzzle. And, perhaps the most terrifying thing of all, its once beady eyes gleamed the same light that now slowly dimmed from the magic stone and sharpened into that of a monstrous predator.

Luchs nearly felt his heart stop when the horrific creature looked ready to pounce. And when it leaped in the air, he fell back on his rear, covering his face in fear that it would rip his head off. Nothing tore at his flesh, but something petite bumped into his knee. A small pebble rolled away from the chipped rubble that used to be the mace-like stone.

The fox, dropping a few grains from its vorpal fangs, stepped proudly back to Vandelas as it became surrounded with the cerulean light once more, reverting to its petite, far less menacing fluff of a body. The lad caressed its cheek and scratching the underside of its neck, treating the creature as if it were a harmless pup.

Luchs watched in awe, fright, and dismay while the lad teased the little creature.

Did it— H-How— What in the gods' names is this beast!?

"Luchs!" Again, as if reading his frightened thoughts, Vandelas grabbed his attention before he panicked again.

Of course. He had to remain calm or risked letting his Second Verse rage and destroy the islet: Vandelas' cold gaze said that much. Emiet was small enough for a simple earthquake to sink it. After a few deep breaths, Luchs exhausted his adrenaline rush, cooling his blood.

Upon seeing so, Vandelas calmed down as well. "Put it back together."

What remained of the stone were pieces fairly small, the size of a slim phalange at the most, and in several shapes. Hopefully, he was not expecting it to be reassembled in the way he found it in.

"Not like that."

The moment he reached out to pick up the first pebble came another rebuke.

"Sit down. Relax."

With a sigh, Luchs let his knees buckle and dropped to the ground with a loud *plop*. "Hope we're not just going to be resting on our laurels while the rest of the country makes ready for war."

"You may find this more strenuous than expected. Now, enough complaining. Close your eyes."

It was hard to believe anyone would find lounging around strenuous, but humoring the lad thus far offered plenty to be surprised over. They had one month. How bad could it be to spend a few minutes relaxing?

A few deep breaths calmed him enough to let his eyes fall shut without feeling disgruntled. Bleak darkness one minute, then the outside sunlight let the briefest blurry blobs of bright hues flash inside his closed vision. They became quite clear when he ceased needless thought. Then, when he completely relaxed, the lights flared with incredible luminance and almost seemed to take form. One shimmering cerulean light took the shape of a human.

Startled by the sudden change, Luchs threw his eyes open.

Vandelas sat where he found the light. He would have dismissed it as his imagination playing a prank on him had it not been for the knowing look on his face. Intrigued, Luchs closed his eyes again.

The light returned to his closed vision, moving like rays of sunshine against a glossy surface. It moved around the human silhouette in small waves. It stretched to the left, crafting another silhouette, one of petite stature, and shifted into a gentle mauve shade that dazzled eagerly around what little remained of the cerulean light at its crown. They were of the quiet lad and his pet.

"Is this your first time seeing it?"

His eyes fluttered open when Vandelas spoke again. "What was that?"

"Valsara: the energy that flows through all life—people, animals, plants, even the earth itself. Nascitte are able to see its flow through what is called magic sight should we desire, and since your control is over the earth, you may see the flow in the ground easier than in either of us."

Eager to find out, Luchs shut his eyes once more and turned his head to the ground. He was right. An enchanting ginger glow gathered much quicker than had the light of Vandelas' and the fox's life energies. Being surrounded by the glow comforted him, burying the unease and anxiety he felt earlier. Not since the times of his life forgotten had he felt so composed.

But it was not that way the entire time. As the comforting sensations set in, so, too, had a vibrant, thrashing pressure that pulsed around his own valsara—at least he thought it was against his valsara, not quite pounding against the body but someplace deeper. It soon became harsh enough to spook him from his trance, sending shocks through his body so menacing that his heart and lungs raced. He could barely sit straight his body shook so.

"Keep calm."

Right. Calm. Take it in ... then get it out.

Keeping himself in check after that took more focus than he thought. That pressure was nothing like he felt before. It did not feel particularly powerful or heavy, but it happened so suddenly that neither body nor mind could keep up.

"What did you feel?"

Luchs tried to assess that for himself. "Something like ... thousands of clubs bashing into me. And not just that." The thoughts were difficult to put into words. There was a grating at his head, something like two rough stones shifting against one another. His legs trembled even without standing on anything, a raging pulsation rushing through them.

"Hm... Conditioning yourself to it can be done, but it will take time. It is not the same stress I experienced, but I might know some tricks that can help you."

"Not the same? What'd you go through?"

"A few different things. Sometimes, I heard animals speak throughout the day and night."

Luchs blinked. "Animals? Speaking? Are you jesting?"

"You've torn an island in two and can't expect another to understand animals?" Those cold, dry words were as close to snide comeback as Luchs heard from him thus far. Noticing the small fox at his side stir, he raised a hand and stroked its back kindly. "I've had a way with them even before my death and learned to communicate with them shortly after. Having my senses grow so strong made it a simple matter listening to them even through walls. I lost many nights of sleep before I could get used to it."

Before his death... When he heard of a previous death, be it his own or another's, something gnawed at him. Small though it seemed, it was still bothersome, grating.

"How did it happen?"

Vandelas glanced back at Luchs, narrowing his gaze. "Questions for later. For now, focus on the rock. Look at what's inside."

Instead of pondering on what was inside, Luchs took a look for himself. The space of the rock's silhouette appeared devoid of anything. For whole minutes he sat there, eyes shut, magic sight fixated on it. Nothing extraordinary happened. Then, just as he was about to give up, he found these minuscule specks of dim brown light. There was valsara within the broken pebbles, the thinnest traces flickering in the void.

"Ignore the world around you and focus on the flow inside. Find every trace there is, then pull them together. Force it all to come together."

"No pressure," Luchs groaned. "Not like those walls are any bigger than a sliver."

That was not the only issue either. He was supposed to pull the valsara together but not lay a hand on the pebbles, yet he could not help reach them out a little. Controlling the flow could not possibly be so simple as to pull them with imaginary strings.

He was left with little choice but to try.

Moving his fingers did not do any good, neither did pressing at the air over the pebbles. Physical movement did not solve anything. He tried to offer a little mental push, but that did nothing either. There had to be a way to make the valsara inside the stone move.

"Will it." He made it sound so simple.

Will it? What does that even mean?

Before frustration could rile him up further, Luchs took another deep breath. It could be done. If a lad like him could do it, then so could he. All it took was a little trial and error.

In attempting to "will it," he kept pushing his hands forward thusly, curling his fingers and unclenching ever so slightly. And in each attempt, there was this soft pang against his valsara. It was as if his very spirit was getting sore, like when one pulled a muscle. He did not exactly know what he was doing, but there was something that seemed to be working in controlling that weak flow.

The pieces of valsara were beginning to converge. Those pulses of light were moving, pushing against the shells they were contained in and slowly beginning to cluster together. There was something else too. While struggling to get a clear look at what happened, he saw another hue begin to glow around the dim brown. It looked familiar. That lively, crisp umber light—it was his own valsara.

He was doing it! He was controlling the flow.

At least, he was for a brief time. The pangs became stronger, more straining, and crept into his head. It shocked him from his trance, leaving his skull throbbing. Luchs' hands darted to his temples to rub them angrily. That was more than just a headache.

"Stop," Vandelas said gently. "Take on too much and you won't be in any condition to train. Rest for a moment."

Luchs was not planning on arguing, not with the pressure crushing his brain. It had to pass after a few minutes, at least he thought so. The longer he sat there groaning underneath the sun's heavy rays, the more strenuous it became.

The softest smack of lips sounded from where Vandelas sat, and when Luchs looked to see what he was up to, the lad dragged the back of his hand across his forehead. The patch of ice he sat on had thinned drastically. It was little more than a thin sheet over a puddle.

"Perhaps ... some water would do us both good."

"Right. And where are we going to find drinkable water?"

As Luchs said that, Vandelas stood without any complication from the ice. "I've been smelling fresh water for a while now, someplace to the southwest. We should reach it in no time." He marched in the direction he mentioned and the little fox followed him as always. He stopped a moment to look back, not too concerned about his pet but the company he kept. "Come along. We may find something to eat as well."

"I'm not a child, laddie! Don't go talking to me like one."

Food sounded good, though. He had not eaten since they came ashore.

Luchs got back up, grunting throatily, trying to shake off the bothersome fatigue. While following the lad, he could not help look back at the thin sheet of ice and the puddle slowly being absorbed into the soil. Had he truly been occupied for so long? It barely felt like time passed at all.

It occurred to him to check the sun's position, but he decided not to. With all that went on, it seemed best not to know for a little longer.

After marching further inland, away from the islet's northern edge, the moisture in the air changed. It was not as heavy and tasted less salty, more refreshing.

Vandelas was right. There was fresh water nearby. It was strange for him to say he smelled it, though.

More fruit grew within the islet, and they looked tastier than the ones growing near the shoreline. Tempting it was to reach out and take one, but they would be there when they went back.

The sun glared viciously overhead. With the source of fresh water and the heavy doses of sunlight, the plants all prospered well. The soil was different as well, softer, if only so slightly.

Past an arch of sparse trees was something truly enchanting. There sat a spring with two levels, one small pond that sat on a ledge over the larger pool, both connected by a small waterfall gently flowing into the pool. Lush grass grew around both levels, as did some flowers. It was a delightful spot for a rest.

Luchs joined Vandelas by the larger pool of water for a drink. He crouched down by it, cupped his hands after dipping them in the water, then pulled them up to his lips. A single sip made him want more. As he quenched his thirst, a sudden splash at the foot of the small waterfall alerted him they were not the only ones there. A few fish had gathered in the upper pond, swimming in the confined space before leaping over the waterfall and into the bigger pool. One after the next, they came flying out of the water, spreading their scarlet frilled fins like gull wings, then pulled them in and plopped into the waters. The pool they swam in was not the deepest, but it met their needs. At the bottom of it grew this thin, fuzzy green seaweed that the colorful fish fed on. First there was nothing, then came the fish, and they vanished not long after having their fill through a small opening in the deepest end. More appeared through a hole like it in the upper pond.

Seeing the small creatures put a smile on Luchs' face. After watching them swim around, he eagerly took another handful of water—he froze when he saw his reflection.

Something had changed. Something about him had changed. Very few times had he ever looked into something as luxurious as a mirror, but his appearance remained fresh in his mind in the time that he had. Broad skull and girth, shaggy brown hair—those remained the same. But his eyes were different now. They were supposed to be green, but fretfully looking back at him were two thick, earth-brown irises. Getting a closer look showed they resembled plots of fertile soil.

They were not natural. They looked just as unusual as Vandelas'.

Another splash sounded from the pool, this one too large to belong to the little fish. Vandelas sat crouched over the edge of the pool, eying the fish with notable interest, an interest one would see on a hungry animal. He picked his right hand up, holding his fingers like sharp claws, and waited. Then, as fast as one would blink, he thrust it into the water and caught two fish that were feeding together. The little things struggled for but a second before their captor crushed them in his grasp. He set the fish aside, handing one to his pet, then thrust a hand in again to catch another.

He crushed it swiftly, "Here," then tossed it to Luchs. Forgetting the water in his hands, he jumped and caught it. It did not look like much but would offer a bit of meat.

Even so, Luchs scoffed at the offering. "I doubt this wee thing will fill me up. A real man could catch a bigger fish."

Vandelas picked himself up, urging his pet to pick up what it had not yet eaten and follow. "If that keeps you from taking control of your Second Verse, you may as well destroy Emiet now."

"Wha—" Luchs was aghast at the lad's words. Destroy the islet? He had such little faith in the newly awakened Nascitte. "Stow it, you gangly runt! Just 'cause you've got the hang of your power, that doesn't mean you're better than me. Where do you get off thinking I'll just up and sink the islet like some oaf?"

Vandelas was quiet for a moment, just staring into space with a serious countenance. He was not ignoring Luchs, more like he was trying to hear something. Then, when he found what he needed, he glanced back at Luchs with dispassionate eyes. "'Twas something I overheard."

"Overheard? So someone else said I'll destroy the islet? All right then. Do tell. Who?"

"I didn't care enough to know who they were."

"They? They who?"

"A handful of men who claimed to have seen the fissure open. I think they were frightened you would end up breaking the rest of Prévinn. When they heard you would be sent here, they thought you'd make it our shared grave."

That could not be. It just could not. If it was true, then was it just those few? Everyone had seen the gash in the earth.

Was it arranged so Emiet would be his final resting place should he fail to take control?

"The Second Verse is dominion over nature itself," Vandelas continued, "and your power over the very earth could be the most inherently dangerous. Would you want someone else with that power anywhere else if they could not control it?"

Although Luchs refused to say it aloud, it made sense. If another fissure opened up or the earth suddenly shot into the sky, how many more would perish? And that was just the beginning. There was more to the power than what he saw so far. He could feel it.

Vandelas took a few steps his way and put something hefty in Luchs' hands, crushing the fish in them. "You've gotten a decent start. Keep it up, and we will return alive."

When his hand moved away, Luchs saw what had been put in his hands was a small rock. He looked down on a smooth surface even though a rough, bumpy one grazed his palm. Taking it into one hand, he saw the rough side looked like it had been broken. Curious, Luchs closed his eyes and dug in to find the valsara inside, and found it to be the same stone that the fox crushed.

It was only half the size and much lighter than it once was. The rough side was poorly put together, but the smooth side appeared as if it had never been broken.

Luchs could not help staring at the fragmented stone in amazement. While he failed to fully put it back together, he learned that he could. It was a start.

~ Ninth Chapter ~

Pressure

The next few weeks passed without much complication. After his first attempt at controlling the Second Verse, Luchs had been working diligently to improve it. He kept the rock he barely managed to lump together close, wanting a reminder that forced him to improve.

Day in and day out, his little teacher had a rock broken and instructed him to piece it back together. As promised, it was much more of a challenge than anticipated. His mind strained with each attempt to fit those crude puzzles together, and it became more grueling the longer he endured.

Struggling to will something to happen without exerting any muscle, despite how difficult it truly was, left him bored and agitated. "Ack! Fie! Fie! Nonsense, all of it. There's got to be another way to better myself than to sit here like a stump," he complained constantly.

Vandelas dismissed those complaints time and again coldly, no words in edgewise.

Then out of the blue came a small surge of energy. A spire of ice suddenly formed beneath Luchs' feet; it would have skewered his skull had he not toppled back. He doubted he could have sensed it in time were it not for the training.

"I've had it with your complaints. You want an exercise?"

A triad of ice spires shot from the ground aiming at Luchs' neck, torso, and heart. Upon pivoting and avoiding them, another three appeared on a tree's branches and narrowed in at the top of his skull. Luchs ducked back and fell, dragging against the ground.

A stinging glare worked over his face as he looked at the lad.

"I've seen that Ederean men like dangerous exercises. I'll try not to disappoint."

Seeing him forcefully tug his left arm down, Luchs dove forward before a thick ice mace could crush his skull. For a moment, he thought Vandelas was genuinely trying to kill him, but that could not have been it. The energy released when he sculpted the ice was too intense. He was purposefully using so much power so that it could be detected.

It was just as he claimed—a dangerous exercise.

"That all you got, laddie?" Luchs taunted.

Vandelas spared no words. He instead clenched his fists, causing the ice he sculpted to shatter into thousands of powdery flecks. As the white cleared, several more ice spires shot at Luchs again, each one crafted barely a second apart from the last. Luchs was never that quick, but the rush of adrenaline made him spring into action fast enough to avoid getting impaled.

The ice formed in somewhat of a rhythmic pattern—aim for the heart, legs, neck, then shatter. Heart, legs, neck, and shatter. Heart, legs, neck, and shatter. Luchs read the timing until finally matching it perfectly, and when he did, he rushed to the side, circling around Vandelas as he continued crafting and breaking ice spires. One last shatter in the pattern, and he hurled himself at the lad to knock him to the ground.

But Vandelas was prepared. When Luchs got close, he grabbed his collar and pushed against his stomach, then easily tossed him aside.

Luchs saw the sky, then the land, and then suddenly his vision failed him when his skull hit something hard.

Suddenly, it was much easier to believe that the small lad had plucked him from the abyss.

The world flickered between darkness and the environment around him. Taking the focus needed to keep his vision from going strained his brain.

The magical eruption that felled him before left more of an impact than he first thought. Since then, pain lingered much longer than it ever had. He used to be able to shake anything off, from scant scraps to severe beatings. But what he experienced now was not as easy to ignore.

He did not want Vandelas to know what he managed to do to him, though, so he gritted his teeth and crawled back onto his feet.

"Don't go getting big-headed now."

Instead of letting him talk back, Vandelas crafted another spire on the tree beside him, shooting it straight at the fumbling Luchs, and stopping it just a centimeter from his nose. Although the ice did not touch him, the bitter cold brewing from it almost felt as if it had pricked his skin.

Luchs tried not to move so as not to rouse him to attack. If it was a real fight, he would have already lost. It was a reflex to stay put and admit defeat when unable to react. Maybe it was because he remembered how everyone sparred back on Des Meurtal, or maybe it was the look he saw in Vandelas' eyes.

It dawned on him to keep struggling and use his Second Verse, but he hesitated. He dreaded his power inadvertently destroying Emiet since learning of the possibility. Nothing happened so far, but he never used the Second Verse to do anything more than put rocks together, and he had yet to do that right.

When he knew the fight had left him, Vandelas shattered the ice, its frost flecking over Luchs' full face. Without the ice protruding over his nose, Luchs allowed his body to loosen up and go limp against the tree behind him.

Vandelas walked to the other side of the tree and sat against it.

"So, whose turn was it again?"

Recently, the two have been talking to each other during times of rest.

Luchs did not like it at first, but it was a great help. At night, when he slept, he uncovered more of his past through his dreams. He learned more about who he was, his family, how they lived, how his home thrived. Some questions were answered, but it was a lot to take in at once. Keeping it to himself did not do any good since it made him more anxious, the thoughts distracting him.

Vandelas saw through his tough façade, claiming it was a trick he picked up by seeing into the valsara of others. He did not look like he cared personally, but asked Luchs what was on his mind. After going back and forth about it, they came to an agreement where each would share something about themselves.

Luchs learned quite a bit about the strange foreigner.

True to the rumors, he came from Vermalio at the request of Princess Camellia: to serve a man who desired an exceptional squire. Something did not add up even though his words rang true.

"Why would Executioner Sörrign want a squire?" Luchs asked.

"I don't know," answered Vandelas. "But I don't need to, as long as he can train me to be stronger."

In respect of their accord, Luchs told him of his first dream. It reminded him of his place as a simple village child in a peaceful home not known to any other. His people isolated themselves from the outside world to avoid the conflicts that others made with each other. Very few outsiders came, but those that did were not driven away, nor did they prevent those who wished to leave from doing so. All that mattered was that those who called the village home could live their lives safely.

The day after that, Luchs asked about the fox. It could change its shape, size, and take monstrous strength using the small stone implanted in its forehead. He wanted to know how it happened. Snowflake always clung to Vandelas' side like a tick. Vandelas considered it family, so he would not turn it away even when ordered to do so by Executioner Sörrign. Instead, he was given the option to artificially strengthen its body by infusing it with magic—or rather, his Second Verse. The power was gathered into a lump of aurichalcum, an alloy which naturally absorbed and retained magic, and the aurichalcum was then melded to the fox. The process was dangerous for both him and his pet.

Luchs thought it insane to put that much strain on a little creature after feeling what it was like himself.

"If'n you're family, why make it go through that?"

"She wanted to stay with me, and Executioner Sörrign wouldn't allow it unless the procedure was done. Since she chose to go through it, I didn't argue."

The beast choosing? Luchs' sides split from laughter after hearing that. He likely said that to hide any guilt he had over it.

The dream from the other night was rather humorous. It mostly involved him spending the day with his sister, Hilda Lau. They were walking through the village in search of the man who herded the sheep flock for their share of mutton. The lass ran about up and down the path, having the time of her life while he chased after. Everyone looked delighted to see them both but were especially fond of her.

She was not always a joy to be around.

When they found the sheepherder, he was in the middle of a dispute with another villager—something about needing more meat for his growing spuds. Luchs did not recognize the loud man, but his sister did and went to support him, shouting louder and spitting more than either could. She bellowed louder than any stout man when she wanted to win an argument.

It brought him great comfort knowing more about his forgotten family than just their faces.

As the days passed, more memories flowed through his mind like a river. He remembered every face from every person he met in his old home, and even the ones from those who took him away from it. It was not much to go by, but he recalled the word *Pterna* when thinking of the men who abducted him. Elderly Jean-Luc Vertueux once uttered the same word when regaling others with stories of the wars he fought in.

Whoever they were, they invaded his home, took him from his family, and intended to make use of him in some way; that much he was certain.

But why? And who else did they hurt?

Such a tale was not worth telling over a little rest, and certainly not to him. Vandelas would not let it go, so instead Luchs thought of something a little cheerier to talk about. "Ah, I've just been thinking about my family."

"Your family?"

"Aye, family. You know, laddie, the people who raise you before you're grown, clothe you, give you food and shelter. You got one yourself, aye?"

"So your dream?"

Always to the point. It was a good trait, though, so Luchs got right to it. "'Twas nothing special—just good old times before I lost my memory, then some others after I did."

Vandelas raised an eyebrow. "And those good times were so much of a distraction?"

"You'd know if you let yourself have any." He leaned against the tree's rough surface and looked to the clear sky. A few stray clouds floated above, looking as lax as carefree children. "It used to just be fun and games with the people I cared about. Now... Well, you fought at Prévinn. Don't get me wrong: I enjoy a good bout as much as anyone, but this is different."

It was war, and that battle was but a prelude, the beginning of something they have yet to truly experience. Even without that declaration from their high priestess, the enemy soldiers all readied themselves to make the ultimate sacrifice for their cause.

Silence encircled them for a time. Nothing but the wisps of wind disturbed it. Luchs thought Vandelas would say something snide and condescending hearing such weak words. Showing weakness was never admirable. But the lad did not focus on that.

"One sister and four siblings who consider you family." That was no judgmental jab, just dry words on a wistful breath. "Never alone, are you?"

Luchs laughed. "Nay, not when I lived in the mountains or even now that I am with House Vertueux. A good lot, they are. Sometimes, I dream my two families one day meet." Impossible as it might be, a dream was a dream, and some were too good to let go of. "How about you? Have you any siblings?"

"Just Snowflake."

Luchs looked back at the part of the tree Vandelas rested against.

Must be lonely being an only child.

"And, in case you planned on asking about my parents, they are wonderful people—strong, devoted, proud in their own ways. I am lucky to be their son."

"Oh? What does your father do?"

"Father was a knight of Vermalio. Mother still is."

"Wait, your mother, a knight? Hah! Now ain't that a laugh! No wonder you're so off."

"Aye, aye. I'm familiar with how you Edereans see warrior women," Vandelas said, clearly unamused. "Tigresses, I heard they are called. It's just another way of saying you don't accept it." He must have heard similar things time and again and grew tired of it, judging by the cynical tone.

"Can't say I get it myself. A woman's place just isn't on the battlefield. Men are stronger, so we're better suited for war."

For a moment, Luchs thought he was hallucinating. He heard Vandelas start to laugh, soft and feeble as it was. It was the first time he heard him laugh.

"Yet one of Vermalio's most famous knights is a woman, one who would skin you alive if she heard what you just said."

To that, Luchs laughed. "Sounds more like a beast than a lady."

"Believe what you want." Growing tired of the topic, Vandelas stood and circled the tree, eying Luchs with the same dull eyes. Cold and dreary as they appeared, there was a temperate spark behind it now. "Enough rest. I'll fetch you another rock."

"Nay, I'm bored of rocks. Let's go another bout. I haven't had one like that before."

Vandelas stopped in place before Luchs could stand again, looking oddly bothered. He then cupped the squire's shoulder, pushing him back on his rear. "Stay here."

"Wha—"

Before another argument could break out, Vandelas reached for the waterskin at Luchs' waist. "I need this." He took it and strode off in the direction of the spring.

"Oi! What're you taking my water for?"

"Cup the back of your head. Keep it there until I get back."

And he was out of sight before he could explain why. Luchs thought to follow him, but was spooked by this warm feeling that crept down his neck. Terrified, knowing the thickness and warmth, his hand flew behind his head to catch the thick liquid. It oozed between his fingers.

Blood. The moment he pulled away he saw blood crawl across his palm, and more still flowed out of him.

This never happened before. Every time he got hurt, every time he had been injured, the bleeding never lasted for so long. Even when in captivity, blood was spilled, but the wounds always closed in no time.

Behind his head was a small smear of blood on the tree trunk he had been thrown against. He had been bleeding for that long and did not realize it.

Death did not just make his body weaker, it robbed him of the durability that made so many recognize him. Maybe it really was the work of magic like everyone believed. Regardless, he relied on that durability more than anything.

And now, it was gone.

It was hard to believe. He did not want to believe it. First his home, his family, then his memories, his taste buds, and now his impressive durability—one after another, he kept losing more of himself.

"Apologies, Luchs." Vandelas returned about as quickly as he left, carrying the waterskin he took as well as a small rag. "Perhaps I should have held back a little."

"Oh, don't flatter yourself." Even in that position, Luchs would not let weakness show. "That love tap didn't even tickle. I've been hit by breezes harder than that."

Vandelas did not bother listening to him as he took the pilfered waterskin and poured some water on the rag. A quick wring, then he pulled Luchs' head back, setting the rag there to soak up the blood. While wincing from the stinging irritation, Luchs felt his hand being moved over the rag and made to hold it in place.

The lad waited until Luchs calmed down before speaking. "I don't think it is that bad. It just needs time to heal."

It irked Luchs that he had to sit down and wait for the bleeding to stop. Other Ederean lads got back up after getting hurt, especially when someone else hurt them. He did not want to be seen as lesser than them. "Nay! I can still train. I'm fine." His free hand pressed at the ground, ready to push himself up, but Vandelas cupped his shoulder and shoved him down again.

"Then you will—with the rocks."

Luchs was not about to argue, not while strings of blood crept over his hand. All he did in response was groan before Vandelas went to get another rock.

He did not go far past the tall trees bearing the delectable red bananas. At the foot of one said tree rested a fair-sized stone. He picked it up and propped in front of Luchs forthwith. No orders were given, probably because they have done the routine to death.

But he did not have the rock broken yet.

"What?" Luchs growled.

Vandelas sat down. "Is there something else on your mind?"

Once again, he managed to catch Luchs wide-eyed and off guard. "Ack! How do you always do that?"

Vandelas tapped the space over his right eye, his icy gaze undaunting. "Finely tuned magic senses can detect subtle changes in valsara, such as changes in emotion. Mine isn't the most keen, but I've learned how to see when a person is distressed."

"So there's no way I can hide anything from you, eh?"

His eyes gleamed rather viciously. "We've been over this, Luchs. Your Second Verse is still without reins to control it. Any emotional upset you have will affect your power, and when it does, in this state—"

"Then we're sunk, along with the islet."

The tired sigh Vandelas gave showed how irritated he was with having to explain again. "Assuming your reach only extends to the one we're on." Quiet as he was, Luchs heard him clearly. They went over how dangerous his power was not just to them, but to everyone many times. Anything could happen.

"Loss," Vandelas muttered. "You've lost something?"

That was oddly specific for someone who could only vaguely read emotions.

The silence seemed to confirm his suspicions. That glint in his eyes grew sharper yet had not suggested any hostility. It was rather somber. "Loss is inevitable," he boded in a tone heavier, grimmer than he had previously. "Time passes, and with it, everything is lost to the wind, sometimes on their own breeze, sometimes together with another. I may not know what you are suffering from, but I know loss is painful. But whatever is plaguing you now, Luchs, cannot be allowed to interfere with the goal at hand." Vandelas reached out and grabbed his shoulder, gripping it firmly. "The time for lamenting is over. Now you must press forward or risk being consumed by your weakness."

The severity in his words alone could have crushed the rock.

Looking into his eyes, sitting in his sights, Luchs felt the weight of what plagued him. He had seen the same deathly countenance before, in the company of soldiers who themselves experienced loss.

What must he have lost to have those eyes?

Seeing the message had gotten through, Vandelas took his hand from Luchs' shoulder and sat back down.

When he backed away, Luchs caught a glimpse of his sleeve, torn and the same color as the rag he held against his head.

"Snowflake."

The beast beside him had long since shifted into its monstrous form, perhaps sensing its master's intensity and waiting for a need to strike. It calmed after he had, but the mere mention of its name sent it into action. It lunged at the stone and, faster than one could blink, shattered the rock, then returned to Vandelas' side while reverting to its natural form.

"Now, continue your training."

Luchs, having lost the urge to resist and complain, nodded and turned to the rubble. A few breaths and a pull at the scattered energy was all it took to meld the first pebble back to its body.

How ... did this happen?

The training was going so well. Luchs finally managed to meld an entire broken stone back together, lopsided and bulbous as it was. He got better at distinguishing the valsara of plants from that of the land. And yet, despite the progress made, it all seemed for naught.

When the sun began to set, the ground trembled and hungrily ripped open before Luchs. In the hysteria, he swore he heard the land itself screaming while the ground beneath him shifted against itself. It was no natural occurrence. He sensed the Second Verse react as the ground violently shook. It was only out of desperation for survival that he managed to still his power before it could raze the rest of Emiet.

A fair chunk of the land had been swallowed by the sea with only a meager peak of it left protruding over the water. A chunk of the ground stretched from Luchs' feet before crumbling into the water. He could not help scuttling away from the new cliff.

They were lucky no one fell in. Vandelas was nearby, having sprinted away from the collapsing land before it broke apart beneath him. He was quick on his feet and knew how to react to that falling tree that nearly took him with it.

Luchs sat uneasily away from the cliff, in a fragile state.

He felt it again—the thunderous beating against the land. It happened before the quake hit. Somehow, sensing the beating made him lose what little control over the Second Verse he clung to. His power went berserk, surging through the ground before the quake began.

Something about the beating bothered him. It was stronger than before, much more intense. It reminded him of when he felt the ground shake from soldiers charging into battle.

No, that can't be it!

Luchs forsook his dread back at Des Meurtal. Bringing himself to kill without crumbling was one of the most difficult struggles he ever endured. He could do it. Nothing held him back after that.

The thought of battle could not still be holding him back.

Vandelas approached him and grabbed his shoulder, drawing him out of the harried storm of thought that raged in his head.

"Are you calm now?" he gently spoke.

It was difficult to say so while feeling his body tremble as the ground had. The blood drained from his face, leaving him lightheaded and a little nauseous. He brought himself to nod only after knowing he could stand without toppling over.

"Good."

Without warning, Vandelas shoved Luchs back to the ground.

Standing back up was harder than before. His legs would not stop shaking, their muscles weaker than old, rancid custard. His arms were not in any better shape either. When he tried picking himself back up, he tumbled and landed on his face.

"Stand."

If there was ever a time Luchs thought Vandelas a teacher in any way, it stopped there. That way he carried himself was much too infuriating to take in such a tense moment.

If only so he would not be looked down upon, Luchs clung his fingers into the soil, clenching his muscles in response, and mustered the strength to push him back onto his feet. The frightened, pale complexion of his shifted into one of red fury.

"Just how badly do you want a beating, laddie?"

"If you can't even stand, you won't be able to control the Second Verse."

A simple scare tactic, but it worked. The ground opened up in front of them and nearly swallowed the islet because of his sudden slip.

"Has there been damage to the rest of the island?"

Letting a groan pass his lips, Luchs kneeled and pressed his hands against the ground.

A few days after learning how to sense valsara, he was instructed on how to focus on the entirety of the life energy across Emiet. It was originally a means of testing how far Luchs could sense the minuscule energy within soil and stone, but using it to track changes in the land was not so difficult. Closing his eyes and concentrating painted a picture of the islet's structure in his mind. The strain it caused was minimal, either due to the size of the islet or Luchs having gotten used to it.

From the surface of the ocean and above, Emiet was shaped like a long, narrow arrowhead with a corner at the south-southeast chipped off. After the quake, another massive chunk had been torn away, shaping the islet into a tear. There was this slight trembling from the layers of valsara underneath the waves, showing a continuing instability, but the land itself was slowly settling.

They were safe for now.

"Not too much damage all around, but there might be aftershocks."

"Were there any drastic changes? Anything?"

As his closed eyes cringed and his brows furrowed, Luchs' magic senses broadened to survey the islet. Nothing seemed abnormal aside from the missing chunk of land. Beneath the surface, however, where the valsara wavered frantically, there were gaps between the ruptured stones that looked ready to cave in at any moment. The worst of it seemed to be around the spring. He found a small underwater cave formed beneath there—the place where the winged fish dwelled. The tunnels connecting it to the ponds had been eroding long before their arrival. And after the quake, they barely held together.

"The spring ... 'tisn't going to last." It was hard to admit, dread welling in his throat.

"Then that is where we're going."

"Wha—" Luchs jolted up from the ground, shocked and disturbed, and stared harrowingly at Vandelas. "You can't be serious! We go there, and we're sunk. Even that wee body of yours alone could make it plunge us down into the deep."

"How long before the land collapses?"

"Hard to say, but it might not last a week more."

"That isn't enough time."

The captain of their ship was under strict orders to not return to Emiet until a month passed. Another twelve days still remained.

Luchs sighed brusquely, knowing full well what the situation dictated. "So I either use my power there or we sink."

Vandelas nodded. "Can you do it?"

That was the question, but Luchs did not even acknowledge it. He *had* to. Too much remained at stake to plummet into the depths with a dying islet.

Neither of them spoke as they marched to the spring. With the land in such a ruined state, they had to focus on what lay under their feet to ensure it would not swallow them. It was a pain for Luchs, who had so much he wanted to get off his chest.

Every time Vandelas came within his sight, he recalled all the obscure training methods he had to engage in: putting puzzles of stone together, wasting time staring at pebbles to see the differences in the dormant energy within them, just sitting and breathing without using the Second Verse at all. He acted so dead set on training him and barely lifted a finger.

"Oi." It was only because they found a spot with enough stable earth that he decided to let his guard down and speak up. "Tell me the truth: do you know what you've been doing since we got here?"

"No."

A quick answer. No hesitation wavered in his voice; it did not bother him sharing that.

It was hard to tell whether he wanted to laugh his head off that someone would willingly admit defeat without a fight or charge angrily at him for letting the fool lead him around.

"You're some kind of daft, laddie," groaned Luchs while bitterly shaking his head. "Why've you been making me do all this malarkey when you don't even know if'n it works?"

"We're not dead yet. It must have helped somehow."

Never had he done anything that made any sense. All those tedious wastes of time could have been just that, yet he spoke so assuredly. Those fools who acted like they knew everything always infuriated Luchs the most. He would have said so, sternly, had he not heard a deafening crack beneath their feet. They had just arrived in the safe zone, and already they left it.

Once more they took light steps across the chipping landscape to avoid being swallowed.

A place that looked almost like something from a fairy tale had been left half-decimated, the spring torn in two. The upper pond still carried flowing water, which poured into the crevasse that opened, a crevasse that tore the lower pool from the upper one. Several trees had fallen, been scattered, and were even crushed into splinters.

His magic sight still needed tuning if he thought that looked fine.

Getting closer any closer than they had was unsafe. The thinnest layers of soil separated them from a fall into the abyss, dirt crumbling speck by speck the longer they stood there breathless. Not much time remained.

In his breathless daze, Luchs waited for any advice Vandelas could offer like he would usually. But he did not say a word. All he did was stare at the tear in the earth.

Curious, Luchs looked into Vandelas' valsara. Anxiety and fright flickered within—he was right about them being some of the easiest emotions to read. Something else went on in him apart from the fear of plummeting into the seven hells, but Luchs could not read it.

Once he broke his focus, Vandelas looked back the way they came, probably looking for the fox that did not follow. "I hope you're ready." He turned to face Luchs. "Consider this your final test."

"You done blathering? I've an islet to save."

Bold words from the robust squire, but they were nothing more than that. Deep down he was more afraid than he ever had been. He melded tiny stones together for many a day, nothing bigger. Miles of fragmented, unstable stone needed to be pieced back together by nothing more than Luchs willing it.

Stubborn pride refused him to show any weakness.

Just another rock. It was the only thing he could think of to keep him calm. *Just another rock...*

Inhaling deeply, Luchs closed his eyes, switching to magic sight so he may see the valsara around them. The rigid ground beneath their feet covered much of the real damage—a gapping, ugly tear that stretched for miles. Jagged stone sheets protruded out of the crevasse walls, barely holding each other together. The energy flowed weakly at certain points, wavered, flickered where the shells were ready to break.

In keeping his calm state, the Second Verse flowed uninterrupted with his tame valsara and smoothly spread in an area surrounding him where he could better influence the earth's energy. The near-inactive valsara flared to life when encircled in the spreading power, something Vandelas called an area of influence, just as the rocks' energy had when attempting to mend them.

Luchs began with an easy movement from his left arm, ushering a thick slab near the spring to pull upwards. Beneath that slab was a layer of a thick mineral that seemed liable to detach and fall into the depths if left alone. Lifting his other arm, his power took a hold of the layer and positioned it gently to where both would remain stable.

The ground trembled subtly when the fragmented earth had been moved, enough for them to notice something was happening underneath.

The process seemed relatively simple, moving slivers of earth from one place to another to promote stability. The crust looked to be in good condition thus far, but after resetting half of the stones dangling from the crevasse walls, he knew it would not be enough. Too much damage had ensued the raging Second Verse. Something else had to be done.

"What's wrong?"

Although it pained him to admit it, he needed help.

"The foundation's too broken up. I can't patch it up."

"Don't patch it up then. Pull it together."

"Can't you make sense for one blasted minute!?"

"Remember, the Second Verse is dominion over nature itself. If the earth won't stand on its own, force it to come together. Use the stable

~ 176 ~

ground to hold up what isn't."

He sounded more confident in Luchs' abilities than Luchs was. The sentiment was generous, but it did not keep the ground from shaking. It was not nearly as bad as the first quake that hit, a mere aftershock from the land attempting to settle on its own. But they still needed to remain vigilant. The trees rattled from the leaves shaking so excessively, and the crevasse uttered a deathly moaning, something ravenous.

"Are you mad!? I do anything else and it'll tear Emiet apart!"

The ground began to shake more tumultuously from the aftershock.

"There's no choice. We're out of time. I know you can feel it!" With the crevasse bellowing so horrifically, Vandelas needed to raise his voice or go unheard. Even then, it was hard to get the message through. "Are you going to shackle this island to your will and sail off it a proud Nascitte, or will you let your power conquer and devour you?"

Just before Luchs could process what he heard, the ground opened up, dragging the unsuspecting Vandelas down into the widening crevasse. Luchs tried to spring into action and grab him before he fell, but his arm could not reach in time.

As he watched the lad plummet, he also saw him bear his hands like claws and drive them into the rock wall, clinging stubbornly to it. Rocks and dirt flung at his face until he finally came to a stop. Crimson trickled down his russet hands and glided down his arms while he struggled to hold on.

"Hang tight!" Luchs shouted. "I'll get you out!"

"Don't! Finish what you started!"

Those words made Luchs tense up. It was bad enough that he could not keep what was left of the land supported, but seeing someone caught into what his power caused rocked him to his core.

"I'm not letting you put your death on my head!"

"Then don't let me! Hurry and pull the land together now!"

Just as quickly as the last, another aftershock ran across the islet, this one more spiteful. The crevasse grew evermore, swallowing more of the islet. And in the wild consumption, the stone around Vandelas' right hand weakened, until his grip failed. "Luchs!" The hand left anchored into the wall trembled having to hold up the rest of his body. His endurance and persistence were admirable and served him well until the stone he clung to chipped off the wall.

"Vandelas!"

Seeing the helpless lad fall drove Luchs to act. Bolting back onto his feet, he flung his arms across his torso, pulling them tightly as if attempting to desperately keep hold of something. The Second Verse spread throughout Emiet, flowing without restraint. Throughout the entire islet the quaking worsened, spreading the waves of seismic energy that even made the waters stir.

It finally happened. He let his anxiety run wild. Emiet was going to sink into the sea.

...Huh?

But it didn't. The devastation never came. The islet still stood.

The quakes stopped, the crevasse grew no further, and the bellowing within it was slowly silenced. The ground remained beneath Luchs' feet. And the strangest thing of all, after a few soft stomps for inspection, then a firm one, he found it much stronger than when they first arrived.

But how?

In his daze, Luchs nearly forgot about Vandelas. He rushed to the cliff and peered into the darkness.

Dirt and dust blanketed the space, a bronze cloud brewed in the quakes keeping him from seeing anything. It was too thick to know what became of him, and going in to find out without knowing what still stood was dangerous.

Soon, the cloud faded, revealing the crevasse had been completely sealed by hard stone ripped from the walls, almost completely concealing the darkness beneath. And lying atop the hard stone was Vandelas, alive albeit injured from the fall.

They were both alive, as was the islet they walked on. And it was because Luchs finally found control over his Second Verse.

~ Tenth Chapter ~
Struggle and Repose

After nearly rending Emiet asunder, Luchs followed every regimen Vandelas put him through without question.

Aftershocks hit the islet frequently, but never another full quake. Everything was merely trying to settle into place. The seismic activity across the islet was more noticeable when the sun rose while the aftershocks seldom came at night. The pattern occurred due to Luchs' Second Verse, the power being more active while the Nascitte was awake. It made Luchs nervous knowing his power still acted on its own accord.

Vandelas disagreed that it was just the Second Verse. He gathered that Luchs still controlled it, although less consciously, since the power had not yet to run rampant. For as little sense as it made, it made more sense to Luchs than much else.

This power—the Second Verse—was something even the Nascitte who controlled it could not fathom.

There was less for the squires to eat after the big quake. They needed to carefully ration everything they found. Water stopped flowing from the decimated spring six days afterwards, and since there was no other source of fresh water, they needed to be innovative. Vandelas froze the water in the air and put it into bowls Luchs carved from coconut shells; by the time they finished training, the ice had melted under the sunlight and was ready to drink.

A few weeks later, the ship returned for them.

Being on a ship, riding over the high seas, felt much better than walking atop Emiet and, at times, much steadier. Unlike the vague training regimen on the islet, the tasks assigned to the crew were clear and direct, and there was a more rowdy and delightful bunch to interact with in hearty scuffles and over filling meals. Sleeping aboard the ship was much more pleasant too, the vessel swaying in a relaxing motion on peaceful nights.

After their time together, Luchs had better notice of Vandelas distancing himself from everyone whenever possible. It was much harder to ignore after getting to know him as someone other than a gloomy child.

One night, when the crescent moon hung in the sky, Luchs awoke and got out of his hammock in the ship's berth, and made way for the main deck. He did not sleep well; another dream of his past had been interrupted by more incessant beating against the land echoing in his mind. They have been occurring more frequently as of late.

At least he was not alone. Vandelas was awake as well. He was leaning against the ship's railing, his head in his arms, in the company of the clingy fox lying beside him. He stared at the moon and waves, calm and relaxed.

When Luchs climbed the stairs, the lad looked more alert but remained perfectly calm. "You'll need to work on your silent approach."

"Are criticisms all you know how to give?" Luchs asked while ascending to the top of the steps.

It was quiet until he closed the distance, making certain they did not need to shout to each other. Neither said anything for a short time. It was rather peaceful taking in the brush of the waves, basking in the glorious lunar light, feeling the ocean air over their bodies.

"Why are you still up?" Luchs chose to break the silence.

"I don't take to water as well as an Ederean."

"Not every Ederean loves a good boat ride the day they come into the world. Give it time. You'll learn to love it."

"And what of you?" Vandelas changed the subject. "Are those memories giving you trouble?"

"Nay, but these blasted headaches keep me from a decent rest."

That seemed to catch Vandelas' attention. His crystalline blue eyes glanced Luchs' way, noting his discomfort. It was nothing but staring for half a minute. That creepy, cold gaze made the nonverbal questioning awkward.

"Perhaps the Second Verse is involved."

That thought crossed his mind more than once. It never happened before his demise, then they tormented him so constantly that it became tempting to slam his head into a boulder to make it stop.

Nothing being said after that, Luchs glanced at Vandelas curiously.

"So you really didn't know what you were doing, eh? You just made me play with rocks while you trained those twigs you hilariously call arms."

Those provocations did little more than bring Vandelas to shrug. "I am a child of ... four-and-ten years?" he said as if speculating whether or not that was the proper way to say it. "The training I took to control my Second Verse was guesswork as well, and barely any offered to help. Everything I've done has all been conjecture, so I could only do as much when training you in your element."

Those quiet words failed to move Luchs. Modesty was not just unbecoming of him after what he saw him do, it was ridiculous.

"Malarkey! You've made ice and snow come out of thin air and use it however you see fit. If'n what you say is true, then how can you do what you do?"

"How indeed..." As Vandelas thought on it, the fox beside him stirred from rest and stretched its body out. Eying its master, it crawled over to him and licked his cheek, barely missing the thread sticking out from the plush scarf around his neck. He let out a chuckle and reached out to pet the fox's fluffy white scalp. "I've wondered that myself many times. Perhaps it was through the diligent training I put myself through. Or it could have been the deathly situations I've found myself in over the years, survival instinct taking control. Or..."

"Or?"

Vandelas mulled over it a little longer, then glanced back at Luchs. "Or perhaps it was because of the power itself."

"Eh? You lost me."

"When you died, a fissure opened beneath you. When I died, I froze what I came in contact with. In both times, our power reacted while we were awakening as Nascitte. Could it be that the Second Verse, when being infused with our souls, takes time to adjust, to settle itself? Then it could be that it uses itself to keep from going out of control."

That made less sense than anything else he said before. The power keeping itself from losing control, but much of it reacted and fluctuated depending on the mental state of the Nascitte.

Luchs thought to say something on how confusing Vandelas' reasoning was, but decided against it. They both had a limited understanding of their enigmatic power. They survived, they learned, and they would continue to learn until bringing their power to higher levels.

"Well, however it works, 'tis under control now."

"For now." Vandelas stood up straight and turned to Luchs, looking him in the eye. "Once on land again, you'll need to continue exercising your control over the Second Verse. At least once a day should suffice."

A cynical grin wormed over Luchs' face. "So more playing with rocks?"

"It's not my concern any longer. Do as you wish so long as it doesn't pull the archipelago underwater."

Turning his attention back to the fox, Vandelas' cold eyes showed more comfort as he closed in to scoop it into his arms. No matter how many times Luchs saw it, he could never get used to it. Even with the scarf wrapped around the lad's face, he could tell when he smiled at the fox. He almost looked normal so long as the jinx had his attention.

"Remember what I told you."

"I know, I know: I'm a mage, not a Nascitte."

Of the few things he explained clearly, that was what had been brought up the most. Very few knew that Nascitte existed, and those few needed to keep it that way.

A Nascitte was born when someone died.

People feared death. Whether it was because they did not want their life to end, or they worried what pain led to it, or even that they were skeptical of what happened to them afterwards, people feared death.

But what if someone were to learn they might be able to revive from the dead and return with the power to bend the world in some way? There were some in the world who would give anything, take any risk, in exchange for power.

Vandelas started to walk off, then stopped to face Luchs again.

"And Luchs, should you have any trouble with the Second Verse, seek me out. I'll be glad to help."

The generous offer caught him off guard. A month in his company and Vandelas only behaved taciturn, distant, cautious. In that moment, though, he treated Luchs as an equal and showed a somewhat kindly expression. The briefest glance at his valsara revealed no hostility or ill emotion whatsoever. He honestly wanted to help.

In seeing that, Luchs' smile became sincere. "I'll keep that in mind."

After crossing the tranquil ocean, their vessel reached Shoafond harbor. As usual, the hearty sailors took to the land with loud, boisterous laughter that caught the attention of the dockhands who went to greet them. Curious about the two lads among the lot of hirsute men, the dockhands greeted Luchs and Vandelas with firm slaps on the back and words of praise for surviving the voyage. Their comments were patronizing, and that likely would not change until they grew into men.

A couple of the soldiers guided Luchs back to Castle Ederea, leaving Vandelas to wander the streets all by his lonesome. Luchs questioned why they did not take him with at first, but after glancing back, he saw the lad wandering around the docks like a green foreigner.

Odd.

It was not as unexpected as what Luchs found upon returning to the castle. After crossing the southeastern drawbridge and passing through the curtains of mist rising from the falls, he noticed a small group waiting at the garden plot creating a fork in the path. The parting vapor revealed those waiting were of the Vertueux family—his meister knight, Ulrin, the loving Liliiun, even Jilié and Agnes.

The moment energetic Jilié saw him emerge from the mist, she ran his way and leaped at him for a hug. The others followed suit after seeing the lass cling to him. His guides went on their way while the familial lot crowded together in embrace and laughter.

A broad smile stretched across Luchs' face but began to slip when he saw a few tears slip over Jilié's cheeks.

"O-Oi, Jilié. What's eating you, lass?"

She refused to speak up and shook her head in denial, claiming that she was upset in the least.

Sympathizing with her little sister, Liliiun bent down beside her and gently cupped her shoulders, holding her close. "'Tis my fault," she spoke ruefully. "I told dear Jilié about the condition you were in before ... you woke up. 'Twas so upsetting when I first saw it myself, and the dear kept asking when she came to visit. I only terrified her. She's been worried sick about you ever since and insisted on being here when you returned."

It was a relief knowing her tears were only out of concern. Not wanting to leave the lass with any more qualms, he leaned down and gave her a big smile just as Ulrin ruffled her curly hair. "Those tears are clearly blinding you. I look all right, aye? Nothing is out of place." Once he had her attention, he leaned in a little more, feigning offense. "Or are you saying I've been in the wild so long I'm looking like those puffy wildcats? You remember that one cub we saw, the one that wandered into the chateau gardens years back?"

Mentioning that once lost wildcat rid Jilié of her tears and etched a big smile in between her freckled cheeks, a wonderful laugh escaping her. That wildcat looked adorable in her eyes while it thrashed about in the flowerbed it found itself in, even when the rest of the family wanted to get rid of it before it found a way inside. She calmed down again.

"It means a lot you'd all come to see me," said Luchs, turning to the delightful family, then stopping at Agnes. "Figured you'd be too busy managing things on Untaseau. How're Sir Trenent and Cael fairing?"

The children's mother smiled. "My husband is well, and Cael is actually here, inside the castle being tended to."

"Oh? Then I should go see him." Before moving toward the castle, he looked up at Ulrin. "That is, if my meister knight doesn't mind it."

Ulrin chuckled before playfully shooing his squire away. "Get out of here, you little buzzard!"

With his meister knight's permission, he followed Agnes inside.

The halls were relatively calm as always. A few soldiers and servants crossed their path now and then, along with a few visiting noblemen tending to their own affairs.

The silence bothering her, Agnes asked Luchs how he was recovering, and did so with a steady, comforting voice. Her placid composure was not so much for him as it was for herself.

Luchs claimed to be faring well, not willing to admit anything else. Like the proud baroness, he, too, wanted to appear strong.

Many Edereans were familiar with a credo: survival means strength, to survive means to be stronger for it, and to be stronger means to be able to support those held dear. It served as a reminder that everyone owed it to more than themselves to be strong—in many ways.

"You think the lad will try hiding from me again?" Luchs asked in an attempt to change the subject.

Agnes tried not to laugh at his attempt at escape. "Oh, hush now," she teased. "Cael likes you. He's just shy, 'tis all."

They eventually made it to a near-empty room being tended to by one of the maids. It was concerning to only find her since the lad had been left there with a couple of attentive, albeit tentative, servants.

"Ah, Lady Vertueux," the remaining maid uttered before worry troubled the noblewoman. "A few of the servants took your son to a

~ 185 ~

different room. They thought it a bit dreary in here; not as much sunlight gets in, you see."

The room did have a gloomy air without much natural light gleaming through the window. Regardless, it still irritated Agnes hearing her child had been moved somewhere else in the massive domain without her knowing.

Having understood that, the maid abandoned the task she had been assigned to showed them to where Cael was. They all stepped outside and walked farther down the hall. Eventually, they came across the vestibule where Luchs first met the general, then climbed the steps and made a turn down a hall awash in sunlight. The sound of the crashing waterfalls had somehow diminished a little in those halls.

It was both impressive and surprising that within a castle surrounded by waterfalls hundreds of feet tall there were places that carried less of the tempestuous sound. It might have been due to what was used to make the castle ages ago.

Perhaps only the gods would ever know what mysterious materials the castle had been made with.

It was very interesting to think about. In the rare moments he had to search for where he came from, Luchs found old documents written by scholars who believed the castle had been built in the fabled Old Age. Many thought the scholar's findings absurd, as the Old Age was a time when mythical creatures walked the world alongside mankind. Even children barely believed in those ancient tales.

Shortly after crossing the halls to the northern side, the maid showed them to a spacious room fit for a duke. The furnishings and ornaments within were elegantly designed and complimented one another. A small table paired with four chairs sat near a large window overlooking the gardens and one of the falls looming high above the castle. Beside the comfortable-looking bed dressed with carnelian sheets, its tasteful canopy donning thin, transparent vermillion fabric, stood a tall armoire. And beneath the veil of comforting light beaming from the window lay an old rug with vague depictions of a long-forgotten war at its outer ring. It was an intriguing contrast to the two children playing a clapping game on top of it.

Cael looked to be having a fun time with his unexpected company.

Just as they noticed the lad, they got a good look at who he was playing with: Princess Camellia.

They put their game on hold when the door opened. Cael looked directly up at the people entering before a smile returned to his face, and he ran to his mother. The maid who escorted the two tensed up at the sight of the princess slowly turning their way. She curtsied as she excused herself, leaving to return to her tasks.

"Oh, might you be this young one's parents?"

She must not have gotten a good look at Luchs.

One of the maids in the room with them took the princess' hand, helping her off the rug. The princess faced her company with a delicate smile, her big eyes aglow with a charm enchanting.

Agnes looked taken aback to see the royal heir, but she kept her gracious demeanor to show respect. "'Tis been a long time, Your Highness. Mayhap you don't remember meeting me. I am Lady Agnes Vertueux of Untaeseau." The noblewoman took her hand from her child's head and curtsied to her princess.

Princess Camellia let go of the maid's hand and curtsied as well, returning the respect given to her. "Well met, Lady Vertueux." Her voice was so amiable, so pleasing to the ear—soft like cotton and sweet like fresh honey. It made the songs birds chirped at the dawn of spring sound grating in comparison. "My apologies. I recall Father telling me I've met many noble families before, but much of them were in my early years."

"Think nothing of it, Your Highness."

The princess looked rather chipper, then turned her gaze toward Luchs and, suddenly, expressed surprise. She blinked a couple of times, trying to assess what was before her.

Luchs bit his tongue before he uttered a word. Speaking out of turn to one of royal blood would not leave him in anyone's good graces. "I-Is something wrong, Your Highness?" But he could not keep quiet for long.

After hearing him speak, the young lady regained her composure and smiled again. "Nothing at all. My apologies. You looked rather familiar for a moment."

The two have never so much as locked eyes before. Hearing her say such a thing made Luchs feel awkward, but he quickly dismissed it.

"Might I have your name?"

A sudden request, and one that stunned Luchs. Normally when formally introducing himself to a woman, a man took her hand and planted a light kiss on the back of it. The custom was a strange one to Luchs, who learned it in his time with the Vertueux family. One look at the suddenly irate maid holding the princess' hand let him know that no one was expecting such a gesture. Following that reasoning alone, Luchs just bowed to the princess. "I am Luchs, Your Highness. I was ... taken in by the Vertueux family." That was the introduction he could give. It did not seem right to say he was of House Vertueux nor was it an opportune time to introduce himself as a Lau. At the very least, he was not being rude by failing to mention a family name.

Whatever the intent, it definitely got her attention. The princess' thin brows lifted somewhat. "Taken in? You are not of House Vertueux yourself?"

"Nay, Princess, but we care for him as our kin." Agnes stretched her hand to cup Luchs' right shoulder, holding onto it as kindly as she had her youngest.

There seemed to be no further need to clarify things. Confusion slipped away from the petite lass' countenance, replaced with a bright smile like the one she wore in the gardens. Her expression and brief silence showed she did not quite understand but liked seeing how close they were.

There was a gentle knocking at the door before the princess could say anything else. A gussied-up man entered pushing a cart that carried a tea kettle and matching cups along with a small, wide basket of assorted baked goodies. The sight of the treats made Cael's face light up.

"Thank you very much, Gerald."

The servant bowed to his princess, a kindly smile on his face, before taking his leave.

"Lady Vertueux, would you care to join us for some tea? We've plenty to share."

"I'd be delighted. Of course, if Your Highness wouldn't mind Luchs here accompanying us as well."

It was kind of her to include him, and he would have accepted were it not for the burden he had been given. He had been out at sea for days without any opportunity to train with the Second Verse. Measures needed to be taken, and he could not do so while sipping tea and nibbling on snacks.

Unfortunately, Princess Camellia seemed to like the idea.

Luchs worried he would be making a mistake in rudely rejecting the offer, but he could not stay. "A-Actually, Agnes, I should probably head to the training grounds. I need to keep in shape—"

"Oh hush, lad! You've been training on that wreck of an islet for a whole month. It won't kill you to sit with us for a bite." Agnes' tone was firm but kind all the same. She was insistent he remained, which showed when she began tugging him and her child toward the table.

The maid holding the princess' hand let go once her charge got comfortable. She then went to the cart, picking up and placing everything onto the table one object at a time. She kept to a certain order for efficiency—first the little costar plates, then placing the teacups atop them, and then setting the pastry basket at the center of the table. The tea had not been poured until everything was set in place.

Cael could not sit still while looking at the pastries put before him. He tried hiding his impatience, but Luchs could see how bad he wanted one as he grabbed tightly his seat and swung his little legs. When everything had been set, Luchs took a crepe and handed it to the lad.

Gleefully, he took the treat and crammed it into his little mouth.

When his mother called him out, the lad pulled the crepe away and timidly looked up at the big, burly squire. "Um ... Thank you, Luchs." His voice was meek yet adoring, something most parents did not think kindly of from their sons, but the lad was young enough for it to still be charming. It would probably be another year or so before more would be expected from him.

The princess uttered nary a word until tasting the tea for herself. She sighed blissfully upon sipping the hot liquid. Its flavor left her in a comfortable trance for a moment. "Mm, savory. Such rich herbs. And a hint of honey, I believe."

The fine commentary made the experience more enjoyable for Luchs. He barely noticed the tea when he drank it. His cringing was from not expecting the beverage to be so hot rather than recoiling from potential bitterness. All he felt wash over his tongue was a bland flush of steamy water. He missed being able to taste.

From the looks of it, though, he was not missing much; Cael barely held down a sip out of politeness.

"That Gerald certainly knows what he is doing. Rarely do I partake in tea so refreshing," Agnes praised.

Perhaps the flavor was for more mature sorts. It said a lot about the young princess who drank it like a heavenly elixir.

She turned to Luchs once everyone gave their opinions on the refreshment and snacks. Her big eyes stared plainly at him, almost analyzing him. Had it not been for her youthful countenance or the captivating sparkle in her eyes, it would have unnerved him.

"Luchs, Lady Vertueux mentioned your return from an islet. Would that, by chance, be Emiet?"

"Aye, Princess."

"Then you must be the new mage Father received word of."

She must not have known his true fate either.

"You performed an extraordinary feat in battle, I heard," the princess chirped. "Tore the ground open, separating both forces, just as the enemy unleashed a dreadfully powerful spell! 'Twas quite the spectacle General Esperance and your meister knight made regaling Father with what took place."

It was also partially exaggerated. They must have needed to report some sort of good news after the devastation in addition to delivering the declaration of war. All the while concealing the fact that he was now a Nascitte, it seemed.

Keeping a straight face after she said that was impossible. She was so excited by what she had been told. Bragging about it would only make him a liar and keeping silent would arouse suspicion. The only thing he could do was smile, nod, and say "Aye," however steadily he could.

"I am curious: how does it feel to wield such power?"

That was something Luchs could not lie about. "'Tis like carrying a double-edged sword in a way, one I have a difficulty wielding properly ... and cannot ever put down."

The description worried her for a moment, as well as the rest of the company, but the princess kept her smile. "Magic can be a fickle thing, at times having whims of its own. But worry not. It shall come naturally to you given time."

While ignorant of his power being the Second Verse, her words offered some comfort.

The princess was just as curious about the rest of her company, sharing her attention with everyone. Cael was not one for conversation, so he said little. Agnes told a great deal about the strong trade on Untaseau and how happy it made the people. The hallowed isle fared well, even after the brawl that broke out between the dockhands and a few guards belonging to a visiting nobleman. Mention of the sea goddess, Untae, brought the princess and her maid to humbly lower their heads and clap their hands together in a silent, second-long prayer.

The conversations were not as rough and rowdy as those with men and lads Luchs' age, but it was still enjoyable, and also relaxing. Without the shouting or barking or abrupt fighting, stress practically melted off Luchs' fatigued body. It was a chance to be at ease.

But as he picked up another crepe and brought it halfway to his waiting maw, the room and everything in it began slowly swaying. The colors and forms merged and blurred with one another in whichever way everything moved, the world smearing like paint on a canvas.

No one else seemed to notice the distortions.

Uh-oh!

Once again, the incessant thrashing broke out inside Luchs' skull. As it had on Emiet, the pain came suddenly, tearing at every crevice in his vulnerable brain, trudging across it as if it were being trampled by horse hooves. Every nerve in his body tensed up. Recoiling from the tremendous stress, he dropped the crepe he held and gripped both hands to his head, hunched over and grunting agonizingly. He gritted his teeth together in hopes of muzzling those weak, unsavory grunts. It was pointless, though. The others clearly saw something was wrong with him.

Agnes and the maid constantly asked what troubled him, their voices failing to breach the raucous thrashing in his mind. There was nothing they could do for him. It would come and pass.

The pain he could endure, but not what came with it. If he did not maintain control until the migraine passed, the earth beneath them would be torn asunder.

The pressure soon came to its apex, burrowing into the very center of his brain. He could feel his power begin to fluctuate, and it continued to worsen.

He could not do it. A quake was going to hit!

The valsara in the earth several floors beneath them began to reverberate, and that passed almost as soon as it was noticeable. The danger had suddenly subsided along with the pain.

When Luchs found the strength to open his eyes again, he looked up beside him and saw the princess, her small hand, surrounded in a veil of beauteous light, held just above his cranium where the pain agitated him the most. The light shone brightly, but did not blind, and left him at ease.

Once his mind finally settled, the light faded from Princess Camellia's hand, and she began to lose her balance. The maid noticed and stepped up to catch her, gripping her hands against her shoulders to support her. She was drained, something her gaze gave away, but the princess was okay; her smile reassured everyone of that.

"Luchs ... do you fare better now?"

Finally bringing himself to let go of his head, he found the thrashing had stopped, the discomfort brought to a minimum.

Luchs was in awe at her power, still breathless from witnessing the light. He got a hold of himself quickly so as not to discourage her. "A-Aye, Princess... Thank you, Princess." That was as much gratitude as he could muster at the moment.

Although the damage had been prevented, he worried what effect the Second Verse did have. His training had been put off for much too long. It was time to take back control. "Please excuse me."

Agnes tried to stop him as he took his leave, but Princess Camellia quickly called on her to stop, allowing Luchs to step outside. He rushed through the halls, making his way to the gardens.

~ Eleventh Chapter ~
Striking Back

The empty patch of earth at the edge of the Crown Plateau was the perfect place to practice with the Second Verse. No one went there, which guaranteed absolute privacy. The soil there was loose and moldable. Veils of mist blanketed the air, thick enough that inhaling rehydrated and revitalized the tired body. Only the sound of roaring waterfalls filled the area, a loud yet serene noise that put the soul at ease.

Luchs spent many hours at that plot. He mostly concentrated on focusing his magic sight and seeing how the valsara in the ground reacted to his influence. When he felt brave enough to attempt it, he began to sculpt the stone and soil into walls. They started out small, insignificant, brought up only past his ankles, but soon the practice strengthened his control and allowed him to do more.

As the days went by, he had been plagued by more thrashing migraines that disrupted his focus. No earthquakes broke out, fortunately, but anything he sculpted crumbled under the stress. Eventually, he learned why it happened.

It was another effect of the Second Verse. Through Ulrin and General Esperance he heard reports of soldiers moving throughout the archipelago. Wherever a battle ensued, the earth lightly shook from the collective vibrations, enough for Luchs to feel them. It was strange to sense movement against the ground from such incredible distances.

Figuring that out gave Luchs more reason to condition himself to the pressure. As a soldier, he would rush into countless battles and needed to be ready for it all. He would not progress unless he learned to deal with everything that troubled him.

He stubbornly kept at it. Whenever the pain returned, a battle ensuing, he forced himself to mold anything of the earth around him and maintain its shape. The effort put great strain on his mind, leaving the body weary. When the thrashing was at its worst, any figure he forged would shatter, the fragments scattering. So many struck at him that he went numb. So many times he nearly passed out from forcing himself to endure stress both physical and mental. It was almost like he had been putting himself through a torture all too familiar.

It was not until after two weeks of practice that he managed to condition himself to the vibrations and keep what he made together.

One day, Luchs asked Maxime to help in his training. His request was a simple one: Maxime would fire arrows at Luchs while he erected walls to shield him. It did not take much convincing for Maxime to agree. He needed to work on his aim, and he felt he owed him for what happened in Prévinn.

They put a fair distance between themselves before beginning, one standing where the grass stopped growing and the other surrounded by soil and stone. Maxime held his bow in hand and reached for an arrow from the quiver on his back, giving Luchs time to prepare.

Allowing the valsara in him to flow more freely, it left him feeling almost as empowered as he once was yet also feeling he could be crushed at any moment.

They began once Luchs signaled he was ready. Maxime quickly nocked an arrow and fired, aiming directly for the torso. Luchs responded swiftly, holding his right hand as if roughly grasping something and jutting it upward. He pulled a rugged slab out of the ground before him. The arrow bounced off the stone and flew off the cliff.

Maxime circled the slab as soon as the earth shifted. He did not want to leave any opportunity to react. Another arrow was nocked as Luchs caught sight of him. Lurching backward, he held onto that unusual grasp just as the arrow was shot, and threw his arm left. Another slab tore from the ground in an oblique curve, bouncing the arrow between two large stones near the plateau's cliff.

The cycle continued for a little while, and each shot fired was closer to meeting its mark than the last. It did not stop until Maxime had been stumped about how to penetrate the scale-like wall protecting his adversary.

The delay bored Luchs, his adrenaline dropping from inaction. After getting shot at so much, he wanted to start fighting back.

He concentrated his power and clenched his fists, then hurled his arm in the direction of the slab before him, causing its base to shatter and launching the fragments at the archer.

Maxime barely reacted in time before getting hit. He dropped to the ground, the stones flying into the mist. Instead of being furious with the sudden attack, he looked thrilled to see some retaliation. He got back up immediately, running with a spring in his step as another barrage of stones flew his way.

The two kept exchanging attacks one after the next. Neither gave an inch, neither lad wanting to lose, until finally an arrow flew past the stone defenses and pierced Luchs' right shoulder. The thin edge tore through the leather mail he wore, driving into him deep enough for the arrowhead to be buried in his flesh. He fell to one knee, and writhed in trying to get the arrow out.

Having never seen Luchs react so grievously to what he used to treat as a minor flesh wound, Maxime hurried to his side, kneeling beside him to see if he could help.

Blood oozed from the wound, something he was not used to seeing, at least not from him. "Guess you weren't jesting when you said you lost that thick skin of yours. Won't your old faction be surprised."

"Stow it and get this arrow out of me."

"Not here. We rip it out where we can patch you up. Come on, let's get back to the castle."

The injury was minor, so there were no complications. All he needed were a few stitches and the time for the wound to fully close.

The knights of Shoafond focused on attending to the needs of the civilians as the rest of the military combed the archipelago searching for the Convent of One. Individual soldiers were sent into the city every day to ensure everyone was content with their ordinary lives. Knights and squires performed a multitude of deeds—helping the merchants set up shop, escorting young women, children, and the elderly, offering friendly banter to bored passersby, even chasing after runaway chickens brought in by farmers.

It was all to keep them from focusing on the attacks across Ederea.

The king needed his people to believe they were still able to maintain their peaceful lives despite the threat plaguing their waters. Keeping them content, as General Esperance explained to his and Ulrin's squires, kept their faith in the military and morale strong. And seeing the good people work hard during the chaos motivated the soldiers to keep up the good fight.

It was important for everyone to keep in high spirits since the threat posed by the Convent of One was so great.

Reports proved it was no stroke of Lady Malute's misfortune that animals suddenly appeared to attack Prévinn. It happened everywhere the Convent of One reared their heads, on every island, in every town, forest, and even in crossfires at sea. Somehow, they managed to seize control over animals and used them as their pawns.

There were also mages in their ranks, much more than there were in service to the crown. All Ederea had were a handful of apprentices still learning the craft from an elderly mage who had seen better days.

The enemy had distinct advantages despite their debut. If left unchecked, they would overwhelm Ederea and leave it in ruins. That was why every general and their vast number of soldiers worked themselves ragged searching for the Convent of One's hiding place.

No matter where they struck or how many there were, their forces always managed to disappear as if never there. The Convent soldiers never focused on taking territory. They only attacked, left devastation behind, and vanished without a trace. They were provoking the Ederean forces, spiting them as they sowed chaos.

Whatever the enemy left behind offered the Edereans little information. Their weapons were unmarked by any unique sigil or name that proved who created them. Anyone captured for interrogation was soon found dead from a spell placed on them—one that Ederea's mage failed to identify. Effective in battle and impossible to track, the Convent of One was a truly terrifying force.

There was talk among the castle patrol that they were closing in on something, though.

One night, King Godefroy summoned many of his generals to inform them of their next move.

The king waited patiently for the available generals to arrive in the throne room, sitting on his throne with a rather intense stare. The attacks have left him tense and stressed, as they had for many.

Princess Camellia did not join them this time. There was instead another man standing proudly beside the king, a bald man wearing robes most would see donned by clergymen. General Esperance and Maxime explained that he was the king's royal advisor; the general's rough tone boded that he did not trust the man.

The rest of the assembly gathered in little time at all. It was then King Godefroy loosened up and stood from his throne. "My generals, 'tis good to see you all here this night," he spoke in a voice stern and proud. "We have been under siege by this enemy for some time now, and you've all taken great measures to oppose their atrocities. I thank you for all you have done thus far.

"Thanks to the efforts of General Aigle," said the king while gesturing to a man still recovering from ghastly injuries, "we now know something of these heretics."

The men took a moment to boisterously praise General Aigle and pat him on the back and shoulder. A few forgot to be careful of his wounds, ushering hearty laughter from the others.

"His scouts managed to track the movements of dozens of enemy ships. Many heroes lost their lives, though not in vain. Their sacrifices allowed General Aigle to tail them to Ciecime, the archipelago's northernmost island."

Luchs learned quite a bit about Ciecime while reading in the archives. That landmass was almost too large to be considered an island, and it supported more life than any land in the archipelago. However, the land was also perilous. It had remained largely unexplored due to the number of surveyors who have gotten lost there. A military base built there to serve as the surveyors' base of operations had long since been abandoned.

And it had been discovered and commandeered by the Convent of One, from what General Aigle reported. "We managed to take it back, but the enemy retreated inland. They used the mountains for cover, they did. We could only track them so far, but they're still there, lying in wait."

King Godefroy looked grievously intense for a moment but shook off whatever it was that bothered him, reclaiming his fierce mien. "Then we know what must be done. General Esperance, review the findings General Aigle provided. On the morrow, you shall take your forces and bring the fight to our enemy. Find whatever den they are hiding in, then torch it and leave nothing standing. Strike down everyone and don't let a single enemy escape to tell the tale. 'Tis high time this Convent of One paid the price for raising arms against Ederea!"

His zealous order brought the soldiers into a spirited uproar, everyone shaking their fists in the air and cheering. General Esperance took his leave upon receiving orders, his subordinates following him. They overheard King Godefroy give the other generals their tasks: to remain on high alert and expect heated retaliation.

Rather than wait until sunrise, General Esperance had everyone prepare for departure immediately while he reviewed the intel. Every soldier and squire gathered whatever necessities they required, storing it to be taken to the warship the coming morn.

Luchs' mind wandered when it came time to sleep. He could not help think he might disappoint the general and make Ulrin look bad again. All he needed to do was remain close to his meister knight, but he still worried. This mission they were given was different than their last.

It was impossible to sleep that night.

At sunrise, every available soldier from the Sea Drake Company boarded their vessel. Preparations were completed quickly, their general eager to complete his task with haste. Soon, the gangplanks were drawn in, the sails were unfurled, and the order to sail had been given. Their vessel left the bay before the merchants set up their kiosks.

The seas were lively as of late. The waves swayed the boat strongly and the winds struck the sails firmly. It was nothing but the expansive ocean blue underneath the clear skies for much of the voyage, barely a cloud to cast shade.

On occasion, they would pass an island a few of the knights called home. They rushed over to the side of the ship when that happened and shouted excitably to the land as if expecting a reply. It was a common thing to do among knights who have not set foot on their home soil for some time. Many believed that Zyleec, the child god of the wind, would carry their voice to distant loved ones they could not yet see.

Seeing them left Luchs longing for a place he could shout to.

Everyone had been hard at work from sunrise to sunset. The crew awoke at dawn to ensure everything was shipshape. Once that was out of the way, the knights took turns sparring with one another, putting one soldier against another; two would face off and the winner would continue without rest until he himself lost. The other knights put Luchs through more strife than usual, but he still left an impression.

Much of the ship went to rest at dusk save for the few keeping watch and the general and lieutenant reviewing battle strategies.

General Esperance received a crude map from General Aigle depicting the terrain they tracked the enemy through. Their squires looked over their work, taking notes. They used chess pieces to represent theirs and the enemy's troops and to hold the parchment down. Much of what they did was guesswork since they did not have an exact location of the Convent or knowledge of the terrain, but immediate changes could be made once in the situation.

The general gave serious thought to potential traps and ambushes laid out for trespassers. Mages were to be expected also. So many things could go wrong if anyone made a single misstep.

Zyleec treated the voyagers well. The strong winds ushered the warship to sail at great speed, bringing them to land in record time. And what they landed upon was breathtaking.

Ciecime comprised of colossal mountains stretching almost high enough to pierce the heavens. There was very little beach to the shores, grass growing several feet from the salty waters. A once-abandoned stronghold stood not far from the water.

General Esperance announced his arrival upon docking and checked in on the man overseeing the stronghold while the troops unloaded their gear. He found out plenty about the Ciecime from him. While a map was helpful, actual directions offered by people who had experience traversing the landscape were invaluable.

Horses would be of no help unless they planned to take them for a few hundred yards and then leave them to fend for themselves. Too much uneven ground and trees lined the only open footpath into the mountain range. Every step led to higher and higher ground, the path soon becoming pure stone.

When General Esperance and his soldiers began the climb and scaled the path, they found a mountain wall that split open into a usable passage past thick layers of tall grass that stretched up to the squires' necks. It took a while for everyone to squeeze through.

The flora grew more rampant past the earthen wall. They had to chop down the vines and tall grass in front of them or risk going in blind.

The expedition grew more difficult with their vision becoming obscured so constantly. Everyone needed to remain together, and those in the rear had to blindly follow the ones taking the lead.

A compass did them no good. The needle spun like a wheel on a runaway wagon. It was a strange phenomenon everyone with the tool found after crossing the mountain barrier. The navigator got flustered and almost threw it away, forgetting it hung on a string around his neck.

The party spent hours moving to higher ground so they could get a better layout of the terrain. More stone lined the bumpy path from then on. Exposure to the fresh air and open gusts was refreshing yet irritated the exposed skin that rubbed against tall grass and thick plants for so long. The path was relatively clear, but it thinned continuously. They were often trapped between a stone wall and a steep slopes with a long drop.

They rested when the moon rose. On the first night, they camped atop a flat upland with the perfect viewpoints to see any incoming threats and boulders that provided fine cover. Most of the soldiers found it difficult to breathe after going so high up. The air was different there compared to the highlands across the archipelago.

Everyone was so exasperated, but Luchs felt perfectly fine. In fact, the environment agreed with him. Resting up for about twenty minutes or so was nice after all that climbing, but he could still go much farther after the brief rest.

Although unused to the thin air, the party managed to keep going the next morning. The terrain brought them to even higher ground, giving them a better look at the land but straining the soldiers' lungs further. They needed to rest much more often.

One evening, when Luchs contemplated asking if they should turn back for everyone's sake, he looked down from the mountain at the glorious ocean waters turned golden by the setting sun, the lower peaks shimmering in the light. It was a beautiful sight.

He wondered if it were possible, if they scaled to the highest peak, to see all of Ederea.

The next day, after moving north of Treasure Point, as Luchs chose to call it, they discovered a shadowy footpath that led to lower ground. They were at a crossroads again. Should they take the more concealed path, they would give up their aerial viewpoint. It would be a risk, and one that they soon agreed was worth taking. A scout was sent down the path and returned with a torn up white flag in hand. It bore strange black markings that together resembled a runic eye—the very same many have seen branded on the Convent of One's warriors.

They were on the right path.

The mountain path converged with a lowland copse within the valley. When the sun began to set again, they found themselves atop a tall hill overlooking a quaint settlement tucked in with the trees.

A village?

From where they were, they could see it was not recently built; development progressed too far for that. Plenty of humble buildings stood, and there was a well dug. There were stone walls in place, but they were no taller than a few feet, used to keep out wildlife.

Luchs looked upon the village confused and uneasy. A place like that meant there had to be more there than the enemy they set out to find. Others lived there, others that probably never picked up a sword.

Everyone remained on standby while General Esperance evaluated the situation. He stared down at the village with a spyglass, his severe expression never changing.

"No one's outside," said the general while putting his spyglass down. "They must be at rest."

"There's no visible guard. And they didn't even bother with ambushes," Maxime blurted out.

"Or countermeasures to keep Aigle's men from following them as far as they did," Ulrin added curiously.

"Mayhap they are just acting cautiously," Luchs boldly stated.

"If'n that's so, then they would have something to show they fear being discovered. They would at least have a patrol set up, something to alert everyone of a threat."

General Esperance nodded. "Aye. The Lieutenant is right. Something is amiss, but that won't change what must be done. Advance to the village! March swiftly, but remain alert to aught you come across. The enemy is cunning and merciless. Grant no quarter in return!"

The general drew his sword and raced down the hill quick as an agitated boar.

Ulrin chuckled while taking his spear in hand. "Always the reckless one, that lout. Let's advance in waves then." He rushed to his general's side after giving orders, wanting to make sure he caught up with him.

Luchs and Maxime followed along with a handful of knights. The archers allowed the others to make some distance between them before following with bows in hand, ready to let arrows fly at any moment.

Luchs made sure to get to the bottom of the hill first. With the enemy unaware of them, it meant they could change the raze mission to a capture mission. No knight would attack anyone unarmed, after all. The only chance he had to limit bloodshed was to convince the enemy to surrender, and capturing their leader would promise just that.

Everyone soon reached the base of the hill and breached the village walls without any interference. They took their steps vigilantly, observing everything around them. With his magic sight, Luchs peered through every house to see the activity inside. He did not need to know what went on in a person's valsara to see it.

He only saw the energy in the surrounding plants and earth.

General Esperance stepped up to a small, shoddy hovel and fiercely tore the doorknob off. He barged inside only to find the cramped space was empty. No one was there. Everyone remained on alert in case anyone decided to jump out of hiding while they were confused.

But nothing happened. No one came out of hiding. And, from what Luchs could see, no one was hiding at all.

That could not be. There had to be someone.

Tracks were seen hither and thither, but there were too many to follow. There were what appeared to be kiosks past the first row of houses, each one with some sort of good lined on shelves or sorted in baskets. A lit lantern was left lying on the side of the road with a little bit of oil still left inside. Signs of past human activity were everywhere, and yet it looked like they stepped into a ghost town.

More soldiers joined in the confusion upon arriving. They were just as startled to find the village empty as the rest of them. A few squires, wanting to prove their mettle in actual battle, looked disappointed that there was no one to fight.

A few scouts searched the other houses and returned with nothing.

"There's really no one here," one of the soldiers exclaimed.

"Could it be General Aigle was misled?" asked another.

General Esperance leered at the questioning knights. "General Aigle studied under the kingdom's finest spymaster before becoming the leader he is. He doesn't make careless mistakes, nor does he allow them of his soldiers."

"Then where are they?" asked Maxime.

The sun came to rest against the mountain tops, its glare rolling over Luchs' eyes and obscuring his vision. When he raised his hand to cover his eyes, he noticed a faint fuchsia glimmer in the distance. It was a little farther down the road, inside the village.

He ran toward the valsara he sensed without a word. His meister knight rushed after him, as did others.

Down the path, standing before a large chapel with an unusual symbol over its doors, was a man donning dark leather garb that blended in well with the shadows, his arms crossed. He was lean, his eyes imposing, and he was armed with two swords, one sheathed at his right hip and the other against his back.

"Wait, is that—"

Ulrin caught up with his squire and looked surprised by the man's presence. "Executioner Sörrign?"

Luchs took an immediate step back when he heard that name.

An executioner? Here? But why?

When General Esperance laid eyes on the executioner, his gaze became more intense, his valsara flaring enough for Luchs to feel his disdain.

Executioner Sörrign shifted his dry glance at the general and stared him down for a moment. "I was wondering when you would arrive, Eurieg." His voice was rough yet clear and calm, projecting his words powerfully throughout the area.

"What are you doing here, Executioner?"

"I could ask you the same."

That snide, vague response only elicited more fury from General Esperance. The man was not pleased with the constant surprises. He wanted answers and intended to get them. He looked ready to snarl another question, but he withheld from speaking, beginning to ascertain what his presence meant.

Some thought he came to personally wipe the enemy out. Luchs feared as such for a moment, but he knew it not to be true. Death's malignant odor did not pollute the air. There were no bodies or bloodstains anywhere. Executioners were responsible for eliminating individual threats to the country. Had he taken on the mission assigned to them and killed so many, he would not be able to erase the evidence, as expected of his role, in time. There would have been signs to show for his work.

"Dastard!" General Esperance barked. "Where are they?"

"They?"

"Don't play coy! The heretics! You warned them we were coming, didn't you? Where are they!?"

General Esperance's words left his party too shocked to react. An executioner, one of the kingdom's most loyal warriors, turning his back on Ederea and siding with the enemy? It was unthinkable. No one could believe anyone given that position would perform such an atrocity. Everyone knew Executioner Sörrign was not Ederea-born, but it was still hard to think he would do such a thing.

Even facing the general's ire, Executioner Sörrign remained calm and nonchalant. "After going through all the trouble, what makes you think I'll just hand them over?"

That was practically a confession. He blatantly admitted to aiding the enemy.

"Traitor!"

"You've only yourself to blame, Eurieg. Had you arrived half a day sooner, you might have been able to carry out your orders and offer us a little trouble."

"*Us?* ...Where's your squire?"

"Van? I lost track of him a while ago. He probably went to look after those Kyrovide. That kid is too sentimental for knighthood, let me tell you."

General Esperance took a tighter grip of his sword, his fist shaking, the metal rattling from how much strain his muscles used. The valsara around it became so intense, so fierce that Luchs flinched, unused to feeling such malice. "He won't need to worry about knighthood, nor you about him. We'll tear apart all of Ciecime to find them all if we must, after I take your head!"

He charged at the executioner, fully intent on doing as he exclaimed.

Executioner Sörrign did not so much as flinch. As the general closed in, he quickly held his left hand for the onyx sword at his hip and drew it skyward, intercepting the general's attack and knocking him back. The soldiers were in awe watching him overpower the hardened general.

The general's arms were trembling uncontrollably after impact. It took a great deal of willpower to force them still.

"Seize him!"

A wry grin drew over Executioner Sörrign's face, and a cold, ghastly laugh passed his lips. "Yes," he uttered as he drew his free hand for the hilt behind his head. "Come at me. Show me what you can do against these!" Fast as lightning he drew a scimitar, and its blade became engulfed in brilliant flames. The weapon was enchanted.

As was the other one. A glance at it with his magic sight allowed Luchs to see a veil of energy spiraling tightly around the onyx sword. It was little wonder he could throw the general back so effortlessly; it had enough power inside to fend off ten men in a single swing.

No one dared approach Executioner Sörrign carelessly. With two magic weapons at his disposal, he could ruin them all. General Esperance and Ulrin remained stalwart, as have their pages and a few soldiers attempting to circle him.

"Aye, good. Cut off any escape. The rest of you, set this place ablaze! Leave the heretics with nothing to come back to!"

Those too intimidated of their foe followed General Esperance's order and scattered, lighting torches and setting fire to every structure. The sight was disturbing, but Luchs put it outside his mind. There was no one inside. No one was dying. They were just keeping monsters from coming back. He faced the traitor, shield up and sword at the ready, trying to convince himself they were doing what was right.

Several knights bravely charged the executioner. He tossed them aside effortlessly, feigning with the flaming blade and slamming the onyx sword where they left themselves open.

He was only playing with them.

He looked more villainous as the flames grew around them, the light twisting his amused countenance into something nightmarish. Those who had yet to charge stood petrified, fearing they were about to go toe-to-toe with an actual demon.

Their wills began dwindling when the infernal flames around them lost their heat, a chilling gust sweeping through the air.

Luchs lost focus of the enemy before him. That wind was not just unnatural, it felt familiar.

The wind picked up, blowing across the village, slowly building in strength until it howled. The fires were quickly snuffed out.

Executioner Sörrign looked to be more interested in the wind than swatting at his foes like flies. He kept looking back to where it blew. "Hm. Looks like he made his way back."

The gusts, guided by an ethereal power, kept getting stronger, never letting up. Many trembling against them, unaccustomed to the chilling cold. They had to keep moving, though, because if they did not, frost slowly crept up their legs and threatened to freeze them.

Despite the deathly cold, some kept attempting to burn the houses. But it was pointless. The flames they lit barely lasted longer than a second.

Suddenly, in a near instant, walls of razor-sharp ice tore across the road, blocking the soldiers off from the houses. From those walls, another mass of ice clustered around the warriors still opposing Executioner Sörrign, trapping the general, Ulrin, Luchs, Maxime, and several others with him in a frigid colosseum.

There was a ferocious valsara, surging in sync with the gusts of wind, overhead. Its source closed in fast, looming directly over Maxime with a sword in hand. Luchs took fast action, racing to his comrade's side and stood between him and the assailant. He held his shield up to meet the weapon that nearly split Maxime's head open.

The assailant was Vandelas Kronas.

Sparks flew from the colliding metal and the impact pushed Luchs a little. The lad was stronger than his sinewy arms and thin body led on. And his eyes—harrowing. There was great ferocity in his stare, and as the moon began to ascend, there was a glow to them that made him appear demonic.

"Craven whelp!" Maxime charged at Vandelas, who stood with a sword in his right hand and its scabbard in his left, and hurled his sword at him. The svelte lad brought his scabbard to meet the attack, its dull surface colliding with and dragging the sword off its mark, throwing Maxime off balance. Vandelas spun and rushed at Luchs with his sword held low, preparing to draw it in an uppercut. Not wanting to remain on the defensive, Luchs hurled his blade in a horizontal swing. He put all his strength into it, but somehow had been overpowered and flicked aside while the lesser man danced about.

Overwhelmed by disbelief and frustration, the squires rushed after him together. They raised their swords and threw them down in unison. Vandelas leaned low and darted to the side, twisting his body and narrowly slicing Maxime's hip.

Luchs barely managed to keep from colliding with and tripping over his comrade.

His wound was small and the bleeding slow, not enough to cause concern yet.

What is he doing?

While Maxime charged again, bent on taking revenge, Luchs waited and watched how Vandelas moved.

Again, a direct assault proved ineffective. As if sensing how and when he was going to strike, Vandelas met the attack with his scabbard, disoriented his foe with a small spin, then countered with a blunt strike at Maxime's upper leg. The control he had of himself and his weapon was uncanny. His sword always fell somewhere away from the torso while still inflicting pain. His strikes were not random, not with such precision and timing.

Was he just playing with them like his meister?

Luchs felt in his gut that was not true. He was holding back. But there was something about him that was deadly serious.

"What game are you playing at?" Luchs asked.

Vandelas looked his way after smacking Maxime aside again. "You think this a game?"

"Why're you doing this? Why betray us for the Convent?"

Maxime got up again to attack but held back for a moment. He was in a similar situation with Luchs once before. They circled the lad, the cold becoming too much for them to remain still.

"I've no desire to aid the Convent of One."

Maxime held his tongue before speaking, then thought of something. "So he forced you? You're just following your meister's orders then?"

"I came here of my own will. I wanted to save the villagers."

"You're not making sense, laddie." Luchs retorted. "The people here are the Convent of One!"

"You're wrong!" His voice was heavy and stern, much different from how he normally spoke. Vandelas stared them down with ferocity befitting a beast ready to pounce, a cold vapor wafting around his body. Before the squires went on the offensive, he breathed deeply, condensing the vapor. "They may worship the same god, but those people have nothing to do with that cult. They've done nothing to Ederea. They are innocent!"

"Innocent!?" barked Maxime.

"Didn't you notice? This isn't a military base. It's just an ordinary village. The people who call this place home are no threat. They don't deserve to be invaded."

That was all the general's squire needed to hear before going on the attack again. He attempted to catch him off guard while he spoke, charging at his side and raising his sword high for decapitation. It was for naught. Vandelas moved out of the way quickly, spinning, taking power from the momentum and jabbing his scabbard in the back of Maxime's head, knocking him to the ground. The blunt blow did not keep him there, but getting back up to fight only resulted in the same thing, again and again, until finally a swift kick to the torso knocked the wind out of him, and his sword from his hands. Maxime collapsed to the ground, falling unconscious.

It was just Luchs and the dancing sword now.

"They don't deserve this."

"How do you know?"

"Wolfram told me everything I need to know."

"How does he know?"

"He led me here. He showed them to me. The people here aren't killers. When he told them your company was coming to destroy them, they were terrified. They all thought they were going to die."

"The Convent came here, right? They came to this village."

"And that's all it takes to condemn the people who live here?"

"You protect them knowing they harbored the enemy?"

"Razing another's home won't save Ederea. Saying it will is just a weak excuse to justify slaughter."

Luchs was speechless. They were following the will of the king, and he called it weakness.

"Unknown people came into your home, Luchs, and took you from all you knew. Are you willing to go a step further than that and take everything from these people?"

Those words made Luchs close his ears to him. Hearing him compare his torture, an experience he told him about in confidence, to those who involved themselves with the force trying to destroy his new home nearly made Luchs froth at the mouth. "They're not me. They're heretics, monsters who destroy everything in their path!"

"They have never left this place, never taken up arms against anyone, least of all Ederea."

"Shut up."

"The villagers aren't the monsters here. You, and your general, and the king all—"

"Shut up!"

Enraged, Luchs rushed at Vandelas ready to take the kill.

To use the moment he lost it all, to talk to him as though he understood what he felt, it made him burn with rage, a rage that guided his sword to the traitor's heart.

Again, Vandelas caught the attack on his scabbard and danced around his foe, but Luchs did not falter from the bizarre movement. He caught his footing and turned to face him just as he readied for another attack. He kept at it, hurling himself at Vandelas with full force.

No matter how he attacked or where he struck, Vandelas defended himself accordingly. Each failed attack infuriated Luchs further.

How tempting it was to use his Second Verse and tear apart the ground from underneath him, or use the stone beneath him to tear through him. But it was too risky. There were too many nearby he did not want to be caught in the carnage.

It took a few tries, but Luchs managed to figure out how to move when thrown by Vandelas' attack. He caught himself from the distraught momentum by the heel and turned to face him while he still spun. Taking his sword in both hands, he rushed at Vandelas to run him through.

As Vandelas slowed, though, he kicked at the ground to keep spinning. That crazed movement brought his blade against Luchs' with incredible strength, enough to knock the weapon from his grasp. The scabbard slammed against his chest, knocking him against the icy wall. While slowing down, Vandelas returned his scabbard to the holster at his hip, then reached skyward when Luchs' sword fell over him, effortlessly catching it at the handle, and held it directly at its former wielder.

Luchs became rigid seeing his sword turned against him. There was nothing he could do. If he tried anything, Vandelas would use that sword to keep him there; the enraged look in his eyes assured him of that.

It was hopeless. He lost. All he could do was hope his meister knight had better luck in his fight.

The furious brawl around the traitorous Wolfram Sörrign subsided, leaving only General Esperance and Ulrin still opposing him. Both of them were fighting for breath, covered in cuts and burns, and struggled to keep control of their own arms. Their adversary, on the other hand, still stood tall with nary a scratch on him.

A smear of blood drew from Ulrin's forehead, trickling over his right eye. "I take it this is why His Majesty dubbed him 'Wolfram the Iron Will.' I admit, the title suits him."

"Don't give him any credit," General Esperance ordered. "Without those weapons, without his magic, he'd be dead."

No response from the executioner. He stared his enemies down, carefully monitoring their movements, waiting for them to pounce. Like his squire, he had nothing to lose in taking the defensive. The only time he drew his attention from them was to examine the fiery blade in his right hand. The flames never wavered despite being bombarded by the frigid winds.

Then his gaze shifted to the onyx sword in his left hand. "Hm..." With deathly slow movement, he drew the fire-coated sword up and returned it to the sheath behind him, the light swallowed up. "Shall we finish this?"

His insinuation that he could crush them both with just the onyx sword wounded their pride and drove General Esperance and Ulrin to charge at him together. Once more did the executioner draw the sword at his back, reigniting the flames with more forceful heat than it had earlier. Dragging his foot across the ground, he spun while pulling the fiery sword dangerously close, scarcely dodging the thrust of Ulrin's spear, and drew it across the onyx sword, dragging their flat sides along each other. The flames grew ever brighter and were hurled in an explosive wave across the colosseum of ice, the blast shaking its walls and making it crumble.

The blast sent General Esperance and Ulrin, and even Vandelas, flying and crashing into the remains of their prison. Wolfram Sörrign still stood at the center, the scattered embers flittering across the air around him. The scarlet scimitar's flames were extinguished in that one maneuver.

He sheathed both of his weapons and walked to where his squire had flown, letting the wind slowly snuff out the small sparks on his sleeves. "Stand up, kid," he ordered. "We still have work to do."

For a moment, Vandelas only responded with heavy huffing, a hoarse voice riddled with pain. The vapor he exuded earlier now covered his entire body in thick clouds.

"Stand!"

By the order of his meister, he found the strength to move, but his body shook and his legs wobbled. It was surprising that he could keep himself up at all. Seeing Luchs still conscious, he limply trudged across the crumbled ice, mindful of the fallen nearby. He stopped before Luchs tensely, then he clenched his fist and rammed it into his gut.

Luchs' vision blacked out, his consciousness slipping away.

~ Twelfth Chapter ~
Small World

Somehow, General Esperance's party ended up in Ciecime's stronghold. No one was missing or dead, just injured.

The general had trouble moving without the aid of his squire, who merely suffered a slight concussion. He refused to back down against the traitor who saved the heretics, and that determination earned him grievous injuries. Ulrin fared better than his superior, but his burns needed constant attention.

And, adding insult to injury, the ones who brought them to the stronghold were the traitors themselves.

The soldiers of the stronghold saw Executioner Sörrign and his squire bringing the unconscious soldiers down the mountain path in pushcarts. At first, they simply claimed they were not successful in their mission, but further questioning brought the executioner to confess they attacked the Sea Drake Company. They were detained in the dungeon without a fight.

As soon as General Esperance learned what transpired, he organized a party of the stronghold's men and sent them to torch the village. They were shown the exact paths taken to get there, but could not find their way.

The village had completely disappeared. There were no buildings or even the rancid stench from the stables to show they were close. Everything was gone.

General Esperance interrogated Executioner Sörrign personally, shouting heinous slurs and barking demands for five hours straight until losing his voice. He knew the gossip about the man's knowledge of magic, about the hexes he cast in secret, with the king's consent no less. It was all rumors spread about the recluse who only showed himself to make a kill, but the general believed them to be true.

Again, Wolfram had no trouble admitting what he did. He did not bring with him two magic weapons; there was a third he used to mask the village's location by distorting the space around it. That was all he cared to share, though. He said nothing about how to undo the spell, no matter how General Esperance threatened him.

Some of the squires took it upon themselves to question the other prisoner. Vandelas was more taciturn than his meister. Nary a word left his lips. He would not say anything about the spell, why he would not talk, or whether or not he was scared about his imminent execution. One of the squires, growing agitated from the silence, took the flaming sword confiscated from the executioner and threatened to make his body a giant, festering burn scar if he did not talk.

The fire made him cringe, but he did nothing more than that. He kept his silence.

If it were not for Luchs' intervention, that squire would have kept good on his threat. There were a few moments he wondered why he bothered to defend him. He was a traitor, after all.

But he doesn't deserve that. ...Does he?

Since they were not getting answers, Ulrin suggested they return to the court and have King Godefroy deal with the traitors, as their protocol dictated.

The soldiers boarded their warship, their prisoners tossed into the brig, and were on their way back home. Everyone was constantly on edge worrying about their prisoners potentially escaping and causing havoc. There was not a soul among them who believed the two simply turned themselves in after fighting them all off.

On the third night at sea, when the waters were calm and the winds gentle, many inquired with the general and lieutenant of what happened to them in their bout against Wolfram. Proud to a fault, General Esperance would not humor his subordinates and chastised them after being asked, then put them to work for pestering him. Ulrin, on the other hand, knew well not everyone would accept going without an answer, and told them all he could remember.

"Treacherous though he may be, that executioner is incredibly skilled. He made sport of us mostly, the lout. Sometimes he'd make a feint with the black sword and hit with the fiery one, sometimes the other way around. Honestly, the enchanted steel wasn't the worst of it—made tolerating that freak storm much easier, it did. But he never left any openings. And whenever we tried to intervene when he clashed with another, he moved fast as the wind and pushed the one he crossed blades with into the other, then punished us with that black sword. That accursed thing... It left my arms numb and wobbly whenever meeting my spear.

"Still, 'twas quite a bout. Were the circumstances different, I'd love to go against him again in single-combat."

The recognition from their lieutenant, while unexpected, left everyone in awe. Perhaps it was his strength that brought the king to deem him worthy enough to be his executioner.

How unfortunate that the choice led to this.

Word had been sent to Castle Ederea regarding the treason via carrier bird days earlier, long before they arrived in Shoafond.

King Godefroy stood from his throne the moment General Esperance entered ahead of the knights guiding Executioner Sörrign and Vandelas by the manacles. Beside him stood six other men donning garb similar to their prisoner, and—not as important—standing smugly by one of the pillars was the king's advisor.

It was customary for executioners to execute one of their own together should he betray the crown. Although rare, the formality served to represent the king taking responsibility for trusting him. They were each armed with an enchanting ceremonial sword that shimmered in the light.

However, before sentencing, a trial was held so that the guilty could confess their crimes and reflect upon them.

King Godefroy glared at the two chained while those restraining them forced them to kneel. He approached them and stopped close enough so that the traitors could see his frustration and disappointment.

Both of the prisoners looked the king directly in the eye, neither appearing intimidated. Despite their positions, they were still resolute.

"Wolfram," spoke King Godefroy gravely, "in the twenty-five years you served me, you've proven yourself loyal time and again. Yet after all this time, you choose to defy my word and sabotage General Esperance's mission. Why? What possible reason could you have for protecting our enemy?"

"I've gone only to test my weapons, Godefroy. Nothing more."

No one was pleased with such a dry response, and the informality he addressed the king with made the other executioners look like they were ready to skip to the sentencing. King Godefroy, however, kept his disappointed stare as he motioned for Luchs to step forward. For some reason, they were informed he wished for the weapons Executioner Sörrign wielded to be brought to the trial.

Carrying both carefully, Luchs brought forth the weapons held in his arms on an old cloth. King Godefroy looked them over for a moment, then took the onyx sword, unsheathing it, and held it a hair's length from its owner's face.

"I've seen you wield Avvär before. An intricate sword, truly. If'n I remember it so, it disrupts the flow of magic it cuts through and breaks the control a man has over his muscles, even indirectly. I doubt you merely went to test your creations in bringing this."

Creations? Did he make those swords himself?

Executioner Sörrign smirked and chortled. "You always had such strange ways to describe my weapons."

"The traitor takes this for a game of sorts," declared the king's advisor. "You have been graciously granted the opportunity to repent for your sins, Wolfram Sörrign. Answer your king. Did you just lie about your intentions?"

"Fine. You caught me. I didn't go to test Avvär—just Anktung."

The advisor glared at Executioner Sörrign and looked like he wanted to continue, but one look from King Godefroy made him stay silent.

"You once told me of how you arrived in Ederea," King Godefroy continued. "After sailing from the north, you became shipwrecked in Ciecime and wandered the landscape. You met the natives before making your way to this very isle. Is this true?"

"'Tis as you say. As it happens, that village we evacuated was where I rested and restocked supplies. A fine people—not concerned about the outside, just their practice and their own. Their religion was difficult to understand; they thought the same of me, but they paid me no mind. They simply offered me a place to stay and food to eat before sending me on my way." The executioner spoke wistfully of that time, showing his experience to be enjoyable. "They and I are alike, in a way. We care more for ourselves than others." An odd thing to say after speaking so fondly of them. "Regardless of the situation they're in, I have my own matters to take care of. I've not forgotten the accord we made together years ago. I grant you my strength and a small share of my work, and in exchange, you secure and provide the materials I need to forge my magic weapons. Our mutually beneficial relationship lasted so long to fulfill that purpose.

"But this kid here can be amusingly persuasive."

Everyone was aghast with his claim. He was putting the blame for his actions on Vandelas, his squire. Those who looked his way noticed the lad neither denied nor reacted to those words, but kept staring at the king.

"After I told him what I knew about the Kyrovide, he was livid, outraged even, demanding we put a stop to your attack. 'A fool's errand

and a waste of time,' I told him, but that was before he claimed 'twas a wonderful opportunity to test my newest creation. And he certainly wasn't wrong. The Drake Fang's fire is sublime. And because I brought Avvär along, I was able to find a new—"

"That is enough!" the royal advisor interrupted shrilly. He marched up to the king and the prisoners. The way he overreacted almost made it seem like he was the one being mocked, not the king.

No wonder General Esperance did not approve of him, the way he carried himself thinking he was in control.

"Most illustrious King Godefroy, this trial is a farce. Wolfram Sörrign has already admitted to sympathizing with the heretics, to defying your order, and now claims to have allowed a child's emotional prattling to sway his already flawed judgment. What sort of man lets his own squire pull the reins?" After appearing tyrannical and raving, he turned to face the king and looked at him as if to express sympathy. "Mayhap you chose him, Your Majesty, but a man's choice can only influence so much. His actions revealed his true colors. He has chosen to meddle with your righteous cause, further risk the lives of good Edereans, and to interfere with justice and mock the noble goa—"

"Noble? Noble!? What do dreck like you know about being noble!?"

That was not the executioner who howled so heinously, but the small, quiet squire who had yet spoken anything in their defense. His voice echoed callously throughout the throne room, the hate it carried a potent venom. He shot daggers at the king's advisor, bringing him to freeze in place, while the once tame valsara within him suddenly ran erratic, threatening to destroy the shell containing it. Everyone near him backed away, as if fearing a beast would pounce and tear their throats out. "You think setting fire to a village, destroying people's homes, is noble? Or slaughtering those who never took up arms? Do you realize how demented that sounds!? Retaliating is one thing, but these men were sent to end their lives just because they worship a different god! That's not justice!" He shot his gaze at King Godefroy, who stood there horrorstruck. "They very nearly committed genocide in your name!"

Luchs never saw Vandelas so angry or heard him speak so loudly, so ferociously before. What he said resonated with the soldiers, all of them turning to one another, silently questioning what they had almost done.

With his rage and hostility in the air, Vandelas' valsara started to calm, leaving a child where the beast once was. "Such destruction only breeds hatred and contempt. If we allowed that attack to happen, then those you branded heretics in Ciecime would seek to condemn you to the same loss."

The dark lad stopped a moment, then thrashed about, startling the soldier holding him in place. The effort was only to shed the amber scarf from his neck, freeing his jaw and revealing these arrow-shaped crimson brands beneath his eyes. "My homeland was razed, my people burned, all by a force I know nothing about. And every day I go without answers, every waking moment spent without knowing why the Kindhrin were forced to face that cruel fate, my hatred continues to grow." The moment of vulnerability passed, and Vandelas quickly bore a resolute stare at the king. "You knew they were there. You might not have known where, but you knew those people were there all this time. And you've done nothing to them up until now. If mindlessly slaughtering innocents truly was your plan, then I was a fool to believe you were a ruler worth following!"

The soldier pinning him in place shoved him to the ground harder for showing such disrespect.

The king's advisor stepped furiously up to Vandelas and shot him a nasty glare, then leaned down and slapped his face. "You forget your place, child," he hissed. "This misguided child understands nothing. The heretics, the Covent of One—there is no difference between them! They worship the same so-called god and wish us all dead because we refuse to do the same. Our way of life has been threatened by these devils, our people endangered and killed, our oceans infested! If allowed to act without correction, they will destroy Ederea. We cannot allow sentiment to lead us astray. We must not—"

"Enough!"

King Godefroy silenced his advisor and drew everyone's rapt attention back to him.

Silence befell the throne room. Long moments passed as everyone stared at the still King Godefroy, waiting for him to make his decision. He looked to the prisoners, then at the onyx sword in his hand. With resolution in his eyes, he sheathed the sword and faced everyone again.

"Release them."

Everyone was awestruck by his decision, but the guards, respectful of their king, did as commanded. General Esperance looked ready to speak up as their manacles were unlocked, but he restrained himself. It was the king's will, so it would be done.

The only one opposing that choice was the royal advisor. He was completely stunned as Vandelas bent down to retrieve his scarf and rewrap it around his neck and face, trembled and clenched his fists when Wolfram Sörrign reclaimed Avvär from King Godefroy. Then, as the forgiven executioner was about to retake his sword, the advisor marched up to the king in a huff.

"Your Majesty, you cannot be serious! They interfered with a holy mission—"

"Nay, Muir. They put a stop to a foolish endeavor before it began. And for the better, says I. Even the conquerors before my time would frown upon such a cowardly act."

"C-Cowardly?"

"Aye, cowardly. Only scum seek to endanger the innocent to hurt their enemy. Listening to you about this almost sullied my name as King. I'm only still worthy to rule *because* they rejected the choice I made out of fear of the enemy."

"You are right to fear the Convent. Everyone does. They seek to destroy us!"

"Silence! I am the king! My word is law! And I refuse to allow my judgment to be clouded anymore—by fear *and* by you! Guards, take this bishop to his chambers and keep him there until a ship to La Kriod arrives."

The same soldiers who restrained the former prisoners dutifully marched to their king's side and restrained Muir. The disgraceful man was dragged out of the throne room kicking and screaming, behaving no differently than an undisciplined child.

How did someone like him become a bishop? More appropriately, how did he manage to win King Godefroy's trust and earn the role of his advisor?

With the verdict passed, the other executioners took their ceremonial swords and left the throne room along with most of the other soldiers. It was discouraging to see most of the people came just to see an execution. Then again, everyone was so convinced of their guilt earlier. And they likely did not accept their innocence yet either.

Castle Ederea was much livelier for the next few days. Word spread about the king showing mercy to the two traitors, and many were not happy about it. The king was seen in a better light, but people also became more pessimistic about those he forgave.

Luchs was leaving the archives when he saw Maxime leaning against a windowsill overlooking the training grounds. He watched as a group of squires below fought with Vandelas.

"They still at it?" Luchs asked when approaching.

Maxime nodded. "Since dawn, one after another, and more keep showing up to give him a piece of their mind. I'd wonder how the foreigner could last so long if not for—" One squire rushed at Vandelas at that moment, only to be countered in a few steps and get smacked aside. "Well, that. What's he doing, fighting or dancing?"

"'Tis effective, whatever you call it. Knocked us on our arses, it did."

From the looks of it, the other squires had as much luck against the strange technique they did. All it took were a few swift swings of the sword after countering them and they were swept off their feet.

The memory of their fight against him did not sit well with Maxime. His fists were clenched together and his eyes displayed an uneasy rage. "Cheap tricks, that's all they are!"

For a time, Luchs wanted to believe that. Tricks only fooled people for so long, though, and looking down at the brawl, he could see more to his technique than mere trickery. Vandelas saw what they were doing. He put strength into his attacks, and not just his own. Somehow, his movements allowed him to use the strength from an attacker to stop them in their tracks, disorient them, and hurl it back at them.

He fought the squires with a silent fury similar to what had been shown at Ciecime.

Luchs let out a dry chuckle listening to his friend's discontent. "The laddie's got to have something, aye?"

"Aren't you angry, Luchs? Losing to him, after everyone you've faced, all the beatings you took from foes bigger than him? He's just a gangly runt."

"And he chose to stand against us all despite that."

Maxime made no retort. He was much too flustered to keep putting the dark lad down. Sighing, he looked back down to the squires getting smacked around as if they were nothing.

"I know how they feel. Everyone was expected to follow the mission, do as His Majesty decreed and as our general ordered. It might not have been the best way, but we followed them and were ready to do what was asked of us. Then that foreigner and his meister just show up and undermine them, completely oppose our cause, and even trounce us. To think he actually thanked them... They were acknowledged for betrayal while we stood by him the entire time. Little wonder they are all frothing at the mouth and going for his head. If'n I wasn't to act by example, just like General Esperance, I'd probably be down there too."

On that, they agreed. Everyone in the company almost had to give a piece of their humanity following the king's will, and they did so willingly. Their commitment had been completely overlooked because someone was willing to oppose the bloody order.

In a sense, even though they were all so upset with him, they were all rather similar.

To know a person's anger is to know something about them.

Ulrin said those same words not long after the trial. He seemed amused, satisfied to have witnessed Vandelas' fit of rage because, even though his actions were different, he proved he cared for Ederea.

Protecting their people was important, but so was protecting their values.

"Honestly," said Luchs, "I'm much too relieved to be mad. Lives were spared, and now, with the king more determined than ever, we're focusing on securing real peace again, not further stoking the flames of war."

Deciding to see how the brawl would end, Luchs leaned against the windowsill beside his friend. Maxime, for some reason, looked more focused on something else. He stared at Luchs, curious and worried.

"Hey, Luchs," he spoke uneasily. "Back at Ciecime, just before I conked out, I heard Vandelas say something. Something about your—"

"Oh right, almost forgot!" Luchs suddenly blurted out, turning to face Maxime. "Ulrin and the general questioned Executioner Sörrign earlier, aye? Did they find out anything?"

It was a sudden topic change. Normally, that would have been thought of as rude. But after staring him down for a moment, Maxime turned back to the brawl and answered him. "Executioner Sörrign knows a great deal of those here—" he paused to clear his throat, "the Kyrovide. He even questioned them on what happened before saving them. They did harbor the Convent soldiers who escaped into Ciecime, but not for long and not exactly by choice."

"What do you mean?"

"Do you remember what His Majesty told us yesterday?"

After the trial had finished and the execution was cancelled, King Godefroy gathered the generals currently in his court and informed them of everything he managed to uncover about the enemy.

The Convent of One came from Ciecime.

Before the du Joiec conquerors took Ederea, two groups of people inhabited the country: the Vainte and the Kyrovide. While the Vainte first chose to oppose the Abioan invaders, the Kyrovide wanted to avoid the fighting. They took refuge in Ciecime and hid from the world.

The Kyrovide were content practicing their faith in solitude, away from violence and war. But that changed when the Convent of One decided to reveal themselves.

After Des Meurtal was destroyed, a party of soldiers had been sent to an island near Ciecime, following intel on where the magic storm that razed it came from, but they never returned. When someone went to investigate, they found the island deserted. The Convent of One was there, that much they knew, and they considered Ederea's intrusion an act of aggression. They acted on that aggression, deciding it was their turn to conquer.

"Some of the Kyrovide don't condone the Convent's violent actions, but they still honor their own beliefs. They harbored the Convent soldiers out of respect for what parts of their religion they did agree on. 'Those who follow in the ways of Kyros never turn each other away when in need,' says he. 'Tis something of an unspoken vow."

Judging by his conflicting tone, Maxime did not believe they did it for the vow alone. It was reasonable to consider that threats from the strong Convent soldiers could have swayed their decision.

They watched the fight below while thinking about that. Few remained standing to oppose Vandelas, and those few hesitated to make sudden moves.

"A party was sent to investigate the village after the questioning. They'll repair what we destroyed and find out whatever they can. I hope they're still as open to visitors."

Luchs listened to his friend as Vandelas knocked down the last squire opposing him. He realized Vandelas did not even fight with swords. The sun's glare reflected not off of metal, but ice that had been frozen thoroughly enough to not shatter upon impact.

With the entertainment out of the way, Luchs walked down the hall, returning to his meister knight for a sparring session. He was suddenly in the mood for some action.

Night veiled across Ederea's sky as the day came to rest. The clear skies glimmered a treasure trove of stars hanging alongside an incandescent full moon. A cold chill brushed across the castle, bringing relief to the weary soldiers who spent the entire day under the hot sun.

Luchs almost could not fall asleep without that chill. Sparring with Ulrin completely tuckered him out. With the gentle brush of cold air, he could fall asleep just by closing his eyes. But sleep did not come easy.

Ack! What now?

His head was buzzing, his magic senses warning of an abrupt change. A tremendous energy surged from somewhere on the Crown Plateau. He doubted it involved the Convent of One but was still tempted to investigate.

Squires were expected to follow a curfew. They were not allowed to leave the castle unsupervised after moonrise. Breaking it would be costly, but it was well worth a few hundred squats in his skivvies beneath a small waterfall if it meant subduing an intruder.

Sneaking past Ulrin was simple as he had dozed off after drowning himself in ale. The guards on patrol were not so easy. Scarcely anyone patrolled the castle since only the foolish would scale the plateau, but they always remained alert nonetheless. If they saw so much as a pebble out of place, the castle was put on high alert.

Remaining hidden took some effort, but it was done. No one saw him slink into the shadows or sneak by. Thanks to the years spent on Des Meurtal, he knew how to evade detection and keep hidden.

After stepping outside, he shuddered and stumbled. That annoying buzz became more erratic as the energy he sensed was clearer to him. It was not just any energy.

It was toward the western edge of the plateau. As he followed a stream leading in that direction, Luchs tried determining whether or not that flux of energy boded danger; with him, it was hard to tell. No guards patrolled that area, oddly enough, meaning the two souls ahead were the only ones about.

Two?

Luchs stopped and closed his eyes, allowing his magic sight to change his view of the world. He still could not read the valsara well, but he knew who they belonged to. It was doubtlessly Vandelas' valsara flaring up. But what was he doing? And what of Executioner Sörrign?

He approached the two quietly, moving quickly to keep hidden behind the trees that stood nearby.

At first glance, they appeared to be training.

With a thick sword in hand, Vandelas charged and clashed with the executioner, who wielded the fiery Anktung. They crossed blades for a moment before the weapon's fire threatened to burn its foe. The lad leaped back before the flames could touch him, vapor permeating from his bare skin.

He fought differently than usual. Instead of holding the sword in one hand and its scabbard in the other, he gripped the handle with both hands. His form was sloppy, and he trembled while moving as he had. But there was still something about him to be cautious of.

Vandelas moved on the offensive and roared a frightful battle cry when he attacked, and his eyes showed a rage and hostility almost feral.

"You still can't take the heat, kid?" Executioner Sörrign taunted.

His squire only growled, rather threateningly.

"You know how you should move, but you're neglecting your weapon. It has a way it wants to move too. Listen to it. Move with it. If you can't do that, you will never find the strength you're after."

Infuriated, Vandelas threw himself at the executioner again with his weapon held for a low blow.

This was not just an exercise. He went after his meister with intent to kill.

But, of course, Executioner Sörrign would not let him do as he liked. He brought his fiery sword to meet his student's in every swing, letting Vandelas get a few strong hits in, until deciding he had enough and slammed its flat side at his exposed hip.

Vandelas fell, crying out in pain, and clung at the injury.

"Your form still needs tempering."

It did not look like the beastly child was finished. He pushed himself up, struggling to ignore the pain, and glared at his meister. Although he struggled to stay standing, he clustered ice in his left hand, crafting a short sword with a thick, jagged blade. Instead of attempting to futilely stab the executioner, he flung the ice at the tree concealing Luchs. The blade pierced the tree straight through its bulky trunk and popped out scarcely a centimeter from his head.

"Step out of hiding!"

The sound of ice clustering was an excellent motivator to make Luchs' shaky body move. He stepped out of hiding with his hands up.

Vandelas was none too happy to see him. "I warned you never to approach me during a full moon!"

He remembered hearing that once on Emiet. "I didn't think you were serious, laddie," Luchs defended. His gaze turned to Executioner Sörrign, who remained perfectly composed despite the intrusion. "Don't you think 'tis a little late for training, Executioner?"

"Go back to bed then. The kid doesn't have a problem with nighttime exercises. He even relishes in it."

That nasty grimace Vandelas bore hardly resembled delight. The way he carried himself like a creature on the hunt was chilling. Those piercing glacial eyes, eyes that faintly glowed in the darkness, underneath the light of the moon, were his most intimidating features. Whatever the full moon was doing to him, it left him almost unrecognizable as the quiet lad he usually was.

That ferocity did not seem so dissimilar from that outburst he had in the throne room.

The executioner sheathed Anktung as he walked to the trees, leaning against one for rest. "Take a break, kid. Lick your wounds, then we can get back at it."

Dissatisfied as he was with how he put it, Vandelas obeyed and limped toward the stream. He sat by it and started splashing water at the burn while gently freezing it over. The white fox sitting in the shadows came out of hiding after seeing its master tend to his wound and sat by his side.

Taking a breath, Luchs approached the beastly child. What he was about to do would likely not mean anything while he was so riled up, but that did not matter. Now that he had Vandelas before him, it was time to say what needed to be said.

The fox turned and growled at Luchs, eliciting Vandelas to turn and leer. He did not want to talk, but Luchs did, and he needed to know.

"Vandelas, yesterday you mentioned Harah Krid." He paused a moment as the lad's gaze turned more gruesome, then continued. "I thought Vermalio was your home."

Nothing was said. He remained silent as he stared Luchs down, those violent eyes glimmering with unsettling hostility. The heavy atmosphere between them felt crushing. But he calmed down. Vandelas turned back to the water, letting Luchs breathe again.

"I was raised in Vermalio until coming here. Harah Krid was where I was born."

The fox turned back to its master, forgetting Luchs' existence, and nuzzled its head against his arm.

Luchs did not entirely believe the animal noticed it, but there was no ignoring the forlorn strands in Vandelas' valsara.

"Vermalio became my home after Harah Krid was destroyed."

"Destroyed!? How—"

"What little I know I probably shouldn't. It all happened when I was just ... a bairn." He paused a moment, possibly wondering whether or not he said the word correctly. "I shouldn't remember, but somehow, I do."

Far-fetched as it was, Luchs believed him. "What do you remember?"

"A city being consumed by flames, horrifying men attacking the Kindhrin, the Kindhrin screaming as they ran for their lives ... their cries being silenced by those who hunted them..." Every detail uttered made him tremble until he pinned his arms down to keep still. The trauma, the one he thought he should not have known, had been etched into his very muscles. "I hear them some nights," he muttered. "I hear them calling out for help—help that never came."

A terrible weight formed in Luchs' heart. He never felt so horrid in his life. After what he said to him, claiming what he did, it was brutal just making him endure his presence. He lost everything too. His life had been completely changed in a cruel, terrifying way.

"I ... I didn't—"

"I never wanted anyone to know."

Luchs wanted to keep going, to say he was in the wrong. An apology was rightfully owed, but Vandelas did not want to hear it.

He raised his hand, curling his fingers around the scarf wrapped around his face. "I thought there would be no need to hide anymore, but I was wrong. There are still Vermalians in this court, and Vermalians hold nothing but contempt for the Kindhrin." Taking a moment for breath, he glanced down and pulled the scarf down just enough to reveal the crimson marks beneath his eyes. "I can wear my natural skin only because this scarf buries these brands, the salient features of a Kindhrin. But I am still careful to avoid Vermalian ambassadors and keep to myself so fewer people talk about me." He paused to pull the scarf back to where it was. "It was only out of luck that there were no Vermalians there when I had my outburst before the king. They know I am here, but none of them know what really I am, and they must never know. If you truly want to make amends, then keep your silence."

Such strange things he mentioned: being able to wear his natural skin, the Kindhrin's salient features, those of the country he was raised in not knowing what he was. A few of his words were spoken with relief, the others with spite and fear. It was as though he was trapped.

Regardless of what any of that meant, he offered Luchs a way to apologize, so he did what was asked and said no more.

The violent wavering in Vandelas' valsara eased just a little. Exhaling another breath of cold air, he stood and turned to face his meister. "My training must continue. If you want something else, it can wait."

Luchs looked on to see Vandelas picking up the sword he dropped and the executioner rising, ready to take Anktung in hand again. Something nagged at him that he should not be there, but he could not resist. This was the perfect opportunity to have a good look at the way they fought without being battered.

Neither of them argued. Or more appropriately, they did not care.

~ Thirteenth Chapter ~

Vainte

There was plenty to learn in watching Vandelas and Executioner Sörrign spar. Off-putting as it was to see them try to kill each other, it was impressive how they danced with their blades. Meister and squire fought one another for what seemed like hours before stopping to rest.

They were not much for conversation, but Luchs was able to get a few things about Wolfram Sörrign out of Vandelas. The executioner himself said nothing; they doubted he cared.

But his squire did care, even though he tried to hide it.

True to the rumors, Wolfram Sörrign did know magic. But he did not spend his time perfecting hexes, contrary to everyone's fears. He was not a conventional mage; he was a blacksmith, and those enchanted swords he showed off were his creations.

Those weapons were made with "seeds" of his magic. He crafted each seed as he prepared their vessels and imbued them into the material once he grasped how they would grow. Then the weapons would be completed as the seed sprouted and merged with them, giving them forms suitable for their power. He had been making weapons that way for years, and would continue to do so until he forged 1,000 magic weapons.

That was what Executioner Sörrign meant when he spoke of an accord between him and the king. That was why some unknown man came to serve King Godefroy.

But why go that far? What was his goal in making those weapons?

Unfortunately, Vandelas never learned that himself.

Wolfram scoffed when Luchs got the stomach to ask. "If I cared to let anyone know about my motives, you'd likely have heard of them by now. They shouldn't matter to you."

He was not as indifferent as he led them to believe.

Regardless, if he would not speak of it, there was nothing Luchs could do. He had his reasons, whatever they were—just as the squires had theirs in striving for knighthood.

Weeks have passed without incident. The Convent of One remained silent and hidden. Not so much as a pirate ship was seen sailing Ederea's waters.

Many in the court were concerned with the lack of action since taking back Ciecime's stronghold and nearly making matters worse with the other Kyrovide. They dreaded what would come next. The generals used every resource at their disposal to comb through the archipelago but have yet to find the Convent of One.

As for Luchs, training only kept him busy for so long. His body tired out after a while, leaving the mind to wander and question the enemy's plan. Waiting for the letters from the Vertueux family to know they were safe left him anxious. In such times, the only thing that kept him calm was the time spent in the archives.

After remembering what happened to him five years ago, Luchs kept rummaging through the archives for anything that could lead him to his old home. It never sat well with him how little he knew about his village, even before his kidnapping. There were just the houses, a river, trees, the mountaintops, and the livestock—but nothing beyond that.

But there has to be more.

He needed to make connections. It was the only way he might one day find his lost home. He had to see it, even if just for one last time.

Desperate for answers, Luchs finally decided to ask Maxime his help. After hearing him out, Maxime could not let him take the arduous task on alone. He even brought one of the new recruits, Levin Ciellic, to help them search the archives.

The three spent many a day going through the archives one book at a time. Every new search began with them checking different areas of the vast library. Few people ventured that far beneath the castle, so they were free of interruptions until someone came looking for them.

They never found anything of interest. It did not help that the village he grew up in had no name; everyone always thought such a thing was unnecessary. In hindsight, it probably was since barely anyone left the village and they seldom received visitors.

"Nothing again," Levin groaned as he slammed a tome shut.

Although a year younger than Luchs and Maxime, the lad was much taller than them, almost six feet. He never bothered to keep his brown hair kempt. Much of his effort was put into his training, as the well-defined muscles along his body proved.

He worked hard, just like everyone else, but he did not enjoy reading.

"I'm all for finding a lost village, Luchs, but we've not found a thing for a fortnight now. This blind search is becoming tiresome."

"Imagine how I feel."

"I did promise this wouldn't be easy," Maxime interrupted, arriving with another book in hand.

"You dared me, sir. How could I have refused?"

The general's squire must have carried more authority than the lieutenant's for him to speak more respectfully to him.

Knowing this, Maxime cracked a smile. "Then you know well you can't back out of it," he stated. "Last a while longer and you can have some of my honeydew candy stash."

None of the maps revealed anything useful. The military papers available to them brought nothing to light either. At some point, Luchs became picking out tomes at random. More often than not, he ended up with one of the apocrypha containing the text no one could read. Each one had worn, aged leather binding unlike anything he ever saw, the corners tinged a golden color and pages written on in a strange red ink.

Seeing so many illegible works made him grit his teeth.

At least, that was how it was at first. Glancing over so many of those pages riddled with illegible scribbles made him notice every apocrypha had similar writing on their first pages. A waste of time perhaps, but Luchs decided to give one another look.

He glanced over this one line again and again, and every time he found himself muttering these loose, unusual syllables. Soon enough, much to his surprise, he started to recognize a few symbols. It was not long after that he deciphered the first phrase:

Tiavin.

Although the meaning eluded him for a moment, he figured out it meant something like "told by." The word after that was difficult to pronounce, but he deduced it had to be someone's name—the author.

Having gotten that far, Luchs attempted to further decipher the text. It was hard to know whether he actually understood the words or if he had lost his mind looking for answers and made up meanings. But everything seemed to make sense the more he read.

"Oi! Wake up already!"

A thick leather smacking the back of his head broke Luchs' focus. The room spun and the waterfalls fell silent until he shook his head and pulled himself together. Maxime stood beside him, holding one of the tomes and looking irate.

"Get your nose out that book! General Esperance is calling for us," he said impatiently.

Still a little dizzy, Luchs took a moment to stand. The books he took from the shelves were already put away in the proper order, most likely by the one who took the tome he was reading and shelved the last two.

"I'm surprised you've been here the whole time. Dinner is about to be served, you know."

That came as a shock. It did not feel like much time passed, but after turning to the crystalline wall, Luchs saw the sun already setting over the horizon. Translating the text was surprisingly engrossing.

"Maxime, you might not believe me, but ... I was reading it."

Naturally, he laughed. "So have plenty of others. Don't beat yourself up. Even the brightest scholars couldn't translate those—"

"I'm serious! I was reading it. I understood it."

Maxime turned back to face his comrade with a disturbed expression. As hard as it was to accept, he believed him. Real men did not lie to one another, at least not about anything serious, and Maxime knew Luchs held firm to that belief. He went back to the shelves and took one of the apocrypha he put away. "He's going to want to see."

They made their way back up the castle. No one got in their way aside from a few soldiers on patrol. They returned to the general's quarters just as he and his lieutenant were stepping outside.

When the squires told them of Luchs' discovery, they were confused and unsure of how to respond, then drolly laughed. A natural response.

So, to prove it, Maxime sat them back inside and threw the hefty tome onto General Esperance's desk for Luchs to read. From the ivory-hued cover, Luchs knew that was not the apocrypha he was reading. It made him a little uneasy knowing that, but upon flipping to the first page, he read. Again, he read the words for "told by" and then someone's name. After that were the same few lines he deciphered from the other apocrypha:

"These pages contain fragments of the most precious of treasures and the most powerful of weapons: knowledge. Without it, one is but a savage, unable to understand the world. Treasure the information within above any jewel and never abuse the power gained from it."

Or something like that.

The room was silent. Ulrin and General Esperance stared at Luchs with owl eyes and hung their mouths ajar as they listened to him speak in this cryptic tongue.

It took a while before he could finish the section, although no one seemed to mind. Their meister knights had the same expressions of shock, disbelief, and baffled amazement that Maxime showed before.

"This ... This is incredible!" The proud Ulrin went up to Luchs, wrapped an arm around his neck, and roughly mussed his hair. The last time he did that was when he said he wanted to be a knight.

Though not one to dole out praise often, General Esperance smiled and patted Luchs on the shoulder. "Incredible, indeed. A shame we've no use for you as a scribe now, otherwise I'd have you translating those relics below. How do you know this?"

"I'm not sure. I just started reading, then ... it all came together."

An explanation without much substance. Normally, that would not sit well with the general, but seeing as they were missing dinner, he decided to let it go for the time being.

Many of the soldiers dined in the barracks. There was plenty of space for the men to eat and be as rowdy as they pleased. It was a place where the soldiers could relax and enjoy themselves after a day of hard work.

As always, the men were loud, boisterous, and reveled like it was the dawn of the kingdom. The tables were covered with plenty of delectable food prepared by the castle's chefs. The men quenched their thirst with the finest rum and mead and sated their hunger with the most succulent mutton, pork, fish, and sea slugs. And practically everyone fought for the dishes they wanted; some got injured more often fighting over food than during training or in actual combat.

Those brawls were hysterical to watch, but fighting for a fish almost made Luchs want to give it up. No one dared give up anything they were after, though, since no one wanted to be called craven.

It was not just some loud, anarchic scene. The men always took those wonderful moments to chat, engage with one another without weapons, and just see how they were doing. Soldiers though they were, they were also people who cared for one another.

One of the soldiers often took out his old lute and played the merriest of melodies for everyone. He used to be a minstrel before taking a knight's shield. No one understood why he chose to become a knight when he had hands so talented; he never bothered to share.

In a way, the soldiers were all one big, crazy family.

The long silence was a ploy. After nearly two months, the Convent of One made a devastating attack on La Kriod. Many soldiers and men and women of the cloth died. News of the attack spread fast.

Survivors had fled from La Kriod on a small ship heading south of the isle, but they were all overcome with fear. There were soldiers on board as well, but most of them had long since passed.

The news devastated all who caught wind of it. La Kriod was not just any island; it was one of the four isles that formed The Chain, an impregnable defensive perimeter around Shoafond. Each isle of The Chain—La Kriod, La Bou'est, La Sceaud, and La Vioes—was a fortified garrison. And the waters between them were obstructed by a magic barrier that deterred all vessels not granted permission to pass.

A fleet of fifty ships immediately set out to take La Kriod back only to reclaim an abandoned isle. The enemy was gone. No traps were left to eliminate the cavalry. And the spell for the barrier had not been tampered with, or even discovered.

They just appeared, slaughtered, and vanished.

More attacks followed northeast of La Kriod. The people on those islands were not as well protected and suffered terrible casualties. Each island's militia did what it could to secure their territory, but each one had its own vulnerabilities, each one exploited by the Convent's forces.

More warriors were needed. The Edereans needed more manpower if there was going to be any hope of fighting back. Ordinary fighters would not be enough either.

Fortunately, Ulrin had a solution. Before taking his shield, he trained on La Vioes, a part of The Chain that was home to some of Ederea's first inhabitants: the Vainte. The Vainte were warriors born, possessing fierce strength and uncanny skill. The prowess Ulrin demonstrated in battle, what he learned from them, what earned him his position at such a young age, proved their aid would be a boon.

However, despite being part of the kingdom at present, the Vainte rarely responded to requests from the king. The only thing that could convince them to help in this crisis would be someone they once trained.

And so, General Esperance sent Ulrin and a small party to La Vioes with an offering to entice the Vainte into negotiating. Parley with the Vainte chieftain would not be possible without something valuable for tribute, which, incidentally, Executioner Sörrign provided.

Ulrin questioned the executioner but found no reason to reject him joining them. "Just following His Majesty's orders, it seems."

His squire was not with him this time. It was only him.

Aside from the discomfort everyone felt having the executioner aboard, the voyage was pleasant. The winds blew against their ship instead of with the sails, so they were left with little choice but to pull the sails up and travel at a less than satisfactory speed. But the ship had been pulled into a current flowing in the direction of La Vioes, minimizing the loss in speed. The sun shone brightly that day, keeping everyone in high spirits until they arrived at their destination.

The sun hung high when La Vioes came over the horizon. Its dazzling light made the land resemble a giant golden serpent from the distance. A squire saying as much put a wistful smile on Ulrin's face.

Whether from a distance or up close, the island was truly serene. The grass was a lustrous green, a trait shared by the leaves belonging to the gargantuan trees strongly rooted in the fertile soil. The land sloped upward from the sea around the edge they docked at, keeping most of the island inaccessible except from that point, a spot Ulrin called the tail of La Vioes. The rest of the land was bordered by slopes too steep to climb and a waterfall that flowed out from the other end. Even if the invaders did decide on striking The Chain from La Vioes next, the only feasible point of entry was on the inside of the barrier.

Stone walls had been constructed where the grass began to grow, but they were not very tall compared to barricades in most military facilities. The only sign of outside influence on the island was the other warships sailing near it for protection, all of them waving Ederea's flag. It was difficult to see at first glance, but Luchs noticed the ships were enveloped in mystical energy—something protective.

"Are there mages here?"

Surprised as he was that his squire noticed it, Ulrin nodded. "None of which the Vainte will share. But they're skilled and, since nearly everyone here is raised a warrior, capable in a fight."

Ulrin led some of his men into the jungle, leaving the rest behind to watch over the ship.

Many of the paths looked the same and were blocked by small bushes. Some were constantly guessing which way to turn. Fortunately, the man guiding them had the lay of the land committed to memory.

The ground undulated beneath them constantly, creating hill after hill, offering plenty of spots for cover for potential ambushes. The birds sang vocally for their feathered kin. A few colorful ones flew overhead, one dropping a few berries from a twig held in its beak. The air was fresher there than outside of the jungle, crisp and clean, with a delightful taste to it. It smelled of something sweet like honey.

It was hard to believe a place so serene also served as part of a major defense network.

When attempting to see how healthy the environment was through his magic sight, Luchs found they were not alone. Someone was near, hiding in the trees overhead, and began moving as Ulrin approached.

"Ulrin, look out!"

His meister knight, who was casually twirling his spear around, took a step back upon his squire's warning and hurled his weapon upward. It met with a similarly crafted weapon wielded by his assailant. The assailant fell backward and landed unsteadily in the dirt. To everyone's surprise, it was a woman.

She crawled off the dirt, gripping the spear in her hands tightly while Ulrin kept this in hand, ready for a fight. Much of her messy red hair had been held beneath a veil over her scalp. And her face, while smudged with a little dirt, was lovely. Her violet eyes, however, beamed with a rigid temper at her target.

Ulrin gave her a sly smile. "Wonderful to see you again too, Rah'ta."

Those who thought to grab the woman before she made another move held back when their lieutenant spoke familiarly to her.

The woman spat at the dirt. "Don't act so stalwart when you need a lad to see me coming. You've gotten complacent."

"Or you just got better at hiding," Ulrin teased. "As fun as this little dance is, I take it you're our guide."

Rah'ta turned to the soldiers accompanying him with a distasteful look. Perhaps she noticed how a fair number of them looked at her. "The chieftain awaits us and he isn't patient. You'd best hope your tribute suffices." She marched past Ulrin, not bothering to wait for anyone to follow.

Many of the soldiers felt a bit uneasy following her. The graceless descent aside, she carried herself like a natural warrior, one that did not care for their presence. Those unaware of how the Vainte lived had been briefed about it beforehand, but they still could not get used to seeing a woman carry a weapon. It was a foreign concept to them, making women into warriors, one that few Edereans accepted.

Luchs wondered if everyone would be able to mind their manners and keep from saying anything foolish.

The walk was peaceful, apart from Ulrin flirting with Rah'ta.

Every time the lout crosses a woman, Luchs silently complained.

A point came when the trees almost entirely blocked out the sunlight. Every direction looked the same when the way back had been swallowed by shadows. No one panicked since Ulrin and Rah'ta kept moving. They did not even slow down. Many wide turns were made circling large trees and the occasional cliffside, enough that everyone would have gotten lost were it not for their guides.

Rah'ta kept going without caring who remained behind her. She moved in response to every tree, ledge, and bush before they came into view.

Soon, the light shone through again. The parting darkness gave way to a clear path leading to a structured settlement. They have arrived.

The Vainte settlement was impressive. A powerful stone wall protected everything inside the claimed land. The buildings within were simple huts put together with excellently carved stone, each big enough for a family or two. Most appeared to be homes, very few showing any sign of use for business aside from the obvious booth. Near every few houses or so stood torches used to light their way at night. At the center of the settlement sat a huge pile of freshly-chopped wood surrounded by spears lodged into the ground. Many children were outside at play, but their parents herded them closer to their homes as the visiting soldiers entered their settlement.

Rare as it was, there have been instances when negotiations with the Vainte turned intense. They obviously have not forgotten how their guests tended to cause trouble when they did not get their way. Since Ulrin was there, he could put an end to any conflicts before they got out of hand.

There were a few friendly faces among the working masses, all of them looking at Ulrin with smiles. They waved and called out to greet him, then returned to their work when he gave them a friendly "Hello!"

At the edge of the settlement stood a large keep that resembled a small castle. In addition to the stone foundation, it was plated with countless skulls both animal and human plastered against the walls.

"They're trophies," Ulrin explained. "When the time comes for a chieftain's heir to take their rightful place, they must prove their worth by demonstrating their strength. Those trophies must be of a hated enemy or a monstrous creature."

"And should they fail?" asked Levin, who joined their party.

"Then all hopes then rest on the next heir," answered Rah'ta.

How cold.

Luchs bit his tongue before giving voice to his thoughts. He needed to show respect.

Their conversation came to an end when a man appeared from the bone-covered keep. He stood at a tremendous height any Ederean man would kill to grow into. The vest he wore did not cover all of his iron abs, grandly defined with years of training. Many scars had been carved into his body from the battles he fought in. Long, matted red hair complemented his rugged face and the short, shaggy beard on it. He was the Vainte chieftain.

A seasoned warrior without question. And someone among Ulrin's men thought the same thing.

"Young Ulrin," the Vainte chieftain greeted the lieutenant of the visiting party with a deep, ragged voice.

Immediately after speaking, the chieftain was beset by the swift Executioner Sörrign wielding a polearm. Noticing the attack before the soldiers even had, the chieftain took the reinforced spear at his back in hand and met the attack. Despite the obvious size difference, their spears pressed against each other, their strength perfectly matched.

A few knights rushed to intervene, but were stopped by Rah'ta's outstretched arm and Ulrin's hand signaling them to stand down.

Why stop them? Executioner Sörrign was attacking their ally, their leader no less!

The Vainte chieftain forced the executioner aside and moved in to strike. Executioner Sörrign spun his polearm before bringing it against his spear, blocking the attack, then slew his blade along its shaft. If he pulled back a second later, the chieftain would have lost his hands. The executioner kept spinning his weapon dexterously, showing off, waiting for the chieftain to take the offensive again, then countered and swatted him in the gut with the shaft of his polearm.

As the spectacle dragged on, the chieftain began losing his footing and made clumsy approaches. The crowd they drew in was baffled by the chieftain's crass movements and enfeebled stance. It was as if his strength suddenly vanished. Stranger than that, some people in the crowd began to feel weak and uneasy just watching. They kept swaying and losing their balance, and some held their heads feeling themselves spinning.

Luchs could barely keep his eyes on their clash without tottering over himself. At some point, he stopped watching until the conflict came to an end.

The onlookers were stunned to see an outsider had the chieftain on his knees, holding a sharp edge of his weapon to his neck. Now that the polearm was held still, everyone was given a good look at it. Instead of a single blade, the weapon had two strong, slender blades, one attached to each end. Those blades were shaped like diamonds and appeared just as durable, and etched on their sides were strange symbols. Perhaps the most captivating feature had to be the red and blue gems on the shaft. They were the same color as the eerie wisps of light that were seen when the weapon was spun.

"The Distortion Wheel, Porlande," Executioner Sörrign uttered. "When spun with enough force, the jewels radiate a faint yet trenchant light capable of distorting one's senses, thus bringing the enemy to its knees." He pulled his weapon from the chieftain's throat and waited for him to stand again. When he did, he then held Porlande at its side, presenting it to him. "Mayhap such a trick isn't to your way of fighting, but a real warrior must be strong in both mind and body. This weapon tests the wielder as much as their enemy. What do you say? Do you think you have what it takes to use it?"

The chieftain looked curt and riled up for a moment, then smirked and laughed, and accepted Porlande.

The Vainte preferred to create and use their own weapons, finding their craftsmanship superior. As such, the Edereans normally offered magic charms or other items to entice the Vainte into cooperating. For their leader to accept an outsider's weapon, magical or not, it meant it was too good to refuse.

"You've a warrior this skilled and yet you feel the need to ask for more?" the chieftain jocularly put.

As much as the others did not like hearing the executioner's praise, Ulrin looked tickled by the response. "Astute as always, Chieftain Ta'roh."

"Has your king ever requested anything else of me, child?" asked Chieftain Ta'roh. He laid his weapons against his shoulder and allowed Executioner Sörrign to excuse himself. "I fear you've wasted your time and resources making your way here. We have our own problems with our mutual enemy."

"I thought the barrier your shaman erected prevents foreign vessels from penetrating your part of The Chain."

"It does. They cannot reach us. But this Convent, their power is great. They use a vile magic that drives the animals here to attack us on their behalf. Alone they are no match for our might, but while organized under the Convent's influence, they pose a terrible threat."

It unsettled Ulrin's men to hear that spell could control animals even without their mages physically being present. It was the first time they had heard of it. So that meant any animal near them could become a potential enemy, no matter where they were.

At least one Convent mage was targeting the Vainte, likely because there was so much wildlife in La Vioes.

"We have our own troubles to bear here. We cannot help you."

To those stern words, Ulrin smirked. "We'll see." He approached the chieftain casually, then turned to face his party. "You lot help out around the village while we negotiate. I'm sure Rah'ta will find something to keep you busy."

The tigress clicked her tongue while the lieutenant followed Chieftain Ta'roh into his keep.

The history she had with him must not have been a pleasant one.

Crossed as she was with him, Rah'ta did put the knights to work. There was plenty that needed to be done: repairing damaged barricades, making salve for the injured, fetching medicinal ingredients for the shaman, skinning and preparing the boars brought in by the hunters. As for Luchs, he was tasked with fetching water from the nearby spring.

Two men, two women, and a lass were already chosen for the job, and Luchs joined them. Everyone was given a pole to balance the two buckets needed to carry the water.

The spring was not too far from the settlement.

Everyone filled their buckets quickly, but Luchs had to take in what he found. Rather than a puny pond, water drew out of the ground into a pool almost large enough to be a small lake and deep enough to bathe in. Smooth stones covered the perimeter of the spring. The crystal clear water flowed from the pool and into a little stream that travelled northward.

As he got to work, he noticed something intriguing. The spring was artificial; someone at some point in history created it. The placement and the octagonal shape of the stones beneath their feet could not possibly be natural.

Who could have made it? And how?

Answers to such questions were out of the Vainte's hands. It must have stood the tests of time, much like Castle Ederea.

Deciding to leave such queries behind for the time being, Luchs hung the buckets on the pole and rested the pole against his shoulders. He did not think the water would slow him very much, but he filled the buckets so much that every swaying motion spilled some water. And the longer he carried them, the heavier they felt.

Every now and then, a Vainte glanced back at Luchs to ensure he did not fall behind. He had no trouble keeping up. The trek was not much different than the initiation he had as a page, carrying a boulder on his back.

Many gathered at the edge of the settlement. No one appeared very thirsty or dehydrated, just eager for their share. They each brought a cup that would hold enough water to last until the nighttime and waited for their turn.

While he was handing out water, Luchs noticed something about the Vainte that he earlier overlooked. Men, women, children—everyone was wearing a leather skirt that reached down to their knees. It was unusual seeing them show their legs when they were not even in the water. He tried not to pay attention to the strange garb so as not to mention it and risk offending anyone.

Cautious as they were when he first entered their home, the Vainte were very friendly. Everyone greeted the outsider helping them as kindly as they had their own and thanked him for his help.

One person in particular was especially happy to see him.

"That you, Luchs?"

He looked up from his bucket to find a familiarly goofy grin beneath a pair of blue eyes, messy black hair, and rosy cheeks. It was Rufus.

Distracted, Luchs dropped the cup in his hand and went up to greet his friend with a playful jab to the shoulder.

"Good to see you, mate!" said Rufus while jabbing Luchs back. "What's it been—four, five months now? You look good."

"Same to you. How'd you wind up on this rock?"

Though the two were having fun, the workers did not appreciate the distraction. Luchs returned to his task as Rufus motioned that he would be waiting by the houses nearby.

After apologizing, Luchs did his part, excused himself, then found the lad playing with a pack of children crowded around him.

The little ones enjoyed wrestling with him. Rufus let them pile onto him as they wrestled. He kept playfully saying, "I give, I give!" after they tripped him and dogpiled onto him. The children only let him go when they thought they won. Just for further amusement, he pretended to be sore and pained after getting up, all the while keeping a gleeful smile. A few of the children seemed worried, but he assured them that no harm was done. They scampered off to get their water once the crowd died down.

"The children like you, it seems. Never took you for a caretaker."

The jokester chuckled. "I just look after 'em when the shaman's protégés are busy. They usually watch the children while their parents hunt, forage, train, et cetera."

"Right. Now, before you tell me how you became a nanny, how about explaining what you are doing here?"

The two could not help share a bitter laugh after Rufus said he was brought here after the chaos on Des Meurtal. "The others had an easier time getting accepted. Every knight thought me too unstable to train, so Commandant Brunlier brought me here, said they would look after me, see if I am worthy to be made into a real warrior."

"And do they?"

"They didn't toss me off the isle yet."

"And there will be no need to." Someone walked in on their conversation, a charming figure with a small, polite smile and kind eyes. This one looked to be about their age yet thin and frail, unfit for battle. Unlike the other Vainte, the one in front of them wore a long robe that reached down to the ankles. Around a slender neck hung a few charms carved from wood and stone that appeared to be sacred.

She carried two cups in her petite hands and offered one to Rufus.

The lad, with a smile on his face, accepted the cup. "Thanks." He brought the rim to his lips and took a slow drink. It was strange how he did not greedily gulp it all down like he always had. When he came back up for air, he looked back at his friend. "Luchs, this here's Tal. He's a protégé to the shaman."

Huh? He?

Disbelief was etched all over his face.

Those eyes, the smoothness of his face, the slender stature, even those lips. Had Rufus not mentioned it, Luchs would have kept thinking the protégé a lass.

The little laugh Tal gave seeing the impression he left almost made him think so again. "Every Ederean has the same disbelief at first," said the effeminate protégé. He did not seem insulted or upset, at least.

"Uh ... sorry, Tal. 'Tis a pleasure." As shocked as Luchs was, he attempted to show respect and extended his hand to do so.

Tal gripped both of his petite hands around Luchs', then jarred it up and back down before letting go. "A pleasure indeed. I must attend to the children now, so please excuse me." And with that, Tal walked off in pursuit of his charge, carrying his water carefully in both hands.

Rufus waved the protégé's way, stopping only when turning to face Luchs.

Luchs looked back at the lad and shook his head, confused. "I don't know how you can look on thinking that's normal." That did not sound like the right thing to say, but it was all that came to mind.

Rufus shrugged. "Strange it may be to you, but Tal is far from abnormal to the Vainte." Deciding to not stand in place, he pivoted on his heel and leaned against the wall of a house, relaxing against the rough surface and taking another drink of water. "I'm not privy to all they know, but Tal explained a fair bit. His place as a shaman protégé actually has something to do with his looks. The Vainte see lads who grow feminine and lasses who grow masculine as blessed."

"Blessed? By who?"

"A formless god they call Tapal."

Luchs raised an eyebrow. "I never heard of it before."

"'Tisn't one of the Gods of the Natural Order. The Vainte worship it in a place on par with Lady Sundralla." Rufus rubbed his head, still unsure if he understood it himself. "I did mention Tapal was formless, aye? Well, it took a form at some point, then changed again, and again, and so on, changing shape to suit its needs. Some of the Vainte still worship the god like the others, and Vainte born a lad or lass are blessed by Tapal if they go through a 'transformation,' just like Tal.

"Those blessed by Tapal possess great spiritual power, so the Vainte embrace the transformation the blessed go through, encourage them to follow their role. It helps them reach some sort of spiritual harmony with themselves, or something."

Now Luchs rubbed his head. The erratic workings of magic became much more complicated to him, assuming anything he was told was true. Hearing Rufus laugh at their mutual confusion made his headache subside somewhat.

"And you don't think this unusual?"

"Not too strange for me. Tal's still a person, and a good one at that. He's kind, reliable, and, I've got to say, pretty fetching."

That last word caught Luchs off guard, but he did not say much in response.

It was not uncommon in Ederea for men to develop romantic relationships with other men, or for women to love women. Luchs saw such pairings several times before.

Despite it being an accepted norm, though, he could not wrap his head around the idea of someone courting another of the same sex. He always tried keeping an open mind but found it difficult to understand.

Such as it was for seeing men kiss the hands of women they met for the first time, or men in skirts, or women who carried weapons and fought alongside men, or a lad who dressed like a lass.

It was strange and more than a little confusing, but it put a smile on Luchs' face nonetheless.

There were so many different people in the world that lived and presented themselves in their own ways. Although they differed, they still found the means to coexist and interact with one another. And since they were different, they could learn from each other and grow together.

Discord would be inevitable, but such discord led to progress.

Luchs was glad he decided to see more of Ederea, of the world, and the people in it. Had he not chosen to follow the path of a knight, he might not have learned as much as he had.

"Well, good on you, mate. Glad to see you're doing well."

"You not going tell me your story?"

Luchs flashed a toothy grin. "Get your arse up and show me around then. That tigress put me to work, remember?"

After Ulrin's meeting with Chieftain Ta'roh ended, his party set sail for Shoafond immediately. From what his soldiers understood, it was less of a meeting than it was two old friends having drinks. His squire had to haul him back to the ship since he could barely remain upright on his own.

Thankfully, they got him out of there before Rah'ta got her claws into him. Being drunk did not help his flirtatious behavior.

The lieutenant hung over the railing during the voyage back and let the ship's captain take charge while the liquor worked its way through him. As impressive as he was in a fight, seeing Ulrin drunk or flirt just made Luchs shake his head.

"How did you become a lieutenant to the First Company again? Or any company for that matter," the lad japed.

Ulrin chortled heartily. "Funny. Let's see you try refusing Vainte generosity. See where it gets you." His speech was well kept together for someone so drunk he could not walk without swaying. Perhaps he just wanted to slack off before returning to the capital.

"So I take it the negotiations didn't go well?"

The drunken lieutenant shrugged, letting the armor on his arms grind against the wood beneath him. "Not in the way expected, but we got something. They're not letting anyone on La Vioes go. The Vainte across the archipelago, on the other hand, are another story. The chieftain of La Vioes has authority over the Vainte throughout Ederea, so what he says goes. They'll comply with us if we show them proof of his order."

"And you have it?"

"'Course I do! You think I'd leave without it? Who do you think I am, little Luchs?"

"Right now, a drunk arse."

The two shared a laugh together until Ulrin nearly slumped over the railing. His squire had to do all the heavy lifting hauling him back onto the deck, which gave the soldiers watching a laugh themselves.

As impressed as Ulrin was with his squire's rescue, Luchs wished he would be more careful.

When everyone had their fun, Luchs, Levin, and Levin's meister knight managed to convince the lieutenant to take a rest in the captain's quarters. With him at rest and out of the way, everyone's work around the ship would be less complicated.

Everything was quiet for some time, just the serene ocean breeze above and the sound of the gentle waves beneath brushing against their ears. A few gulls passed every now and then, making their way across the isles, sometimes taking rest in the crow's nest. The only thing to defile the silence was Ulrin losing the alcohol late at night as he leaned against the railing again, moaning like an ailing yak.

As much as they wished it, that was not the most disturbing thing to happen on the voyage.

When they were halfway to their destination, they came across a horrifying sight: a ship graveyard that was not there before. What little remained of a dozen ships littered the once clear ocean. Most of the vessels had been rent asunder, entire hulls and masts torn and scattered in the water. Corpses were seen floating hither and thither, a few still bleeding out, their lifeless hands clinging to broken planks. The only ship that still managed to keep afloat was one that desperately waved the Ederean flag.

~ Fourteenth Chapter ~

Distress

The kingdom went into an uproar.

The dark times wrought by the Convent of One led the royal family to take more action. Princess Camellia herself planned a voyage to go and put the terrified people at ease. But she was attacked by the Convent, the fleet assigned to escort and protect her decimated. Most of the soldiers died, and those who survived suffered terrible injuries, including their charge.

Had it not been for the efforts of the mage in her company, no one would have survived. His sacrifice saved the heir to the throne.

Word of the tragedy spread when Ulrin's party returned to the capital with the survivors. The soldiers attempted to shield Shoafond's populace from seeing their princess in her critical state; it was not something they should have seen. The soldiers themselves could not bear to see her porcelain skin stained crimson and battered black.

The king was more than enraged. His perpetually stoic persona crumbled upon laying eyes on his daughter. He trembled with every move, overwhelmed by seething pain and anger. He could barely still his hand to caress her blackened cheek. The malevolent valsara he exuded seeing every bruise, cut, and burn on her was enough to shake the hearts of everyone in his presence.

Soon, the entire country knew of the attempt on the princess' life. Everyone went into a panic and many rioted in demand of answers as to what happened. The soldiers did all they could to calm the people, but it was no easy matter.

Edereans were a hot-blooded people. Hearing their princess, someone they called their shard of sunshine, had been hurt put them at odds with themselves and their leaders. They were losing faith in the military because they could not protect her. She was *that* precious to them.

It was amazing how one person could affect others so.

After that disaster, General Esperance fortified Shoafond with as many able-bodied soldiers as possible and bolstered their defenses.

Attacking a royal was a sign of terrible things to come. The silence would soon end, making way for the real battles to begin and the casualties to form mountains.

And Ederea's military minds were just realizing how low their chances of victory truly were. The Convent's ships travelled through and met with the princess' fleet inside The Chain, the most secure perimeter in Ederea. It would take a full-frontal assault on any side to get past the warships guarding those waters. Even if magic came into play and somehow compromised the magic barrier, word of an attack would still spread. The only way the Convent would be able to pass undetected was if someone let them through The Chain.

Luchs could not believe something like that happened. The Convent of One opposed all of Ederea, threatened their way of life, and slaughtered countless people. No one in their right mind would do anything for them.

They must have done something, used some ghastly magic, to breach The Chain.

Unfortunately, there were those who suspected seeds of treachery were beginning to sprout. Everyone worried that those close to them could be enemies, and of being accused themselves. No one would dare speak their accusations aloud, thankfully, if only so solidarity among the soldiers would remain strong.

Whatever the case, it changed nothing. They got through, they attacked the princess, and morale throughout the kingdom crumbled. They needed to find the Convent's den and put an end to the war before Ederea became further divided.

The question was, how?

Every investigation led to dead ends. No traces were left behind. All of the captured Convent soldiers died, a spell put on them by their mages killing them so they would not talk. Every island in the archipelago had been combed for Convent activity without uncovering anything.

How could they cause so much mayhem and vanish like ghosts?

Many of General Esperance's men were plagued with doubt and terror, affecting their productivity. A week after the attack, once they believed Shoafond fully secured, their lieutenant attempted to ease their qualms by treating them to a hearty meal at a popular tavern in the city. Everyone needed to step away from the castle and lift their spirits for a little while. Were a battle to ensue in their fair haven, they would need to feel alive again beforehand. A popular Ederean saying went, "Feel dead, and you may as well be." Soldiers without morale often forgot what they fought for and lost hope when the situation worsened, leading to their demise.

The tavern between the markets and the residential district was large enough to house every soldier who accepted Ulrin's offer. Every table on the ground and upper levels was full, all the chairs taken by soldiers and regular patrons. The atmosphere was lively, what with the servers and even the tavern proprietor interacting with the customers like old friends. A violinist sat between the staircases playing an old but pleasing melody.

While everyone had scattered, Ulrin and Luchs sat together at the bar being tended to by the proprietor, a hearty man with dark skin and a scar around his nose.

"Let me guess, the usual for you and your lad?" spoke the proprietor in a low, strong voice. He and Ulrin were well acquainted, it seemed.

Ulrin responded by pulling out two silver lev and handing them to the man. Knight and squire sat and chatted while waiting for their meals to be prepared. Luchs wanted to know more about the war effort, anything he cared to share now that the tight-lipped general was not around. But all Ulrin wanted to talk about was the dish he ordered. It was hard to say whether he did not speak of it because the lieutenant could not divulge that kind of information in public or simply because he was so enamored by the dish.

Their host, Dray, walked back behind the counter and brought them each a thick meat slab on a plate. Luchs thanked him for the food before he felt the need to skewer his meister knight with a fork just to make him stop talking. Dray lingered a bit longer to stare at the squire and wait for his first bite, just as Ulrin was. Bothersome as their speechless motion was, he came to eat. He grabbed his fork, carved off a decent chunk, and jammed it into his mouth. The flavor was lost to him, but there was more to enjoy. The meat was cooked evenly enough to make the surface crunch while the inside was tender and juicy. And the melted butter slathered on top gave the meat a nice texture as it slid down his throat.

Before he realized it, his plate was cleared and licked clean. Ulrin had a laugh seeing his squire eat to savor the meat yet with such gusto. "What'd I tell you? Dray, another plate over here!" The dish filled Luchs to the point he almost refused the second course, but he could not resist having more.

Suddenly, things did not seem as grim. The men looked much livelier, too, after sitting down, taking a breath, and enjoying a good meal in good company.

Breaking away from reality for a moment was just what they needed.

After realizing such, Luchs decided to keep his thoughts off the war for the time being. Letting the mind rest could give them all better insight later on.

In addition to the new plate, Dray brought out a cup of ale for Ulrin and another filled with ivory juice for the lad. "The drinks are on me."

"Mighty generous of you."

"Just 'cause you always pay your tab, Lieutenant. Don't get rosy on me." The tavern proprietor turned toward Luchs, offering a friendlier smile that showed a few missing teeth. "I've been wanting to meet this squire you kept blathering about." He looked him up and down, eying the muscle and the little visible burn scar at his neck. "Strong, and he has some experience under his belt. Looks like he could take my son on in a scuffle."

Ulrin pulled away from his drink to say, "High praise considering he's all you talk about."

To which Dray laughed. "Poke fun *after* your squire here takes a position like commandant. You knights and squires are like kids and parents in a way, aye?"

"We're more like brothers, but aye."

The two shared a few more jokes Luchs could not quite understand and laughed together, passing a few stories while he ate his fill. When Dray remembered what he said of the squire, he explained how Ulrin frequently visited the tavern while his squire was on Emiet.

"He was oft worried, asking if he made the right choice."

"In what?" Luchs asked.

"Letting that little lad lead your training," Ulrin answered. "Eurieg got in my head while you were away, saying that executioner's protégé would only make matters worse."

It made sense considering how unpredictable Executioner Sörrign behaved altogether. Luchs did not say anything for or against it. All that mattered was that neither of them got killed and returned to make things better. So far, the latter had yet to happen. There was still much he needed to learn about his Second Verse and how to use it without upsetting the land.

But such dreary thoughts did not need to be brought up for the time being.

More customers arrived following the mirth that echoed from the merry tavern. Drinks were ordered and passed around while the violinist began to play a sprightlier melody. A few of the men took out some swords and dropped them to the ground in crosses, then started a swift dance around the sharp edges. Watching them put the patrons in good spirits.

Several of the new people were knights on patrol coming in for a glance at the sudden burst of noise. Once they figured out it was just the tavern returning to its naturally vibrant self, they stayed for a quick drink before returning to their posts.

A few women stepped inside, one instantly recognizing Ulrin and seeing if she could get his attention. At noticing Ulrin gladly gave it, Luchs decided to seat himself elsewhere.

He enjoyed the music with a few squires he recognized and joined the calls for an encore once it ended.

Enjoyable as the brief respite was, it could not last long in their state of emergency. Everyone returned to their duties, ensuring the peace was kept.

As soon as Lieutenant Ulrin completed his tasks the next day, he took Luchs straight to the training grounds where they practiced with every weapon they knew how to wield.

The lieutenant proved as proficient with the sword, axe, and mace as he was with the spear. He knocked Luchs on his back more times than either cared to count.

He did not always have as much time for his squire as other meister knights did for theirs, but the change in events led him to make time. He did not want to risk losing Luchs in battle due to lack of training, so he intended to be intricately thorough in molding him into a warrior.

Fortunately, Luchs was a quick study. After taking an attack head-on, he mimicked the technique and used it on Ulrin, who then demonstrated effective counter maneuvers that threw him back.

"Didn't think I'd make this easy, did you?"

Luchs grinned. "I was hoping you wouldn't." Easy training would not provide the strength to save Ederea. He needed Ulrin to be brutal.

Readying himself for their next clash, Luchs held his sword resolutely and readied the shield on his arm to intercept any attack. It was the stance he most favored out of the others Ulrin taught him. He stared down and circled his meister knight, careful to watch how he moved his sword. Making the first move against him was foolish, but Ulrin was patient and would not react without reason to. He carried his weapon confidently in his right hand, leaving his left side exposed. Smart as it might be to attack that weak point, there were several ways to counter approaches like that.

Waiting for an opportunity made him restless, so, after bringing himself around the exposed left side, he charged at his foe. Ulrin pulled his sword in before his squire's got too close and swiftly intercepted the attack, then flicked him aside before thrusting for his head. Luchs lurched to the side before the tip of the blade hit, then moved in and for another swing. With a confident smirk, the lieutenant swiftly drew his sword close, holding Luchs' weapon in place using the guard, and strongly pushed against him.

It was not easy, but before he was pinned down, Luchs pulled his sword away from Ulrin's, held the weapon close, and put all his body into a quick lunge. That did not work so well either. Ulrin swiveled around him, then ducked low and tackled the lad, knocking him into a nearby stream.

Luchs spat out water upon resurfacing. "Really? The water?"

"I thought a quick dip might clear your head. You'll need it to keep up with me, little Luchs."

"Would it kill you to stop calling me that?" asked the drenched squire as he crawled out of the stream.

"I suppose not, but I still can't help looking at you as the sad little lad Father rescued years back."

"I'm not that lad anymore!"

"Oh?" Ulrin taunted. "Show me how you've grown then. Don't just mimic me. Fight like a real Ederean!"

Those words spurred Luchs to attack. First showing his student a grin, Ulrin then blocked the bold strike and met the full force thrown into it with his own. "'Tis wise to fear the witch god of death's cold grasp, but a warrior must face it head-on." He shoved Luchs away, letting his sword's tip swipe against the hard ground. "Never remain on the defensive for long. Fighting on the defense shows your enemy that you need to. If you must, ward them off quickly, then take the fight into your hands. Otherwise, the flag you serve under will be stained by your blood and weakness."

Luchs dove in close to make another strike, this time a horizontal swing at the shoulders that came close to slicing the neck. Surprised as he was at how close that attack came to hitting, Ulrin was mostly impressed.

"Very nice. Keep this up and you might actually need to hold back. As for me—" A grunt escaped Ulrin as he shoved the lad back again, following a swift turn that guided the pommel of his weapon into Luchs' gut. "I'm not quite ready to stop."

That was checkmate. Recognizing that, Luchs dropped his sword, showing he gave up. Only then did his meister knight take a more relaxed stance, took ten steps back, and readied himself once again.

It went the same way until it came time to stop: the squire rushed in, took a little beating, then seized the courage to take control before ending up in a position that would normally be fatal. For someone who went on about taking the offensive, Ulrin showed off a lot of flashy moves while keeping his student at bay. It was probably because he could. Many veterans knew of ways to disable enemies they fought without killing if they could afford that luxury, and preferred it.

They continued sparring with one another until nightfall. Luchs was almost too sore to move afterwards. Training with Lieutenant Ulrin made him yearn for his lost durability. Thankfully, the man reverted to his kindly self when he needed a hand up.

Things were settling down in the castle by the time they went inside. Only soldiers on patrol and servants sprucing up the halls walked about. The generals would likely be the only other ones awake, and if not, then just General Esperance.

"That lout always forgoes sleep when times get serious," Ulrin claimed.

Before turning in, they decided to check on their general and see how he handled the stress put on him. Knowing him, he would not rest after everything that happened. It was one of the reasons Ulrin became his lieutenant, he often jested—to keep the general from keeling over from exhaustion.

The halls leading to his quarters were clear and the luminescent crystal lamps lit them in pristine light enough to see. Light from the bright waxing moon shone through the windows they passed, a tranquil, comforting glow.

Upon approaching the general's quarters, Luchs felt he could walk on his own.

Ulrin opened the door to find the general deeply engrossed in countless documents spread sloppily across his desk. The general never looked their way. He stared at the parchment as if his mind was worlds away. That could not have been good.

"Ho, Eurieg! You in there?"

That loud shout only made the general scowl Ulrin's way. "I heard you enter, Lieutenant."

"Could have fooled me with you not so much as scowling our way." Ulrin casually walked over to the desk and glanced at the documents. "What's this you're reading?"

"Letters depicting the attacks made on Ederean territory by the Convent of One." Although he kept his voice steady, those words he spoke were unfortunately heavy. "A messenger bird brought word of another travesty due south-southeast of here. General Aigle is dead."

The air, once smooth and easy to breathe, became lead upon hearing the terrible news. A general dead. An entire company lost the guidance of their leader. And judging by the way General Esperance looked at the letters, he must have read that the army was not in good shape with their lieutenant in charge.

Ulrin lowered his head and pounded a clenched fist over his chest out of respect for the dead, a motion his squire mimicked.

The general flipped to another page. "I anticipated there to be a pattern to the Convent's actions, so I've been reviewing these documents to find it. Alas, none of them are consistent with each other. Every battle they engage us in, the Convent uses tactics that are completely unique to each other. Their militia should be unbalanced, and yet they keep overcoming us with their guerilla attacks."

Ulrin raised his brows. "So they've some military brains on their side. I thought we've already gone over this."

"That can't be all there is to it," the general firmly proclaimed, his stern voice shaken. "They breached The Chain, came out of nowhere to attack without warning, led us on a wild goose chase, and even eliminated Aigle, a brilliant general. The only victory we've had thus far—if'n you can call it that—was the battle at Prévinn."

Luchs cringed at the mention of that fateful day. So many perished when the vile magic rained down upon them, so many were forced to experience hellish torture as they faded.

"Eurieg, you're not thinking—"

"What else could it be but betrayal?"

The lieutenant grasped his general's shoulder, attempting to offer some comfort. "I understand what happened to Her Highness shook you, but—"

"'Tisn't only the attack on our fair Princess Camellia, Lieutenant. They know our every move. Our military has been ambushed sailing across the archipelago and the safety measures made for the civilians compromised. Either spies have miraculously slipped into our midst or we are betrayed. Betrayed..."

No one liked going to the worst-case scenario, but General Esperance looked absolutely certain of that possibility. A paranoid thought, to be sure, but neither Luchs nor Ulrin corrected him. His hands trembled while crushing the letters in his hands.

"I know it. I feel it."

Always trust your gut. Ulrin often told that to his squire since before he became that, something he must have learned from his mentors, maybe from the conflicted general as well.

What could the Convent of One do to make anyone a turncoat? They attacked innocent people and ruined lives. Homes were destroyed, families broken, and orphans made because of them.

Trying to appear composed, Luchs stepped up to the general's desk. "General Esperance, are you sure of this?"

The general looked up from his letters to the squire. "Don't wish to doubt your own, lad? Noble, perhaps, but 'tis also foolish. Men have weakness in their hearts. Some overcome it, but there are those who cannot help but succumb." After saying that, he finally noticed frustration had tightened his grip. He let the parchment go and used that hand to rub the tension in his forehead. "I don't like thinking that way either, but nothing else makes sense. They've magic on their side, aye, but even mages have their limits. They still cannot move across the archipelago without our knowing or surprise our armies so spontaneously." While pinching his index finger and thumb between the space over his eyebrows, General Esperance seemed much tenser. He sighed and said, "I've had this feeling for weeks now and tried to think about it in a multitude of ways. But every thought gainsays all we've come across. I know we've been betrayed ... and we need to find out by whom."

It was hard to hear and much harder to accept. Ulrin scowled in frustration, then glanced back at the flag that hung over their heads with conflicted eyes. The country was united under that flag, or at least it used to be. "We'll find the traitor one way or another, General. And he will be brought to justice."

No one else knew of General Esperance's suspicions. There was enough tension infecting everyone without mentioning it.

Lieutenant Ulrin kept a careful watch over his soldiers and those roaming the castle. He approached soldiers and servants with a friendly face as always, but if they were doing something out of the ordinary, he would subtly question them, see if they were up to anything.

Maxime wanted to keep his distance from others but knew he could not afford to. A general's squire needed to appear as resolute as the general he served, and he could not do so if he hid from everyone. Since learning of the potential of a traitor in their midst, he began behaving much like the skeptical, tired lad he was on Des Meurtal again.

General Esperance did not express any empathy for his squire or his fellow knights. They were soldiers, and as soldiers, they were expected to face the trying times with their heads held high, their chests puffed out, and their will unshaken.

Few moves were made against Ederea, which invited skepticism and brought on an unsavory thought. Everything they had done—the attack on La Kriod, luring Ederean forces to Ciecime, perhaps even the attempt on Princess Camellia's life—was merely to toy with them.

Luchs could not comprehend why the Convent would waste so much time, resources, and lives simply to pester Ederea? All of that unrest and suffering, he reasoned, only served to bolster their cause.

But Maxime saw it differently. He believed the Convent of One wanted to put Ederea through as much pressure as possible until the country broke from the strain. Pressure might have made diamonds, but everyone had their limits and not everyone had the strength to surpass them. The riots that resulted after the attack on the princess were but a prelude. If things became worse, the Edereans would lose their will to fight back and give in to their fear, to the Convent of One.

Although he still did not want to believe someone betrayed Ederea for the Convent of One, Luchs began to have his doubts.

As their meister knights began their search for the traitor, the squires were told to focus on their training. Unfortunately, there was much less time for their mentors to instruct them personally because of the crisis. A few other knights recognized by the general and lieutenant both offered to teach Luchs and Maxime alongside their squires. They gave some useful advice on how to use their favored techniques both with offensive and defensive measures. Luchs was especially fond of swinging his shield around like a mace, a method that definitely served in a pinch if used properly.

Many squires gathered every now and then to have at each other in massive brawls behind the castle. They met each other's weapons, socked, headbutted, and beat each other until unable to continue.

Working out and working themselves over was excruciating. But resting while everyone gave it their all made Luchs feel weak, so when he was not strengthening his body, he was strengthening his mind. Observing others in combat had its merits, such as seeing how they responded to attacks aimed at their weak points.

There were occasions when the remaining generals occupied the castle archives while searching for information that could have been tampered with or stolen. After everything that happened, they could not yet rule out the possibility of someone infiltrating the yet impregnable Castle Ederea.

One day, Luchs caught Levin on his way to the archives. He claimed to see Maxime suspiciously making way for the area beneath the castle, lurking in the shadows and looking hither and thither as if on the lookout. Just to ease the eager squire's curiosities, they went to the archives together and found Maxime hiding in a corner and reading from a pile of documents.

Even if he tried to hide it now, it would not do him any good.

"Ho there, Maxime!"

He turned back with a surprised look, surprise which immediately faded when he saw who found him.

"What's that you got there?"

Maxime looked back to the parchments he had in hand. "General Esperance's classified documents, or duplicates at least."

"Duplicates?"

"Every general writes copies of their records and hides them throughout the archives in case of an emergency requiring the originals to be destroyed."

Levin arched an eyebrow, bewildered. "Sounds complicated."

Maxime nodded. "'Tis a protocol that's been followed since the days of the conquerors. Best to remember the old ways in case those times return."

"And what will General Esperance say when he finds out you've been prying into his secrets?" Luchs asked.

Considering that made Maxime nervous, but he did not give it much thought. "Meister knights should keep their squires in the know. How else am I supposed to learn?"

Luchs understood how he felt, but going through classified information was a serious offense. "And if'n you get caught, then what? I doubt General Esperance will forgive you for that."

"I'm not just going to stay quiet and keep training. I want to help our cause, to keep more from dying. If I can figure something out from General Esperance's documents, then hopefully we can end this war all the sooner."

With that kind of mindset, it would be hard to convince him to stop.

But how did he find them? If the generals hid their documents in such an unrestricted place, they had to have put them someplace that no one could easily access.

Bringing that up made Maxime tense up and even look a little guilty. "I might have had some help."

He let someone help him steal military secrets? That sounded more boneheaded and irresponsible than he would usually behave. It showed how desperate he was.

...No, *that* showed how desperate he was.

Out of everyone in the entire castle, the one who came up to them with a pile of parchment in hand was Vandelas, squire to the man his general detested the most. And, of course, tailing him as always was the petite snow-white fox.

Having never seen the jinx before, Levin jumped. He was almost as surprised by how the others underreacted to its presence.

Rather than explain what a fox was doing there, Luchs thought to find out what the lad was up to. "Didn't think you'd put down your sword for a few parchments," he said to the dark lad. "What're you doing here?"

Vandelas glanced Maxime's way. "I was trying to read, but your friend was being loud. Helping him seemed like the best way to quiet him down."

Cold as always, but there was something off about him. He had a harshness to his voice and a more reserved demeanor than usual. If sunlight were not shining through the clear crystalline walls, Luchs might have assumed the full moon was out.

"And did Maxime tell you what might happen if'n you do?"

"It doesn't take a genius to figure out what stealing a general's documents will get you. Like I said, I just want him quiet." He handed Maxime the documents. "These were stashed underneath the shelf with the foreign history texts. Another enchantment kept them hidden, but it reactivates itself like the others."

"Are there any more?"

"None that I can find." Vandelas walked back into the labyrinth of information with his pet in tow.

How odd to see he knew where he was going. Luchs ventured beneath the castle dozens of times and never once saw him. Plenty of others came and went, but never the Kindhrin lad.

Now Luchs was curious. Leaving Levin to entertain Maxime, he followed Vandelas. He found him reading an old tome, its pages open to a well-detailed drawing of what looked to be a land of gold. He tried to get closer and see what the text on the page beside it said, but stopped when the fox saw him and started growling.

One word from its master was all it took to quiet the fox. Since he did not bother shooing him away, he must not have cared about the intrusion.

Taking a few steps closer, Luchs saw a few strange words in the text: Harah Krid.

"So you came here to learn about your homeland. That's your homeland, aye? Harah Krid?"

"Maybe once." The tone of his valsara darkened when he spoke. Vandelas' gaze never left the pages, his gloomy, glacial eyes sparking an intrigue that grew with every syllable he read. The text contained the history of the country, it seemed. As grim as he appeared, he showed a yearning to understand where he came from.

It was something Luchs could relate to.

Seeing him look content with the read made it easy to understand how callous he was earlier. "So you're finally taking a breather?"

Irritated by the continued interruption, the dark lad glanced at Luchs. He never said a word, staring at him with a piercing gaze that ushered him to speak on.

"Talk about you has been going around as of late. Barking at the knights, thrashing anyone who gets close whenever you have a sword in hand—you're more belligerent than usual. A crazed beast."

Blunt, but Vandelas did not seem to mind. His gaze remained steady and unmoved before Luchs finished talking, and upon weighing what he heard, it turned back to the text. "And what of it? You're suddenly worried for me?"

"Worried they'll choose to cage you is more like it."

"They're welcome to try."

"You sound so sure of yourself."

Luchs hoped to reel more out of him, but he would not say much more voluntarily. That was how it looked at first anyway. When he turned the page, his firm expression suddenly appeared forced, his eyes reflecting a frail sadness. He continued to read on with intrigue but grew distracted. Sorrow plagued him, a sorrow that grew stronger as he struggled to bury it.

At his leg sat the little fox. It stared at its master, then, once prim and patient, began gently pawing at his pant leg for attention. His focus broke and drew down to the beast at his foot. He locked eyes with it, then bent down and picked it up into his arms. The aloof, cynical child once again resembled an actual human being while paying attention to his beloved pet.

That mirth did not last. A cold sigh passed his lips and through the bulky scarf. "I have to get stronger," he quietly said. "So that I can protect her."

The fox brought out a vulnerable side of him that he often kept hidden. He was cloistering himself inside the tome for something other than intrigue or rest. He was struggling to distract himself from something grave. Those once stone-cold eyes began to show dread and fear.

All for the princess.

Luchs knew it was her he thought of. Those two, for some reason, were rather close.

He once saw them together. It was a calm day, nothing out of the ordinary. He went up to the princess as if she were an ordinary lass. Her handmaidens did not mind his presence in the least. They spoke with one another familiarly, and he looked genuinely happy all the while.

"You truly care about her, don't you? The princess, I mean."

Having seen Luchs at his worst, Vandelas could not quite dismiss him after their roles reversed. He kept quiet a moment and looked the burly squire's way a few times before closing the tome.

"Princess Camellia has done much for me since we met, more than I can hope to ever repay."

"How so?"

He remained hesitant a moment, then spoke. "Being what I am ... put me in a compromising place in Vermalio. There was much I wanted to know and do there that I was not allowed to. If I stayed there after all that happened, I don't know what I might have done. When Princess Camellia offered to bring me here, my path didn't look so dark anymore. She saved me from a home that was slowly turning into a prison before it could ruin me."

There was a soft sentiment in his voice, yet the way Vandelas spoke made Vermalio sound like a hell in some way. It was hard to believe such a venerable kingdom would seem like a terrible place. They were trustworthy enough to be close comrades with Ederea for half a century, even when tensions were high during the war against Pterna.

Then, as Luchs looked back to the old tome beneath the dark lad's hand, he began to understand what he meant.

Having had his moment to feel vulnerable, Vandelas placed the fox atop the shelf and reached for the tome, picking it up into his arm. "I was not there to protect her before, but I intend to be strong enough for when I will be. When next we face the Convent of One, I'll slaughter them all."

He walked past Luchs with purpose and put the tome back in its proper place.

There really were many ways to cope with grief, even bracing for what else might feed it.

Luchs did not see him off yet. "Off to pummel some more squires?"

"Or a knight, if I can get one to take me seriously."

"Leave them be, varlet!" Luchs chortled. "Let me get my gear and I'll amuse you for a while."

Vandelas was neither amused nor irritated, and went on without giving a response. Whether he took him seriously or not, Luchs intended to show him he was not alone. He was just as serious about stopping the Convent of One.

~ Fifteenth Chapter ~
Precautions

Attacks from the Convent of One escalated as methods were put into place to stop them. Enemy ships sailed across Ederea, mirages that could attack others, as if they owned the country. The military barely managed to keep them from sacking the islands they called home, but suffered countless casualties in every attack.

General Esperance had been hard at work attempting to figure out where the Convent of One was hiding and who the traitor aiding them might be. Spies from the Kelpie Company constantly met with him to deliver whatever intel they collected. Since spying on the enemy was impossible, they mostly relayed on the state of the restless Edereans. If they found anything on the Convent of One, it would likely not remain secret for long.

Luchs unintentionally intruded on one of those meetings. At the time, General Esperance was in his quarters being handed a letter by a woman. The squire stepped out the moment he realized what was going on.

He was curious to know who the woman was. There was something about her eyes—those hard, imposing eyes—that left him petrified. Was she one of the spies, or merely delivering a message for one? He thought he recognized her, but did not understand how.

While the generals searched for ways to take the upper hand, the soldiers put their focus on combating the enemy's callous attacks.

Hearing of the atrocities committed by the Convent of One made Luchs restless. He wanted to join the battle, to help protect the people, but he still needed to ready himself.

Every day when Ulrin dismissed him from his duties, Luchs went behind the castle to exercise control of the Second Verse. His focus slipped more often, distracted by the terrible changes that further met the Convent's desired outcome. He barely managed to pile the earth onto itself.

The tricks he learned failed him. His focus on the enemy made his already volatile emotions run amok and weakened the control he had. Psyching himself up only made the structures he barely managed to shape crumble into gravel, eventually crushing them into sand. He kept trying again and again until finally breaking down, falling to his knees, and pounding the ground in a violent rage.

His power, adjoined with his rage, surged through his hammering fist, making thick cracks in the ground, cracks that spread into the plateau's foundation. The frightful *boom, boom, boom* that resounded went unheard by the one causing it.

The damage stopped spreading when a hand reached out and grabbed his wrist. What caught his attention was not the hand being strong enough to restrain him, but rather how slim it was.

He turned back to find a woman in frilly garb grasping his wrist only to release when he unclenched his fist. She was not alone. Accompanying her were a few other women dressed in similar garb and—

"Princess Camellia!"

Concern was clear in Luchs' voice when he called out her name. Barely three weeks passed since she received her ghastly injuries, but she stood on her own feet with only the hand of her servant to support her.

Luchs stood up, albeit a little shaky from the reckless use of his power.

"Princess, are you all right? Your injuries—"

The little lass smiled. "They are nothing to fret over. Time and rest have rendered them a mere discomfort, certainly tolerable enough to be about." Her radiant eyes showed mirth, but it quickly passed. "'Twould be imprudent of me to remain bedridden whilst my country faces this crisis, certainly after the tumult it caused."

It was hard to forget how the people reacted after hearing of her condition, let alone seeing it. Her words remained steady and her tone gentle, putting Luchs at ease. Everyone would fare better after knowing their shard of sunshine had as well.

She approached the shaky squire, guided by the lady holding her hand. Despite the outburst she so clearly witnessed, the princess smiled upon him and her eyes reflected a soothing radiance.

"You are not alone. These harsh times trouble us all."

Those words were a gentle embrace that wrapped around him.

A little worn out from his fit, and suddenly aware of how acted, Luchs groaned and rubbed the top of his head. He could not bring himself to look her way, embarrassed by what she witnessed.

He was more than just troubled, and the princess could see that. She tenderly placing a hand over his shoulder, grasping it kindly. "Their tricks shan't last. These people shall be found and their power cut. Father has been working tirelessly to ensure that, as have the fine men protecting the kingdom. All will be well again."

It was hard to believe her words despite how absolute her claim was. No conflict resounded in her voice and her expression remained unchanged, never showing any telltale signs of uncertainty.

It was charming albeit foolish to assume all would end well.

Luchs could not help but chuckle. "You do any dancing with the angels in your rest?" After recalling he spoke to royalty, he hung his head and gave the lass with an apologetic look. "Beg pardon, Your Highness. I just—"

The princess chortled seeing him struggle to recompose himself and appear respectful. It made Luchs blush. Still, it was better than her being upset with him.

"...How can you be so optimistic after what happened?"

The princess' moonlit irises were briefly eclipsed by a blink reflecting confusion. Whatever it was about, it did nothing to damper the brilliant glimmer in her valsara. "I believe in our people and those who fight for their sake: the soldiers, their superiors, our allies, and you."

She stepped forward with the handmaiden holding her hand and looked at Luchs with a comforting gaze as she held out her other hand in asking for his. Confused as he was, Luchs followed her gesture and put his hand over hers. Her gentle little palm sunk into his when she cupped them together, her fingers lacing around the strong hand. Then, before he could ask what that was about, a veil of beauteous light enveloped the maiden's hand. The light surprised the squire but soothed his distraught mind while reinvigorating him all the same. It was an enchanting glow that made the moon and stars of the night sky pale in comparison, one that could only be called holy.

Luchs remembered seeing it before and knew it was meant to help him.

After the light faded, Princess Camellia's hand slowly slipped from Luchs' and her body slipped backwards. The handmaiden connected to her quickly lowered herself and caught her.

The spell restored Luchs' strength while, consequentially, sapping the princess of hers.

"P-Princess—"

She smiled as her servant helped her to her feet by the shoulder and hand. "A momentary fatigue, I promise. 'Tis but a side effect of my magic."

"Magic...?"

"Rejuvenance. It heals wounds and diminishes strain on the body and mind." She stopped a moment to take a breath. "But this gift at times weakens me and renders me quite vulnerable."

Why would she use it on me then?

After going so far as to exhaust herself for him, saying the thought aloud would only be an insult to her kindness. He aimed to oppose it silently, but her widening smile spoke how well she saw through him.

"You go through much strain to control your power. I know how you insist on using it for battle. 'Tis only right that I lessen that burden, however fleeting that may be."

"But why should that fall onto you? Why burden yourself to help me?"

"It pains me to see another suffer. And moving forward with something alone tends to worsen that suffering the longer it lasts." Something told him she was not referring to his training. Her luminescent eyes peered through the muscle and bone, into what lay beneath, the conflict that ensued inside. They reflected the chaos that left him so uneasy. It was stupefying. And she saw it all.

But it was the first time Luchs realized how he truly saw himself: vulnerable, weak, and afraid.

"No one should have to endure their ordeals alone. And since not many understand your power, I thought to share my own."

Luchs was at a loss for words. That little lass before him was nothing short of kindness, generosity, and purity incarnate. It was little wonder why everyone in Ederea loved her so.

"I would be grateful if you kept this between us. Father prefers my magic to be kept a guarded secret."

With her words of encouragement given, the handmaidens guided their princess back to the castle grounds.

Luchs watched the princess go, still stunned by the ray of hope that shone upon him. Then, one of the handmaidens looked back at him.

It was the woman General Esperance met with before.

That ferocity, that hardened look in her eyes revealed she was no mere servant. The mightiest warriors bore those same eyes, the eyes of someone familiar with engaging death, and delivering it.

And she stared at him as though prepared to dance with the witch god no one dared name.

"Oh, and Luchs!" Princess Camellia called back to him, already sounding a little better. The handmaiden guiding her stopped to allow her mistress to turn and face him. "Please do restore the plateau to its proper state. 'Tis our home, after all."

No words passed his lips. The squire just flashed a forced grin.

She must have understood his intent. They were all on their way again, all except for the frightening lady who remained a second longer to hold up her finger, gesturing her demand for silence. A shiver went down his spine, interpreting it as a threat rather than a request.

It embarrassed him how he lost control of the Second Verse. That said, having the princess' faith motivated him to keep it together.

The damage was not severe. It would not take long to fix.

A month had passed without a whisper from the Convent of One. Their sieges ceased and no one had seen a sign of them. Despite how relieving that should have been, no one could relax knowing full well how dangerous their silence was. The princess never left Shoafond after fully recovering for that reason.

The attack on Prévinn, then La Kriod, the attempt on Princess Camellia's life. What horrifying atrocity would they commit next?

Every military faction across the archipelago became more precautious during the calm. Seeing as no one knew where the enemy hid, they sought to prepare for any eventuality conceivable. King Godefroy even recalled ten thousand soldiers from the mainland east and west of Ederea to confront this threat.

The enemy had never once attacked the mainland territories of Rivieredell and Cragfill. They were not always a part of the country; Rivieredell was ceded to Ederea by the other Abioan kingdoms after the days of the du Joiec conquerors came to an end, and Cragfill had been granted to Ederea by Vermalio to recognize their countries' friendship.

It seemed they only had interest in claiming the Ederea they knew.

It frustrated Luchs that all he could do was train, but he put that frustration to good use. His combat abilities improved drastically with the guidance of Ulrin and his helpful followers, and he found out how effective their efforts were after enough practice.

One sunny afternoon, many squires and knights gathered in the training grounds, as they have done regularly, and attacked each other in small groups. Many paired up in groups of three or four, but Luchs partnered himself with only Levin. Everyone was given weapons with their blades shaved down.

To begin the exercise, the leading knight picked a center point for the battlefield and had everyone take a hundred steps away from it in different directions, then they charged at one another. Several squires struck each other hard using their momentum in their attacks. A knight attacking Luchs aimed for his neck, and Luchs met the strike by holding his shield up, then pushed against the ground and rammed his entire body into the man, knocking him to the ground. In a real battle, any warriors following his lead would likely have trampled the man. Since he survived, though, he got back into the rhythm only to be smacked aside the head by the hilt of Levin's sword.

Anyone recognizing they had been hit by a "fatal" blow dropped their weapons and left the battlefield to wait for the bout to end.

Fourteen warriors still stood by the time every group clashed with one another. Maxime was fighting strong alone against two other lads. Meanwhile, Luchs and Levin opposed an adept soldier, Levin's meister knight, Stewart Halbrek, who wielded a thick sword. As heavy as the weapon looked, its wielder guided it with a deft hand and had plenty of muscle to refrain from any unwanted staggering. Getting close to him was not easy with how he waved that massive sword about.

But Sir Stewart had a weakness both of his opponents knew how to exploit. Capable as he was, he tended to slow after haphazardly throwing his sword so many times.

One. Two. Three. Four. Five. Six.

There!

Seeing his stamina wane, Levin brought his sword to meet his meister knight's and held it in place long enough for Luchs to circle the man. Sir Stewart shoved his squire aside and hurled his weapon at the burly one. But the blade swept past Luchs as he stepped around it, giving the squire the perfect opportunity to hurl his shield into the knight's gut.

Everyone loved how Luchs used his shield with a throw of the fist, even those on the receiving end. Although he lost his astonishing durability, he had grown strong and learned to fight like a warrior. And his peers came to respect him not for who his meister was, but for how passionately he fought.

Still, he felt he could do better.

"So, what do you think the general wants?"

One cool night, Luchs and Ulrin made way for the throne room after being summoned by General Esperance. Why they were not instead informed to head for his quarters instead, they did not know. It had to be important to take up the king's time.

Ulrin shrugged in response to his squire. "Hard to say. Mayhap he'll finally admit the pressure cracked him."

It was not likely given how stubborn that man was, but the thought made Luchs chuckle. Proud people made the most outrageous faces when they lost their composure and struggled to maintain it.

The halls were empty that night. No servants wandered the halls having finished their tasks, resting for the early morn ahead. Luchs never realized how the collective *clop*, *clop* of boots and people's gabbing drowned out some of the waterfalls' roars. It was hard to believe they could be drowned out at all, almost as hard as it was to believe the falls sounded different at night. They had a rather serene ring, something like a whale's song, one that steadily faded as they approached the doors to the throne room.

When opening the doors, they found not just General Esperance, his squire, and King Godefroy, but also a few executioners.

Whatever their meeting was about must have been unorthodox.

The chatter ceased as soon as they entered, and no one spoke a word until the throne room doors were closed again.

"Well, doesn't this seem important? Mayhap too important for a mere lieutenant," Ulrin jested.

The king chortled. "Yet General Esperance thinks it best you be here, and I trust his judgment. Besides, it leaves more for the lads to learn."

"Shall we get on with the briefing, Your Majesty?" an executioner uttered. Most of his face was concealed beneath bandages, but his left eye, a hard dark blue bead, was left exposed. Judging by the harsh redness in places the bandages did not cover, the injury mostly consisted of burns. "Time is of the essence."

"Aye, aye." The king stepped toward his throne, perhaps out of habit rather than intent, then faced his men with a stern gaze befitting a war hero. "Since Jarl is so eager, I'll get to the point. The Convent of One's carelessness in freely prowling our waters has done more than insult our might. It left them exposed. They've grown too complacent to keep their secrecy, enough that we may take advantage of it.

"Four days prior, a letter arrived from Commandant Soless of Levia Fossa containing detailed information of where and when an enemy fleet would arrive. Every detail—the number of ships, soldiers, even their ammunition count—was spot on. With that intel, our troops routed the lot of them, destroyed their vessels, and took the survivors prisoner in our Cage Falls. And this morn, we received another letter from Levia Fossa, this one coming from the Commandant's source."

"The first piece of intel was a means of proof, reassurance that the source is genuine," General Esperance stated.

"Meaning said source is willing to share more?" his lieutenant inquired.

"Aye, according to Commandant Soless."

The other executioner, a bald man casually lying an axe against his shoulder, looked impressed at first, then was struck with disbelief. "Who's the man's informant?"

A wry grin crossed over the king's face. "A survivor from La Kriod. The good commandant came across him whilst defending his shores from an attack and freed him from an enemy vessel. Seems this soul overheard a fair deal of secrets during his incarceration, playing the helpless prisoner as he had."

"A hopeful priest who prayed to be saved," uttered Maxime.

"A reason why we must keep our faith, lad. Now, to the point, you must take a party and make for Levia Fossa to meet this source of Soless'.

Get as much as you can from him, anything that may prove of use against the enemy. He may be the key to crippling these monsters."

"And us, Your Majesty?" Jarl prodded.

"Protection. You two shall ensure our informant's survival."

"All due respect, sire," said the axe-wielder, "we're not bodyguards. We're executioners, slayers of the treacherous."

"Consider anyone who targets him a traitor then. With how Lady Malute has eclipsed Lady Sundralla's boons as of late, the Convent may well target him."

Whatever argument either executioner had was dropped. The situation was much too dire to think about titles or proper roles, and they knew it well. Everyone wanted the war to end before it claimed too much.

"Our time is nigh, friends. Let's not waste it."

To conclude the audience, the subjects bowed to their king and went their separate ways. General Esperance looked much more at ease with the executioners absent, though still appearing disgruntled. He and his subordinates left the throne room together.

That sour look on his face made Ulrin grin.

"Not one word, Lieutenant."

All the man did was snicker, not speak.

"I'll make the arrangements forthwith. Should all go well, you'll arrive at Levia Fossa within a couple of days."

Ulrin glanced at his general, looking perplexed. "You're not coming?"

"There's something important I must see to here. I have faith you three shall represent our company well nonetheless."

Maxime turned to look at his meister knight. He seemed hurt, a little crossed even. All that kept him from speaking out of turn was the respect he swore to have for his meister knight.

Sudden as the change was, Ulrin accepted it with a shrug and nod.

The order went out shortly after the meeting with King Godefroy for the Sea Drake soldiers to depart for Levia Fossa. Three warships set sail through what used to be waters infested by Convent vessels. Theirs were the only ships to move across those waters. The goddess of luck was shining upon them for a change.

But that did not convince Lieutenant Ulrin that all was well. He remained his rare yet stubbornly skeptical self throughout the voyage, and made second guesses the farther out they went. The lack of an enemy threat was making him paranoid. Of course, no one blamed him, not with the madness that had been sewn across Ederea. It kept him on high alert, as he should have been.

The seas were calm, but the wind slammed against their sails. Dark clouds rolled in, absconding with the sun's brilliant light. No storms assailed them, though, nothing so awful that they needed to change course.

Luchs could not relax for much of the voyage. The restless valsara around him made him feel the same. The valsara in the water behaved similarly to that of the land: faint and seemingly inactive. But for some reason, the ocean's valsara spiked erratically every so often, bringing him small pangs of stress much like the migraines he felt on occasion. He kept a constant lookout because of that abnormality just to be sure there were no surprises.

One evening, he found Maxime leaning against the railing on the quarterdeck, admiring how the fading sunlight shimmered against the horizon. He seemed peaceful enough but still looked despondent.

Maxime turned around before Luchs could speak up. The *creak* of the floorboards he stepped on gave him away.

"A right beauty, eh Maxime?" Luchs asked when he faced him.

Maxime nodded. "Aye. A fine masterpiece the goddesses Untae and Sundralla created together."

"Didn't take you for a poet."

"'Tis something the general's wife said once."

"You met his wife?"

"When she came to visit him. She's a fine lady, very kind."

He kept his voice strong if not tired, trying to hide the dreariness he felt. He was as proud as any Ederean.

"He's no Cain."

A smirk drew along Maxime's face listening to Luchs. "I thank Lady Sundralla every day for that. The man values his troops too much to treat them like cannon fodder."

"He's a smart one too—has to be to wrangle this pack of bampots."

That smirk twisted and opened wide into a hearty laugh. They knew all too well how foolhardy the men they worked with were. The craziest thing either of them saw was that one man who tried to make himself into a living cannonball.

"Then you know he's smart enough not to get rid of you."

His laughter suddenly cut off. Try as he had to cover up his surprise, it only made him look more sheepish and ashamed of having such doubtful thoughts.

It was hard not to chuckle seeing those saucer eyes grow wider still like an owl's.

Despite how obvious his mood was, it did not seem likely he would lay what plagued him bare. *He wouldn't understand*, he probably thought. It was reasonable thinking given how Luchs himself was never rejected by those he cared for, or even feared the rejection.

"If he really wanted to get rid of you, he would have by now."

"Why'd he send me off if he didn't deign to come himself?"

"Why does he pickle the minnows he buys from the fishmongers? The man is as odd as the troops he leads, he is."

That remark shook the gloom off Maxime, bringing him to laugh again. Brilliant a general though he was, the man had strange taste.

"Guess that explains his excessive reliance on Lieutenant Ulrin."

While not the best choice of words, they did not sound at all hostile or malignant, simply an observation of strange behavior. But what sort? The general seemed about as reliant on his subordinate as ever.

"What's that supposed to mean?"

"You don't know? General Esperance has been using this war to test Lieutenant Ulrin's capabilities—not just in combat, but also in decisive decision making and more. He wants to know how he'd handle managing the army himself once the time comes."

"Wait, he wants to make Ulrin a general?"

"Aye, someday. Like he did when making me his squire, he wants to ensure his choice won't be a mistake." Reminiscing on that part for a moment, Maxime laughed at the constant hesitation unbefitting of an indomitable veteran. "You'd think after six years he would have nothing more to prove."

If General Esperance knew Ulrin the way Luchs did, he probably knew of the man's faults all too well, particularly were he distracted by a fetching maiden as he had been every so often. And he had a hard time pulling away from his ale too.

His faults aside, Ulrin had qualities worth someone considering offering him such a position. The only mistake would be refusing him simply because of his human shortcomings.

Their discussion dying down, Luchs began to realize how late it was, the sun almost completely sunk over the horizon. Most of the crew not on lookout were already in the berth readying for a meal before the day's end. They agreed it was best to join them before all the good food had been taken.

But Maxime stopped halfway to the main deck, his eyes fixated on the darkened space ahead. Luchs thought to see for himself what caught his friend's attention, but he only saw dark blue waters and a near-black sky. It was relieving to see no strange ships sailed their way. He insisted something was out there and walked briskly to the beak of the ship to get a better look. While there still appeared to be nothing out of the ordinary, as Maxime walked, he looked much more excitable.

"Land! Lieutenant, Admiral, land ho!"

Land?

There was absolutely nothing on the horizon.

Luchs ran up to where Maxime was before he rushed back the way he came to get their captain. He had to strain his eyes fairly hard to even get a glimpse, but there it was. There was the smallest stretch of land slithering past the border between sea and sky.

Good gods, he has some peepers on him!

The swift squire reached the ship's captain and found he had fallen asleep, his body slumped against the wheel. He grabbed the man's broad shoulders and started shaking him awake. "Confound it, Admiral! Get your lazy arse up already! We've reached Levia Fossa."

And he was *much* livelier than usual, more assertive. Where did that melancholy go?

Irate as he was when shaken from slumber, the admiral lightened up upon seeing the smudge of land with his own eyes. Although, he did start spewing some colorful language when he saw his lookout had also fallen asleep.

It did not take long for the crew below to hear the news. Luchs helped one of the soldiers unfurl the sails, the evening winds strong enough to carry them to shore by the time the sun had set.

None came to greet the military ships with dusk long passed and the town's curfew in effect aside from the perturbed dockmaster. It took some convincing to assure him that they were the Sea Drake Company while Ulrin stood there still noshing on the sea slugs from dinner. Fortunately, they had a letter stamped with the royal seal to ensure their stay.

Whether not to seem rude or simply to get them off his dock, the dockmaster showed those who preferred to sleep on land the way to the inn. It was a welcome change from sleeping in the ratty old hammocks between the ship's cannons.

When the sun rose, everyone retrieved their mounts from the horse transport and rode straight for the military facility north-northwest of the town. The sun shone brightly that morn and the skies were clear, offering fine weather for a ride. The island was abundant in rich greenery: tall, healthy grass, trees with full trunks, the occasional patch of golden flowers along the path, bushels of bushes. Herds of yaks peacefully roamed the wide landscape.

The land was beautiful, serene. But there was something strange about it. Every mile or so they traversed, it felt like the path descended into a slope, the land receding ever so slightly. Ahead of the company was a clear view of the land arching downward below sea level. It was breathtaking to see everything the land had to offer from that angle, but the phenomenon left something to be desired: a tall, protective wall, for instance. If a tidal wave were ever to hit the island, it would likely drown from the impact. Many of the troops speculated the same thing, but for some odd reason, storms never reached Levia Fossa's waters.

A few soldiers were reminded of the legend of Levia Fossa as they rode along the sloped land.

Ages ago, there was a terrifying giant serpent that ravaged the great seas, devouring everything in its path. It threatened to lay waste to all of Avariu until a great acolyte of Lady Untae confronted it. The acolyte opposed the colossal beast with incredible divine power, granted to her by her goddess, in a conflict that tore through the central continent, forming the Ederean archipelago. The battle lasted for many a day until the acolyte finally bested the beast, sealing it in a bottomless pit formed in the ruins of their conflict. That pit was in the center of Levia Fossa, its seal undisturbed for millennia.

Perhaps the monster's very presence kept the storms at bay.

It was a shame they would not get the chance to see the seal, but there were more pressing matters ahead of them.

The path the party had taken led them down a rough hillside that looked to be pieced together by boulders. It took a while for the horses to adjust to the terrain and gallop through it without trouble. Past that was a clear, smooth path that led to a long stone bridge connecting to a massive fortress.

The military facility stood proudly overhead, the shadow it cast blocking out the sun. The bailey surrounding it promised absolute protection, its foundation almost as impressive as that of Castle Ederea. Beneath the base of the walls was a rocky cliff that was much too steep to scale. Several guards armed with crossbows kept watch from atop the gate, ready to rain arrows down on anyone bold enough to invade. The guards noticed the party's approach immediately, and instead of taking aim, they looked to be conversing about something. When they finished, the iron gates rose to grant the party entrance to their facility.

The courtyard within was filled with dozens of knights, squires, and even pages all performing repetitions with swords and spears. A drillmaster oversaw it all from atop a flight of stairs leading to the gate of the secondary bailey.

It was clear how organized the facility was compared to Des Meurtal.

Luchs was already jealous to find the facility so close to a populated area, but to see the pages receiving proper instruction made him a little sour.

Ah well. At least I know I'm ready.

Shortly after entering their facility did the drillmaster notice the visitors. He watched them a moment, then gave the order for those training to continue their reps without interruption. From the tone of his voice, it sounded like his words carried a subtle yet vague threat. Odds were the trainees knew what it was.

Ulrin smiled as their host came to greet them. "Hate to interrupt the exercises, Commandant. Mayhap we should return another time."

The troops all groaned despite knowing it was only small talk.

Commandant Soless was a rather robust man. He wore his red hair beneath a sharp-looking helm, its visor lifted to expose his big black eyes. Impressive as his thick girth was underneath his yak hide leather armor, most of his body was lean, rippling muscle. The man bore a big, jolly smile when approaching his guests. "Nonsense, Lieutenant Ulrin! You and Eurieg's men are more than welcome in my facility. Come, we've much to discuss."

The training men and lads continued their exercise, never stopping to observe their guests. Once they reached the stairs, the commandant called on one of the men on duty, a young-looking thing barely out of his squiring days, and instructed him to watch over the exercises and call out anyone who slipped up. "Remember: loud, powerful voice. Let it come from your belly," he said. It might be a difficult task for him considering the man barely had any belly at all.

A group of soldiers took their guests' mounts to a massive stable built on the other side of the secondary wall for rest and feed.

"I don't mean to question how you do things, Soless, but are they really going to listen to him?"

The commandant chuckled at Ulrin. "Probably not," he admitted shamelessly, "but should anyone pull me away from our business, there's space for them on my wall."

The bald executioner, Reur, joined in the rough laughter. Those who shared an aversion toward executioners hoped he did not think their host serious.

Most of Ulrin's men were dismissed as soon as they reached the facility's main keep. Only Ulrin, Luchs, Maxime, and Executioners Jarl and Reur remained in the company of Commandant Soless as they followed him through the busy halls. Servants, soldiers, and students all scurried hither and thither following one task or another, scarcely stopping for a moment's rest. Footsteps echoed through every hall, tuning out any hushed conversations one might have.

"I see everything is as bustling as ever."

The commandant nodded. "Aye, and more so than ever since the threat of that blasted Convent. There's always much work to be done securing our waters and land all the while ensuring our pages have the chance to learn before rushing off into a real battle."

The bandaged Jarl coughed to interrupt. "Speaking of which, where might the one we came here for be?"

"Ha! I like this one. Right to the point, he—" Commandant Soless paused a moment, losing his breath after seeing the executioner. He had not gotten a good look at him until now. "Ralias' gauntlet, man! What happened to you?"

His only exposed eye twitched at the man's spontaneous reaction. He did not look too pleased to be reminded of his injury. "Never you mind."

"I'd steer clear of that, mate, unless you want to find that out firsthand." Unlike other executioners, Reur was a more sociable and vocal sort, not to mention informative.

The commandant took that warning to heart. "Er, right... Right then, our little informant. We came across him after claiming an enemy ship. He was their prisoner—not their only one, but the only one the Convent hadn't yet questioned before killing. I take it they thought him the least in the know compared to his comrades. But the man spent enough time left alive to learn plenty about them."

How that could even be possible when someone was a prisoner boggled them all. Fortunately, they did not have to wait long for answers. While they were talking, the commandant brought them to the room where their informant had been placed.

The room was somewhere on the fourth floor past the soldiers' barracks. It was spacious enough to house three people and had plenty of furniture to keep its occupants comfortable. Judging by the quality of the fabric of the bed covers and the rugs and curtains, it must have been a guest room meant for visiting nobles. But the guest was far from noble.

No one expected the informant to be Muir Dubois.

~ Sixteenth Chapter ~

Strain

"The bishop?"

Everyone was as surprised as Luchs. Given how Muir despised the Convent of One and their opposition of the Gods of the Natural Order, it was astonishing they kept him alive at all.

The crotchety priest turned to face his guests with a look of relief as his impatience dissipated. "Ah, now don't you look familiar. Weren't you with the First Company's general?"

Remembering his manners was trying given who he was addressing. He could not even keep a smile. "I'm his lieutenant."

Muir mused over that for a moment, trying to remember exactly where he had seen him before. The priest was likely too preoccupied shouting and thrashing about when he was being dragged out of the throne room to remember anything else from that time.

Not wanting to wait for answers, Maxime nudged Ulrin, urging him to remember why they were there. He might have interrogated the man himself if General Esperance had not left Ulrin in charge.

"You tipped us off about the Convent's attack?"

"Indeed."

"With what? Commandant Soless says you've been held captive the entire time."

A dark reaction rolled over the bishop's face, his scowl spreading the already depressing wrinkles on his face. He tried to muster words but failed to say anything right away. The bony hands he kept atop the table he sat at trembled. "Held captive, aye..." Stopping for a moment to smack his dry lips, Muir took a deep breath before continuing. "After La Kriod fell, many of the survivors were captured, myself included. We were kept in their leaky brig until this slack-jawed, broad-headed, putrid barbarian came up to us, smacked us with a riding crop, and demanded we tell him who maintained The Chain."

"He must have thought you knew of a way to pass it."

"And all he snared were humble men and women of the cloth. Without the Grand Acolyte, we were of no use to him. But the heathen did not let our suffering end there. He questioned everyone individually while the rest of us were put to work. Everyone was killed one by one, each failing to give him what he was after.

"My time had almost come when brave Soless liberated me from that ghastly ship. Had it not been for him, I would have joined my brothers and sisters in the Elysium."

Jarl groaned loudly. "That still doesn't explain how you pulled more of his comrades down with him."

Muir laughed dryly a moment. "Ah, yes. 'Twas a trifle. You see, the heathens had foolishly loose lips—spouted every little thing they heard to one another, they did. They seem to have a surplus of crystals in their possession that allows them to communicate with their own across the archipelago. 'Twas the same day I heard of the plan to strike La Sceaud that Commandant Soless rescued me."

As if the Convent didn't have enough magical help, Luchs thought.

Fear gripped the Ederean soldiers whenever they learned that the enemy had yet another use for their arcane power. This time was no different. Before the dread could settle, Ulrin cleared his throat; this was not the time to sink into hopelessness.

"Glad as we all are that you yet live," he spoke with a sincerity everyone else knew to be false, words spoken for courtesy, "you know the crisis we face in allowing them to roam free. Do you know anything more about our enemy?"

Muir gave a stern expression as he nodded. "Plenty."

"I'll start with the most important question then: do you know anything of the hole they hide in?"

The bishop shook his head, then appeared hesitant. "Hm... I did hear talk of some place their captain seemed fond of. But the name ... it eludes me." Realizing that was not what the lieutenant wanted to hear, he quickly attempted to reassure him of his usefulness. "B-But I do know more of their plans of attack. A cowardly lot they are, but with the scale they plan on proceeding in, the siege may well cause The Chain to fall."

"So they finally have a grand siege planned to wipe us out. Sounds like more magic will be at play." Shaking off the concern that taking root into him, Ulrin turned to the squires with a smile and eyes feigning ease. "This'll take some time. While I handle this, I need you two to survey the fortress, make sure it'll hold in case of attack. Think you can manage?"

The squires eagerly grinned and pounded their chests in salute to their lieutenant. They excused themselves just as the bishop began complaining about why the executioners had yet to leave.

Surveying Levia Fortress did not require much effort. All they had to do was explore the facility and see what it had to offer. Since he was better with numbers and making records, Maxime went to inspect the stronghold's stockpile of weapons and rations while Luchs got a better look at how Soless' soldiers maintained their defenses.

The fortress was massive, perhaps the size of the capital city. It was so grand that the island's entire population could potentially fit inside. The tall walls somehow looked more imposing on the outside of the keep than from within, and atop them were several ballistae capable of hitting anything well past the bridge. There was always at least a dozen men on watch above the gate. One of the knights informed Luchs that there was usually never a need to drive away intruders by force seeing as how their fortified walls kept everyone out. And for anyone to force their way through the gates would take the strength of a giant.

Levia Fortress was built shortly after the conquest of Ederea over a hundred years ago to serve as the home for the du Joiec family before Castle Ederea had been discovered. It would take a devious mastermind to infiltrate such a stronghold.

Having finished his survey so soon, Luchs climbed to the top of the gate, where he had an excellent view of the soldiers training in the courtyard below. Those performing repetitions did so in perfect sync with each other, and the ones who were sparring fought with vigor, ferocity, and control.

With such solid defenses and fine men to arm them, even the Convent of One would have their hands not get inside so easily.

Ulrin would be pleased to hear that.

But before he would make his report, Luchs went to check on Maxime and see what he found.

Commandant Soless provided the general's squire with precise instructions on how to find the weapon storage. From there, all he had to do was find a man named Golbern and ask him for what he needed. And if politely asking did not make him work, he was instructed to state, "Get off your laurels and get to it!" Arrogant as it would sound coming from a squire, everyone in the facility knew how fond their commandant was of using that phrase, and how he told his messengers to use it too.

It would have been amusing to see a grown man scamper to work for a meek lad, but they likely already got the formality out of the way.

Luchs got a few chuckles in while walking back the way he came. The halls were quiet enough for one to hear the breaths of air whispering from the windows. It was a pleasant little hymn that unraveled only when disturbed by distant voices.

He heard a conversation being made across the hall, an argument it seemed. Leaving it be and passing it by would have been the best course of action, but the direction he headed in did not branch into another hall. Before he thought to turn back and wait for Maxime to meet him, he realized one of those voices belonged to Maxime.

Without making a sound, Luchs traced the voices to its owners, then hid behind a wall where the conflict could be heard clearly. A brief peek past the corner showed no fists being thrown, just the lad and a gruff, stalky man shooting daggers at one another. The man had thick blonde stubble growing around his chin and looked down at Maxime with stern, sharp green eyes. He did not wear any armor, just worn, rustic clothing.

What was a civilian doing in a military facility? And what did he do to get the normally meek Maxime so upset? The last time Luchs saw so much disdain in his droopy eyes was when he fought for his life on Des Meurtal.

The squire mumbled something too quiet for Luchs to pick up, but the intensity in his shaken voice carried over clearly—so much frustration and sadness.

Then the man uttered something. "—never amount to anything that matters like that," was all Luchs heard. After those biting words, he turned his back on Maxime and left.

Those eyes of Maxime's froze wide in a painful daze and his mouth dropped open in frightful disbelief. A light rattling resounded from the metal on his trembling hands, hands that closed into fists. He leered at the silhouette disappearing ahead of him. "You're wrong. Wrong! I'll show you! I won't just take my shield; I'll become a general and make my name renowned across the land. I'll become a man that actually knows what it means to have pride!"

Those words might not have fazed the man, but they certainly shook Luchs. It was the first time he heard such vigor, such fury from him. And it left him gasping desperately for breath. Saying what he did must have been trying.

It was obvious he knew the man rather well if he brought himself to bellow as he had. Saying he hated the man seemed somehow inaccurate despite the tension and hostility he carried. There was something more to it, something akin to longing. And in that moment, that desire began to turn into something else, something oppressive, something that twisted his once still valsara into a mass of hate.

After going his way and turning the corner, Maxime swept that frustration aside upon seeing he was not alone. Neither squire said anything to the other as both, now face-to-face, were still affected in some way by the tension.

"Luchs ... how long were you here?" Maxime tried to sound casual and loose, but failed to hide his stress.

As fine an attempt as that was, Luchs was not letting either of them leave without some answers. "Long enough. Who was that dastard? Why were you howling at him?"

Maxime held his tongue and looked away for a moment, sorting through some complex thoughts. He took a deep breath, sighed, then looked to Luchs with morose eyes. "That was the town's mayor, Adan Sauvor."

"I'd say 'tisn't very smart talking so rudely to a man like that, but you know him, aye?"

The lad shrugged. "I have the 'privilege' of calling him Father."

So they were family, and not very close judging by the vile way he uttered *privilege*. He had more brass than Luchs thought to speak so brazenly to his parent; he could not even oppose Cain when he was still alive.

"He came here to discuss matters of security for the town, not to see his me. 'Twas but a coincidence we met here."

"'Tis not like you gave any notice. We've done nothing but focus on the war effort since it began."

"Notice or no, the man would not see me of his own will."

"You make it sound like he doesn't care."

"Because he doesn't. He sent me away because he doesn't care." Maxime closed his eyes and breathed deeply in an attempt to keep calm. Then he took his fist, pressed it between his clavicle, and clenched it tighter still: a silent prayer for resilience. "It's been this way since Mother passed. After she left this world, I stopped meaning anything to him. I was less a son than a termite in his home. No matter how I tried to do good for him, it was never enough. In the end, he sent me to Des Meurtal."

Luchs almost could not get his next words out. "You endured Des Meurtal, became a soldier, to prove your worth to him."

Maxime nodded and tightened his fist more. "And, as you might've heard, 'twas all for naught. He will never love me. And I will never know pride from him." His fist began trembling from how tightly he gripped it. Soon, blood seeped from between the gaps of his vambrace.

His dedication was wavering. Being an errand boy for the lieutenant and general did not help his confidence grow. And now he finally accepted that his father rejected him.

A halfhearted soldier was doomed to die the moment he stepped foot on the battlefield.

Luchs stepped up to his friend, gripping of his shoulders in both hands. "You're going to let it end that way then? When you have so many others relying on you now?"

And Maxime shook his head, letting his bloody fist drop. "Not on my life! I got this far without the dastard's praise. I don't need it! I'll help bring this war to its end. I'll become a knight. I'll be more a man than he ever was." Those words were spoken with as much passion as he had uttered for his supposed father, except there was no hate or anger. Every word he said to Luchs burned with conviction, stilling his wavering heart.

Happy to see his friend still empowered, Luchs patted his shoulders. "Aye, you will."

Ulrin was pleased with what he learned from Luchs, Maxime, and (possibly) Muir. They had enough weapons to supply a small army. No gaps were seen in Levia Fortress' defenses. They were well prepared for a Convent attack.

Many still feared being struck down by magic, but Commandant Soless assured them that they would be safe. Before the Sea Drake Company arrived, a Vainte shaman visited the fortress to apply a magic shell that promised to shield it from spells used for malintent. Magic passed down through the Vainte tribes was especially complex; only someone brandishing magic as powerful as theirs could hope to dispel the protection. Their walls were as good as safe from the Convent's mages.

The night they arrived, the Sea Drake Company was treated to a feast. The banquet hall had been filled with tantalizing food fished up from the bountiful waters of Levia Fossa. The men gorged on mountains of fish, piles of sea slugs, plates of oysters, and tankards of ale and rum. Some of the lads were disappointed that there was no mutton, but they kept quiet so they would not bother the drunken adults.

As wonderful as the food, Luchs did not stay long. A feast could not make him forget the possibility of an attack or what awaited should they fail.

Maxime joined him in the courtyard outside, as had a few other ambitious lads hoping to make a difference. They got together to spar with each other barehanded. Eventually, they broke into two teams to keep things interesting. The Levia Fossa pages and squires were strong and resilient, their skills on par with the Sea Drake squires. The only thing to separate them was how they used their wits.

Several knights looked on from the rather wide windows. The brawl entertained them so much that they began betting on which ones would be left standing. Several of them lost their bets as soon as they were placed. The Levia lads proved too much for many of the Sea Drake squires. Only a handful of them continued to struggle.

Those who remained were the cream of the crop. The meister knights showed their faith and pride in them in their cheers.

"Go on, Luchs! Mash 'em!" Ulrin shouted, his voice a little slurred.

Not wanting to disappoint him, Luchs went on the offensive. His recklessness broke the Levia lads' formation apart, giving the rest of his teammates a chance to pick them off one by one. He got back on his feet quickly and charged at the nearest lad, grabbed him, and gave him a strong headbutt, knocking him out. A few squires tried grabbing Luchs from behind, but he shook them off and fought back, punching a taller one in the gut and slamming a bulkier one to the ground with his other arm.

Soon enough, it was just him, Maxime, Levin, and several other Levia lads going at one another, their teams dissolved.

The ruckus died down once everyone lost the energy to go on. Their limbs were soft as sponges. From the looks of it, one of the Levia knights, the one Commandant Soless earlier left in charge of the exercises, won his bet. He earned a shiny silver lev piece from each man who participated in the gamble. The lads helped one another up while offering firm handshakes and pats on the back, showing respect for each other's skills.

Some of the men were proud of their trainees' efforts, others were not too thrilled by their failures. From looking at the disappointment on the knights' faces, the lads could tell their failures earned them a rousing training session the next morn.

Despite the exertion, Luchs did not sleep much that night. The war often kept his mind active, as it had for many others, drawing it to more unsavory thoughts. He required distraction.

With the general's permission, Luchs was allowed to borrow one of the apocrypha from Castle Ederea's archives. No one else knew how to read the text in the ancient tomes, so it would not be missed for a time. From what little he managed to decipher, he found the text depicted a tale of great and powerful beings: "those who weaved the light," it read. They were creatures said to have paved the way for growth and understanding. Much of the writing was still difficult to read and required more than a few weeks to decipher. Even so, he had a few ways of learning the archaic writing.

Much of the night was spent staring at those pages and attempting to pronounce the strange words. While it was trying for some part, learning the language relaxed him enough to eventually fall asleep. There was something about it that made him forget the war for just a moment.

The rest he had was, although short-lived, so refreshing that he woke the next morn full of energy.

Confident as he was in the squires' findings, Lieutenant Ulrin wanted a look around the facility himself. It would take some time to replenish their ships' supplies, which Commandant Soless generously offered to compensate, so they had plenty of time on their hands.

Naturally, after a night of conditioning his mind, Luchs sought to exercise the body. He convinced some other lads to spar with him by bringing up their lousy performance the previous night. The Levia lads' skills with weapons were more impressive than their bare-handed combat. They were tough to fight, especially when they suddenly decided to interrupt a match and attack in groups. But Luchs proved his sword-and-shield techniques to be the more effective against them all.

After working out for an hour or so, he left the rowdy lads behind in search of a place to meditate. Most places in the facility were occupied by loud knights and their trainees. There was, however, an empty, open yard nearly everyone avoided save for visiting clergy from the shrine at the center of the island.

It was a breathtaking space, not very spacious, but the air was delightfully crisp. The grass was kempt and trimmed below ankle-length and the plants well cared for. At the center of the yard stood tall a grand willow tree with branches like long locks of hair, and its trunk—to Luchs' surprise—had the outline of what appeared to be a woman, a beauty at one with nature. It was as if Great Gaia herself sat there with him.

Believing the goddess' presence might sharpen his concentration, Luchs sat before the deific tree and breathed gently, slowly, clearing his mind of unnecessary thoughts. He placed a dense stone bigger than his meaty palm in front of him. It seemed better to use that for practice than risk tampering with the soil and ruining the tranquil scenery. He still detested the exercise, but it always helped improve his focus.

His breathing steady, Luchs focused on the faint energy inside the stone. Holding out his hands, he broke the stone with his power by barely flexing his fingers.

A few fragments kicked up the tiniest clouds of dirt. A small layer of the soil was loose enough to almost be dust. Thinking he could use that, he began concentrating on the soil too. It was slow work, but the loose soil began to gather around the pebbles.

Then an idea hit. As soon as he pulled the stone fragments from the dirt, he began piecing them back together while packing some soil into the cracks and over the surface. It looked like a mess, but with his magic sight, he found that the minerals started compounding and getting denser when more force was used to pack them together.

The mass of dirt and rubble did not appear very stable. Most of the foundation looked like it would easily crumble. When he leaned in to touch it, it felt durable, perhaps suitable enough to use with a catapult. Barely any of the soil flacked onto his palm.

Curious about how well it would hold, Luchs grabbed the stone and stood with it. There was much more heft to it than when it was just a rock. When he got used to the weight, he began tossing it into the air like a ball, gently at first before seeing how far high it could go. Catching the stone after it soared high enough to block out the sun almost made him drop it.

He wanted to see what he could do with it.

Lobbing it at something was the first thing to come to mind. But at what? The Goddess Tree was out of the question. Throwing it against the wall seemed wasteful.

In the end, he decided to take it to the archery range.

The instructors did not seem very bothered by the lad carrying an ugly stone through their training yard. A bulky man with eyebrows as bushy as his beard seemed to be in charge. When Luchs asked him how sturdy the dummies were, the man chortled. It was hard to say whether he was amused with his idea of training or doubting he could actually hit the frame given how awkwardly he carried the stone. Whatever the case, he allowed Luchs to find out for himself.

He set the stone aside for a moment to grab a dummy and set it in place about twenty feet away. Picking up the stone was not as hard the second time around; he even managed to haul it to his shoulder. He held onto the stone with the right hand on the back of it and the left on its sandy underbelly. As he pictured the wooden dummy as one of the Convent's soldiers, Luchs took three strong steps forward and hurled the patched-up stone through the air, smashing it directly into the dummy's abdomen. The lumpy projectile shattered upon impact, but the "strong as iron ore" frame, as the instructor called it, had split in two before falling to the ground.

Several people looked his way baffled. Luchs was just as amazed. Those dummies looked to be the same as the ones used at the castle. Arrows could barely puncture the dense frames, and overgrown men that tried to break them could barely make a dent in them. But the mess he clumped together tore one apart.

It was amazing. That was not just ripping rock from the earth and moving it as he saw fit. He found a new use for his power.

The instructors were as impressed with Luchs as they were aggravated with him for breaking the hard-to-make training dummy. Showing them how he got such a destructive projectile made their complaints stop. The demonstration of his power left the men in awe and caused an uproar of cheers from the pages.

Word of the lad who could move the earth spread throughout Ederea since the battle at Prévinn. Many thought such a person did not exist, so it shocked the nonbelievers all the more when they saw him pack soil and stone into one dense mass with his mind.

Everyone kept asking what else he could do with his power. While he still did not have much confidence in his control, he could not rightly say as much to them. Perhaps it was not the best choice, but he boasted of how deep the scar left in Prévinn was—leaving out the part about how he did it while dying. It was enough to leave them wanting to hear more.

Luchs managed to avoid many questions by saying he needed to get back to training, just like everyone else.

It was so exhilarating to learn a new way to use his power that he had to find out what else he could do. He continued his exercises for hours, though he did not find out anything new. His control, however, progressed exceptionally.

He lost the strength to continue after sunset, fatigue softening his muscles and dulling his focus. He pushed himself to go on until he could no more, then rest against the Goddess Tree. The branches danced in the gentle breeze. A sound much like a faint humming was heard echoing from small openings in the trunk. The tree—the goddess it embodied—sung to him as a mother would to her child.

Such a soothing melody. It lulled him to sleep before he even realized how relaxed he was.

In his slumber, Luchs recollected a precious moment from his lost past.

He and his sister were energetic children, always running around until their bodies gave out. Once, when they were both small, they fell asleep in their mother's lap underneath a beautiful willow tree, their heads resting adjacent to one another. At the time, when he awoke and found where he was, he pretended to still be sleeping. He liked where he was, who he was with, and they were at peace there.

For a moment, their calm breathing reached his ear, as if they were still with him.

They remained on his mind even as he awoke. *Ma... Hilda... Where are you?* He would have dwelled on it longer if possible.

A loud, deep bellowing echoed throughout the area. It was the warning horn, the one blown only when the fortress was under attack. An uproar broke out from the inside.

Shaking off his fatigue, Luchs took his sword in hand and rushed straight toward the commotion.

His heart raced, confusion overtaking him, as flashes of valsara filled his magic sight. There were so many, too many inside the fortress walls for them all to be Ederean soldiers. He could not believe his eyes when he saw his comrades fighting the Convent of One.

Luchs staggered at the sight of Convent soldiers overwhelming the armored knights, charging inside.

'Tisn't possible. How did they get in!?

There was no time to dawdle. More enemies charged through the gate, its bars protruding inward from the archway, the seared tips smoking from the blast of an explosive spell.

If enough forced their way in, nothing they did would save them.

Since the enemy still overlooked him, Luchs focused on the earth outside the fortress supporting the bridge. The first few sets of support were hundreds of feet from him. He had to widen his area of influence to the point his mind almost snapped. Keeping his concentration was grueling, especially since he was already exhausted, but Luchs forced himself to keep going until he could sense the earth beneath the bridge's support, then tore it apart. The bridge collapsed in seconds, taking every person still on with it.

The tremors spread across the fortress, throwing everyone off balance for a moment, but it did not keep the warriors from lashing at each other.

Destroying the bridge stopped the enemy's advance, for however long it was worth. The armored guards gave their all to force the intruders back, eager to shove them down the cliff.

Letting his power loose cost Luchs terribly. His body became heavier, his muscles practically turning to stone. He was barely able to lift his sword when an enemy broke from the crowd and rushed his way.

The man looked to be running from the fight given how perturbed he was to see Luchs guarding the archway.

Luchs held up his sword. He was not about to let a craven Convent cur best him. The "warrior" stared him down, unintimidated, probably assuming he would fare better in a fight with him than a grown man.

The Convent soldier stepped in quickly and swung his sword for Luchs' head. The preemptive strike bounced off his shield, leaving the enemy exposed. Had he the strength, Luchs would have swiftly thrown his sword across the man's torso, but he only managed to meet their swords. They exchanged swings of the blade until the enemy threw Luchs against the wall, knocking the sword from his hand.

Almost as desperate to land a fatal hit, the soldier rushed at him only to be stopped by a figure leaping from above and crashing into him. The new arrival, a squire judging by his size, pinned the man to the ground, piercing his heart with a spear upon impact. The squire remained where he was until certain his foe was dead, then pulled his spear free.

Luchs could not believe his eyes. "Aloysius?"

The squire stepped off of the corpse and turned around, looking about as surprised to see Luchs as he was to see him.

Aloysius hurried to his friend's side while wiping away the blood spattered on his face away. He had grown since they parted ways, about a head taller, and sprouted some stubble over his lip and on his chin.

He grinned as he helped Luchs back to his feet. "Good to see you, mate," he said while handing him the weapon he dropped.

"You too."

Overjoyed as they were to be reunited, they had not forgotten about the battle. A few more men charged at the squires, wanting to avenge their fallen comrade. Luchs rushed at one and bashed him with his shield while Aloysius faced the other one. The enemy confronting Luchs took his attack like it was a lovetap, then grabbed his shield when it came at him again. Seizing the opportunity, Luchs stepped forward and ran him through, ending his life.

Aloysius disposed of the threat before him just as quickly and looked to his friend with a smile. "Look who learned to kill."

Luchs give Aloysius a sour look as he pulled his sword free of the corpse. *So he knew...*

The Convent forces still fought to overwhelm the Edereans. Without their numbers constantly increasing, the Edereans managed to stand their ground and keep the fight within the outer courtyard.

But they did not keep the enemy from infiltrating the fortress.

The horn that called everyone to battle bellowed once more, then fell silent during the second blow. Luchs looked to the tower to found the valsara of two people: one quickly fading, the other slinking back down the tower.

There was no time to lose. Luchs made his way back inside the fortress through a hidden passage Aloysius showed him. Everyone stationed there, soldiers and servants alike, committed to memory every possible exit in case of emergency. And this certainly qualified as such.

Crossing through the passages was like going into a cave. They were small, cramped, and dank, and it felt like they were going in circles at every turn.

None of them connected directly to the chamber the bishop hid in. The closest they could manage was the servants' chambers halfway across the same floor.

Bracing for the danger to come, the squires hustled through the halls ready to swing their weapons at a second's notice. Assassins were still on the prowl in search of their target. Their lives could be taken at any time by an enemy stealthy enough to slip past the brawling soldiers. They had to be prepared to do the same.

The pungent scent of freshly spilled blood permeated the air.

They picked up the pace hoping to save whoever remained. In their haste, they found one of the slain. At the bottom of a staircase was a large man lying on his stomach, swords protruding from his back, his blood staining his skin. And the garb he wore was that of an executioner.

It was terrifying to think someone there had what it took to kill an executioner, but there was no time for fear to set in.

Clang, clang!

The sharp ringing of blades clashing broke the silence. The squires did not stand idle. They followed the sound of conflict, listening to the rhythm as it began to gradually slow, the grunts of the fighters growing louder.

The dying rhythm continued past the room where the bishop once hid, down a trail of blood droplets. Dozens of corpses led them toward the direction of the conflict, ending with a maid impaled by a spear.

Soon, they found Executioner Jarl locked in combat with another maid who resembled the impaled one.

They would have stepped in to stop the executioner (somehow) had they not noticed the woman had the upper hand.

The maid met the knives she wielded with the sword Executioner Jarl scarcely managed to keep hold of. Blood seeped from the man's side, and he barely managed to keep from falling over his wobbling legs. While he appeared to be on the offensive, the maid quickly lashed at him with ferocious speed, carefully aiming for the vitals the executioner scarcely managed to protect. When a knife met with the sword, she dragged it along the blade and moved in to draw it across his abdomen, forcing him to step aside before she carved through him.

Her technique was too precise, and her reflexes too sharp, for her to be a mere maid.

"She's one of them," Aloysius warned.

There was no other explanation. Edereans did not train women to use weapons, not for anything outside of self-defense. But she fought with enough skill to show she knew how to take a life in an instant. If her opponent was anyone other than an executioner, she would have.

Past the fight, in the shadows at the side of the hall, was the bishop. Muir clung to the wall, walking unsteadily against it with a limp on his left side.

Luchs rushed past the assassins to aid the injured. Executioner Jarl moved to the side in an attempt to shield him, but he was stabbed and shoved aside by the woman, who set her sights on the lad.

She threw a knife at his back. It missed his heart by just an inch, but slowed him down enough for her to catch up to him. She held her last knife over his neck, ready to finish him off.

But it never made contact.

The wall beside them broke apart and the stones, guided by his Second Verse, flew at the woman, pummeling her to the floor.

The assassin's knife dropped to the floor from her limp hand, and she lay dead under the rubble.

Luchs was overwhelmed by his shock, both at seeing the woman nearly stab his neck and seeing his power react in such a way. He did not even think about using his Second Verse; it just happened. It reminded him of when he began to swing a sword on impulse, not thought.

Use of the Second Verse was starting to become second nature.

Aloysius rushed to the wounded executioner's side. "Sir, are you all right?"

Executioner Jarl ignored the squire as he struggled to get back on his feet. His arms and legs trembled with every move. Despite that, the executioner forced himself to stand, leaning against his sword like a staff. He gruffly approached the bishop who still limped against the wall to escape. He picked up the pace as he took the knife the assassin dropped and hurled it at Muir, piercing his hip.

Luchs froze with disbelief. The man assigned to protect the bishop was now attacking him.

"Craven snake!" Executioner Jarl caught up with Muir before he could react. He grabbed him by the collar and hoisted him up, then slammed him into the wall, the impact dislodging the knife. "Why in the gods' names have you sold us out to the Convent of One!?"

The bishop quivered in his grasp but said nothing.

"You devote yourself to the Gods of the Natural Order, then swear fidelity to the king ... and now you forsake both your faith and loyalty by sneaking heretics into the fortress to slaughter us!" Not waiting for an answer, Executioner Jarl lifted the frail man up and slammed him into the wall again. "What are you after? What in the seven hells are you after!?"

The bishop grunted and wheezed trying to cope with the pain. The squires watched in bewilderment. They thought to step in and stop this until Muir let out a dry laugh. Whatever shred of dignity he clung to had been erased by the dreary, sinister gaze he gave Executioner Jarl.

"Faith... Loyalty... Such trivial things matter not in this world." His demeanor completely changed. He acted much like he did when he was the advisor to the king—haughty, spiteful, looking down at everyone before him. "I acted to attain power, something King Godefroy and the gods lack."

The squires could not believe their ears. No Ederean ever accused their king of harboring weakness, but as he revealed his true self, Muir gladly did so with a venomous tongue. And he was supposed to be a clergyman, yet he committed sacrilege by slandering the gods he revered.

Executioner Jarl tightened his grip around the bishop's collar. "How dare you!"

"Easily," Muir snapped. "You treat such paltry things like they'll sustain you for life. But that could not be further from the truth. Only power can promise life and prosperity. And the Convent of One has it—devastating power! I was promised a share, just like their mages, assuming I provided them the means to topple Ederea's might. It disappoints me to no end that General Esperance was not here to join us, but for his lapdog to deliver two executioners and the whelp who decimated their forces in Prévinn!" The bishop interrupted his tangent to laugh like a madman, actually taking joy in the chaos he helped to create. He then looked to the man holding him captive with pity. "Your king is a weakling who rejected the noble ideals of his ancestors. Ederea has lost what made it strong, a leader that united through power, thus leaving it beyond hope for prosperity. No gods can save you now. You are all—"

Whatever the traitor hoped to say was silenced by the executioner's sword piercing his chest. Although his hand was unsteady, rage fueled Executioner Jarl with the strength to drive his weapon through his captive and puncture a deep gash into the wall behind him.

"The only ones beyond hope are spineless fools like you!"

In drawing his weapon from the corpse and letting it drop to the ground, Executioner Jarl took a few uneasy steps backward before stabilizing himself. He held a hand to his head, trying to wipe away the sweat being absorbed by his bandages. "Damn those wenches and their poison." He gripped at the bandages concealing his face and tore them away. Neither squire could look away from the grotesque burn scars that seared his face red or the fleshy mess where his right eye should be. He already looked like he belonged to the witch god of death. Despite his injuries and obvious weakness, Executioner Jarl stepped across the hall toward the battle cries heard outside. He was still fully intent on fighting.

"Executioner, you've got to stop," Luchs insisted. "If you keep fighting, you'll—"

"Reur died because of that snake. And I won't be the only one to join him if the heretics aren't expelled from this place. If I can't fight, then I'll shield someone who can. But I won't stop. I refuse to."

There was no stopping him. Even if they tried, he would exert himself in brushing them aside. Faith, duty, vengeance—everything that kept him alive gave him the power to keep fighting. Stopping him meant depriving him of his final wish. No warrior would do that to another.

Seeing him continue on, the squires knew they had to do the same. Young as they were, they were warriors too.

~ Seventeenth Chapter ~
Tragedy

The battle was bloody. Although the Ederean soldiers remained strong throughout the conflict, they suffered terrible casualties. So many perished in the siege that the pungent stench of blood stained the air.

Many survivors sustained terrible injuries that would keep them out of battle for a long time—their bones crushed, their limbs lacerated. Even Commandant Soless lost the use of his left arm.

What was once the most prominent military facility in Ederea emerged from the chaos as little more than a husk.

Had it not been for Executioner Jarl's resilience, they might not have won the day. He fought alongside the soldiers, slaying every enemy that crossed him, and gave many disheartened soldiers a chance to fight back. Many owed their lives to the executioner who died a hero.

"Get back to Shoafond... Warn Godefroy..." Those were his last words.

When Ulrin heard what caused the chaos, he was livid. He ranted on to himself about how he had been so blind, how he should have never questioned General Esperance's judgment of the bishop—a wretched snake.

It was the first time Luchs saw him scream and wail about in such a rage.

Once their warships were prepped, the Sea Drake Company returned to Shoafond. Luchs did not want to leave Aloysius behind, but he was needed in Levia Fortress, especially with his meister knight was injured.

Lady Untae was not kind to them during their return. The salty winds were rough, and the waves grew large and rancorous, slapping around the ships and keeping them from a straight course. Dark clouds rolled in and loomed above, spread further out than anyone could see. It was as though the goddess of the sea was punishing them for allowing heretics to defile her waters.

A heavy rain fell as they closed in on the capital. The mariners had a difficult time keeping their ships stable in the dark tempest until they sailed beneath the towering cliffside and safely rolled into the docks.

Fewer people worked the docks than normal, and those who did were not their usual boisterous selves. They hung their heads as they worked, downtrodden and disheartened, incapable of holding their spirits high.

And there was a valid reason for that. Shoafond had been invaded in their absence.

The enemy came out of nowhere before they knew what happened. No unknown ships sailed through their waters. Somehow, the Convent of One marched from inland and laid siege to the city. The militia attempted to protect the civilians and evacuate them to safety, but bodies kept falling.

The streets were barren and littered with destroyed stalls, debris from crumbled walls, and belongings abandoned in the chaos. Spilled blood had dried over the ground and smeared the sides of buildings. A few people were still gathering the dead.

Some eyes watched the returning soldiers survey the damage behind near-closed window shutters. They wanted to greet them but were too afraid to leave the safety of their homes.

Ulrin ordered his troops to scatter and help the other knights attend to the civilians as he readied his horses. They moved out with haste, a few calling out the names of their loved ones, while their lieutenant, Luchs, and Maxime raced down the trail to Castle Ederea.

They came from inland, from the direction of the castle.

When they crossed the waterfall trail, they found stray pieces of armor and weapons scattered about, signifying a struggle took place. Dread ate away at them the longer it took to reach the castle.

It was much worse around the nearby bridge. Stone had been chipped off the sides from heavy pressure. Burn marks could be seen through the mist. The drawbridge gate had been left open, the chains that held it up torn off and the towers where the guards resided destroyed.

So many knights were on guard at the ruined drawbridge that they formed a wall in the path. They raised their weapons immediately upon seeing silhouettes in the mist and only lowered them when they could identify Lieutenant Ulrin.

An audience was made with the king quickly. They learned all that transpired from him.

To start with, King Godefroy explained how Shoafond came under fire. A ship of Convent scouts was found sailing within The Chain. It was immediately intercepted, its soldiers captured and imprisoned in the Cage Falls to be tortured for information. They would not give any answers despite the inquisitors' best efforts, and were left in their cells to rot.

A day later, it happened.

The Convent of One appeared out of nowhere with a massive army en route to the castle. Squadrons were dispatched to intercept the enemy, but several Convent warriors split from their army to attack the city, forcing the knights to further divide their power to protect the citizens.

They held the line well until a powerful mage joined the fray: the one calling herself Gatreah, high priestess of the Convent of One. Her harrowing magic obliterated everything before her and allowed her forces to fight their way into the castle.

King Godefroy himself joined the fight armed with Avvär, the onyx sword given to him by Executioner Sörrign. With the magic weapon, he was able to compromise the witch's spells and fight her on even ground. He kept her occupied, the two leaders facing each other, while his knights routed the Convent forces. The Edereans used the complex architecture of the castle to their advantage, tripping their enemies up and gradually thinning their numbers.

Alas, they did not take victory.

The Edereans were beset by one of their own, cut down by him without remorse or hesitation. A hundred good men fell to the traitor's blade, and, much to the sorrow of the king, he knew who it was.

Vandelas Kronas.

After his treachery earlier in the year, no one was surprised to hear he turned on them again. He had sympathized with the heretics, and, in the end, betrayed Ederea for them.

Ulrin muttered a curse under his breath, wishing he trusted his general like he failed to do previously. Another person he did not trust had betrayed them.

"The Convent of One appeared before me so to end this drawn-out game of theirs and claim their dominion over Ederea. And they might have were it not for the brave warriors who fought beside me, who shielded me as I had them... We were fortunate their high priestess had grown weak during the battle and retreated the way they came."

He spoke of how the high priestess used one of her own as material for a terrible spell. A single touch from her set the sacrifice aglow in a ghastly light that consumed his body and opened a rift in space. The Convent forces fled through the lingering light, the traitor providing cover while he carried Gatreah to safety. They vanished through the rift, leaving nothing but destruction behind.

Ulrin gritted his teeth and hung his head shamefully. "If only we were here..." Realizing there would be another time to regret what happened, he pulled himself back together, ready to get to work. "They will attack again once their leader has recovered. Where is General Esperance? We need to devise a plan immediately."

An anguished King Godefroy said nothing. He kept staring forlornly at nothing, then he looked to the sky and took a deep breath. Upon exhaling, he turned his stern face to Ulrin. "Before that, there's a matter I must discuss with you." This caught him off guard, but Ulrin listened carefully to the king's words. "The attack on our capital left a void in my military. It must be filled before action can be taken. You have a marvelous set of skills, I noticed, and words of praise from your general leave me to believe you are the most suited for the role." The king took a step forward and extended an open hand. "Ulrin Vertueux, prithee ... take the role of my first general."

Time stopped moving for Ulrin in that moment. His eyes shot wide open and his mouth hung ajar when he realized what was asked of him. He was trapped in disbelief, unable to cope with the new knowledge or rationalize how to proceed.

It hurt for Luchs to see his meister knight this way. He wanted to do something to snap him out of it.

But what could he do? This was not something that could be met with smiles or carefree words. He could not simply say to seize the opportunity or that it was what General Esperance would have wanted. Ulrin lost more than a leader; he lost a mentor and friend.

A decision needed to be made, and with a heavy heart, Ulrin forced his hand to stop trembling and take the king's in a firm grip.

Shoafond was in chaos since the attack. Many people knew how hard times have been and that they would only get harder, that they must stand together and pick each other up. But many were overwhelmed by what had happened and became unhinged. The people, in their fear and desperation, raged and lashed out at everything around them.

Not only had the enemy infiltrated The Chain, they attacked the capital. Shoafond had never once been attacked before. Those rioting saw this once-in-a-lifetime disaster as a result of King Godefroy's weakness.

Efforts were made to quell the riots. They were mostly made up of men too inebriated by rage and grief to think straight. Thankfully, they tended to die down after someone tired out the angriest ones in their midst. Crude as it was to knock some sense into the men and restrain them, it worked. Once they were subdued, the other soldiers worked to pacify the rest of the people with peaceful rhetoric.

In times of unrest, everyone needed to stay together. And they came to remember that truth.

Luchs was supposed to be resting after he helped stop a riot, but he could not keep still after all that happened. Instead of lounging about, he took a walk in the gardens behind the castle. He needed to clear his head of all the hate and fear he saw on the people's faces.

It made him think of Executioner Jarl.

"Get back to Shoafond... Warn Godefroy..."

He knew. The moment Muir's allegiance was made clear he knew what was in store for them.

Others must have come to the same conclusion, but it did not matter. The traitor was found and punished too late.

And now they had Vandelas, a Nascitte and deadly fighter.

Luchs felt like a fool. He valued him as much as his other peers. He trusted him to teach him how to hone his Second Verse. He believed that he cared about the fate of Ederea.

Despite the pain in his heart, he refused to give in to despair. So long as there was life, there would be hope. They would find a way to defeat the Convent of One and free Ederea of their madness.

When the sun was at its highest, he found himself in the field of radiant flowers. Their aroma was enchanting as always. Just one sniff and the storm in his mind parted. Every sound around him became so much clearer. The birds sang beautifully. The winds brushed against the leaves and the flower petals, their rustling joining the singing animals in a pleasant chorus.

There was something to the symphony that made him uneasy. A rustle in the bushes drew his attention and made him reach for his sword. It was small, so it was likely just a squirrel scavenging for food, but he still could not relax. They could control animals, even from afar.

The noise became louder as whatever caused it approached at a startlingly slow pace. Luchs looked to the bushes with his magic sight. He could not make out the valsara, but it definitely belonged to something small, and there was something odd about it. He recognized it as a small paw poked out of the bush.

"Snowflake?"

The diminutive fox stepped out of hiding, its legs shaking and its body swaying with every move. Its once pristine white coat had been covered in leaves and twigs stuck to patches of dried blood. It walked up to Luchs slowly while keeping its left hind leg off the ground. By mistake its leg touched the ground, forcing out a painful yip and causing it to collapse.

The beast was injured—and without its master.

Unable to turn away, Luchs reached down and picked it up into his arms. He felt its weary heartbeat weakening by the second.

Someone had to help it, but everyone who recognized it would have it killed, and anyone who did not would want the jinx thrown out of the castle. There was no one he could think of who would help except—

Without another thought, Luchs rushed back to the castle. He used the mist for cover from guards on patrol and anyone else happening to stroll by. He could not let anyone spot him until the fox was safe.

Once inside, hiding became much more difficult. Most of the halls were without much ornamentation. He had to rely on the sound of footsteps or chatter resounding against the walls and move away from them accordingly. After spending so much time on the Crown Plateau, he became rather skilled at tuning out the falls when he wanted to. A few guards who noticed his presence grew suspicious and almost found him. Instead of turning back, after remembering what he did in Levia Fossa, he made use of the Second Verse by hurling pebbles in the direction opposite of him. It worked like a charm.

He dodged guards and skulked through the halls, careful to remain unseen. The effort had brought him to the most heavily-guarded tower in the castle. Difficult to infiltrate as it was, the only one he could rely on had been there since the attack.

He was so close. He felt her valsara above.

On the top level of the tower was a singular hall that led to a singular door guarded by two very large, very intimidating knights. Getting past them would be the most difficult part. The trick used on the other guards would not work there, not when there was no other path to misdirect them down.

Right. Guess there's no choice then.

Gathering his courage, Luchs charged up the stairs shouting "Princess Camellia! Princess, please come out!" at the top of his lungs. The guards reacted immediately moved to restrain him. Luchs pushed against them with all his strength but could not match them. "Snowflake needs help!" He kept the knights off the fox as best as he could, jutting his head about and jabbing his thick elbow at their guts.

It did him little good.

One of them swiped Snowflake by its scruff while the other dragged Luchs back down the stairs. The poor thing could not even cry out as it was hoisted to the window at the edge of the hall, a window that opened to a heart-stopping drop to oblivion.

"Cease this instant!"

The princess' abrupt command forced both knights to stop in place and turn to face her and the handmaidens leaving the room. Without the need of a command, the servant holding the princess' hand marched over to the knight holding Snowflake and snatched it from his meaty hands. She brought the fox to her mistress, who held it like a mother cradling her injured child.

Luchs breathed a sigh of relief. He doubted he could do it, but he did. Snowflake would be safe with her.

Princess Camellia did everything she could to heal Snowflake with her magic alone. At some point, she sent her handmaidens out for supplies needed to clean the fox's fur and wounds.

It was just her, her patient, a single handmaiden, and Luchs in the princess' secure chambers.

While the ladies continued attending to the fox, Luchs waited patiently at the edge of the room sitting by a massive window with a good view of the lowlands. He was alone with his uneasy thoughts for some time.

He never thought that he would worry about Snowflake. Every time he encountered the fox, he only saw it with contempt like everyone else.

And yet when it looked at him so pleadingly, so unlike the angry beast it always behaved as, its well-being was all he could think about.

And when he thought about the fox, he thought of its master.

By the time her servants returned, the princess had done everything possible for her patient. She, guided by the one who watched over her, walked to the window for some rest and sunlight while they cleaned Snowflake. Princess Camellia sat across from her guest and relaxed in her seat. "My magic can do nothing more for her."

"Will it live?"

The princess glanced at the fox with melancholy eyes. "'Tis up to her." She tried to hold back a few tears, her stare sparkling sadness. Her dainty hands gripped her dress tensely, frustrated she could not do more. "Most of the injuries are internal—very trying to treat. Her leg had broken in a few places. My ladies need to hurt her a little more to ensure it heals properly, something they promised they know how to do." She looked back at Luchs after she finished her diagnosis. "Truly, 'tis a miracle she survived."

A miracle it survived, even with what it could do to its body.

"It'll live. It's a tough little beastie."

Luchs' positive outlook did little to lighten the mood. The air was so tense it was hard to keep from choking on it.

"Travesty upon travesty..." the princess boded. "An attack claiming the lives of countless good men, the loss of General Esperance, Executioner Sörrign leaving the fight in this dire hour, even—" She could not bring herself to go further than that. The princess looked ready to sink into despair, the weight of each tragedy pressing down on her as though she was being crushed by mountains. But she chose to proudly hold her head high, much like her father had when faced with unfavorable odds. Although her eyes reflected grief, her demeanor boasted strength once more. "Our ancestors faced matters as grave as this long ago. They survived then, as shall we now. We must all remain strong."

Those words were strong, held together, but also monotonous and without much conviction. It sounded like a mantra she used to force that conviction to rise within her. And yet to not crumble under the chaos, to believe—or try to believe—there was a ray of hope somewhere in the darkness took immense strength of will in itself.

Allowing herself the time and silence to breathe and clear her thoughts, the grief and despair in Princess Camellia's eyes cleared, and in its place was an even more lustrous radiance than before.

When she looked back Luchs' way, she seemed anxious and uncertain. "Kind Luchs, do you believe what they said about Vandelas?"

Luchs froze, not because the question was so preposterous, but because he came to doubt what he heard himself.

Finding Snowflake all alone made him question everything. Nearly every time they met, Vandelas always had his pet jinx by his side. It stubbornly followed him everywhere, even if it was out of sight. Less made sense than before.

He protected the Kyrovide before, but that had more to do with the scar he bore than anything else. To suddenly start fighting for those more genocidal than the soldiers who sailed to Ciecime...

It did not make sense.

"Forgive my asking, but why do you trust him so much?"

The princess did not seem to mind his question. She even smiled again, although it was a fragile smile. "I know of the things the knights and squires say about him. No one voices their concerns to me directly because they worry they will slight me." She breathed softly as she spoke. "I came to know him in our two years of friendship, and he is not the monster they say he is. Vandelas Kronas is kind, someone who treats his dear Snowflake like family. He is generous, someone who gives his own time to aid the people and even my servants with their problems. He is just, someone who would never tolerate anyone forcing the innocent to endure cruelty."

Kind? Generous? That was the first time Luchs heard anyone say such things to describe the quiet, harsh, antisocial foreign lad. It was difficult to imagine him going around the city and willingly interacting with troubled townsfolk. Then again, he did volunteer to help Luchs when he needed it most.

The princess turned to the window and looked down at the lower levels of the castle. "I sensed his valsara during the conflict. He fought strongly at first, but something dark, *twisted* crept its way inside of him, shackled him. They did something to him—of that, I am certain."

The princess' voice wavered, but not with fright or worry, not entirely. In her words was rage, a fury that made it hard for Luchs to see her as just a gentle princess. She desired action, but without the authority of a queen or the means to meet her desires, she tried not to let it show.

Thinking on what stirred the princess' hidden fury, Luchs looked over to the fox. The handmaidens treated and bandaged its wounds, and set it into a little basket lined with a fluffy blanket to rest. Its abdomen rose and fell shakily. There was a spark in its eyes; he swore he recognized what it was, and seeing it made it hard to look away.

Princess Camellia cupped his broad shoulder with her small hand. "Rest assured, I will do everything in my power to save her."

Luchs knew there was hope for Snowflake. With that to ease his mind, he began to focus on what else he had been told.

Night came with the rise of the crescent moon. Little light illuminated the way for those traversing the shroud of darkness since the new moon ended the night prior, and the clouds above obstructed what little radiance the moon and stars offered. Carrying a lantern was a must if anyone wanted to safely find their way.

The castle was under much heavier guard after sunset. No one knew if there were any remnants of the Convent of One still about after the confusion they made. Most of the soldiers could not sleep, not with the devastation still fresh in their minds.

Everyone thought the newly appointed General Vertueux was out ensuring defenses remained strong that night. But that was not his main focus.

Luchs informed him of a deserter hiding someplace on the Crown Plateau, a fact the king validated and clarified on when asked. Ulrin only saw red when he realized such vital information had been kept from him. Every casualty of the battle that took place in Shoafond had been relayed to the generals, but this was the first time anyone mentioned an executioner, Wolfram Sörrign no less, deserting the war effort.

It was unforgivable. For a warrior to forsake his duty when their kingdom was in need, it was nothing short of treachery.

Hoping to rectify this slight, Ulrin stamped through the southwestern edge of the plateau down a small, forgotten path across the cliffs that could only support a few men at a time. Luchs followed to keep his meister knight from doing anything he might later regret, though with some hesitation. The ground they struggled to cross was damp as a marsh and without any railing to keep anyone from plummeting into the waterfalls' basin. If anyone were to fall from that height, their body would be shredded on impact with the raging waters below.

The climb continued for a while before they found an old shack built inside of a crevice on the side of the plateau. It was impressive enough knowing Executioner Sörrign went down that crumbling path to return to his living quarters without knowing that ancient, mildew-ridden hovel was his living quarters. It had windows, but they were boarded up. The only ventilation the hovel seemed to have was a wide chimney, which at the moment spewed a thick cloud of smoke that brewed out of the crevice to be dissipated by the mist outside.

Ulrin did not wait to rush at the door. "Sörrign!" he bellowed. "Wolfram Sörrign, open this door! You'll answer for your cowardice now!"

The only thing to answer him was the loud sound of clanging metal.

Whether his voice was drowned out by it or the executioner was outright ignoring him, Ulrin did not care. Instead of waiting, he threw the unlocked door open hard enough to slam it against the wall inside.

Luchs followed his meister knight inside and stood at the door in awe. On the walls inside hung a myriad of weapons with a great many shapes, colors, and sizes—swords, daggers, spears, bows, maces, axes, shields, and so many others he could not even name. They were all displayed in a way that they almost concealed the wall behind them.

The hovel was lit by a fire brewing mightily from a hearth in the back. Contrary to what they saw outside, the inside was oddly spacious. Much of the space was occupied with tools large and small. Boxes full of numerous minerals and gemstones sat near the entrance, much of them appearing to contain amber-colored stones called aurichalcum. If anyone were to make off with just one box, they would be able to live prosperously for the rest of their days.

Clang! Clung!

That sound came from the back toward the hearth. Beside it stood Wolfram Sörrign in front of a grand anvil with a thick hammer in hand. Instead of the typical garb he wore for his position, he dressed in breathable clothing underneath a heavy-looking smock. The thick gloves on his hands protected him from the sparks that flew upon him striking the hammer against a blade of white-hot metal.

That place, the entirety of his living quarters, was a forge.

Something caught Luchs' eye when the hammer fell. The sparks, for the briefest moment, shimmered an enchanting light before dying out. It was a light similar to the man's valsara, a light that extended to the hammer he tempered the white-hot metal with. The energy he exuded slowly melded with the metal, infusing it with power.

He was creating another magic weapon.

The display did nothing to impress Ulrin or quell his rage. He marched up to the man with fists clenched. "Sörrign!"

The executioner slammed his hammer against his work once more. "No need to shout, General. I heard you the first time."

Ulrin gritted his teeth. "Yet you don't deign to answer me."

"Only one man may summon me, and you aren't him. Besides, why leave my masterpiece when you let yourself in?"

Ulrin's hand trembled. The temptation to reach for his sword was becoming all the harder to restrain. "You dare say such words as though you still hold them high? I know of your desertion, coward! You outright declared to King Godefroy that you refuse to fight for him any longer."

No matter of tongue-lashing deterred Wolfram's focus. "Aye, I recall.

That was more of a bitter prattling than anything. That defeat did no favors for my thinning patience."

The executioner's words remained smooth and calm, a little difficult to hear over the roaring fire and the falls outside. His focus remained fixated on the wrought metal in front of him, as if nothing else mattered.

And yet, something was amiss.

"Be that as it may, I don't intend to join the fight again until my work here is complete."

For a moment, Ulrin began to resemble the deceased General Esperance he made such an angry face.

"You've taken leave of your sanity if'n you think *this* is more important than the crisis we face! Did you forget how many died when you fought the Convent, or what your rat of a squire did? After everything that happened, you find it best to hide away here and play blacksmith!?"

Bold words to say, as any good leader should to make clear their position and strength. Sometimes, though, they only earned the ire of the one receiving them.

Upon the hammer again striking the metal, a strong pulse of magic filled the room, scattering sparks from the fiery hearth all around. The sparks blinded them for a moment, and when next they could see, Wolfram Sörrign faced them for the first time with his left hand holding the flaming Anktung to Ulrin's neck. Fury burned in his eyes as menacing as the flames from his sword.

"I *am* a blacksmith—the best this world will ever know."

The tongues of fire burning over Anktung lashed at Ulrin's neck but never made contact. He dared not move. If he so much as twitched, the executioner would strike.

Luchs' valsara surged when he saw his meister knight in danger, but he kept his power from running amok. In such a small space, against such a warrior, he could not do anything.

The sword at Ulrin's throat was held steady, its wielder refusing to relent. There was malice in him, a malice that struggled to mask a fatigue that fought its way to the surface.

Wolfram groaned and collapsed to his knees as the flames of Anktung died out. The exhaustion and pain he once hid became all the clearer. He gagged hoarsely, fighting for breath as though suffocating. His left hand lost its grip on the scarlet scimitar, yet his right only tightened around the hammer in it.

Through his magic sight, Luchs witnessed something harrowing. Splotches of an inky darkness appeared in Wolfram's valsara and quickly ate away at it. The emptiness spread gradually. And the more it spread, the more anguish he endured.

In his agony, Wolfram uttered something they could not understand, but those cryptic words were spoken proudly and granted him the strength to subvert the emptiness consuming him. Slowly but surely, his valsara restored itself and briefly gleamed a brighter radiance than before.

Fighting through the fatigue weighing him down, Wolfram picked up Anktung and found the strength to stand again. He glanced over to the mess of wrought metal atop the anvil. "Thirty years I spent crafting these weapons ... nine hundred ninety-nine awe-inspiring weapons none could ever hope to forge, created by my hand. And now the thousandth, my masterpiece..." His magic still flowed into the hammer even while he struggled to keep from faltering, a tantamount to his iron will. Unlike the murderous way he gripped a weapon, his hand held the hammer like it was something precious.

The creation of his weapons meant more to him than they would ever understand.

The executioner's frazzled stare steadily shifted to Ulrin. "My goal led me to Ederea, to serve under Godefroy, who coveted my skills as a warrior. My loyalty was bought by what was necessary to forge my weapons, my means of etching my name into history. Your war, your losses, and that kid are not my concern!" He turned back to the hearth and put down his hammer only to sheath Anktung, then picked it up again. "I refuse to let all of my effort go to waste by failing to reach my goal. Try coercing me further, and you'll find out what every one of my creations can do firsthand!"

His ultimatum given, he tossed Anktung over his shoulder directly at Ulrin's head. Ulrin staggered backward and threw his hands up to catch the weapon.

"Consider that my contribution to the war. Now get out of my workshop!"

Not another word had been spared on them. He went back to tempering the metal, grunting heavily when the hammer fell.

There was nothing more to do there. Ulrin did not have it in him to make an ailing man fight beyond his limits. Although unable to see the ghastly phenomenon happening to his valsara, the weakness Wolfram portrayed could not be faked.

They left the executioner to his own devices, as he wished.

The climb back up the plateau was grueling. The cold air and vapor washed away the excessive heat and bit into them.

Luchs found himself looking back at the forge. He could not stop thinking about the darkness that tried to consume Wolfram. It left him shaking. He did not understand what it was or what it did to him.

Whatever that was ... 'twasn't right.

The cold sapped the two of their body heat after so much vapor draped on them. With the night upon them, they needed to hurry back to the castle before they caught cold.

They went to a nearby guard post. There was a resting chamber inside for the men off duty to relax in, one with a wonderfully massive hearth built in its center. A few men were already relaxing inside, dressed in nothing but their smallclothes, when Ulrin and Luchs entered. Not wanting to be there for long, the two merely shed their armor and sat on a bench near the edge of the room.

Ulrin leaned against the wall, slumping into a more relaxed posture. A lot happened in the past few days. It left the new general weary.

"Are you all right, Ulrin?" his squire inquired.

"Aye, I'll be fine." His breathing was more ragged than usual. He ran his hand over his face and rested it on his sweaty forehead. "Why in the seven hells didn't King Godefroy tell me about his heart?"

A heart attack certainly made better sense than anything Luchs could come up with, but he doubted that was it.

They both sat in silence for a time, taking in everything that had happened to the country and to themselves.

Since the death of the previous general, Ulrin went through an astonishing change. He became more focused on the tasks put before him, harsher toward his subordinates, more easily riled up by surprises and upsets in plans. He was so unlike the man he was not long ago. Drastic as the change was, it was to be expected. He had taken a heavy responsibility after someone he looked up to lost his life in the line of duty, someone he might have been able to save were he not sent on a fool's errand.

He was not alone. Since awakening with amnesia, Luchs saw the world in black and white, and learning of all the different shades that were there was hard to accept at first. There was more than just right and wrong, good and bad. And making mistakes was infuriating.

But they could still make up for their mistakes.

"We just need to find that witch," Luchs muttered. "We find her, then we can tear the Covent apart."

His meister knight chuckled at the notion. Maybe it was not impossible, but it was asking for a lot. Displays of her power showed how dangerous she was. That was not what Ulrin found so funny, though.

Whatever it was went over Luchs' head.

Ulrin looked back to him, amused. "I'll not have my squire marching off to meet the witch god of death before he's ready." Since he brought her up, he assumed Luchs meant to fight her. The power to move the earth and shape it however he pleased—it was likely the only thing that could oppose her devastating magic. "Steel yourself for that time anyway. With our misfortune, it'll likely be soon."

~ Eighteenth Chapter ~
Led Into the Chaos

Stopping the riots took some effort. Every day, another outraged soul would cause a multitude of disturbances both for the knights and for the other civilians scared out of their minds. Although the soldiers were more than capable of subduing the troublemakers, the repetition made focusing on other more dire matters incredibly difficult.

The remaining generals in Shoafond had their hands tied searching for the enemy's den. They failed to learn anything of use from the findings of their lost mage's apprentices. All the mage youths learned about the spell the high priestess used to invade Shoafond was that it destroyed the bodies of the willing to ripe a hole in space. Everything else was beyond them.

All Luchs understood was that the Convent of One sacrificed their own like disposable pawns. The very idea nauseated him.

As for him, he spent every spare moment exercising control over the Second Verse. The talk with Ulrin left him uneasy. Knowing his power could well tip the scales of the war did nothing to ease the strain of controlling it. What happened on Levia Fossa was a fluke, he felt. He could not risk making the next battle his last by relying on subconscious thought.

He needed to know he was ready. He needed to be ready.

Instead of tearing stone from the earth, Luchs used what he learned in Levia Fossa to mold together mineral debris into different shapes and launching them at archery targets with his mind. He ran out of targets after a while; to continue, he formed stone pillars from the ground up. The pillars held together through the Nascitte's will alone. He pitched slabs and spires at the pillars, watched how the stones fell apart, then put them back together without a speck of dirt out of place.

Some squires gathered to watch. Although clumsy in the beginning, Luchs soon turned his exercise into an artful display. The immobile targets posed no real threat, and thus less of an exercise, so Levin volunteered to act as an enemy for him to focus on. No one worried very much for him since he carried a shield as big as he was tall. The metal took a beating but held together.

Levin was not very fast, but made up for that with endurance and cunning. He always got back onto his feet immediately after getting hit and dashed past the stone projectiles thrown his way. And once he got close to Luchs, he delivered unto him a heavy fist to the gut.

It served as motivation to keep his aim precise.

Luchs grinned at his sparring partner when they retook their starting positions and pounded his chest to show he was more than ready.

Rraw! Rraw!

A heinous barking broke through the cheers. Everyone frantically looked around to see where it was coming from. Before they could react, a flash of white flew over the bushes and slipped past the crowd, stopping just before Luchs.

Hard as it was to believe, it was right in front of him.

"Snowflake!?"

The fox stood there perfectly in its monstrous form, no weakness, no apparent wounds. It looked perfectly healthy even as the power within it receded, returning the beast to its small, fluffy, unthreatening state.

It was a miracle. For a moment, he thought it the work of the gods, a boon from Great Gaia to protect her creation. Then he looked to the glowing azure stone lodged into its head.

Even though he found an explanation, Luchs could not believe the beast was already in perfect health. Barely five days passed, five days to heal what would have taken grown men much longer, if at all. It could not have been merely a Nascitte's power. What was it about that stone that allowed it to do the impossible?

"A jinx!"

The squires all stared at Snowflake. It was hard to tell if they were more surprised by its sudden appearance or that Luchs had yet to kill it. Levin, on the other hand, rushed in to take the opportunity.

Luchs stepped past the fox and took his shield, slamming it into his comrade's before he got too close.

The tall squire staggered backward. "You daft, Luchs?"

"Hold, hold!" Luchs bade the squires. "Don't hurt this fox. Her Highness cared for it."

Everyone looked at him like he was crazy. Rumors had spread that the tender princess spent some time caring for a hurt animal she came across, but no one believed it was a fox. Foxes were jinxes, and no one, not even those devoted to Lady Malute, would play with bad luck.

Convincing them not to attack it would not be easy.

Something punctured his ankle before he could explain.

Snowflake, having slipped past the gaps in his shin guard, bite into his ankle, and only released when he looked down. It scampered in the direction of the training grounds, stopping before it could slip out of sight to look back. It waited while the other squires demanded an explanation and insulted Luchs for not acting, then, as if portraying impatience, rushed back to nip his ankle again and ran back to where it waited.

It was almost as if it wanted him to follow. Feeling there was nothing to lose, he chose to see for himself.

The others followed Luchs in his pursuit, roaring as they chased the fox, eager to do it harm. It would do them little good. In its monstrous form, it was nigh invisible; in its natural state, it was faster than a spry hunting dog. How strange it was that something with such small legs could move so quickly.

The fox took them through the castle past several others who attempted to get rid of it. Most of the squires gave up the chase after it went past the bridge, curious as they were about what was happening. It never let Luchs lose sight of it, stopping for him to catch up. When he could not find it after it blended in with the thick mist, it ran back only to let him see before sprinting off again.

Okay, so it does want me to follow.

The others assumed it was toying with them. It stopped being entertaining to them after they were brought to the docks.

The dockhands did not take kindly to the disturbance and threw whatever they had on hand at the fox and squires both.

Snowflake pranced around the things thrown its way without slowing its pace. It was brave to delve so far into the docks and go as far as to board a ship full of panicked seafarers eager to exterminate it. It was as crazy as its master; it rushed through the main deck only to stop right at the bow of the ship. It sat there and stared at the northern horizon.

The remaining squires formed a wall to keep the sailors from getting near Luchs, who tried to see what the fox wanted. They did not follow it through the capital for no reason. Everyone wanted to know what it was after. They were ordered to move and took terrible tongue-lashings upon refusing, the men using every salty word in their limited albeit colorful vocabularies to get them to obey.

Luchs stared down at the fox. "Well, jinx, what's this about?"

Its eyes remained on the horizon, never turning away.

He began to feel foolish for believing, even for a moment, that the beast actually wanted to tell him anything. It was only causing a ruckus, like it always did. Just when he started to see it in a new light, he went back to wondering why Vandelas bothered—

The fox's master! It followed him wherever he went, no matter how far or how perilous the journey. And it always found him.

"Snowflake."

Only when Luchs spoke its name did the little fox look back. Its big, beady blue eyes left a strong impression. The animal could not make any facial expressions like a human, and yet there was something Luchs easily recognizable in its stare: resolve.

The hesitation Luchs had vanished as he crouched down to the fox's level and, imitating the motion he used with horses, held out his hand. The fox only stared for a moment, cautious of him as ever, but Snowflake soon lowered its guard and stepped close to rubbed its head against him. It placed enough trust in him to not be thrown off the ship.

They would need its trust if they were to succeed.

"You've lost your mind."

The Sea Drake Company's new general was as blunt as the last. It did not matter that the one he spoke to was his squire.

They were in the general's quarters discussing what move they could make in their position—or rather, Ulrin was thinking to himself when Luchs barged in with Snowflake. He explained his plan to rely on the fox to track down the Convent of One's whereabouts.

There was no other way. The kingdom was in chaos, its military struggling to maintain a semblance of order, while the enemy roamed free to commit further atrocities. The Convent's profane magic made them powerful and kept them ever out of reach. Even now, while they wasted time picking themselves back up, people across Ederea were submitting to their fear that all they had and loved would be mercilessly torn away.

Time was running out.

"I know! I know this is madness. But it'll work."

"You expect me to believe using a fox, one as devilish as that," Ulrin gestured at Snowflake, "to track down that backstabbing whelp into a heretic-infested nest will fare well for us? You want we should drown what's left of our armies in Untae's Cradle too? Or toss our weapons to the hounds and horses and hope they won't turn on us again? 'Tis suicide. You cannot expect me to approve of this."

"Just listen!" shouted Luchs. "It can do it, I know. Back on Emiet, whenever morning came and Vandelas wasn't there, he left Snowflake behind. It left after I woke and came back with him every time."

"So it's a hound in poacher's skin." Ulrin shook his head, unimpressed. "That happened on a tiny islet with no one else on it. There's no way this thing can track him throughout the entire archipelago, especially not when he vanished with the Convent without a trace left behind."

"Aye, it can. I can show you!"

"Luchs, that's enough."

"But—"

"Enough!"

His patience at its limit, Ulrin threw his fist against the desk he stood by, the loud *thud* startling Luchs into silence. Everything stopped for as long as the deafening sound resounded in the room. It was hard to look at him and see such unsettling rage.

Appearing so furious seemed hard on the general as well, given how easily the façade fell apart. Letting go of the frustration, he walked up to his squire and took a firm grip of his shoulders. "I'm as desperate to end this war as you, believe me. I want the death and despair to stop," he muttered in a languid voice. "Don't think this a lack of faith in you. I have to think about the good of my men as much as the country. Too many have fallen already, and I can't have any sacrifices be made in vain."

And he wanted to keep more from being sacrificed in the process.

No one could not fault him for being so cautious about this. Ederea was being buried in corpses, death staining the land and polluting the sea, and the only way to stop it was by killing more. The question was, how would he keep the ones who died from being those they held dear? He now carried the weight of those choices made thanks to his predecessor's faith in him. It had to be tormenting, suffocating.

When he saw his squire understood, Ulrin went back to his deck. "We will find a way, but until then, your focus should be on helping keep the peace. Leave the life-or-death decisions to me." Giving his final word on the matter, he returned to his desk to finish his business.

There was no way Luchs would leave it be. The chaos affected him just as it had his meister knight. There were times when he closed his eyes and saw corpses of friends and foes alike, the images coming to him much more frequently as the conflicts escalated.

No one could bear anymore waiting.

It was a good thing he thought of another way to approach this.

Knock! Knock!

Ulrin was not expecting visitors, but he tucked his documents away and told them to enter. Surprised as he was, he had a smile when Princess Camellia stepped inside, accompanied by a couple of her handmaidens. The entryway felt a little crowded with four people standing there.

The princess greeted the general with a curtsy. "My apologies for the intrusion, General Vertueux."

"Nay, think nothing of it, Princess. 'Tis always a pleasure to see you." Ulrin forced himself to hide the strain in his voice so he would not make the royal lass uncomfortable. "To what do I owe the pleasure?"

"I come with a request: please accept your squire's proposal."

Ulrin sat in his chair speechless. He could not resist giving Luchs a sour look.

Before going to Ulrin, Luchs bumped into one of the princess' handmaidens readying to leave for an errand. He knew beforehand that Ulrin would not approve of the plan, so he asked her to relay the message to the princess.

Getting her attention was not easy. In fact, she completely overlooked his existence until he mentioned the Convent of One.

"I ... sincerely apologize for my squire pestering you with this matter, Your Highness. What he suggests cannot possibly work."

Instead of simply pressing the matter, Princess Camellia tilted her head in confusion. "Whyever not? It had once before."

Ulrin who was shocked by her response. Luchs, too, looked to the princess with rapt attention, hoping she would elaborate.

The white fox walked up to her. Noticing the creature, Princess Camellia crouched down and picked it up, cradling it in her arms when she stood. "This fox, Snowflake—she is truly remarkable." Her dazzling stare shifted to the men in the room. "When Vandelas first came to Ederea, he had been tasked with proving his worth to Executioner Sörrign. Executioner Sörrign, to that end, took him to an uninhabited isle somewhere in The Chain and left him there with instructions to return here before the month's end. During the time, since he was prohibited to have help from anyone or anything, I watched over Snowflake." Her petite hand gently stroked down the fox's back, comforting it while she went on. "The poor thing grew restless without him, then, after three days, decided to go in search of him. She could not cross the ocean by her lonesome, and only Wolfram knew where Vandelas was left. Two weeks passed and there was no sign of Snowflake, but when Vandelas returned, it was with her by his side."

The story left them speechless. That feat was nothing short of miraculous. He could have been taken in any direction, so for the fox to return with him, it had to have gone wherever he had.

Ulrin intended to interject, unwilling to admit that it would happen again, but before he could, Princess Camellia spoke up, slightly less gentle and more resolute. "General Vertueux— Ulrin, my friend. You know of the things I see, just as the good Eurieg Esperance had." She closed her eyes and bowed her head, taking a moment to remember the lost, before looking back at the new general. "So I ask that you trust in what I see in Snowflake. By whatever means, she *can* track Vandelas to whatever forsaken place he is held in. All you must do is provide her a means to reach it."

It was not likely her royal status that kept him silent. The fight in him faded when she mentioned seeing things, whatever that meant.

He rubbed the throbbing vein in his head, a sign he conceded. "Just my company won't be enough. The Convent will have enough men to overwhelm what we have left."

"I shall convince Father to amass all available soldiers with haste. Once he hears of your plan, everything will be in motion."

"And he will accept it?"

The princess smiled. "The Abioan peoples have used a variety of unorthodox methods to change history time and again. 'Tis the reason we inhabit Ederea to this day. Father shall not forsake this boon and ignore the lessons of our ancestors, especially not after the mishap with Muir."

She took her leave after thanking her general for his time and letting the fox scamper from her arms. The princess was confident and convincing for someone so young. It was not the first time Luchs wondered what made her like that, and it likely would not be the last.

The Sea Drake soldiers in Shoafond were informed to rest for an upcoming expedition and to advise others to do the same. Ulrin remained discreet with the details; it was best no one knew of how events would transpire for the time being. Ships were prepped to sail at a moment's notice. All they had left to do was wait for the word from the king.

Three days passed. It was not until the following afternoon that King Godefroy summoned General Vertueux not to his throne room, but to his personal quarters. The room contained a great many relics from past conquests, time making them nothing more than trophies. Not much else filled the room aside from a long, sturdy table. It was once a war council chamber, but since the previous king took to advising his generals in his throne room, it had not been used for decades. The servants kept the room clean even though no one used it.

The only reason King Godefroy would call anyone there was to give orders for their ears only.

The king approved of the plan whispered to his ear. He ordered General Vertueux to take his mightiest soldiers and hunt down the forces who ravaged Shoafond.

However, he made it clear that the only ones who should know of Ulrin's "special compass" were to be his most trusted and valued soldiers, not the other warriors that would follow them into battle. The superstitious would jump ship the moment they found out the truth.

Messengers alerted the two other generals remaining on Shoafond that their next mission had been decided, and the next morning, soldiers from the Sea Drake, Phantom Osprey, and Kraken Companies assembled, ready to set sail.

King Godefroy and Princess Camellia du Joiec were at the docks to send them off, their presence signifying their best wishes along with the warning that they were about to embark on a dangerous crusade.

The princess did not allow Luchs to leave until he promised to bring Vandelas back safe and sound. It was not an easy thing to do. After all that happened, he did not know if it was possible. But he wanted him back too.

After the attack, they had only a few seaworthy vessels left. A mere three ships left Shoafond, but more joined them from other islands.

A fleet of twenty mighty warships sailed to the north. Each ship harbored approximately one hundred hardened warriors ready for battle, but the flagship commanded by Ulrin only had the necessary fifty.

Even the most dutiful of his company were hesitant to allow a fox aboard their vessel. They might have revolted had the same thing not happened before. Nevertheless, some of them could not help asking the mage youths sailing with them for a magic charm to ward off bad luck.

It was a great risk taking along the three young apprentices who learned under the kingdom's lost mage. They had no combat experience and had yet to take another's life. But they needed people familiar with the ways of the mystic arts if they hoped to survive the next battle.

Throughout the voyage, Luchs kept watch over Snowflake while it tirelessly scoped the horizon. He made it look like he was doublechecking their course for the admiral at the wheel, looking down at the compass he held constantly when someone approached. Not all of them were aware of what truly led them, and the illusion put those who were somewhat at ease.

The fleet rode the rigid waves north-northwest of the capital past the secured ruins of La Kriod. Just like every time they crossed The Chain, every crew member of every ship, those stationed to guard The Chain and those departing, hollered encouraging wishes for luck in their missions at each other.

"Show those dastards who really owns these waters!"

"Send them all down to the seven hells!"

"Avenge our fallen! We got The Chain!"

No one knew where the ships were going, but it was clear what it meant for such a sizable fleet to be advancing, especially after the chaos that ravaged Shoafond. The endgame was near.

Ederea lost many battles against the Convent of One, but the soldiers held dear the faith that they would win the war.

The men grew disheartened after their eleventh day at sea. There was no land in sight, and they had long since passed Ciecime, leaving Ederea's borders. Roaming the northern waters without a clear destination was dangerous, even for the seaborn Edereans. And it was only a matter of time until their supplies would run out.

Snowflake sat at the bow of the ship, directing them to sail onward north. It had not moved in some time and remained ever alert.

Ulrin assured everyone they were still on course, but his words offered less comfort than before. Some of the soldiers started to speculate whether he had what it took to take the place of their last general.

Don't make me regret trusting you, jinx, Luchs irately thought.

On their thirteenth day at sea, the winds tousled the waves and the ships that crossed them. The salty air slapped the seafarers in their faces.

Luchs braved the worst of it making sure their compass did not fall overboard. The little beast endured the raging elements as well as hearty Edereans.

A few of the men argued with Ulrin that they should turn back before they got pulled into Untae's Cradle, but the general did not waver and admonished his soldiers for their cowardice.

It was not the waves or wind that shook them, rather what they carried—an ominous wailing. Every worthy seaman knew all of the harrowing sounds of the sea and the meanings they had. There was something different about what brushed against their ears and sails. It was the cry of a wraith calling out for their souls.

As the winds picked up and the wailing grew louder, the waves crashed against the hull with greater ferocity. A few men clung to the railing to keep from being thrown overboard. One manning the crow's nest fell from his perch, crashing into a barrel of fresh water. The men ordered the squires and mage youths to weather what would come from within the berth. Although the meeker were inclined to obey, everyone remained at their posts wanting to prove their mettle.

The three mage youths joined Luchs at the bow, careful to step lightly around the fox. They seemed focused on something, almost lured in by it.

"Do you think...?"

"This far north? Possibly."

"Wouldn't the admiral know it?"

Whatever they discussed, it sounded important. Nervous tension cracked in their voices.

Snowflake growled while leering in that direction, although it was difficult to hear.

General Vertueux shouted through the wind and joined them when he went unheard. "What're you all doing?"

"We needed a better look," answered Alister, the tallest mage.

While Ulrin questioned the mage youths, his squire stared at the darkening horizon. There was no phenomenon he could detect with his magic sight. All he saw was a mass of swirling dark clouds looming in the distant skies.

They had been visible since the waters began rocking their vessel. The winds were strong enough to stir the mighty ocean, deterring their course, however slightly. A storm had caught them in its snare.

And yet—

I ... don't feel the storm.

Everyone cowered before the winds and the harsh sprays of water, everyone but Luchs. Only he felt a gentle, cold breeze brushing against his face and the faintest splash of mist at his cheek. It was as though the raging elements passed him by.

There was one thing he did feel: the pull of the current.

The ships had all been caught in some unusual current that moved in a manner that felt unnatural. It drew them all toward the vortex of dark clouds, to where Snowflake pointed.

Instead of what lay ahead, Luchs turned down to the waters below. What he saw was faint, but the water contained traces of magic that towed their vessels down the unnatural current formed around it.

"General!" The admiral ran hastily down the deck to meet them. "Something's got the rudder. We lost control of the ship!"

Everyone nearly jumped out of their skin. The mage youths pushed past Luchs to get a better look at the waters themselves. They did not panic and only remained focused on what was in front of them, inspecting it thoroughly.

"It must be the witch's doing," said Fiona, the female mage wearing glasses.

"Got the same feel as the magic that snuffed our teacher, it does."

If Gatreah laid a trap, it meant they were getting close. They were on the right track after all.

Ulrin turned to the mages. "Can you dispel it?"

The short, chubby mage, Seoc, shook his head. "We'd need more time than we have."

The general clicked his tongue. "So she intends to sink us."

"Not sink," Fiona informed. "We're being guided."

"To where?"

"To there!"

Everyone looked to Luchs, then out to the waters ahead. Beneath the epicenter of the swirling clouds, tucked behind the rough waves ahead, was a small, dome-shaped island almost as dark as the stormy skies. Although it appeared barren, life still sprouted and struggled to survive. The shoreline was calm, separated from the chaotic waters by a ship graveyard.

"I'm starting to see where they get their surplus of manpower."

Not many understood right away, but they put together what Ulrin implied quickly. Such a cruel method. The magic drew in ships that strayed too close to the island, wrecked them, then the Convent fished out the survivors and offered the chance to either join them or the dead.

And their fleet was about the meet the same fate.

The flagship jostled, throwing everyone on their backs. The current had forced them to pick up speed.

"Any ideas on how we get out of this?"

The mages each looked at one another, shared reluctant glances, then turned back to their general and shamefully shook their heads.

"We need to get there anyway," Luchs interrupted, "just in one piece. How about getting rid of the wreckage?"

The squire taking the initiative threw the three off, but they admitted that seemed to be their best option. They looked back at Ulrin for an answer on his part. There was no argument from him; he offered a simple nod.

Luchs grabbed Snowflake, enduring the startled bite it gave his hand, and followed Ulrin to the deck, giving the mage youths their space. Much of the crew gathered after realizing there was nothing they could do on their part. They were eager to witness a magical feat that would not threaten to destroy them.

A moment passed with the three standing still with their hands clasped together, time spent clearing their minds and calming their spirits. The display did not appeal to those with eyes unable to see the movement of another's valsara, but Luchs saw it all. Their once calm valsara spread vibrantly like ethereal flames stoked by their will. The radiant colors flared out intensely enough to push back the winds assaulting them.

Then sparks of scarlet energy manifested from their bodies.

They got much closer to the amassed wreckage, teeth of splintered wood coming into view. Fiona, stepping past her peers, held out her hand, concentrating the energy to bubble from her palm. When fully gathered, she shot it out at wreckage. The resulting explosion caused the debris to scatter and fall directly at them. In response, the two other mages shot out several less concentrated sparks of power, incinerating the wood and metal before it hit the ship.

The crew watched in awe, then hollered hearty cheers for the three mages clearing the path.

The raging current kept throwing everyone off-balance, but the mages stood their ground, holding a stance that kept them from falling over. Static light rained down on the makeshift blockade, decimating it layer by layer. They focused on spreading the destruction out as much as possible, ensuring a path for the other ships behind them.

But the demolition grew more grueling after they ripped through the first layer and worked to blast away the older ships that condensed together. The way they were packed together made the wreckage dense enough to resist the rain of energy, and more debris flew at them the more that was destroyed. Sparks from the debris blasted flew back at the ship, getting closer and closer to searing the crew.

At the speed they were moving and the rate the obstacles were destroyed, it would not be long until they became part of the graveyard.

Luchs tried sensing for land beneath the water hoping he could use it to move the ships himself, but there was nothing holding it all up. Somehow, the entire wreckage consisted of flotsam—suspended entirely on the water.

He could not help. It was up to them.

They did what they could, but there was too much to clear away and not enough time. Everyone braced for impact, grabbing onto something in place, in anticipation of the collision.

The ship shook violently, even though they had not yet reached the wreckage. Everyone thought some of the debris had struck the hull, but the ship was completely intact. The water underneath, the current that kept rocking their vessel, and the magic flowing with it grew stronger.

Wait. That's not the witch's magic.

Luchs felt it, and so did the mages. There was another energy coursing through the waters, something serene and mystifying, the antithesis of the witch's sinister magic. Luchs saw the beauteous energy much more clearly than the malignant force pulling them toward land. It was slowly neutralizing the current and removing its pull on them while at the same time using the dwindling energy to pull apart the amassed wreckage.

The three mages quickly caught on to what was happening and shot bursts of their combined magic where the wreckage was splitting, enough for the mysterious energy to tear open a path.

Everyone rejoiced knowing their crusade had not yet come to an end. They rushed to the mages to thank them for their efforts, and were stumped when they humbly admitted to having outside help.

Who was it that saved them?

A small trail of the lingering magic offered an answer. It led to another fleet of ships sailing their way.

The lookout offered his spyglass to Ulrin so he could have a look.

A smirk drew across his face. "What took you so long, Rah'ta?"

~ Nineteenth Chapter ~
The Bold and the Beast

Without the wreckage to block their path, the Ederean forces sailed to the island unimpeded and dropped anchor at the shore. It was strange to find no one there to greet them, no troops waiting in ambush, anything to keep them from advancing. The soldiers took this opportunity to prepare for battle.

Everyone remained on guard knowing perfectly well how cunning the Convent of One was. Meanwhile, a few Phantom Osprey scouts went ahead to investigate the terrain and locate the enemy.

While waiting for the intel, Ulrin met with their reinforcements, the Vainte who saved them from being shipwrecked. It was a welcome surprise to see more able warriors joining the fight. The few extra ships offered a few hundred more men and tigresses, including Rah'ta, Rufus, and Tal. As it turned out, it was their shaman's effeminate protégé that dispersed the magic that drew them toward oblivion.

The excitable knights and squires were eager to give thanks to the protégé, but he humbly denied it was him alone. "The spirits were with me. 'Twas their influence that gave me the strength needed." His modesty only made them prone to offer more praise.

Luchs met Rufus and introduced him to the other squires he worked with. It took some explaining to convince him that Maxime was a decent squire and person, but after that, they got along well. Levin actually reminded him a little of Aloysius, though Luchs failed to see how.

"Now ain't this quaint."

Most of them were familiar with that gravelly, nonchalant voice, and trembled when its owner approached. It was hard to believe no one noticed Commandant Brunlier among them before. While there were roughly four thousand men-at-arms altogether, he was a behemoth among them. "Good to see ye've all made it this far, 'specially ye, lad." Those last words were directed at Luchs, much to his surprise and discomfort. "Heard ye're quite the earth-mover now. I'd love to see that power meself, but don't go ending the battle so soon. No glory in winning the war that way, aye?"

Luchs nodded without thinking.

A shock though it was to see him again, it was somewhat of a relief. With so many mighty warriors, they stood a chance of defeating the Convent of One.

The soldiers got acquainted with one another while waiting for the scouts to return. Some of them knew each other as friends, others as rivals, and there were even those with mortal enemies among them. Whatever their history, they vowed to stand and fight together in the battle to come. After all, everyone wanted to return home alive.

Upon the scouts' return, General Vertueux marched off the beach and climbed onto a large boulder. He carried himself proudly as she faced his army, but his squire could plainly see how nervous he was. A general's role was not only to lead his troops, but also to motivate and inspire them to charge bravely into battle with the confidence they would emerge triumphant.

The eyes of every warrior rested on him with rapt attention. They waited to hear the words that would guide them.

Upon taking a breath, Ulrin seized his courage and took a step forward. "My brothers-in-arms and valued allies, we've come a long way since we settled into Ederea a century ago. Although 'twasn't without sacrifice and strife, we've made more than just alliances and settlements; we formed bonds and came to make the archipelago a home for all of us. We treasure the collective islands, the people in them, and the grand history we made together. And this menace calling itself the Convent of One has spent too long defiling Ederea—our home, our people, our lives—for the sake of their faith alone. They perform acts more profane than any sin to turn us against each other, to ruin the legacy we've built, all so they can make an Ederea that fits their design alone, no matter how many—no matter who—they must sacrifice. No more!"

The Edereans howled, their collective cries shaking the quiet beach.

"This night, we bring this menace to its knees! This night, we take back our home! This night, we show the Convent of One that we will never bow to them!"

The mighty proclamation energized the army. Their valiant battle cries were echoed by praise for the general and their king, and they shook their weapons in the air.

General Vertueux took his halberd in hand and slammed its pommel against the boulder. "Let's go! To victory!"

And thus, the Ederean forces marched through the unknown land ready for war. A steep uphill climb brought them inland. Every step across the tough terrain kicked up dust. The few mounted atop their blindfolded horses advanced as easily as those on foot.

The air was unsavory and a little hard to breathe. It had a stagnant, unsettling odor that would have made eyes water had the bountiful flora growing there not masked it, their pungent aroma not very savory but still invigorating.

The barren land felt different from anyplace in the archipelago, Luchs felt. He sensed these veins of intense energy coursing throughout the island, spreading to nearly every corner, keeping the ground warm to the touch. He had doubts about what it could be, but when he stepped over one, he felt it connect with him momentarily. His whole body spasmed frantically and he fell to his knees.

It was nothing like he felt before. When looking at the energy flow with his magic sight, he found it resembled the stagnant valsara within stable ground. But this was not dormant potential energy. The ground beneath the surface was moving on its own.

He came to dread joining the expedition. The shape of the island, the powerful energy coursing through the land, the fairly masked scent of brimstone—they were walking on an active volcano.

Luchs could not use his power now. If his control over the Second Verse lapsed in the slightest, the volcano would erupt. The war would end, but without a winner, without anyone returning home.

Ulrin remained by his squire's while he recovered. He asked what was wrong, but Luchs said he was fine and stated it was just pre-battle shivers. Ulrin did not believe him, but he kept moving with the army. He figured out what it was about and kept his silence. There was nothing he could do to help him, no matter how much he wanted to, and it pained him.

Luchs conditioned himself to the intense energy, although he could not help twitching when he came into contact with another vein. No matter the discomfort, he refused to let it show. This battle was where he would prove himself as a warrior and a Nascitte.

I won't mess this up. It won't end that way. I won't let it!

The army trekked across the jarring hills of the volcanic island following the scouts' lead. They crossed over rough paths on cliffs above the beaches. It was eerily quiet the entire way, the wind blowing monotonously across the island and the waves below soft and gentle. There were no encounters with hostile wildlife or the enemy.

No one believed the Convent was not expecting them, not with the foresight they had throughout the months spent oppressing Ederea.

When the full moon hung in the center of the starlit sky, the army crossed a pass above a grand ravine where the Convent of One hid. A small settlement was built in the belly of the ravine, one with buildings that resembled those from the village in Ciecime. And standing behind the village to the northeast was an ancient basilica. Within the once holy building's walls, a terrifyingly familiar power crackled and lashed about.

The Convent forces amassed outside the settlement and faced the pass. Their leader must have alerted them when her spell had been erased.

A brief look through a spyglass showed that, despite the decrepit living conditions, the warriors were in capable shape and armed just as well as the knights. Their numbers were almost on par with the Edereans.

There were too many of them for everyone to live inside the settlement. The homes built there could not possibly shelter so many. And yet there they all were, waiting for them.

"Look at them. Cornered in their little hole." Commandant Brunlier cackled a ghastly laugh that frightened the young. "That's when rats fight the hardest."

"'Tis their home, after all. But I doubt they question their chances of victory," Rah'ta interjected. "Nay, I wager they're thinking of making an example of us." She glanced at Ulrin, her smile twisted. "Let us get close enough to taste victory, then pull it away and send our bodies back south, strike fear into anyone that dares look for them—for death." She was teasing him to see if he would lose heart.

But the general looked down at the settlement with drive and contempt. No doubt stumbling upon the enemy invoked some vile emotions. "Their intention doesn't matter. They're here, waiting for a fight, and they'll get it." He turned back to the mage youths and Tal, who were well guarded by a group of heavily armored knights. "Where is the witch?"

Alister pointed to the basilica. "There."

Snowflake shared as much interest in the building, never looking away. That must be where they kept him.

"Her magic grows by the second," Fiona warned. "I fear she's preparing a nasty surprise."

"Can you sense any traps, magic or otherwise?"

The mage youths did not seem to know whether or not to say anything in case there were traps they could not perceive.

Tal, on the other hand, looked perfectly certain after opening his big eyes. "The spirits only warn of the one called Gatreah. They say nothing more than that."

"Then the warriors there are the only things standing between us and that witch."

Commandant Brunlier chortled. "What'd I tell ye? Like rats."

Appropriate as his claim was, it did not seem right. The Convent of One always had plan underway while its cannon fodder caused havoc. It was safe to assume the high priestess herself was plotting something to counter the Ederean forces.

And if the flux of power was of any indication, there was not much time left.

General Vertueux called on the captain of his cavaliers to order the horsemen to take formation immediately. The mounted soldiers gathered into different squads, all of them taking arrow-shaped formations with their captain in the lead of the vanguard. Each one was accompanied by an archer that would help thin the herd. They were to kill as many enemies as they could until the main force caught up, then turn their attention to aiding the mages.

"Rah'ta, you're with me. I need your skill to face the witch."

The toothy grin the tigress bore showed how eager she was for battle. "She won't last, not while I have this." She carried Porlande, the dual-bladed Distortion Wheel gifted to the Vainte. Her chieftain entrusted it to her so the crusade would be handled quickly.

Then Ulrin turned to his squire. He looked at him differently than he had the other warriors, showing more compassion and worry. "Luchs." He spoke softly, then steeled himself. "You'll support the faction following mine. Rush into the fray when we find the witch and pick off anyone that gets in the way."

It was a fitting role for the squire to the general, not one that would get him involved in the most fights, but still vital. And it would get him closer to their biggest threats—one of them he would need to handle himself.

"Gilbrand, my squire will be accompanying you."

The behemoth simply grinned. No doubt he saw it as an opportunity to get a glimpse of his power.

Luchs stood uncomfortably with Maxime and a few knights, attempting to hide from Commandant Brunlier's gaze. How strange it was to feel both relieved and unnerved at the same time.

"It ends here. For Ederea!"

Their general's rallying cry mustered incredible fighting spirit from the soldiers as they charged through the pass. In response, the Convent warriors advanced against those invading their sanctuary, screaming praises for their god in hopes it would bring them victory as the Edereans had for Lord Ralias.

The horsemen rode their stallions through the pass, their steeds galloping across the ravine at great speed. They met with the enemy forces first and began mowing down the grunts in front. The enemy kept a strong formation and stubbornly fought the cavaliers, though there was little they could do against the archer at their backs.

By the time the rest of the army caught up and clashed with the enemy, nearly half of the cavaliers had been slain. Although it came at a cost, the assault caused the Convent's formation to fracture. They fell apart in face of the avalanche of Edereans.

Luchs was in the rear along with Commandant Brunlier, Rufus, Maxime, and Tal. They rushed through the clashing forces as the struggle reached an impasse, and picked off the enemies in their path. The faction followed not far behind Ulrin as they rushed for the basilica.

Their forces breaking formation and slowly losing ground only made the Convent of One fight much more fervently. They used the growing chaos to mislead the Edereans, breaking their forces apart.

Unfortunately, Commandant Brunlier's faction lost sight of Ulrin and his men. The separated factions put pressure on the Convent soldiers, forcing them to keep their attention on them and away from Ulrin.

The first to engage with Luchs was a swordsman of impressive stature carrying an equally impressive sword. The swordsman mercilessly threw his weapon down at Luchs. Upon intercepting the attack with his shield, Luchs shoved the sword aside with all his might, then thrust his blade through the staggering man. He withdrew his weapon quickly, ready for the next to come his way.

He noticed how dread did not grip him this time around. Was it from the time spent in battle, his value for enemy life dulling? It was not something he could focus on, not when he fought for the lives of his comrades and everyone they cared about.

Every Convent warrior threw themselves at the Edereans in groups, ganging up on smaller factions in hopes of picking their army apart piece by piece. Luchs fought through a dozen enemies before they began circling him. One rushed at him from behind. "Coward!" But the man was strong, and the force he put into his axe would have cleaved Luchs in twain had he not held his shield up to block it. Had he used his sword instead, the force from the swing would have dislocated his arm and potentially broken his sword, just as it had against a certain behemoth when he was a page.

Fortunately, Commandant Brunlier was fighting alongside him this time, and he easily swatted away all those that surrounded Luchs before they could overwhelm him. "So ye rats fancy yerselves strapping men gangin' up on a lad all alone, eh?" he merrily jested.

Easily seen as the biggest threat, the commandant was the next to be beset by the Convent horde. Their group advances did little good against him. It only took one swing of his massive sword to repulse four men charging together. One came at him from behind, restraining him so his comrades could finish him off. That was a mistake. Commandant Brunlier, flashing a wicked grin, reached back with his free hand to grasp the man's face, then threw him at a group charging his way.

Maxime made sure no one else ambushed Luchs while the behemoth had his fun, the two fighting with their backs to each other. They fended off the enemies pinning them down until the Edereans began to force the Convent back, then fought back fiercely.

Snowflake was never far from Luchs, but went on the hunt when enemies drew near. In its monstrous form, it pounced at the bloodthirsty men, tearing through one before swiftly moving onto the next and so on.

It was very good at distinguishing allies from enemies. It gracefully leaped past the Edereans while ruthlessly attacking those who took what it cherished.

Rufus fell behind only to aid the surviving horsemen that circled back to protect Tal. Anyone who got too close he leaped at like a wiry monkey, swinging his two hand axes like a maniac yet with uncanny precision.

The shaman protégé was no slouch either. Whatever magic he brandished allowed him to throw the enemy back at will. Looking to him with magic sight showed Tal conjuring what appeared to be another source of faint valsara—his spirits, perhaps—and hurling it at the enemy. Some of the victims were simply pushed back, others battered, and some even lacerated. Those pulses of valsara acted independently of the one conjuring them until fading away.

"Watch out!"

Luchs' comrade struck at an attacker at his side, something he might have noticed had he focused on the threats around him. He sliced the man's arm in an uppercut, then quickly angled his sword and plunged it into his back after he collapsed.

"Keep those peepers off the lass and on the battle."

"Tal's a lad." Luchs made up for his blunder by charging at the warrior aiming at Maxime's exposed back, slamming his shield into his gut before slicing it open.

Unimportant as that remark was, it left Maxime surprised enough to ignore his own advice. "Truly?"

"Ask them about it later. Get back to hacking!"

The might of the Ederean army forced the Convent troops to move to their advance. The Edereans kept the enemy off of their general to the best of their abilities as they advanced toward the basilica, circling the settlement.

The battle raged on, both sides colliding with one another like raging waves in a storm of chaos. Neither side relented, both driven to keep fighting for causes justified to themselves. It was not long until they crossed a field of blood just to fend each other off.

The influence of magic gave the Ederean army the advantage, one the Convent of One had long since had for themselves, an advantage they now fought without. No matter how many were cut down, no matter how they neared the settlement, there was no sign of any of the Convent mages.

Something was wrong, and it was about to get much worse.

The malignant energy from within the basilica grew exponentially, until it finally burst, the discharge shooting out innumerable threads of energy across the combat zone and beyond, forming foreboding arcs in the sky. A great many circled back to the basilica; the rest scattered across the island at breakneck speed, one aimed for Snowflake.

Acting on impulse, Luchs dove in front of the fox.

He hoped to scoop it in his arms and roll out of the way, but the magic thread was too fast and shot into his back. He crumbled before the original target, the energy crackling across his nerves.

But nothing else happened.

There was no pain or weakness, just a small discomfort that faded. Whatever heinous power the spell had, it did not affect Luchs.

Then ... what in the gods' names was it for?

When he looked back up, the fox fled back the way they came.

A soldier helped Luchs back to his feet. He seemed relieved to see him unharmed, though remained oblivious to what just happened.

No one else seemed to have been hit by the magic explosion. The battle raged on uninterrupted, not a soul reacting to the apocalyptic light show that encompassed the battlefield. It was for the best. If any other person saw it, the Convent's morale would be bolstered, the spell doubtlessly intended to benefit them.

Since his understanding of magic was limited, Luchs thought to ask Tal what he saw, but he could not find him in the crowd of soldiers.

Turning back was not an option, so he forged on.

The enemy forces kept throwing themselves at the Edereans with abandon, if only to slow them down. They knew of their leader's plan, just not that it had already begun, and kept fighting to secure its fruition.

Enemy reinforcements came from the settlement on horseback. There were about fifty or so, not enough to impact the battle too much.

But the horsemen did not remain on their mounts. As soon as they got close enough to join the fight, they dismounted and swatted their steeds on their hides, sending them into the fray without guidance. The horses ran around the warriors of the Convent and charged after the Edereans, trampling them under their hooves out of pure malice.

And entangling each of their valsara was one of the threads that fell from the sky.

The spell to control animals!

The Edereans' horses remained unaffected for the moment since they were blindfolded, but every other manner of beast there would be after their hearts before long.

The chaotic chorus of war escalated to its peak, the warriors' battle cries, grating clashes of metal, and drum of tumbling bodies drowning out all else. And when it was at its most harrowing, the discord had been surmounted by a terrible howl.

The howling resounded throughout the area simultaneously with a breath of deathly cold wind, both coming from the direction of the basilica.

Luchs rushed past the conflicting forces and cut down all in his way to return to his meister knight's side. Despite distancing himself from where most of the warriors fought, the danger grew exponentially worse.

More fallen were left to rot on the path. The entirety of Ulrin's faction lay dead underneath sheets of crumbling ice. The only survivors were fighting the monster responsible for the carnage ahead.

Before he ran to join them, Luchs noticed something grasped in one of the dead's hands. He froze upon realizing it was the very weapon Executioner Sörrign callously hurled at Ulrin: the Drake Fang, Anktung. The general gave it to one of his soldiers, someone who was trusted to stop a specific enemy. Luchs felt a pang of resentment upon realizing so. Conflicted as it made him, he needed to act, so he grabbed the sword in its amber-like holster and ran toward the conflict ahead.

Only two Edereans remained against one foe. Rah'ta went on the defensive and Ulrin, bleeding from his left shoulder, wielded his spear in his dominant hand, careful of the beast confronting them.

They dared not make any sudden moves against Vandelas Kronas. Though he stood against them unarmed, the casualties behind them were a clear sign they must not take the lad lightly.

No, they did not even look at him as a child anymore—rather as a beast bearing its claws.

There was another watching over the conflict safely from a distance, a woman dressed in arcane robes. Her face and skin were undeniably beautiful. The silver jewelry hanging from her ears and adorned around her neck accentuated her natural charm. Her scalp was smooth, giving her the appearance of a living idol, although her long, pointed nose twisted that image. Under her alluring skin, her valsara, a wicked radiance of violet and crimson, revealed her oppressive nature as much as the beady red eyes leering at the Edereans.

At last, the witch, Gatreah, showed herself.

A pulse rippled through the air around Gatreah—a signal for Vandelas to attack. The beast howled a terrifying scream, further exuding a feral aura, then pounced.

It was hard to see from that distance, but as the beast assaulted the spear-wielders, Luchs found his valsara tangled in dozens of the threads that fell from the sky. The very spell that compelled animals to obey the Convent's will brainwashed him too.

Vandelas coated his forearms in ice, forming frightfully sharp claws as he rushed after the wounded Ulrin. Rah'ta got in his way before he could lay a hand on him, thrusting the shaft of her weapon to repel him. She attempted to spin Porlande and use its mesmerizing properties, but the beast got in close before she could so much as wave it. That trick was not going to work unless she slowed him down first.

He saw every motion made against him before they hit and evaded nimbly, ducking, rolling, pivoting, and stepping away ahead of time.

Ulrin jumped in when he moved his way, thrusting his spear for his abdomen. But Vandelas pirouetted around the attack, then, using the momentum from his spin, pushed against the spear with his right arm and swiped his icy left at the man's chest. He fell back to avoid getting torn apart, leaving him vulnerable to another attack.

Were it not for Rah'ta stepping in, repelling him with a swing of the spear, Ulrin would have been a goner.

Seeing Vandelas move so much showed Luchs what he needed to do. Those threads binding him all connected directly to Gatreah. If he slayed her, and he would be free.

No one noticed he was there yet. He took this opportunity to circle around, using a natural wall of jagged stones as cover. Ulrin and Rah'ta still kept the beastly Vandelas busy, but both were nearing their limits while he kept up the momentum.

Past the natural cover, Luchs saw the witch oversee the weary fighters struggle against her puppet. While she was distracted, Luchs took his sword in both hands and ran toward her at his fastest, the witch not noticing him until the blade was raised overhead. She startled and attempted to move away, rather pathetically, just as a cold wind snapped from the side.

A wave of ice launched across the field in an instant, forming a barricade between Luchs and the witch. The blade, falling against the icy wall, snapped in two, its tip flying past his head, cutting his cheek.

Vandelas ran to meet Luchs, closing the distance with blinding speed. He stood slightly hunched over, breathing heavily, his breath white. His glacial stare, those predatory eyes having found suitable prey, bit at Luchs as harshly as the cold.

The way he reacted showed the witch was not just using him as a weapon, but also as a shield. She did not use a spell to deter or kill her attacker either. The hold she had on her puppet limited what she could do.

And yet, despite having revealed such, Gatreah laughed haughtily from behind her protection, finding nothing had changed. "Bold, but so terribly foolish."

Everything took a turn for the worst. As if having the Nascitte of Ice maliciously stand against him was not bad enough, he was not alone.

Another beast, a wolf, snarled from behind him, accompanied by two others, all of them looking very hungry.

Where did they come from? The island should not be hospitable enough to sustain predators such as those.

It was likely that the Convent brought them, along with who knows how many other breasts, from other islands to be used as their pawns.

Without the need for extra protection, or perhaps simply to have a better look at the squire squirm, Gatreah motioned for Vandelas to remove the wall. A simple clench of his ice-coated fist was all it took for the barricade to shatter into thousands of glittery specks.

Gatreah's venomous laughter thickened the tension in the air. "I pray that your suffering shall allow you to repent," she scoffed. "Go, my pet. Finish the enemy leader."

The threads against Vandelas' valsara tugged him back to where he left Ulrin and Rah'ta. But he did not budge. He stood there, eying Luchs with eyes glimmering a trenchant malice and growling ferally. Rather than being upset, Gatreah hummed with intrigue. "Oh? So this child is a bigger threat than those real warriors?" It sounded more like she was looking down at Luchs than anything. "Very well. Your brethren shall dispose of them."

The wolves obeyed the witch's indirect command and left them to target Ulrin and Rah'ta.

"Now, punish the sinner child!"

This time, Vandelas did not hesitate. Instead of engaging him then and there, though, he raised his arms slowly, then snapped them to his sides and shattered the ice coating them without damaging the skin. He then clenched his fists, forging bars of ice between them, bars that became the handles of two long, toothy swords. He wielded the new weapons the same way as he had with a sword and scabbard.

Wary as Luchs should have been, he saw something when he traded his claws for swords: it was still him underneath those threads.

Luchs smirked after dropping the broken sword from his grasp. "That's right," he uttered. "You're a warrior, not a beast, so fight like one!"

He raised his arm, reaching for the handle behind his back, and quickly drew Anktung, summoning its flames.

The beast winced at the sight of fire. Fright filled his eyes, fright that shifted into ferocity as he faced the sky and screamed a violent howl. Then he charged, swiftly closing the distance between the two, and began swinging. Luchs held his shield firm, deflecting the attacks directed at his torso, sparks flying when ice grated at the hard steel. Vandelas pivoted to his side after that attack failed and swung for his prey's bulky arm. Before ice cut through the protection on his arm, Luchs moved out of the way and threw his shield at the attacker. Nimble as ever, the beast danced around the repulse and moved in for a more vulnerable point to strike. The path of the blade was clear as day. Luchs swung Anktung to intercept, a loud hiss resounding as its flames seared the ice.

Going on the offensive made Vandelas fight differently. He moved faster and carried much more force in his strikes than when calm, but it resulted in forgoing his perfect defense. It became easier for Luchs, who took on the lad's deadly dance many times, to see and follow his movements ahead of time.

Taking the lead did not suit him.

Even so, he was relentless. Shortly after being tossed aside, he rushed back in for another attack.

Luchs refused to remain on the defensive and swung Anktung wide, casting a wave of searing heat that even burned the wielder. The beast dove to the side, rolling in the dirt to escape; a thick vapor wafted from his left knee, unable to pull it away in time. Wanting to keep him pinned down, Luchs swung the Drake Fang again, hurling another wave of embers before he could stand again. But Vandelas used his momentum to throw the frigid air around him at the sweltering heat.

Hot and cold colliding seemed to cancel each other out until Luchs felt the frigid air sweep across his body. Moving took more effort than it should have, his muscles momentarily petrifying. While he endured the cold, Vandelas slid through the blending air undeterred and closed the distance between them once more.

Luchs waved Anktung to fend him off. The veils of heat kept Vandelas at bay, but he kept trying to get around them.

"I know you can hear me," Luchs shouted over the roar of Anktung's flames and the hiss of burning ice.

Perhaps he heard, but he did not answer.

Since he could not get close, Vandelas began to rely on his Second Verse. The air above freezing, a mass of ice spires manifested over Luchs' head and plummeted with a firm pull from the cold Nascitte's arms.

Luchs leaped out of the way before the frozen fangs sank into him.

The fight did not stop even while he stumbled. All he could do while on the ground at first was block attacks with his shield. The strikes from Vandelas' blades became more ferocious as he continuously froze over them. No matter how thick the blades became, he dropped them onto his prey without slowing.

When a blade about as thick as a hatchet slew at his left side, Luchs shoved his shield at it, throwing the beast back a few steps, and swung Anktung groundward at the thinner weapon. Seizing his chance, he slammed their foreheads together, making him stagger further backward. Vandelas' skull was surprisingly hard, but Luchs' was harder.

"You don't want to do this. Fight it! Fight that witch off!"

His words failed to change anything. Vandelas recovered from the headbutt and continued swinging his icy fangs without mercy. No matter how much Luchs blocked his advances, no matter how close he swept the flames to his icy body, he tirelessly kept on the attack, all the while Luchs' endurance dwindled.

The beast, as if sensing that, forced his way through the veil of heat and, when Luchs swung for and missed his shoulder, swatted the blunt edge of an icy blade at his wrist, knocking Anktung from his grasp.

The sword's fire dissipated the moment it left its wielder's hand.

Dreading the next step in the deadly dance, Luchs threw his shield arm into Vandelas' jaw. That move to knock him back also, unexpectedly, pushed the Drake Fang away, kicked away by his heel.

The only surefire way to stop him had been ripped away.

Without the flames to deter him, there was no stopping the deadly dance. Vandelas leered at Luchs as he licked the blood from the corner of his lip, then moved in for the kill. An icy blade curved across Luchs' face, missing by a hair's length when he dove to the ground.

Luchs skidded through the dirt and struggled to get to his feet as the beast came from behind and threw his swords down at him. He turned and raised his shield, bouncing the fangs back, but had been pinned to the ground again. Each fall of the ice hammered at his shield tremendously. A dozen strikes made Luchs' arm feel like it would soon fall off.

Staying put like a turtle hiding in its shell was suicide, and if he moved, the ice would tear him apart. There was no way out.

But Lady Sundralla had not yet forsaken him. Before Vandelas could land the final blow, a long broadsword had been drawn above him. It was guided by Commandant Brunlier.

Knowing him, he wanted to be included in the "fun" too.

Despite coming from his blind spot, Vandelas sensed the attack coming and leaped out of the way before the blade could graze him. The behemoth did not let up and kept on the offensive. The beast, taking a defensive stance again, held the icy blade in his left hand to intercept, but was overwhelmed by his enemy's pure strength. Realizing the difference between them, he swiveled away from the attack just before it connected.

"A spry one! Good, good. This should be fun."

While the two monstrosities fought for control of the battle, Luchs ran to get Anktung. The witch noticed what he was up to and motioned for her puppet to stop it. But the commandant proved too great a threat to turn away from.

Try as he did to move past the heavy weapon, his flashy swordsmanship failed to deter the mighty behemoth.

Although he clung to his swords, Gatreah required a beast, not a warrior, and tightened her grip around the threads binding him.

Letting out a growl, Vandelas recklessly pushed past Commandant Brunlier's guillotine swing and spun with his icy blades, carving them into his exposed right arm and slicing it from its socket.

Luchs picked up the magic weapon in time to bear witness. He watched in horror as the four-foot log of muscle had been torn from its base, a stream of blood spilling from it. The behemoth tottering backward in agony.

To see that happen before his very eyes was more than Luchs could bear. He gritted his teeth and tightened his hand around Anktung.

"Enough!"

As Vandelas held his blades to slay Commandant Brunlier, Luchs sheathed Anktung only to draw it quick as lightning and, the flames burning as bright as his fighting spirit, swung it. More than embers flew from the conflagrant sword; a blade of pure fire shot at the beast, striking true and drowning him in the flames.

Some of the flames scorched Commandant Brunlier, but it was not nearly as devastating to him as it was for the icy Nascitte.

He howled in agony, flailing desperately to put out the fire, and fell to the ground as it dissipated. His trembling body was covered in a thick vapor that dyed the air white.

"Stay down!"

Luchs did not want the fight to drag on. He did not want to hurt him. What happened was not his fault. He was just as much a victim as those the witch forced him to kill.

He vowed to bring him home alive, but he feared it was impossible.

The beast rose, fighting off the torturous pain melting his body, and set his sights on Luchs once more. He moved sluggishly, the fire having slowed him, grunting vilely and keeping those glowing glacial eyes on his prey. Frost coated around his burns, making him appear a frozen zombie. Some ice ran down his right arm and reformed the base of a sword in his palm.

One wave of Anktung would be all it took to put him down. But Luchs refused to do it. He still wanted to keep faith, and only watched him march his way.

It was not until the beast was within five feet that Luchs reluctantly accepted that he had to end it. He watched him weakly hold the icy blade out to the side, waiting for the point of no return, and, just when he thought there was no turning back, recoiled at Vandelas driving the blade into his own thigh.

The lad fell to the ground. He looked to be kneeling as he forced the weapon through his left side. The ice in his grasp shattered after gripping it so tightly, his right hand then wrapping around the self-inflicted wound while the other dug into the dirt. Those eyes of his still radiated ferocity and malice, but flickering in the cracks of his blue irises was defiance.

"What in The Divine One's name are you doing? Attack!"

The witch tightened her hold on Vandelas, the threads constricting his limbs and throat. He screamed as he thrashed about. But he did not budge.

"You dare disobey your high priestess? I command you to attack!" For his resistance, Gatreah tightened the malignant threads until they dug into his valsara. The torture forced painful cries from him again and again. "Rise! Fight! Kill the sinner child!"

His bellowing was so loud that it drew the attention of many soldiers on both sides.

No matter the pain, Vandelas rejected Gatreah. His fingers dug into the ground both from enduring the torture and to keep himself from obeying. The raging valsara inside him pushed against its shell to follow the will of his puppeteer as the shell itself struggled to resist. And through it all, he never raised his head.

Luchs understood why, but again he refused. Instead, he sheathed Anktung, leaving himself open should the witch win. "I'm not giving up on you. You can beat her," he wholeheartedly encouraged. "That wench, she's nothing compared to what you've been through! You defied the will of a king. You opposed an entire squadron with just your meister. You can't let a single witch and her tricks break you. You're stronger than this, Vandelas Kronas!"

Vandelas looked up at Luchs, gritting his teeth until blood trickled between them. His eyes trembled from his struggle with control.

Luchs maintained his show of strength if only to inspire him to show his own. "You stood by me—*trusted* me—when I was at my most dangerous, even when I almost buried you alive. What kind of friend would I be if I abandoned you now?"

The heartfelt encouragement rocked him to the core even as he was being strangled by the witch's spell. Pain and suffering tore his psyche apart as he struggled.

Luchs watched him throughout his torture. It was horrifying, but no matter how gruesome it looked when he shook on the ground, he remained where he was. He needed to be there with him, to witness the moment he broke free.

After what felt like an eternity of torture, Vandelas' throat began reverberating a bloodthirsty growl.

The threads that once dug deeply into his valsara bounced back against the way it naturally flowed. They kept constricting, their manipulator vengefully tightening their hold on him, but his valsara kept reforming and pushing the threads back, a terrifying force pulsating from it. Gatreah stopped her attempts to retake control after she felt it through her threads.

Luchs felt it too, and being so close to it made him want to flee. This heavy force exuded from his valsara like a giant heartbeat.

"I'll kill you..."

He winced when Vandelas spoke for the first time, fearful that he lost his fight.

Pulsations spread throughout the air when he finally found the strength to stand again. As he moved, the threads around him began to strain, their hold weakening.

The spell was losing its power.

Those words were not for Luchs. But somehow, they did not seem directed at Gatreah either.

Vandelas' valsara flared with the freedom he reclaimed. Luchs could not help taking a few steps back, watching the anomaly in awe.

"You will pay ... for what you've done... I'll tear you apart ... until there is *nothing* left!"

He pulled his arms in and grabbed the threads that bore into his very life. And with a primal roar, he tore them away, allowing his valsara to flare vehemently, incinerating the remaining bonds and blinding anyone able to see it.

When Luchs opened his eyes, he stopped breathing. Vandelas' valsara had expanded beyond the prison of his body, shaping into the form of a monstrous beast the size of five men. The left side of it resembled the wolves that stopped attacking to behold the appearance of a beast among beasts, the right appearing sharp and jagged, the claws and fangs frozen over. When Vandelas raised his head, it raised its massive, slender skull. And when he roared, the valsara let loose a mighty shockwave that shook the world.

The winds stirred and debris scattered. Upon hearing the otherworldly howl, the animals cowered and fled. The wolfs turned tail, the birds took flight, the wildcats scattered, and the horses abandoned their riders. Every single animal had broken free of the spell and escaped, fearful for their lives.

Vandelas turned—the quadrupedal shape of his valsara following suit, despite the disproportion of its human shell—to face the witch. He stalked toward her steadily, eying for any movement for escape. But his presence left her petrified. She did nothing but stare horrorstruck at the monster within him.

He only made it so far before his injuries caught up with him. His knee fell to the ground, bringing down the left half of the beastly valsara, the impact shaking the ground. He kept trying to move so to take his prey between his jaws, but willpower was not enough to sustain him anymore. The valsara encompassing him began to recede back into his body as he collapsed. What remained of the valsara before returning to its shell bore a crater into the ground.

It was unfathomable. Valsara was the energy that coursed through all living things, an intangible force. And yet his not only expanded past its container, but also affected the very world around it.

Just how much can Nascitte do?

"D-Demon..." Gatreah uttered, her voice shaken. "I've been deceived... He is a demon in human skin. A demon among us..." Her own valsara began to flare, reacting to the devastating magic power forming in her palm.

"It must be expelled!" The power exploded with a thrust of her arm, shooting at the defenseless lad.

Time slowed as Luchs rushed to Vandelas' side. He ran as fast as his meaty legs could move, which felt deceptively slow as the mast of profane light closed in. He could not get him out of the way before the spell hit. So he did the only thing he could and threw himself over Vandelas' body, using himself to shield him.

~ Twentieth Chapter ~

Retribution

Death mowed over Luchs and Vandelas, but it never claimed them. The sound of searing earth drowned out all else until fading away, allowing silence to loom again. Luchs never felt a thing.

He opened his eyes—that in itself a surprise. Ghastly burns scarred the ground, marking where the profane spell hit. The mark left behind was a pitch-black befitting the touch of the witch god no one dared name, a mark that relentlessly consumed all life it touched but parted and faded once it met him.

Luchs inspected his body for disfigurement as he stood. Every limb was accounted for, as were his fingers, nose, and eyes. He did not even have a hair out of place or burns like on the ground. It was as if the spell never hit.

Gatreah stared him down with her mouth hung open. She trembled and shook her head in denial. "Demons... The both of them—demons!" Magic crackled in her hands, and once more she launched the profane light it formed at him.

Luchs braced himself before Vandelas, still intent on acting the shield, crossing his arms over his face. The light was painfully bright, but that was all the pain it inflicted. His eyes adjusted quickly, and he found the magic washing over him like a steady stream over stone, then parted at his sides.

There was no pain. The blast of light dissipated quickly and left as much damage as the last.

Several of the clashing factions stopped fighting once the witch began her assault, and all were speechless to see someone survive her dreadful spells, none more so than the witch herself.

"I-Impossible... No!"

Gatreah lost what little composure she had left and, refusing to relent that her magic did nothing, began hurling the same spell at Luchs over and over. Nothing changed no matter how much power was put into it. It all parted and broke apart upon meeting Luchs, who stood there dumbfounded.

Although unharmed by the magic, he felt a dreadful familiarity when he came into contact with it. He remembered the endless suffering that came with it tearing his body apart, the terror from the horrifying memories it made him see. It was the same spell that killed him crashing into him, just used to a smaller extent.

But why did the spell leave him alive? It was the same magic, the same destructive force, cast by the same mage. Yet it did nothing.

As much as he wanted to contemplate the impossible, he was still in battle and needed to protect someone who could not do so for himself.

Gatreah wore herself out after throwing a dozen or so blasts. She hoarsely gasped after draining herself of energy and stared at the squire with crazed eyes. That devilish ego of hers was not content with knowing that her almighty magic was so easily endured by the enemy, by a child no less.

Outraged, Gatreah plunged her profane power into the earth. In seconds, the ground shook violently, throwing everyone—Ederean and Convent pawn alike—off their feet.

The natural energy flowing through the island began rising toward the surface as the ground around them gradually chipped apart. At the rate it travelled, the entire island would soon be torn asunder.

That crazy witch is going to kill everyone!

A single panicked thought from Luchs, a tremendous surge of his Second Verse following, stopped everything. The magic moving the earth dissipated instantaneously, the ground becoming still again. It was a surprisingly simple matter to redirect the natural energy back to its original flow. The pressure from the effort weighed against Luchs, but only for a moment.

Life on the island struggled to cling on and flourish. Her own followers were there reaching numbers over the thousands. To make the sudden motion to wipe all of that out—she was cruelty personified.

That's enough.

With a wave of his arm, the ground leading to the witch rose and splintered into columns until one threw her into the air. Her panicked mind was too disturbed to focus on any spells that might soften her landing. She landed on her right arm, the impact from the twenty-foot fall breaking it.

The nearby Convent forces, seeing their leader in mortal danger, charged at Luchs altogether. They were intercepted by what remained of the Ederean forces, who refused for their chance at bringing the witch down to be taken away.

Gatreah picked herself up, cradling her arm, and ran toward what remnants of her army managed to squirm past the Edereans.

If she came into contact with anyone, she would use them to open a rift like she had in Shoafond. She would be out of their reach forever.

Abandoning his role as a shield for the unconscious Nascitte, Luchs raced after Gatreah quick as the wind.

She had already gone a great distance and was moments away from meeting with her legion. No matter how fast he ran, he would not catch her in time. Although he hoped to avoid using his power any further, there was no other choice. He stopped in place and took an abrupt stance while expanding his area of influence, then swiped his right arm, its muscles clenched, across the horizon. The earth between Gatreah and her legion had been torn asunder as though a massive hand dug into it, the debris flying into the air. The resulting fissure was deep, perilous, and had a river of molten rock flowing through it. The desperate witch attempted to run around it, but Luchs collapsed the earth at every side that did not lead to him, forcing her hopes of escape, like the destroyed earth, to plummet into the lava.

He was not satisfied with just that. His reach extended to the scattered rubble that had yet to fall from the sky. With a strong tug, he hauled them down in an avalanche hurled directly at the witch.

Gatreah used her power to form a barrier that withstood the assault while bouncing the debris across the battlefield. It held together against half of the avalanche before the prism-like surface started to chip. The last stone destroyed the barrier, and would have crushed her had she not rolled out of the way.

By the time she recovered, Luchs finally caught up with her.

The witch took a few desperate steps back. Unable to eliminate the obstacle before her or change the terrain around them, she was left with nowhere to run.

But still, she refused to yield. "I am Gatreah, high priestess of the almighty Convent of One and acolyte to The Divine One, Kyros. The one true god blessed me with power beyond mortal comprehension for my devotion. A holy vassal such as myself cannot be bested by an infidel, a spawn of chaos and sin. His world shall be cleansed of you and your decrepit brethren, even if it means erasing the land on which we stand!"

The very air sparked and snapped from the intense power broiling through Gatreah. Her eyes and hands flickered the light of her profane magic as it amplified to devastating levels. The overwhelming force kept Luchs at bay and made it impossible to get close to her. As she raised her arm to the air, holding her claws out as if offering something to her god, the symbols branded on her arms radiated the same stabbing light. The sky above began to ripple from the influence of her magic. With each passing second, a magic symbol appeared above until the entire island was encircled by them.

Just as her power was about to reach its peak, it fell drastically in an instant. She clung her arm around her chest and nearly doubled over, struggling to remain standing. Physical wounds were not what almost brought her to her knees; her valsara, once radiating a smoldering glow of oppression, began to slowly fade from the center out as it was eaten by an inky black darkness. It continued to spread, but the witch remained vigilant and fought through the anguish to retain the flow of her magic. Soon, her valsara began to reconstitute and her power rose again.

Luchs refused to let her regain power. Even with the pressure of her magic keeping him away, she was not out of his reach.

He took Anktung in hand and raised it high, then stabbed it into the ground, guiding the Second Verse through the small indention to cleave the cliff that hung over the fiery fissure. Down the patch of crumbling earth fell, along with the witch. Luchs kept his eyes closed until both her bloodcurdling screams and her valsara had been extinguished.

"May the witch god of death carry your soul to the deepest of hells." With that prayer left to haunt the departed, he pulled the sword from the ground, housed it in its sheath, and turned his back on the river of lava.

While retracing his steps to find Vandelas, he constantly observed the island's condition. When the witch attempted to have the ground swallow them, the delicate balance that kept the natural energy in check flew off-kilter, and the energy threatened to tear through the entire island. But once Luchs used his Second Verse, the damage carelessly made was mended and continued to maintain itself even after ripping open a gaping red scar in the earth. The lava flowing, exposed to the air, moved as if nothing happened.

The Second Verse adjusting itself to its bearer—it sounded much less insane now.

Despite that small comfort, they still walked on an active volcano. So long as they were there, he could not relax.

It was a shame, too, because it seemed the battle was already over.

The Convent of One's forces scattered shortly after the death of their leader. They held on for so long only because they had faith in her terrifying magic. Great fighters as they were, there were obviously no former Ederean veterans fighting for their cause; they would have remained to see the end with honor instead of running. The Edereans chased after the stragglers not to bring them to the blade, but rather to take them into custody.

A few factions scattered to collect and attend to the injured, one of them heading Luchs' way. He hoped they had something to eat. After exhausting himself to the point where moving his legs took all his strength, he desperately needed a pick-me-up.

Fortunately, he had enough strength in him to make it back to his unconscious comrade, who was not alone. Snowflake returned from wherever she hid to tend to its master. No matter how it nudged his cheek, he showed no signs of coming to. He barely breathed and the pulse at his neck was faint, but he still lived.

When he got another look at his surroundings, Luchs realized he was not where he left him. Where he was had been buried the debris thrown in the fight with the witch.

Lady Sundralla was rather capricious with her boons to him.

It did not take long for his faction to catch up with Luchs. To his delight, they were joined by the injured Ulrin and Rah'ta.

"There he is—the witch slayer!" The other soldiers shouted delightful cheers in response to Ulrin. A few even raised their weapons in the air from the excitement. It was hard not to smile at the rowdy display.

The fox, mistaking the soldiers' cheers for aggression, turned and snarled at them.

When the general noticed who the beast protected, his expression became grim. "And him?" he uttered sternly.

Luchs knew he would not overlook Vandelas or his actions. It was hard to respond despite the simple answer: "Alive, just tuckered out."

The general's stare grew colder, and it made Luchs feel like the praise never happened. There was a painful moment of silence.

Ulrin did not seem disappointed or even upset. "I thought it might be difficult for you after your time together. Well, no matter." After bracing for the pain, he released his injured arm and took his halberd in hand. His eyes revealed no sympathy or mercy.

Seeing him move toward Vandelas made Luchs' body feel all the heavier, but that did not stop him from blocking his way. "'Tisn't that I couldn't. I refused to." That was harder to say. It felt like his throat was closing.

The general stared him down. "What is this?"

"I won't kill him, Ulrin. And I won't let you do it either."

The little kindness that remained in the general vanished. "Defending a traitor is nearly as bad as being one, you know. Step aside."

"Nay, I won't."

It became all the more difficult to refuse Ulrin the longer he did. But after everything he went through, he would be a fool to give in now.

"You would stand with that traitor over me? After what he did?"

"But he didn't!" Luchs shouted past the strain in his throat. "If'n I knew him to truly be a traitor, I'd never bother trying to get through to him. But he didn't. The witch brainwashed him, forced him to do as she bade, and he was fighting back the entire time. He even stabbed himself after taking back a shred of control just to keep from hurting me."

"Is that all you've to say for this? Brainwashing?"

"'Tis truth!"

Nothing about Ulrin's countenance showed he believed in his squire. He grew terribly irate the more he continued to disobey. The hand gripping tightly around the halberd's shaft shook violently, a show of the restraint he kept to avoid forcing his squire aside.

He would never have considered such a thing before, but before he was not a general. And as one, he needed to show strength and discipline. Others like him no doubt thought Vandelas a traitor. Should he choose to side with the squire he was so fond of, those vengeful would revolt and attempt to do the job themselves. Whoever those soldiers were, they remained silent to see how their leader would respond.

~ 375 ~

"Step aside!"

"I won't!"

His patience reaching its end, the general stepped in to sweep him aside. But he was stopped by a stone slab half his size jutting from the ground and blocking his way. He looked to Luchs with an expression riddled in disbelief.

"I bet everything on killing that witch to protect everyone here. And I'll do it again if it protects him from you."

A few soldiers thought he was bluffing, but hesitated to make a move. They left their home ready to put their lives into their leader's hands, and they did so again as he confronted the child before him.

"He's already had his trouncing, so let's give him an open hand."

It did not hurt Luchs to see Ulrin doubt him again. He was a squire, a student who needed to learn from the meister. The only way he would be heard was if he stood up for his decision, alone if need be.

Soon, Maxime walked up to Luchs and stared at him sternly. He took a moment to note his comrade's will, then turned around to face the knights, and turn his sword on them.

No one believed what they saw from their last general's squire. It looked like a betrayal to his meister knight, who selected him because he knew the importance of following the chain of command regardless of what happened.

He looked to his current general, determined albeit intimidated and apprehensive. "I did terrible things before... We should at least know what made him do it."

The choice encouraged others to do the same. Rufus stepped away from the crowd to stand beside Luchs, a loyal friend to the end. Then followed Levin, and even Tal.

And when it looked like Ulrin made his choice, Rah'ta took Porlande and held its blade to his neck.

He looked to the tigress, horrified. "You too?"

"Don't tell me you didn't notice. An honorary Vainte warrior yourself, you must have seen it. A lad he may be, what tried to slaughter us was a beast. And 'tisn't any mystery what our enemy did to them." Rah'ta turned her gaze to Luchs. Her eyes were heavy and proud, but in the corner of them was a glint of compassion. "I doubt you picked this child for your squire simply because of your ties. Have you any faith in the one you chose to inherit your will, or haven't you?"

Now that others stood with him, the hesitation and fear of standing against Ulrin faded. The other soldiers became less eager to act before the general, a man who could not come to the decision himself. The conflict in his head raged on and the weight it carried was evident from how his eyes trembled.

After a moment, Rah'ta lowered her weapon. The others thought she had a change of heart.

But the motion showed she knew what he would do beforehand. The general holstered his weapon behind his back, sighing. "Tie him up. I don't want him moving so much as a pinky."

The tigress nodded and took a bundle of rope from one of the knights, then approached the children slowly. She wanted to appear less of a threat both to them and to the malformed fox that kept snarling at them.

Someone attempted to interject but was cut off by their leader.

"You, take some men and attend to Gilbrand. Close that hole in him before he bleeds out."

The soldier looked over to Commandant Brunlier and winced when he noticed the missing arm. He hesitated, but obeyed.

Rah'ta, after staring the beast down for a time, somehow convinced it to return to its plusher form and step aside. Leaving her to her job, Luchs joined those who rushed over to the kneeling Commandant Brunlier.

The behemoth refused to move even when help arrived. All of his remaining concentration was put to lowering his heart rate so it would slow the tremendous blood loss. His only remaining hand clamped over the hole that kept spurting ribbons of blood. It took six men to open his grasp and another two to pull his arm away from the wound.

A stomach-churning sight it was to see the crimson-soaked socket where an arm used to be.

Everyone did their part to bandage Commandant Brunlier up and keep the bandages from falling out of place, but even that was difficult. The bandages were immediately stained and did little to slow his circulation.

The general brought Tal to see what could be done. Unfortunately, there was little the shaman protégé could do. "There is little that can be done here with what we have. We need more supplies."

Supplies that might save him would be hard to come by and difficult to identify. But since they were in the domain of a sorceress, they had a chance. And the most likely place they would find what they needed was somewhere no one wanted to go.

Ulrin took a party to the basilica once he found the mages youths. While alluring from a distance, the building was none too pleasing up close. Its windows were naught but holes after the glass had been shattered. The gargoyles hanging from their perches fell apart after being claimed by time. The only thing on the outside tended to was the garden that grew precious fruits and herbs and the bounty of trees that purified the sulfurous air; the soil was much more fertile there.

Everyone remained on guard while entering the basilica. They knew not who else remained or what sorts of wicked magic protected the place.

It was eerily quiet. No one hid in the shadows or guarded the once hallowed sanctuary.

Perhaps the Convent doubted they would make it so far.

The party split into groups to further investigate. Ulrin remained by the entrance with a scout and the blood-stained behemoth while the others combed the halls. As for Luchs, he sat in the foyer to guard their prisoner.

For the moment, the fight was over, but he could not rest easily. In his time as an Ederean, he had been to many sorts of churches, but the one they were now in did not have the same air of comfort and safety. Two tall columns kept the entryway from collapsing on itself and led to an alter where preachers must have spoken of their god. The many benches facing the dark space—including the one he sat on—were old, decrepit, rigid, and made a discomforting *creak* whenever anything so much as touched them. Lanterns hung from the walls and dozens of candle holders as tall as a person stood around the altar, all of them blown out, leaving the massive statue at the center concealed in shadows.

The statue looked to be of a robed person with the wings of an angel. As far as Luchs could tell, it was an idol of the Convent's god, Kyros. Much of its features were blank and unremarkable; it did not even have a face. It seemed out of place in the basilica too. The rock used to sculpt it was a slightly darker shade than the walls of the monument, which were something close to marble. It was as if it did not belong there.

"Fie... Dead again."

That dry, hoarse voice startled Luchs. He did not expect Vandelas to wake so soon.

He barely stirred, the glimmer in his half-lidded eyes faded and the glow it radiated dim. For a moment, it looked like he would slip back into unconsciousness, but Vandelas clung to his senses and shook his head. "Wait. That ... can't be. The Elysium—" He paused to groan, his mind doubtlessly still drained.

Luchs could not help but chortle. He had to be dreadfully disoriented to confuse the decrepit basilica with the eternal garden.

"Don't let that boggle fool you, laddie."

He gave him the time needed to recover enough to focus. As he watched Vandelas struggle to lift his head, Luchs' magic sight revealed a weak valsara. Such a drastic change from the force once strong enough to affect the material plane. Seeing him like that, it was a wonder Vandelas had the strength to so much as twitch.

The fox tried to take his attention while he recovered, sitting on its hind legs with its forelegs patting at his ribs. It kept sniffing his face heavily enough for Luchs to hear its huffy breath.

Even in his current state, the little beast still made him look calmer. "Snowflake ... you're okay."

It nuzzled into his neck after getting the recognition it wanted. Once it was done showering him with affection and sniffing his neck, it leaped off of his lap and scampered down a distant hall.

The small disturbance it made alerted Ulrin. A nod from his squire was all it took to let him know of the change. He approached the prisoner slowly, cautiously, still concerned he might take his life if given the chance.

By the time he reached the bench they sat on, Vandelas finally found his grasp on reality and took notice of the ropes intricately binding him.

"At least I'm not in the dungeon. And since I'm not, what does that mean for Gatreah?"

Luchs grinned. "She's dead—not a trace left."

That should have come across as spectacular news, but Vandelas looked somewhat bitter. "Shame... I hoped to return the torture she inflicted on me in kind."

The general looked upon his prisoner with mistrusting eyes, but he knew he meant what he said. "Is that how they convinced you to fight for them? Torture?"

Vandelas glanced at the man beside him. It took a moment before he recognized who that was. "Convince? I had no say, not when she used that charm."

"Charm?"

"A gaudy little pendant she used to control the animals." He spoke of the stone around her neck she clung to when she gave him and the animals orders.

Ulrin did not entirely believe him. "And you say she used it on you? You're no beast."

"But the spell shackled his valsara all the same," Luchs objected.

Recalling the experience made Vandelas trepidatious. "A consequence of being brought back from the brink. My instincts became less human, more animalistic. I've had problems before, but I never imagined something like this would happen." Those cold eyes drifted off elsewhere, staring into nothingness. "Her spell ensnared me when she invaded Shoafond. I protected Snowflake from it, but ended up as another of their puppets. She's been trying to bring me back under her heel again since she brought me here. I fought her off for as long as I could, but when the full moon rose again ... I lost all control.

~ 380 ~

"I can't forget that spell digging into my mind, warping my senses, putting the monsters from my nightmares in place of anyone who was a threat to the Convent. A part of me knew what I saw wasn't real, but … I couldn't stop."

It was hard to think of him as he was before after seeing him tremble and snivel over the trauma. Horror was etched in his eyes and rattled in his voice.

Luchs remembered how he froze after Anktung was drawn. He could not help wondering what nightmarish thing was seen in his place.

"How many did I kill?" Neither of them gave an answer, but Vandelas was insistent on getting one, which showed as he turned to Ulrin. "Lieutenant, they were your men, your brothers-in-arms, lost because of me. Tell me! How many lives did I steal from you?"

In the little time since his predecessor passed, Ulrin became an excellent example of what an Ederean general should be: strong, proud, intrepid. "None, lad. That was the witch's doing, not yours." And, like their king, he could not punish someone who was not at fault. "My squire, your brother-in-arms, convinced me."

Those words filled Luchs with more pride than he knew. He finally felt that Ulrin truly trusted him.

But what he said had a different effect on Vandelas. It was hard to tell if his horror grew or diminished. He moved to further protest as Ulrin leaned in to undo his bonds, but realizing they would not listen, he relented and laid his head against the bench.

He would have remained silent had he not seen the weapon at Luchs' side. "Ah, Anktung. So Wolfram gave you something to fight me with."

Luchs was hoping he would not have noticed it. "Aye, in a way." It made him uncomfortable to even think about what he was about to say, but he deserved to know. "Actually, he gave it to us so we would leave him to his work. He thought too much of that weapon he was forging to consider you."

"I see." A quick response, and one that did not sound surprised or hurt. It was shocking how quickly he accepted that. "Between a lifelong goal and a child he barely knows, the choice doesn't surprise me. It's probably for the best. If he abandoned it and left his work incomplete, I'd lose respect for him."

Whatever went on in his head, Luchs left the matter alone. That was just his way of thinking.

When he was freed, Vandelas tried moving around so his senses would fully readjust. Luchs stood up and took his arms over his shoulder so he would not put pressure on his left side. They walked together to the gardens, a path from which the light had been completely blocked out by a massive form.

Stepping into the basilica was Commandant Brunlier taking note of the beast that had robbed him of his arm.

A sudden feeling of claustrophobia overwhelmed Luchs, as though he were about to be crushed. It was tempting to run, but turning their back on him was not an option.

The behemoth stood there eying the both of them with a heavy stare. Instead of appearing malignant or hateful, though, a wide smirk crept over his face and he cackled loud and strong.

Then he stepped away to take a look around the basilica as Fiona tailed behind. "Stay put and heal!" she ordered futilely.

Luchs let out a harsh sigh. They were both in for it once he recovered.

No one realized how much time was spent fighting until the sun rose. An entire night passed since their arrival on the strange island. Many fell asleep the moment they found the chance.

But some could not bring themselves to rest. For some, it was due to adrenaline still coursing through them; others were skeptical about whether or not they were truly out of danger.

The Convent of One had many mages in its ranks, all brandishing terrible power. Every horde sent to terrorize Ederea had at least one among them to keep the scales tipped in their favor, all of them zealots moving at the will of the high priestess who gave them power.

But no other Convent mage had been seen.

Those raiding the basilica soon found something that both reassured and horrified them. Behind the statue of the Convent's patron god, enshrouded by the shadows, was a passage. It led to another room, a grand chamber filled with the light of the glistening morning sun by a crystal-like skylight. Despite the mystifying atmosphere it created, there was a lingering air of dread that would not fade. At the chamber's center was a grandiose, intricately drawn magic circle, and at its edges were the haggard corpses of twenty robed men: the Convent mages. They were all pale white with skin shriveled against their skeletons and expressions of anguish frozen on their faces.

The mage youths ascertained the cause of their deaths was magic related. Whatever it was left Tal too horror-struck to cross into the chamber. The poor shaman protégé babbled in a voice shaken, muttering about a sacrifice.

"The spell that summoned the animals!" blurted out Seoc, who now wore bandages over his abdomen.

"She stole their lives to empower herself," added Alister.

That troubled Fiona. "So she lacked the power to cast it alone."

Given the many magical feats the Convent of One had performed, it was unlikely this was the first time the sacrificial chamber had been used.

It was then that they understood the place of everyone in the Convent of One underneath the high priestess. The zealots had no more value than a sword or horse—used to the point of breaking, then immediately replaced and forgotten. And the promising mages, they were grapes upon a vine that were well tended to until ripe for the picking.

The fallen deserved to be sent off to the afterlife properly, even those belonging to the enemy. So the soldiers took the shriveled corpses outside where graves were being prepared. Non-combatants of the Convent offered to help once they saw their own being tended to.

Luchs offered to take the burlier corpse at the opposite end of the circle. The body was difficult to move, its lifeless limbs heavy as stone. A refreshing breeze blowing in from the outside made carrying it less strenuous. Once it reached the wall behind him, a faint whistle resounded.

Unable to turn away, he abandoned the body to investigate. The wall was strong, steady, but like the statue that concealed the chamber, it was made of a material different from what was around it, built recently. Another passing breeze revealed the whistle came from a small gap between two stones.

"Luchs, what are you doing?"

He focused too much on the wall to pay his meister knight any attention. It blocked yet another path, another secret hidden, and he wanted to find out what it was. With the Second Verse, he broke apart the wall barring his path stone by stone until it was but a pile of gravel.

A new passage had been revealed. It was a short path connecting to a small altar standing underneath a sliver of light. Luchs walked down the passage, feeling much more at ease there than in the sacrificial chamber. At the end was not another tribute to a god, rather a towering tablet made of dark, slick metal. There were depictions of what appeared to be an epic battle, stars falling from the sky, a maiden crying over a dead land, and the maiden's tears stirring the very elements. The beauteous depictions were made of collective beads of color that formed into captivating swirls. Whoever created them must have been a masterful artist in their time.

Luchs was so amazed that he failed to notice his meister knight catch up with him. Others gathered before long.

Maxime could barely take his eyes off the tablet. "What is this?"

"'Tisn't like anything of the Convent's," a knight said.

Ulrin took a closer look while his soldiers bombarded his squire with praise. The squires constantly hassled him to tell them how he found the passage; no one believed him when he told the truth.

Luchs loved the attention, but had to turn it away when he saw Vandelas hobbling through the hall. He rushed over to him before he pushed himself too far. "What in the gods' names are you doing?"

"You used your power. I thought there was trouble."

Reassuring him everything was fine, Luchs tried to force him to stop moving, but when he saw the tablet, he, too, wanted a closer look. Despite the obvious weakness, he still had plenty of energy, enough to force the burly squire off him and keep moving.

Luchs was not going to let a torn-up scrapper push him around, but the thought of restraining him slipped his mind when he saw Vandelas walking without support. The muscles in his leg should have been too damaged to hold him up, but still he walked, stopping only to rest every other step.

It should not have been possible. But then again, neither was surviving the witch's magic.

He seemed to be doing well enough on his own, so Luchs left him be, saying he would see him atop the altar.

As he scaled the flight of stairs, he noticed something odd about the markings on the bottom of the tablet. Once at the top, he realized it was writing—the very same he found in the apocrypha.

"You notice?" Ulrin asked.

Luchs nodded.

"Can you read it?"

He was not certain but needed to try regardless. The apocrypha never offered any clues as to where they originated from, and he was desperate to learn. The depictions showed it would not be what he desired, but he clung to false hope and read.

After taking the time to figure out what the inscriptions said, Luchs read aloud the translation:

The Divine Light, guide and guardian to all life, faced the threat of the Horrendous Dark, an endless void.

The Light's battle against the Dark brought ruin to the land, decay to the oceans, stillness to the air. Our World turned lifeless and cold, left a shell of death and ash. All looked to the skies hoping their Light would return with salvation in hand. Only strands of starlight fell from above.

One strand struck the remains of a dead tree. It sparkled and glimmered, then radiated a golden light that formed a Heavenly Beauty. As the Beauty beheld the faded wasteland once abundant in life, she fell to her knees and wept.

The tears of the Heavenly Beauty reached the rotted ocean and purified its waters, cleansing a second strand of fallen light. From the sorrowful waters emerged a Stoic Angel immersed in the golden light. The Stoic Angel stirred a torrential storm and forged a chariot from the awakened waves. On her chariot she rode to revive Our World's revitalizing waters.

The torrential storm stirred by the Stoic Angel reached the tallest cliff overlooking the ocean. There, the chilling ocean breeze sprayed over another stand. Four great winds raged across Our World as the strand took the form of a Zephyr Child donned in the golden light dashing through the air. The Zephyr Child broke apart the great winds, scattering them, purifying the air and brushing away the ash.

The ash brushed away by the Zephyr Child collected in the maw of a hollow mountain, covering the strand within. From the bed of ashes, ashes melted and ignited into a pool of flames, rose a Molten Giant draped in the golden light. The Molten Giant, boring its colossal hands into the mountain's crust, spread its power across the land, forming mountains from liquid fire. The liquid fire created new lands and restored the fertile earth.

The Heavenly Beauty's tears revived the plants once decayed, restoring all that was lost.

Everything taken away had been brought back. Our World lived again, stronger than ever, under the protection of the voices of nature.

As much as it pained Luchs to learn it was not what he hoped, he found himself captured by what he read.

It was a tale truly enticing. Everyone recognized the beings who revived the world: Moltore, the god of molten earth; Zyleec, child god of the wind; Untae, the goddess of the sea and bringer of ocean life; and Great Gaia, mother goddess of life and bringer of livestock. But the Divine Light was unknown to them, an enigma that—if the tablet was of any evidence—gave existence to the Gods of the Natural Order.

No one knew how the gods came into being until now. They discovered a religious treasure, a treasure the Convent of One must have viewed as a challenge to their beliefs, and thus a threat.

~ 386 ~

"They oppose the gods yet have this?" a knight hollered in disgust.

For the Convent of One, simply covering up the tablet, ignoring it, seemed aberrant. No one believed they did not know it was there either, not with the evidence already uncovered.

Then, an epiphany struck.

It was rash, but Luchs knew no other way to prove it. Confident that his power still maintained the disrupted flow of energy beneath the surface, he took hold of a few large boulders protruding from the ground using his Second Verse. "Step away from the tablet!" That warning was enough to convince everyone to scatter before the boulders were lobbed at the relic. A cloud of dust and dirt blinded the onlookers below. The boulders broke apart upon impact. When the dust cleared, they were awestruck to see the tablet standing without a scratch.

The soldiers were outraged with Luchs' impulsiveness, but the general looked intrigued. Following his lead, he ordered one of the mage youths to join them. All three of them came, each one feeling stronger together.

That was better. "You three, blast the tablet."

"...Sir?" Seoc asked.

"Go on—like you really want it destroyed."

The mage youths did not know what to make of their general's order, but did as they were told. In unison, they clapped their hands together, pouring power into their palms and slowly pulling their hands apart, each forming spheres of scarlet. A thrust of the wrist fired the energy at the tablet. Blinding flashes filled the chamber, searing burns lingering on the slick metal, but the magic flares soon faded, once again leaving the tablet unscathed.

As much as it surprised the others, Ulrin patted his squire on the shoulder, pleased. "They couldn't destroy it, so they hid it hoping it would be forgotten."

Luchs was glad to hear he had done well. He felt accomplished having figured that out himself.

Many came and went after they heard about the hidden tablet, wanting to see the piece of history for themselves. Luchs gladly read the story for anyone who asked. He stayed atop the altar for a long while, reading the inscriptions over and over.

Something gnawed at him after every reading. He noticed how easy it was to read the inscriptions compared to the apocrypha at Castle Ederea. There was also the way the deities were described.

He heard the story before.

The general left after word was delivered that a member of the Convent had information he would offer in exchange for sanctuary. Most of the other soldiers left to ensure no one in the settlement would riot or cause a disturbance, and the rest remained to guard the basilica, which was being used as their base for the time being.

No one spoke. A deafening silence hung in the air, the sound from the outside fading into the soft echo against the walls of the chamber. It would have been a relaxing setting, but somehow, as Luchs continued to read the tablet, it became all the more unsettling to be there alone.

Thankfully, Vandelas decided to remain there while he healed. His pet just returned, carrying in its maw his missing scarf.

"Vandelas," Luchs spoke up, "what do you make of this?"

The lad glanced up at him while coiling his scarf around his neck. "I thought you were as devout to the Natural Orthodoxy as any Ederean."

It was hard to answer, and until he could contemplate what it was he felt, he chose not to.

Those glacial eyes of Vandelas' were as hard to read as ever, but he did not act the inquisitor. Instead, he looked back to the tablet and admired its artwork. "Your guess would probably be better than mine. I lost faith in gods some time ago. Anything I say will hold nothing but doubt."

So neither of them would be of help to the other.

Luchs looked up to the depictions of the gods working simultaneously to maintain nature's order, lost in thought.

Zephyr Child.

Heavenly Beauty.

Molten Giant.

Stoic Angel.

He thought about the words depicting Zyleec, Great Gaia, Lord Moltore, and Lady Untae until his head spun.

The tablet was not the only thing to record those specific epithets; they were written in books, books that were read to him as a child and that he learned to read himself, books written in the same script that towered over him. But his mother and grandfather always told him they were only stories, myths told to inspire.

No one in his old village believed in them because no one there believed that gods existed.

But those who hid the tablet away and those who found it did. They believed in gods and came to fight each other over differences in their beliefs. So many suffered, so many died, over ideals meant to lead the lives of the faithful. It all hit Luchs in one hard, painful instant.

All those countless people could have died from a myriad of other reasons—disputes over dishonor, diseases or famine, attacks from wild beasts, natural calamities. But instead those victims of war, warriors and civilians alike, had their lives cut short because one megalomaniac decided the only way of life, the only way to see the world, should be her own.

With the memories that returned to him came these new feelings. It was not just rage and spite, but also shame and pity for those with views so rigid that they could not exist with any other.

Perhaps that was why the Kyrovide chose to hide from the world. They were afraid of the persecution, the hate, the carnage that followed.

But Luchs thought it time to stop hiding.

When Ulrin returned, Luchs told him everything: his memories steadily returned, that they had been for months, how little he actually knew of his obscured home and his lost family, how he hid everything for fear of what might happen when he remembered who he was. There was a great deal to process, but Ulrin patiently listened to every word and waited for his squire to finish his tale.

Even with everything he heard, there was not much to consider. He patted his squire on the shoulder. "No home and no family, eh, Luchs Lau?" he said while playfully ruffling his hair like when they first met. "Nonsense.

You have us. That won't change even if we do someday find your family."

It was weird hearing someone else speak his family name, but he liked it. And after so long, he felt proud to acknowledge it.

"So, what did the informant say?"

The expression on Ulrin's face was hard to read, portraying both satisfaction and unease. "Not much but quite a lot." Vague as that sounded, he seemed confident. "Apparently, someone was in contact with Gatreah before she declared war."

"What?"

"Dozens of her followers admitted to it. At first, they wanted nothing to do with an outsider, but whoever they were seemed knowledgeable of their god and wished to offer homage to him. That was how it began, then the visits became less of a pilgrimage and more of a rendezvous with the high priestess. This person always came alone and carried nothing more than a letter in hand."

"'This person,'" Luchs interrupted. "They don't even know if they were a man or woman?"

"Not when said visitor wore a cloak and kept their face concealed to all but their leader." It was hard to imagine anyone, let alone Gatreah, could bring themselves to trust someone who would not even show their face. "I'd like to have seen the confusion that caused among her apostles. They were wary when their meetings left lasting impressions on their high priestess, making her behave strangely."

"What of the letters?"

"The one I spoke to had a peek at them once, though he didn't know what to make of them. But he blamed them for her choice to declare war." The general glanced back at the passage with a gaze impatient. "The men are searching for them now. If'n what we've been told is true, we may have more to worry about than we were led to believe."

An outside force manipulating the Convent of One from the shadows. From how high the priestess held their faith, it was easy to think she sought control of Ederea herself.

It did not make sense. Those who worshipped Kyros kept themselves hidden from all Ederea for the longest time. Barely anyone knew they existed until the war began. After going through all the trouble to remain hidden, she chose to open her arms to an outsider unknown to them.

Was simply knowing of their god enough to grant them such trust?

As they discussed the unusual circumstances, Tal entered the chamber and scampered up the steps to the altar. He carried a thick stack of parchment barely contained in those small hands.

"Anything?"

The shaman protégé shook his head. "No spells or poison. Whatever the man saw must be in the writing."

Ulrin accepted the pile of parchment just as it was about to pour from Tal's grasp. He took a look at the one on top, then skimmed over several others after giving them a few seconds of attention.

"Odd. Most of it looks to be poetry."

Poetry used to convince a madwoman to bring war to a powerful nation. There was always something unusual to be found.

"Anything catch your eye?" inquired Luchs.

"Nay, nothing. Each one is about something different, but nothing significant." Just when Ulrin looked ready to give up and conclude the informant was not to be trusted, he paused once he got to the bottom of the stack. "Hold a moment... Interesting. Listen to this, lads:

"'As the sun comes to rise, so must it set. As man is born into the world, so must we rest. Nothing lasts eternal save for The Divine One; change is imminent. Still tides will rage and darken without the golden glow. Valiance shall be predated by despair. But the way of Kyros is absolute and his Acolytes of Light must lead the way to his radiance.'" Ulrin paused a moment to groan in disgust. "He was right. Gatreah was being nudged toward war."

Luchs did not understand, but came to as his meister knight further explained. Ederea was also known as the Land of Golden Tides for the unparalleled beauty of its majestic waters gilded by the light of the rising and setting sun.

How the poem mentioned "tides" and "without the golden glow" boded a dark omen.

But what did "Valiance shall be predated by despair," mean?

The tension in the air was thick with a deathly chill suddenly brewing. Luchs tried to keep from reaching for his weapon when he sensed Vandelas' valsara flare once more. He looked to him fearing the witch's curse still had some hold over him, but the threads did not bind him.

His Second Verse reacted to the sudden flux of his valsara, thin layers of frost forming at his feet. A trembling arm worked its way to his left leg, its touch forming a layer around the bandages wrapped over his self-inflicted injury.

"General Vertueux," he said unsteadily as he stood, "you are right. Our troubles are *far* from over."

Ulrin suspected something was wrong with Vandelas, taking note of the unease from his squire and Tal, but he calmed when they noticed he was merely riled up by the discovery.

"Mayhap they aren't, but the day is ours. When we learn who else wishes to threaten Ederea, we'll deal with them then. For now, we've won."

~ Epilogue ~

Word quickly spread of the Convent of One's defeat.

The knights who fought beyond the archipelago returned to Shoafond and were hailed as heroes. Their fear doused and hope again restored, the people cheered for the warriors and their bravery, showering them with praise and flower petals.

The king and princess went to the city to welcome the conquering heroes once they received word of their return. They were elated to see so many return alive after the losses they suffered.

Princess Camellia was delighted to see Vandelas safe but feared for his well-being. Dozens of soldiers who saw him threatened to run him through until King Godefroy's fierce voice silenced them.

Those who stood up for Vandelas moved to shield him from the king's wrath, but there was no need. He saw that the child standing before him, ashamed of the harm he caused, was not the one who went berserk that day, and welcomed him back as heartily as he had the rest of the army.

If there were any objections, they were left unspoken.

After so much time spent living in fear, it was time to celebrate. A grand festival was held throughout the city that went on for two days and two nights. The heroes were shown the respect worth warriors of their caliber.

No one mourned for the fallen Ederean warriors. They were praised as much as the living to honor their valor and sacrifice. Everyone sang of the deceased with loud, proud voices so they would hear from the Elysium how thankful they were for them.

And near the end of the festivities, many requests were made so that the last song sung would be of Luchs, who slayed Gatreah the Wicked, the incarnation of evil. Everyone loved the idea.

The bards sang of he who tore the earth asunder, who pushed through the dark magic undeterred, who stood beside his comrades and became their unwavering shield.

It was embarrassing to be so overly praised, but Luchs grew accustomed to it and celebrated with them like an Ederean. He danced over dropped swords and with lovely young maidens, threw hatchets at painted targets, stuffed himself with the best food, and drank from a chalice his fill in mead.

For as much fun as the squires had partying, celebrating that the knights now saw them as men for surviving the war, Maxine was not as content. He lost his meister knight, after all.

In losing his respected mentor, he was further away from the coveted knight's shield than before. When a meister knight was lost, the squire would need a new one. At the end of the festivities, he would be taken to a training facility and remain there until another knight chose him.

Many of his peers tried to cheer Maxime up, told him how well he had done for himself. They did not want him giving up.

He put on a good show for his comrades, but they knew it was only that—a show. It was hard to know whether it was to honor General Esperance, to show he still had the spirit to be a knight, or to keep himself from crumbling under the burgeoning pressure.

He needed something to distract him.

A young maiden Levin met tried to pull him back into the crowd to dance, but he sent her Maxime's way, and when she learned he was a general's squire, she pulled him into the crowd instead to introduce him to her friends. The lovely lasses each tried to keep his attention, asking him questions and flirting with him. And all he could do was stammer and offer an awkward smile.

His friends had a laugh seeing him turn so bashfully red.

There were no frowns from then on. It was important that everyone enjoyed the celebration, for when it ended, their normal routine would repeat itself once more.

The sun remained radiant with colors of hope as Ederea healed. It was perfect weather for the people of Shoafond to be out restoring their city.

Remnants of the Convent still caused havoc across the archipelago. But without their leader, they were disorganized, easy to pick apart.

After defeating Gatreah and claiming the enemy's land, much of the Sea Drake Company remained on standby. The other companies were more than eager to snuff out the rest of the attackers in their place.

Luchs felt uneasy waiting for word on the effort to finish the enemy. He kept busy by helping other squires and knights with their exercises, tending to his meister knight's gear, following the patrolmen, and going into the city to see how businesses and families were holding up.

Thoughts always drifted back to how the other soldiers were doing.

One day, after he finished polishing his new sword and Ulrin's collection of spears, a servant knocked at the door of their bedchambers. "General Vertueux requests your presence," she said. It was unusual for him to send a messenger.

He needed something else to do, so Luchs followed the kind lady.

It was a beautiful day. Golden rays brought warmth and comfort to the land. The veils of mist surrounding the plateau shimmered in the sunlight. The birds serenaded the gardens with their lovely voices.

New beds of flowers and shrubbery have been planted hither and tither, along with some patches of grass that looked slightly darker than the rest. Some flowers still had blots of blood on their petals. Try as they had, the landscapers could not quite erase the evidence of an attack.

It was still tranquil enough for a small group to relax on the grass.

There sat Ulrin with Princess Camellia and a couple of her faithful handmaidens atop a blanket, having a conversation over tea.

Luchs joined them after thanking the servant for showing him the way.

"There you are." Ulrin was the first to notice him. He patted the open spot beside him and a familiar handmaiden, inviting him to join. "Come here, take a load off."

The blanket was soft to the touch. At the center of it was a silver platter carrying a teapot and matching little cups, a small pitcher for cream, and a jar for sugar. The handmaiden closest to the princess took the last empty cup in hand and poured Luchs some tea. His nose told him it was a blend different from the one he shared with the princess previously.

"Gracious! What happened to your eye?" asked the handmaiden as she handed him his tea.

The fresh shiner on Luchs' left eye was too swollen for anyone not to notice. He thought no one would ask about it since squires often got into fights.

"'Tis nothing, really."

He did not want to admit it was not much of a fight.

It occurred when Luchs happened to cross Vandelas in the halls. The lad walked up to him and suddenly rammed an unforgiving fist into his face. The act did not anger Luchs as much as it shocked him.

It was not to instigate a fight, but rather to convey his ire.

At Vandelas' hip hung a simple white sword with a large blue gem embedded between the guard and the blade.

That sword was a memento from his meister.

Rumors had spread that Wolfram Sörrign disappeared without a trace. No one had seen him since the crusade to topple the Convent of One. Many suspected he fled Ederea, but King Godefroy crushed the rumors when he made knowledge of Wolfram's death known.

Although he did not say it aloud, Luchs found it hard to believe the man put so much effort into such a plain weapon, a canvas left blank. But he did regret telling Vandelas what he did.

He left the most important weapon he made to his squire.

Instead of dwelling on it, Luchs tried to relax. A sip of tea washed away some of his stress.

"Not that I'm not grateful, but what did you call me here for?"

His meister knight smiled. "So you can take a load off, like I said. A knight always on edge can't do his best." He took another sip of tea, sighing after parting his lips from the glass. "I know tensions are still high, but you've been more frazzled than an angry boar."

Luchs scoffed. "Looks who's talking! I saw you at the festival. You normally flirt with every woman you cross, yet you barely spoke to any these past few days."

Ulrin always accepted how he was. It was odd to see him cringe and try to brush it off. "Oi, lad! Not in front of the princess."

Princess Camellia laughed. "No need to hide it, General Vertueux. I'm quite aware of your habits." Her voice portrayed pure amusement rather than displeasure, treating his reaction as a comedy act. "Why else would my ladies warn me of you when I invited you for tea?"

The hardened handmaiden looked Ulrin's way. Her stare held a particular disdain that made him recoil.

Ready to retort as he was, Ulrin held back, swallowing his words before they passed his lips. Anything he said would be pointless. That woman was not one who would be swayed by charm or flattery, especially not when she was familiar with his reputation.

She looked away only so she would enjoy her tea.

"Take it from me, Luchs: don't take these ladies lightly. Their claws will be around your neck the moment you do."

"Dear Elanor is protective of me because she cares," Princess Camellia defended her servant. The other handmaiden took her cup once it was empty, returning it after having it refilled. She partook in the tea, then gave a satisfied sigh. "There is no need to fret over you, though. You would make a very poor prince."

Now it was Ulrin's turn to laugh. "'Tis been some time since I heard Milady Queen's wit. I oft forget how much of your mother you have in you."

It was rare for anyone to mention the late queen. Luchs did not know what kind of woman she was, just that she touched the people as much as the princess had and died when her daughter was young.

The princess looked to be elsewhere for a moment, perhaps thinking of a memory with her mother. She took another sip of tea, drowning the masked sorrow, and retook her good mood.

"Mayhap the losses faced cannot be changed, but we must always find the strength to move forward. The dead leave this world to the living, so 'tis the duty of the living to do right by them." She glanced over to Ulrin. "Wouldn't you agree General Esperance wishes for the same?"

There was a look of nostalgia in Ulrin's eyes. "Definitely like your mother," he mused. "I think Eurieg would rather I honor his death over a few pints, but," he paused for another sip, looking more relaxed as he savored the flavor, "this certainly hits the spot."

That answer was enough to satisfy Princess Camellia, and it earned a laugh from the less threatening handmaiden. Normally, this would be the time when he would start flirting, but he knew better.

He and the princess continued to have their fun pitching jabs at one another for a few moments. There were some clever ones at the start, but they lost all meaning on Luchs when they went into each other's personal lives and experiences. It was a little strange to hear the normally prudent princess of Ederea speak so loosely with someone despite keeping the proper tone.

After getting the last word, Princess Camellia turned to face Luchs, her smile beaming. "I heard you've regained what was lost, Luchs Lau."

Flinching seemed like the natural reaction. Hiding that name for so long made it seem like there was no better way to respond. But he was not hiding it anymore. "Aye, Princess."

"How does it feel?"

"Liberating, like a weight has been lifted."

"How marvelous. Does that mean you know who you are now?"

That made him think for a moment. Even after confessing, he still was not entirely sure. But when he thought about how he hid his name, how he denied it for a time, it was enough to make him laugh. "I'd like to think I always have."

It was as satisfying to say as it was to see the princess' and Ulrin's smiles upon hearing it. After so long, it finally made sense.

Every decision he ever made was just that—his decisions, his choices. From following and resisting his sister that fateful day, to choosing to pay his debt to House Vertueux by becoming their knight, to defying Ulrin, those actions were refections of who he was, and who he became.

I am Luchs Lau, a shield for those in need. My family and friends are my greatest treasures, each one precious and irreplaceable, and I will protect them no matter the cost.

That acceptance did not mean he chose to leave his past behind him, not after what he went through to pick up the pieces. His mother, grandfather, and sister were still out there somewhere.

Ma, Grandpa, Hilda, don't forget about me. I'll find you someday.

In the time war engulfed Ederea, another page begins her training in Vermalio.

Like her brothers, Veronica is expected to learn the ways of knighthood and protect the kingdom. Many see promise in her, promise that is tempered into skill. Everyone always looks at her strangely, though, because they are cautious of her and her powers.

Despite that, she always looks for ways to help people, even those who leave behind regrets. One of her powers is being able to see and converse with the phantoms of the dead, and she uses it to help them find peace.

Even with so many against her, will Veronica find a meister knight who accepts her? Will she one day find the soul of her lost brother?

Seafarer Page

Third Book of the Aethereal Knights' Tales